D0448570

Emma Miller lives quietly in her old farmhouse in rural Delaware. Fortunate enough to be born into a family of strong faith, she grew up on a dairy farm surrounded by loving parents, siblings, grandparents, aunts, uncles and cousins. Emma was educated in local schools and once taught in an Amish schoolhouse. When she's not caring for her large family, reading and writing are her favorite pastimes.

Marta Perry realized she wanted to be a writer at age eight, when she read her first Nancy Drew novel. A lifetime spent in rural Pennsylvania and her own Pennsylvania Dutch roots led Marta to the books she writes now about the Amish. When she's not writing, Marta is active in church life and enjoys traveling and spending time with her three children and six beautiful grandchildren. Visit her online at martaperry.com.

EMMA MILLER

Rebecca's Christmas Gift

&

MARTA PERRY

A Christmas to Die For

HARLEQUIN® LOVE INSPIRED®

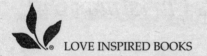

LOVE INSPIRED BOOKS

Recycling programs for this product may not exist in your area.

ISBN-13: 978-0-373-83894-3

Rebecca's Christmas Gift and A Christmas to Die For

Copyright © 2016 by Harlequin Books S.A.

The publisher acknowledges the copyright holders of the individual works as follows:

Rebecca's Christmas Gift
Copyright © 2013 by Emma Miller

A Christmas to Die For
Copyright © 2007 by Martha Johnson

www.Harlequin.com

Printed in U.S.A.

CONTENTS

REBECCA'S CHRISTMAS GIFT

Emma Miller

"For I know the plans I have for you," declares the Lord, "plans to prosper you and not to harm you, plans to give you hope and a future."
—*Jeremiah* 29:11

Chapter One

Seven Poplars, Kent County, Delaware,
Autumn

Rebecca Yoder stole another secret glance at the new preacher before ducking behind an oak tree. Today had been delightful; she couldn't remember when she'd last enjoyed a barn raising so much. Leaning back against the sturdy trunk of the broad-leaved oak, she slipped off her black athletic shoes and wiggled her bare feet in the sweet-smelling clover. It may have been October, but fair weather often lingered late into autumn in Delaware and the earth was still warm under her feet.

She and her friends Mary Byler and Lilly Hershberger had been busy since sunup, cooking, helping to mind the children and squeezing dozens and dozens of lemons to make lemonade for the work frolic. It seemed that half the Amish in the county, and more than a few from out of state, had come to help rebuild new preacher Caleb Wittner's barn, and everyone—from toddlers to white-haired elders—had been hungry.

As adult women, a great deal of the heavy work of

feeding people fell to them. Rebecca didn't mind—she was happy to help—and work frolics were fun. A change from everyday farm chores was always welcome, and gatherings like these gave young people from different church districts an opportunity to meet and socialize. Getting to know eligible men was the first step in courtship, as the eventual goal of every Amish girl was finding a husband.

Not that she would be in the market for one for some time. Technically, at twenty-one, she was old enough to marry, but she liked her life as it was. Her older sisters had all found wonderful husbands, and she intended to take her time and choose the right man. Good men didn't exactly grow on trees, and she wouldn't settle for just anyone. Marriage was for a lifetime and she didn't want to choose in haste. If she couldn't have someone who loved her in a romantic way, she'd remain single.

Rebecca yawned and rubbed the back of her neck. This was the first chance that she, Mary and Lilly, all of courting age, had found to take a break. Here, under the shade trees, they could take a few minutes to relax, talk and enjoy some of the delicious food they'd been serving to the men all afternoon. The fact that their chosen spot was slightly private while offering a perfect view of the young men pulling rotted siding off the old barn was a definite plus.

"I don't care how eligible Caleb Wittner is. I wouldn't want him." Balancing her plate of food, Mary folded her long legs gracefully under her as she lowered herself onto the grass. Her voice dropped to a conspiratorial whisper as she leaned toward Rebecca. "Amish or not, I tell you, I wouldn't set foot in that man's house again, not even for double wages."

Lilly's curly head bobbed in agreement beneath her spotlessly starched prayer *kapp*. "Didn't I tell you? I warned you before you took the job, Mary. I learned the hard way. He's impossible to please, and that child of his…" Lilly rolled her dark eyes and raised both hands in mock horror, causing a round of mirth. Blonde, round-faced Lilly had a sweet disposition and had been a loyal pal since the three of them had gone to school together as children, but Rebecca knew she was prone to exaggeration.

Actually, Lilly and she had been first graders when they'd met. Mary had been older, but that hadn't stopped her from taking the newcomers under her wing and helping them adjust to being away from their mothers all day. The friendship that had kindled around the school's potbellied woodstove had only grown stronger with each passing year. And since all of them had left their school days behind and become of courting age, not a week went by without the three of them attending a young folks' singing, a trip to Spence's Auction or some sort of frolic together. To cement the bond even more, Mary's brother Charley had married Rebecca's sister Miriam, which made kinship an added blessing. So tight was hers and Mary's friendship that Rebecca often worried how she'd stand it if she married out of the community and had to move away.

"Seriously." Rebecca nibbled at a stuffed egg and returned to the subject of Caleb Wittner's mischievous daughter. "She's a four-year-old. How bad could she be?"

"Oh, she's pretty awful." Mary chuckled as she tucked a stray lock of fine, honey-brown hair behind her ear. "Don't let those big, innocent eyes fool you.

Turn your back on that girl and she's stuffing a dead mouse in your apron pocket and tying knots in your shoestrings."

"Together," Lilly added with a grimace. "She tied my church shoes together so tight I had to cut the laces to get them apart. And while I was trying to sort them out, she dumped a crock of honey on the sermon her father had been writing."

"I think you two are being uncharitable," Rebecca pronounced. She eyed one of Aunt Martha's famous pickled carrots on her plate. "And letting your imaginations run away with you." Her attempt at reining in her friends' criticism of Caleb and Amelia Wittner was spoiled by another giggle that she couldn't contain. Mary was terrified of mice. Rebecca could just picture Mary's face when she'd slipped a hand into her pocket and come up with a dead rodent.

"That's not the half of it," Mary went on. "Amelia's impossible, but her father…" She pursed her lips. "He's worse. Short-tempered. Never a kind word for me when I came to watch his daughter. Have you ever seen him smile? Even at church? It's a wonder his face doesn't freeze in winter. He—" Mary broke off abruptly and her face flushed. "I didn't mean…" She shook her head. "I wasn't mocking his scars."

"I didn't think you were," Rebecca assured her. The three of them fell silent for a minute or two, and even Rebecca, who hadn't been critical of the new preacher, felt a little guilty. Caleb had suffered a terrible burn in the fire that had killed his wife. One side of his face was perfectly acceptable, pleasant-looking even, but the other… And his left hand… She shivered. God's mercy had saved him and little Amelia, but had left Caleb a marked man. She swallowed the lump rising in her throat. Who could blame him if he was morose and sad?

"Ya." Lilly took a small bite of fried chicken and went on talking. "It's true that Caleb Wittner is a grouch. And it's not uncharitable to speak the truth about someone. He's nothing like our old Preacher Perry. I miss him."

"We all do." Rebecca sipped at her lemonade, wondering if she'd made it too tart for most people. She liked it as she liked most things—with a bit of a bite. "Preacher Perry always had a joke or a funny story for everyone. What is that English expression? His cup was always full?"

Perry's sudden heart attack and subsequent passing had been a shock to the whole community, but nothing like the surprise of having newcomer Caleb Wittner selected, within weeks of his arrival in Seven Poplars, to take his place as preacher. The position was for life, and his role as shepherd of their church would affect each and every one of them.

"You have to admit that Caleb and Amelia have certainly livened things up in the neighborhood," Rebecca added.

The coming of the new preacher was the most exciting thing that had happened in Seven Poplars since Grace—Rebecca's secret half sister—had appeared on their back porch in a rainstorm two years ago.

Without being obvious, she glanced back at the barn, hoping to catch another glimpse of her new neighbor. There were two men pulling a large piece of rotten sideboard down; one was Will Stutzman, easy to recognize by his purple shirt, and the other was her brother-in-law, John Hartman, Grace's husband. Caleb Wittner was nowhere in sight. Disappointed, she finished the last few bites of her potato salad and rose to her feet. "We better get back and help clear away the desserts before someone comes looking for us."

Her friends stood up, as well. "I wonder if there's any of your sister Anna's *apfelstrudel* left?" Lilly said. "I think I could make room for just one slice."

More than two hours later, as the purple shadows of twilight settled over Caleb's farmstead, Rebecca returned to the trees near the barn to retrieve her shoes. Most of the families who'd come to work and visit had already packed up and gone home. Only a few of those who lived nearby, including her sisters Miriam and Ruth, and their husbands remained. Rebecca had been ready to go when she realized that she was still barefoot; she'd had to stop and think where and when she'd removed her sneakers.

"I remember where they are now," she said to her mother, Hannah, who was just climbing into their buggy. "You and Susanna go on home. I'll go fetch my shoes and see you there." Home was around the corner and across the street. She could just walk.

Mam and Susanna waved and their buggy rolled down the driveway, followed by her sisters and brothers-in-law behind them.

"You want us to wait?" Miriam called as Charley brought their wagon around to head down the driveway.

"I'm fine." Rebecca waved. "See you tomorrow!" As the sun set, she turned to go in search of her shoes.

The barn stood some distance from Caleb's home, which was a neat story-and-a-half 1920s-era brick house. English people had remodeled the house over the years, but had left the big post-and-beam barn to slowly fall into disrepair. Although the roof and siding had deteriorated, the frame of the barn remained sound.

It was the potential of the barn and outbuildings that had drawn Caleb to the ten-acre property, according to Rebecca's brother-in-law Eli. Even though it was quickly getting dark, Rebecca had no problem finding her shoes. They were lying by the tree, exactly as she'd left them. She thrust her foot into the left one and was just lacing it up when she heard a pitiful meow. She glanced around. It sounded like a cat.... No, not a cat, a kitten. Rebecca held her breath and listened, trying to locate the source of the distressed animal. She hadn't seen any cats on the property today. In fact, when she'd been serving at the first meal seating, she'd distinctly heard Caleb say that he didn't like cats.

That had been a strike against him. Rebecca had always liked cats better than dogs. Cats were... They were independent. They didn't give affection lightly, but once they'd decided that you were to be trusted, they could be a great source of company. And they kept a house free of mice. Rebecca had always believed cats to be smart, and there was nothing like a purring cat curled up in her lap at the end of a long day to soothe her troubles and put her in the right mind for prayer.

Meow. The plaintive cry of distress came again, louder than before. It was definitely a kitten; the sound was coming from the shadowy barn. As Rebecca stepped into her other shoe, she glanced in the direction of the house and yard, then back at the barn. Maybe the mother was out hunting and had left a nest of little ones in a safe spot. One of the kittens could have wandered away from the others and gotten lost.

Mee-oo-www.

That settled it. There was no way that she could go home and abandon the little creature without investigation. Otherwise, she'd lie awake all night worrying if it was injured or in danger. Shoes tied, she strode across the leaf-strewn ground toward the barn.

Today hadn't been a proper barn raising because the men hadn't built a new barn; they'd stripped the old one to a shell. Tomorrow the men would return, accompanied by a volunteer group from the local Mennonite church and other Amish men who hadn't been able to take a Friday off. They'd nail up new exterior siding and put on a roof. The Amish women would return at noon with a hearty lunch and supper for the workers.

Rebecca looked up at the barn that loomed skeleton-like in the semidarkness. She wasn't easily scared, but heavy shadows already lay deep in the structure's interior, and she wished she'd thought to come back for her shoes earlier.

She stepped over a pile of fresh lumber and listened again. This time it was easy to tell that a kitten was crying, and it was coming from above her head. Only one section of the old loft floor remained; the planks were unsound and full of holes. The rest was open space all the way to the roof, two stories above, divided by beams. Tomorrow, men would tear out the rest of the old floor, toss down the rotten wood to be burned and hammer down new boards.

Meow.

Rebecca glanced dubiously at the wooden ladder leaning against the interior hall framing. Darkness had already settled over the interior of the barn. It was difficult to see more than a few feet, but she could see well enough to know that there was no solid floor above her. The sensible thing would be to leave and return in the morning. By then, the mother cat would probably have returned for her kitten and the problem would be solved. At the very least, Rebecca knew she should walk back to Caleb's house to get a flashlight.

But what if the kitten fell? Nine lives or not, the loft was a good fourteen feet from the concrete floor. The baby couldn't survive such trauma. And what if it got cold tonight? It was already much cooler than it had been this afternoon when the sun was shining. She didn't know if the kitten could survive a night without its mama. What she *did* know was that she didn't have the heart to abandon the kitten. Making up her mind, she started up the ladder.

Caleb tucked his sleeping daughter into bed; it was early for bedtime, but she'd had a long day. He covered her with a light blanket and placed her rag doll under her arm. He never picked it up without a lump of sadness tightening in his throat. Dinah had sewn the doll for Amelia before the child was born. It was small and soft and stuffed with quilt batting. Dinah's skillful fingers had placed every stitch with love and skill, and Baby, with her blank face and tangled hair, was Amelia's most cherished possession.

He paused to push a lock of dark hair off the child's forehead. Amelia had crawled up into the rocking chair and fallen asleep when Caleb was seeing the last of his neighbors off. He hadn't even had time to bathe her before carrying her upstairs to the small, white-washed room across the hall from his own bedchamber. A mother would likely wake a drowsy child to wash her and put her in a clean nightgown before putting her to bed, but there was no mother.

It seemed to Caleb that a sleeping child ought to be left to sleep in peace. It was only natural that active *kinner* got dirty in the course of a busy day. Morning would be good enough for soap and water before breakfast.

"God keep you," he murmured, turning away from the bed. To the dog standing in the doorway, he said, "Fritzy. *Bescherm!*" Obediently, the black Standard Poodle dropped to a sitting position and fixed his attention on Amelia.

Absently, Caleb's hand rose to stroke the gnarled side of his face where only a sparse and ragged beard grew. The burned flesh that had pained him so fiercely in the days after the fire had finally healed. Now he had no feeling in the area at all.

Some said that he'd been lucky that his mouth hadn't been twisted, that his speech remained much as it had always been, but Caleb didn't agree. Luck would have been reaching his wife before the smoke had claimed her life. Luck would have been that Dinah and he and Amelia could have built a new home and continued their lives as before. A small voice whispered from the far corner of his consciousness that he asked too much of God, that the blessing had been that his daughter had come out of that inferno alive.

He did not blame God. The fire that had consumed their farmhouse had been an accident. A gust of wind… A spark from a lamp. The cause was never truly determined, but as Caleb saw it, the fault, if there was fault, had been his. He had not protected his family, and his precious wife had been lost to him and his beloved child.

"Watch over her," he ordered the dog. With Fritzy on duty, Caleb was free to check that his horse was safe, that the toolshed doors were locked and that all was secure.

Flat, green Delaware was a long way from the dry highlands of Idaho and the Old Order Amish community that he'd left behind. After the fire and the death of his wife, Caleb had tried to do as his bishop had urged. He'd tried to pick up his life and carry on for the sake of his child. He'd even gone so far as to consider, after a year, courting a plump widow with a kind face who belonged to his church. But the bitter memories of his past had haunted him and he'd decided to try to pick up the pieces of his life somewhere new. In Idaho, there had been no family ties to hold him. Here, where his cousin Eli lived, things might be better. It had to be good for Amelia to grow up with relatives, and Eli's wife had six sisters. A woman's hand was what Amelia needed, he told himself.

Caleb left the kitchen and walked out into the yard. All was quiet. His house was far enough off the road that he wasn't bothered by the sounds of passing traffic. There were several sheds and a decent stable for the horse. The old barn, a survivor from earlier times than the house, stood farther back. Caleb was pleased with the work that had been done on it today. Alone, it would have taken him months. There were good people here, people that he instinctively knew he could trust. He prayed to God that this move to Delaware had been the right one for both him and Amelia.

He walked on a little farther, drawn by the sweet

scent of new wood that lay stacked, ready and waiting for the following day. He stood for a moment in the semidarkness and gazed up at the exposed beams. He thought about the laughter and the camaraderie during their work today. Everyone had been kind to him and Amelia, trying to make them feel welcome. And he *had* felt welcome…but he hadn't felt as if he was part of the community. He still felt like an outsider, looking in through a glass-paned window, hearing their laughter but not feeling it. And he so *wanted* to feel laughter again.

Caleb was about to turn back to the house when he heard a thud and then a clatter from the barn. Something had fallen or been knocked over inside the building. Had some animal wandered in? Or did he have a curious intruder? "Who's there?" he called as he approached the open front wall.

"Just me," came a woman's voice from high above.

Caleb stepped inside and looked up to see a shadowy form swaying on a loft floor beam. A sense of panic went through him and he raised both hands. "Stop! Don't move!"

"I'm fine. I just—" Her foot slipped and she swayed precariously, arms outstretched, before recovering her balance.

Caleb gasped. "Stay where you are," he ordered. "I'm coming up."

"I'll be fine." She lowered herself down onto the beam until she was kneeling. "It's just hard to see. Do you have a flashlight?"

"What in the name of common sense are you doing in my loft, woman?" He ran for the ladder and climbed it at double speed. "*Ne!* Don't move."

"I don't need your help," she said, taking a sassy tone with him. Rising to her feet again, she began traversing the beam toward him.

"I told you to stay put!" Caleb had never been afraid of heights, but he was all too aware of the distance to the concrete floor and the possibility of serious injury or death if one or both of them fell. He stood cautiously, finding his balance, then stepped slowly toward her.

"Go back," she insisted. "I can do this."

"*Ya,* maybe you can," he answered gruffly. "Or maybe you can't, and I'll have to scrape you up off my barn floor with a shovel." He quickly closed the distance between them, reached out and swept her up in his arms.

Chapter Two

Caleb carried Rebecca to the end of the crossbeam and set her securely on the ladder. "You got your balance?"

Her hands tightened on the rung and she found solid footing under her before answering. "I'm fine. I really could have managed the beam." She slipped into the Pennsylvania *Deitsch* dialect that was their first language. "I wasn't going to fall." It wasn't as if she hadn't climbed the loft ladder in her father's barn a thousand times without ever slipping. Nimbly, she made her way down the ladder to the barn floor and stepped aside to allow him to descend.

"It didn't look like you were *managing*. You nearly fell off before I got to you."

A sharp reply rose in Rebecca's mind, but she pressed her lips together and swallowed it. Caleb Wittner's coming to her rescue, or what he'd obviously *believed* was coming to her rescue, was almost… It was… Her lips softened into a smile. It was as romantic as a hero coming to the rescue of a maiden in a story. He'd thought she was in danger and he'd put himself in harm's way to save her. It didn't matter that she wasn't *really* in danger. *"Danke,"* she murmured. "I'm sorry if I caused you trouble."

"You should be sorry."

His words were stern without being harsh. Caleb was obviously upset with her, but his was the voice of a take-charge and reasonable man. Somehow, even though he was scolding her, Rebecca found something pleasant and reassuring in his tone. He was almost a stranger, yet, oddly, she felt as though she could trust him.

Meow.

"Vas ist das?"

"Ach." In the excitement of having Caleb rescue her, she'd almost forgotten her whole reason for being in the barn in the first place. "It's a *katzenbaby,"* she exclaimed as she drew the little creature out of the bodice of her dress. "A kitten," she said, switching back to English and crooning softly to it. "Shh, shh, you're safe now." And to Caleb she said, "It's tiny. Probably hasn't had its eyes open long."

"A cat? You climbed up to the top of my barn in the dark for a *katzen?"*

"A baby." She kissed the top of the kitten's head. It was as soft as duckling down. "I think the poor little thing has lost its mother. It was crying so loudly, I just couldn't abandon it." She raised the kitten to her cheek and heard the crying change from a pitiful mewing to a purr. The kitten nuzzled against her and Rebecca felt the scratchy surface of a small tongue against her skin. "It must be hungry."

"Everyone has left for the night," he said, ignoring the kitten. "What are you still doing here?"

Rebecca sighed. "I forgot my *schuhe.* I'd taken off

my sneakers while…" She sensed his impatience and finished her explanation in a rush of words. "I left my shoes under the tree when I went to serve the late meal. And when I came to fetch them, I heard the kitten in distress." She cradled the little animal in her hands and it burrowed between her fingers. "Why do you think the mother cat moved the others and left this one behind?"

"There are no cats here. I've no use for cats," he said gruffly. "I have no idea how this one got in my loft."

Caleb's English was excellent, although he did have a slightly different accent in *Deitsch*. She didn't think she'd ever met anyone from Idaho. He was Eli's cousin, but Eli had grown up in Pennsylvania.

He loomed over her. "Come to the house. My daughter is in bed, but I'll wake her, hitch up my horse and drive you home. Where do you live?"

Rebecca felt a pang of disappointment; she'd assumed he knew who she was. She supposed that it was too dark for Caleb to make out her face now. Still, she'd hoped that he'd taken enough notice of her in church or elsewhere in the daylight to recognize her by her voice. "I'm Rebecca. Rebecca Yoder. One of Eli's wife's sisters."

"Not the youngest one. What's her name? The girl with the sweet smile. Susanna. Her, I remember. You must be the next oldest." He took her arm and guided her carefully out of the building. "Watch your step," he cautioned.

The moon was just rising over the trees, but she still couldn't see his face clearly. His fingers were warm but rough against her bare skin. For the first time, she felt uncertain and a little breathless. "I'm fine," she said, pulling away from him.

"Your mother will not be pleased that you didn't leave with the others," he said. "It's not seemly for us to be alone after nightfall."

"I'm not so young that my mother expects me to be in the house by dark." She wanted to tell him that he should know who she was, that she was a baptized member of his church and not a silly girl, but she didn't. "Speak in haste, repent at leisure," her *grossmama* always said.

Honestly, she could understand how Caleb might have been startled to find an intruder in his barn after dark. And it was true that it was awkward, her being here after everyone else had already left. She wasn't ready to judge him for being short with her.

"It's kind of you to offer," she said, using a gentler voice. "But I don't need you to take me home. And it would be foolish to get Amelia—" she let him know that she was familiar with his daughter's name, even if he didn't know hers "—to wake a sleeping child to drive me less than a mile. I'm quite capable of walking home." She hesitated. "But what do I do about the kitten? Shall I take it with me or—"

"*Ya*. Take the *katzen*. If it stays here, being so young, it will surely die."

"But if the mother returns for it and finds it gone—"

"Rebecca, I said I haven't seen a cat. Why someone didn't find this kitten earlier when we were working on the loft floor, I don't know. Now let me hitch my buggy. Eli would be—"

"I told you, I don't need your help," she answered firmly. "Eli would agree with me, as would my mother."

With that, she turned her back on him and strode away across the field.

"Rebecca, wait!" he called after her. "You're being unreasonable."

"Good night, Caleb." She kept walking. She'd be home before Mam wound the hall clock and have the kitten warm and fed in two shakes of a lamb's tail.

Caleb stared after the girl as she strode away. It wasn't right that she should walk home alone in the dark. She should have listened to him. He was a man, older than she was and a preacher in her church. She should have shown him more respect.

Rebecca Yoder had made a foolish choice to fetch the kitten and risk harm. Worse, she'd caused him to make the equally foolish decision to go out on that beam after her. He clenched his teeth, pushing back annoyance and the twinge of guilt that he felt. What if the young woman came to harm between here and her house? But what could he do? He couldn't leave Amelia alone in the house to run after Rebecca. Not only would he be an irresponsible father, but he would look foolish.

As foolish as he must have looked carrying that girl.

The memory of walking the beam with Rebecca in his arms rose in his mind and he pushed it away. He hadn't felt the softness of a woman's touch for a long time. Had he been unnecessarily harsh with Rebecca because somewhere, deep inside, he'd been exhilarated by the experience?

Caleb sighed. God's ways were beyond the ability of men and women to understand. He hadn't asked to be a leader of the church, and he certainly hadn't wanted it.

He hadn't been here more than a few weeks and

had attended only two regular church Sundays when one of the two preachers died and a new one had to be chosen from among the adult men. The Seven Poplars church used the Old Order tradition of choosing the new preacher by lot. A Bible verse was placed in a hymnal, and the hymnal was added to a pile of hymnals. Those men deemed eligible by the congregation had to, guided by God, choose a hymnal. The man who chose the book with the scripture inside became the new preacher, a position he would hold until death or infirmity prevented him from fulfilling the responsibility. To everyone's surprise, the lot had fallen to him, a newcomer, something that had never happened before to anyone's knowledge. If there was any way he could have refused, he would have. But short of moving away or giving up his faith and turning Mennonite, there was no alternative. The Lord had chosen him to serve, so serve he must.

Caleb looked up at his house, barely visible in the darkness, and came to a halt. He had come to Seven Poplars in the belief that God had led him here. He believed that God had a purpose for him, as He did for all men. What that purpose was, he didn't know, but for the first time since he'd arrived, he felt a calm fall over him. Everyone had said that, with time, the ache he felt in his heart for the loss of his wife would ease, that he would find contentment again.

As he stood there gazing toward his new house—toward his new life—it seemed to Caleb that a weight gradually lifted from his shoulders. "All over a kitten," he murmured aloud, smiling in spite of himself. "More nerve than common sense, that girl." He shook his head, and his wry smile became a chuckle. "If the other females in my new church are as headstrong and unpredictable as she is, heaven help me."

The following morning, Rebecca and her sisters Miriam, Ruth and Grace walked across the pasture to their sister Anna's house on the neighboring farm. Mam, Grace and Susanna were already there, as they had driven over in the buggy after breakfast. Also present in Anna's sunny kitchen were Cousin Dorcas, their grandmother Lovina—who lived with Anna and her husband, Samuel—and neighbors Lydia Beachy and Fannie Byler. Fortunately, Anna's home was large enough to provide ample space for all the women and a noisy assortment of small children, including Anna's baby, Rose, and Ruth's twins, the youngest children, who'd been born in midsummer.

The women were in the kitchen preparing a noon-day meal for the men working on Caleb's barn, and Rebecca had just finished quietly relaying the story of her new kitten's rescue to her sisters.

Rebecca had spent most of the night awake, trying to feed the kitten goat's milk from a medicine drop-per with little success. But this morning, Miriam had solved the problem by tucking the orphan into the mid-dle of a pile of nursing kittens on her back porch. The mother cat didn't seem to mind the visitor, so Rebec-ca's kitten was now sound asleep on Miriam's porch with a full tummy.

Grace fished a plastic fork out of a cup on the table, tasted Fannie's macaroni salad and chuckled. "I'd love to have seen that preacher carrying you and the kitten across that beam," she teased. And then she added, "Hmm, needs salt, I think."

"Keep your saltshaker away from my macaroni salad," Fannie warned good-naturedly from across the room. "Roman has high blood pressure, and I've cut him off salt. If anyone wants it, they can add it at the table."

Grossmama rose out of her rocker and came over to the table where bowls of food for the men were laid out. "A little salt never hurt anyone," she grumbled. "I've been eating salt all my life. Roman works hard. He never got high blood pressure from salt." She peered suspiciously at the blue crockery bowl of macaroni salad. "What are those green things in there?"

"Olives, Grossmama," Anna explained. "Just a few for color. Would you like to taste it?" She offered her a saucer and a plastic fork. "And maybe a little of Ruth's baked beans?"

"Just a little," Grossmama said. "You know I never want to be a bother."

Rebecca met Grace's gaze and it was all the two of them could do not to smile. Grossmama, a widow, had come to live in Kent County when her health and mind had begun to fail. Never an easy woman to deal with, Grossmama still managed to voice her criticism of her daughter-in-law. Their grandmother could be critical and outspoken, but it didn't keep any of them from feeling responsible for her or from loving her.

A mother spent a lifetime caring for others. How could any person of faith fail to care for an elderly relative? And how could they consider placing one of their own in a nursing home for strangers to care for? Rebecca intimately knew the problems of pleasing and watching over her grandmother. She and her sister Leah had spent months in Ohio with her before the family had finally convinced her to give up her home and move East. Still, it was a wonder and a blessing to Rebecca and everyone else that Grossmama—who could be so difficult—had settled easily and comfortably into life with Anna. Sweet and capable Anna, the Yoder sisters felt, had "the touch."

Lydia carried a basket of still-warm-from-the-oven loaves of rye bread to the counter. She was a willowy middle-aged woman, the mother of fifteen children and a special friend of Mam's. "I hope this will be enough," she said. "I had another two loaves in the oven, but the boys made off with one and I needed another for our supper."

"This should be fine," Mam replied. "Rebecca, would you hand me that bread knife and the big cutting board? I'll slice if you girls will start making sandwiches."

Lydia picked up the conversation she, Fannie and Mam had been having earlier, a conversation Rebecca hadn't been able to stop herself from eavesdropping on, since it had concerned Caleb Wittner.

"I don't know what's to be done. Mary won't go back and neither will Lilly. I spoke to Saul's Mary about her girl, Flo, but she's already taken a regular job at Spence's Market in Dover," Fannie said. "Saul's Mary said she imagined our new preacher would have to do his own laundry because not a single girl in the county will consider working for him now that he's run Mary and Lilly off."

"Well, someone has to help him out," Fannie said. She was Eli Lapp's aunt by marriage, and so she was almost a distant relative of Caleb. Thus, she considered herself responsible for helping her new neighbor and preacher. She'd been watching his daughter off and on since Caleb had arrived, but what with her own children and tending the customer counter in the chair shop as well as running the office there, Fannie had her hands full.

Mam arched a brow wryly as she took a fork from the cup and had a taste of one of the salads on the table. "A handful that little one is. I'd take her myself, but she's too young for school." Mam was the teacher at the Seven Poplars schoolhouse. "My heart goes out to a motherless child."

"No excuse for allowing her to run wild," Grossmama put in. "Train up a child the way they should go." This was one of their grandmother's good days, Rebecca decided. Other than asking where her dead son Jonas was, she'd said nothing amiss this morning. Jonas was Grossmama's son, Mam's husband and father to Rebecca and all her sisters. But although Dat had been dead for nearly five years, her grandmother had yet to accept it. Usually, Grossmama claimed that Dat was in the barn, milking the cows, although some days, she was certain that Anna's husband, Samuel, was Jonas and this was his house and farm, not Samuel Mast's.

"Amelia needs someone who can devote time to her," Fannie agreed. "I wish I could do more, but I tried having her in the office and…" She shook her head. "It just didn't work out. For either of us."

Rebecca grabbed a fork and peered into a bowl of potato salad that had plenty of hard-boiled eggs and paprika, just the way she liked it. From what she'd heard from Mam, Amelia was a terror. Fannie had gone to call Roman to the phone and the little girl had spilled a glass of water on a pile of receipts, tried to cut up the new brochures and stapled everything in sight.

"Caleb Wittner needs our help," Mam said, handing Rebecca a small plate. "He can hardly support himself and his child, tend to church business and cook and clean for himself."

"You should get him a wife," Grossmama said. "I'll have a little of that, too." She pointed to the coleslaw. "A preacher should have a wife."

Lydia and Mam exchanged glances and Mam's lips twitched. She gave her mother-in-law a spoon of the coleslaw on her plate. "We can't just *get him a wife,* Lovina."

"Either a housekeeper or a wife will do," Fannie said. "But one way or another, this can't wait. We have to find someone suitable."

"But who?" Anna asked. "Who would dare after the fuss he and his girl have caused?"

"Maybe we should send Rebecca," Grace suggested.

Rebecca paused, a forkful of Anna's potato salad halfway to her mouth. "Me?"

Her mother looked up from the bowl she was recovering with plastic wrap. "What did you say, Grace?"

Miriam chuckled and looked slyly at Rebecca. "Grace thinks that Rebecca should go."

"To marry Caleb Wittner?" Grossmama demanded. "I didn't hear any banns cried. My hearing's not gone yet."

Anna glanced at Rebecca. "Would you consider it, Rebecca? After…" She rolled her eyes. "You know…the kitten incident." Anna's round face crinkled in a grin.

Rebecca shrugged, then took a bite of potato salad. "Maybe. With only me and Susanna at home, and now that Anna has enough help, why shouldn't I be earning money to help out?"

"You can't marry him without banns," Grossmama insisted, waving her plastic fork. "Maybe that's the way they do it where he comes from. Not here, and not in Ohio. And you are wrong to marry a preacher."

"Why?" Mam asked mildly. "Why couldn't our Rebecca be a preacher's wife?"

"I didn't agree to *marry* him," Rebecca protested, deciding to try a little of the pasta salad at the end of the table. "I didn't even say I'd take the job as housekeeper. Maybe."

"You should try it," Anna suggested.

Rebecca looked to her sister. "You think?" She hesitated. "I suppose I could try it."

"*Gut.* It's settled, then," Fannie pronounced, clapping her hands together.

"*Narrisch,*" her grandmother snapped. "Rebecca can't be a preacher's wife."

"I'm *not* marrying him, Grossmama," Rebecca insisted.

"You're going to be sor-ry," Ruth sang. "If that little mischief-maker Amelia doesn't drive you off, you and Caleb Wittner will be butting heads within the week."

"Maybe," Rebecca said thoughtfully, licking her plastic fork. "And maybe not."

Chapter Three

Two days later, Caleb awoke to a dark and rainy Monday morning. He pushed back the patchwork quilt, shivered as the damp air raised goose bumps on his bare skin and peered sleepily at the plain black clock next to his bed. *"Ach!"* Late… He was late, this morning of all mornings.

He scrambled out of bed and fumbled for his clothes. He had a handful of chores to do before leaving for the chair shop. He had to get Amelia up, give her a decent breakfast and make her presentable. He had animals to feed. He'd agreed to meet Roman Byler at nine, in time to meet the truck that would be delivering his power saws and other woodworking equipment. Roman and Eli had offered to help him move the equipment into the space Caleb was renting from Roman. He'd never been a man who wanted to keep anyone waiting, and he didn't know Roman that well. Not only was Roman a respected member of the church, but he was Eli's partner. What kind of impression would Caleb make on Roman and Eli if he was late his first day of work?

Caleb yanked open the top drawer of the oak dresser

where his clean socks should have been, then remembered they'd all gone into the wash. Laundry was not one of his strong points. He remembered that darks went in with darks, but washing clothes was a woman's job. After four years of being on his own, he still struggled with the chore.

When confronted with a row of brightly colored containers of laundry detergent in the store, all proclaiming to be the best, he always grabbed the nearest. Bleach, he'd discovered, was not his friend, and neither was the iron. He was getting good at folding clothes when he took them off the line, but he'd learned to live with wrinkles.

Socks were his immediate problem. He'd done two big loads of wash on Friday, but the clean clothes had never made it from the laundry basket in the utility room back upstairs to the bedrooms. "Amelia," he called. "Wake up, buttercup! Time to get up!" Sockless, Caleb pulled on one boot and looked around for the other. Odd. He always left both standing side by side at the foot of his bed. *Always.*

He got down on his knees and looked under the bed. No boot. *Where could the other one have gone?*

Amelia, he had already decided, could wear her Sunday dress this morning. That, at least, was clean. Fannie had been kind enough to help with Amelia sometimes, and Caleb had hoped that he could impose on her again today. The least he could do was bring her a presentable child.

"Amelia!" He glanced down the hallway and saw, at once, that her bedroom door was closed. He always left it open—just as he always left his shoes where he could find them easily in the morning. If the door was closed, it hadn't closed itself. "Fritzy?" No answering bark.

Caleb smelled mischief in the air. He hurried to the door, opened it and glanced into Amelia's room. Her bed was empty—her covers thrown back carelessly. And there was no dog on watch.

"Amelia! Are you downstairs?" Caleb took the steps, two at a time.

His daughter had always been a handful. Even as a baby, she hadn't been easy; she'd always had strong opinions about what she wanted and when she wanted it. It was almost as if an older, shrewder girl lurked behind that innocent child's face and those big, bright eyes, eyes so much like his. But there the similarity ended, as he had been a thoughtful boy, cautious and logical. And he had never dared to throw the tantrums Amelia did when things didn't go her way.

Caleb reached the bottom of the stairs and strode into the kitchen, where—as he'd suspected—he found Amelia, Fritzy and trouble. Amelia was *helping out* in the kitchen again.

"Vas ist das?" he demanded, taking in the ruins of what had been a fairly neat kitchen when he'd gone to bed last night.

"Staunen erregen!" Amelia proclaimed. "To surprise you, Dat."

Pancakes or biscuits, Caleb wasn't certain what his daughter had been making. Whatever it was had taken a lot of flour. And milk. And eggs. And honey. A puddle of honey on the table had run over the edge and was dripping into a pile of flour on the floor. Two broken eggs lay on the tiles beside the refrigerator.

"You don't cook without me!"

Fritzy's ears pricked up as he caught sight of the eggs. That's when Caleb realized the dog had been gulping down a plate of leftover ham from Saturday's midday meal that the neighborhood women had provided. He'd intended to make sandwiches with the ham for his lunch.

"Stay!" Caleb ordered the dog as he grabbed a dishcloth and scooped up the eggs and shells.

"I didn't cook," Amelia protested. "I was waiting for you to start the stove." Her lower lip trembled. "But… but my pancakes spilled."

They had apparently spilled all over Amelia. Her hands, face and hair were smeared with white, sticky goo.

Then Caleb spotted his boot on the floor in front of the sink…filled with water. He picked up his boot in disbelief and tipped it over the sink, watching the water go down the drain.

"For Fritzy!" she exclaimed. "He was thirsty and the bowls was dirty."

They were dirty, all right. Every dish he owned had apparently been needed to produce the floury glue she was calling pancakes. "And where are my *socken?*" he demanded, certain now that Amelia's mischief hadn't ended with his soggy boot. He could see the wicker basket was overturned. There were towels on the floor and at least one small dress, but not a sock in sight.

"Crows," Amelia answered. "In our corn. I chased them."

Her muddy nightshirt and dirty bare feet showed that she'd been outside already. In the rain.

"You went outside without me?"

Amelia stared at the floor. One untidy pigtail seemed

coated in a floury crust. "To chase the crows. Out of the corn."

"But what has that to do with my socks?"

"I threw them at the crows, Dat."

"You took my *socken* outside and threw them into the cornfield?"

"Ne, Dat." She shook her head so hard that the solid cone of flour paste on her head showered flour onto her shoulders. "From upstairs. From my bedroom window. I threw the sock balls at the crows there."

"And then you went outside?"

"Ya." She nodded. "The sock balls didn't scare 'em away, so Fritzy and me chased 'em with a stick."

"What possessed you to make our clean socks into balls in the first place? And to throw them out the window?" Caleb shook his finger at her for emphasis but knew as he uttered the words what she would say.

"You did, Dat. You showed me how."

He sighed. And so he had. Sometimes when he and Amelia were alone on a rainy or snowy day and bored, he'd roll their clean socks into balls and they'd chase each other through the house, lobbing *socken* at each other. But it had never occurred to him that she would throw the socks out the window. "Upstairs! To your room," he said in his sternest father's voice. He could go without his noonday meal today, and the mess in the kitchen could be cleaned up tonight, but the animals still had to be fed. And Amelia had to be bathed and fed and dressed before he took her with him.

Amelia burst into tears. "But…but I wanted to help."

"Upstairs!"

And then, after the wailing girl fled up the steps, he looked around the kitchen again and realized that his worst fears had come to fruition. He was a failure as a father. He had waited too long to take another wife. This small female was too much for him to manage without a helpmate.

"Lord, help me," he murmured, carrying a couple of dirty utensils to the sink. "What do I do?"

He was at his wit's end. Although he loved Amelia dearly, he didn't think he was an overly indulgent parent. He tried to treat his daughter as he saw other fathers and mothers treat their children. He was anxious for her to be happy here in their new home, but it was his duty to teach her proper behavior and respect for adults. Among the Amish, a willful and disobedient child was proof of a neglectful father. It was the way he'd been taught and the way his parents had raised him.

The trouble was that Amelia didn't see things that way. She wasn't a sulky child, and her mind was sharp. Sometimes Caleb thought that she was far too clever to be four, almost five years of age. She could be affectionate toward him, but she seemed to take pleasure in doing exactly the opposite of what she was asked to do.

With a groan, Caleb raked his fingers through his hair. What was he going to do about Amelia? So far, his attempts at finding suitable childcare had fallen short. He'd hired two different girls, and both had walked out on him in less than three weeks' time.

Back in Idaho, his neighbor, widow Bea Mullet, had cared for Amelia when Caleb needed babysitting. She had come three days a week to clean the house, cook and tend to Amelia. But Bea was in her late seventies, not as spry as she had once been and her vision was poor. The truth was, Amelia had mostly run wild when he wasn't home to see to her himself. Once the bishop's wife had even spoken to him about the untidy condition of Amelia's hair and prayer bonnet, and another time the deacon had complained about the child giggling during service. He had felt that that criticism was unfair. Males and females sat on opposite sides of the room during worship and children, naturally, were under the watchful eyes of the women. How was he supposed to discipline his daughter from across the room without interrupting the sermon?

Amelia was young and spirited. She had no mother to teach her how she should behave. Those were the excuses he'd made for her, but this morning, the truth was all too evident. Amelia was out of control. So exasperated was he, that—had he been a father who believed in physical punishment—Amelia would have been soundly spanked. But he lacked the stomach to do it. No matter what, he could never strike a child.

Caleb shook his head. He'd ignored the good advice that friends and fellow church members had offered. He'd come to Delaware to put the past behind him, but he'd brought his own stubborn willfulness with him. He'd allowed a four-year-old child to run wild. And this disaster was the result.

"Good morning," came a cheerful female voice, startling Caleb.

He looked up and stared at the young woman standing just inside his kitchen. She'd come through the utility room.

"The door was open." She whipped off a navy blue wool scarf and he caught a glimpse of red-gold hair beneath her *kapp*. Sparkling drops of water glistened on her face.

Caleb opened his mouth to reply, but she was too quick for him.

"I'm Rebecca. Rebecca Yoder. We met on your barn beam the other night."

She offered a quick smile as she shed a dark rain slicker. Beneath it, she wore a lavender dress, a white apron and black rubber boots—two boots. Unlike him. Suddenly, Caleb was conscious of how foolish he must look, standing there with one bare foot, his hair uncombed and sticking up like a rooster's comb and his shirt-tails hanging out of his trousers.

"My door was open?" he repeated, woodenly.

Fritzy, the traitor, wagged his stump of a tail so hard that his whole backside wiggled back and forth. He sat where Caleb had commanded him to stay, but it was clear that given the choice he would have rushed up to give the visitor a hearty welcome kiss.

"*Ya.* I'm guessing you weren't the one who left it open." She pulled off first one rubber boot and then the other and hung the rain-streaked slicker on an iron hook. "I'm here to help with the housework. And Amelia."

She looked at him and then slowly scanned the room, taking in the spilled flour, the cluttered table and the floor. Her freckled nose wrinkled, and he was struck by how young and fetching she appeared. "Eli told you that I was coming, didn't he?"

Eli? Caleb's mind went blank. "*N...ne.* He didn't."

"Yesterday. He was supposed to tell you that I..." She shrugged. "Fannie sent me. Fannie Byler. She said you needed someone to..."

He couldn't remember Eli or anyone mentioning

sending another girl. Certainly not the Yoder girl. "They sent you?"

Rebecca's small fists rested on her shapely hips. "You're not still angry about Friday night?" Her smile became a chuckle.

"I'm not angry," he protested. "But you're…you're too…too…" He was going to say *young,* but he knew she was at least twenty-one. Maybe twenty-two. Old enough to have her own child. "Inexperienced. Amelia is… Can be…difficult. She—" What he was trying to say was lost in the sound of Fritzy gagging. He groaned out loud. The ham Amelia had given him was far too rich for the dog's stomach. "Outside!" Caleb yelled. "If you're going to be sick, do it outside!" He pushed past Rebecca and dashed through the small utility room to throw open the back door.

Not quite in time.

Fritzy made it out of the kitchen but lost it on the cement floor in front of the washing machine. "Out!" Caleb repeated. Sheepishly, the dog bounded out into the yard, where he proceeded to run in circles and snap at the raindrops. Now that his stomach had yielded up the large plate of ham, Fritzy was obviously cured.

Caleb returned to the kitchen to deal with Rebecca Yoder. "You have to go," he said.

"Ne," she replied, smiling again. *"You* have to go. Roman and Eli will be waiting for you. There's a big truck there already. Eli said yesterday they were expecting your saws this morning."

"I don't need your help."

"You don't?" She slowly scanned the kitchen. "It looks to me as if that's exactly what you do need." She tapped her lips with a slender finger. "I know what the other girls said, about why they quit. I know what they said about Amelia and about you."

"About me?" The trouble was with his daughter. What fault could those young women have found in *his* behavior? He hadn't done or said anything—

"They said you are abrupt and hard to please." She sounded…amused.

"I am not!"

"Dat!"

Caleb turned toward the sound of Amelia's voice. She was standing in the kitchen doorway, still in her wet and muddy nightgown, her face streaked with tears. In one hand she held a pair of scissors, and in the other, a large section of her long, dark hair.

"Amelia?" He grabbed the scissors. "What have you done?"

"I'll tend to her," Rebecca assured him without the least bit of concern in her voice. She walked calmly over to Amelia, as if little girls cut their hair every day. "This is women's work. Isn't it, Amelia?" She looked down at the little girl.

Amelia looked up at her, obviously unsure what to think.

Caleb hesitated. He couldn't just walk out and leave his daughter with this girl, could he? What if that only made things worse?

"I'll be here just as a trial," Rebecca said. "A week. If we don't suit, then you can find someone else."

Caleb didn't know what to say. He really didn't have a choice, did he? The men would be waiting for him. "A week? *Ya.*" He nodded, on firmer ground again. He wouldn't be that far away. It might be easier to let this young woman try and fail than to argue with her.

"Just a week," he repeated. He looked at Amelia. "Dat has to go to work," he said. "This… Rebecca will look after you…and help you tidy up your breakfast." He looked around the kitchen and shuddered inwardly. "I hope you are made of sterner stuff than the past two girls," he said to Rebecca.

"We'll see," Rebecca answered as she gathered the still-weeping child in her arms. "Breakfast and clean clothing for Amelia…and two boots for you are a start, wouldn't you agree?"

The strenuous task of unloading the heavy saws and woodworking equipment took all of Caleb's concentration for three hours. But when the truck pulled away and he was left alone to organize the tools in his area partitioned off in Roman's shop, his thoughts returned to Rebecca and his daughter. What if he'd been so eager to get out of the house and to his tools that he'd left Amelia with someone unsuited to the task? What if Amelia disliked Rebecca or was fearful of her? What if Amelia had been so bad that Rebecca had walked out and left the child alone?

Once doubt had crept into his mind, Caleb began to worry in earnest. The thing to do, he decided as he slid a chisel into place on a rack, would be to walk back home and check on them. It wasn't unreasonable that a father make certain that his new housekeeper was doing her job and watching over Amelia. It was still spitting rain, but what of it? And there was the matter of the blister on his heel, where his shoe had rubbed against his bare foot for the past few hours. Putting a Band-Aid on the blister made sense. He couldn't afford to be laid up with an infection, not with the important contract to fulfill in the next thirty-eight days.

Caleb surveyed his new workbench and tables. This was a larger space than he'd had on his farm back in Idaho. Once everything was in place—drills, fretsaw, coping saws, hammers, mallets, sanders, planes, patterns and the big, gas-powered machinery—he could start work. Many of his tools were old, some handed down from his great-grandfather. The men in his family had always been craftsmen and had earned their living as cabinetmakers and builders of fine furniture. Only a few of his family's personal antiques had survived the fire: a walnut Dutch cupboard carved with the date 1704, a small cherry spice cabinet, and an *aus schteier kischt,* a blanket chest painted with unicorns, hearts and flowers that would one day be part of Amelia's bridal dowry.

A tickle at the back of Caleb's throat made him swallow. He didn't want to think of Amelia growing up and leaving him to be a wife. He knew it must be, but she was all he had and he wanted to keep her close by him for a long, long time. Impatient with his foolishness—worrying about her marriage when she had yet to learn her letters and still slept with her thumb in her mouth—he pushed away thoughts of Amelia as an adult. What should concern him was her safety right now. He'd abandoned her to the care of a girl barely out of her teens. For all he knew his daughter might be neglected. She could be sliding down the wet roof or swimming in the horse trough.

Slamming the pack of fine sandpaper down on the workbench, he turned and strode toward the door that led outside to the parking lot. He swung it open and nearly collided with Rebecca Yoder, who was just coming in. In her hands, she carried a Thermos, and just behind her was Amelia with his black lunchbox. They were both wearing rain slickers and boots. Caleb had no idea how they had found Amelia's rain slicker. It had been missing for days.

Caleb sputtered his apologies and stepped out of their way. He could feel his face flaming, and once again, he couldn't think of anything sensible to say to Rebecca. "I… I was on my way home," he managed. "To see about Amelia."

His daughter giggled. "I'm here, Dat. We brought your lunch." She held up the big black lunchbox.

"And hot cider." Rebecca raised the Thermos. "It's such a raw day, Amelia thought you'd like something hot."

"Not coffee," Amelia said. "I hate coffee. But…but I like cider."

"There's a table with benches in the next room," Rebecca suggested. "Eli and Roman eat lunch there when they don't go home. I know Eli's there." She pointed toward a louvered door on the far side of the room.

"I helped cook your lunch," his daughter proclaimed proudly. "I cooked the eggs. All by myself!"

"She did," Rebecca agreed. "And she filled a jar with coleslaw. There's some chicken corn soup and biscuits we made. But Amelia said you liked hard-boiled eggs."

"With salt and pepper." Amelia bounced up and down so hard that the lunchbox fell out of her hands.

Caleb stooped to pick it up.

"Ooh!" Amelia cried.

"It's all right," he assured her. "Nothing broken." He followed Rebecca and a chattering Amelia into the lunchroom. He didn't know what else to do. And as he did, he noticed that under her raincoat, Amelia looked surprisingly neat. Her face was so clean it was shiny and her hair was plaited into two tiny braids that peeked out from under an ironed *kapp*. Even the hem of her blue dress that showed under her slicker was pressed.

"What…what did you two do this morning?" he asked Amelia.

"We cleaned, Dat. And cooked. And I helped." She nodded. "I did."

No tears, no whining, no fussing. Amelia looked perfectly content.… More than content. He realized that she looked happy. He should have been pleased—he was pleased—but there was something unsettling about this young Yoder woman.

Rebecca stopped and glanced back over her shoulder at him. Her face was smooth and expressionless, but a dimple and the sparkle in her blue eyes made him suspect that she was finding this amusing. "Do you approve?"

"Wait until I see what my kitchen looks like," he answered gruffly.

Amelia giggled. "I told you, Dat. We cleaned."

Rebecca's right eyebrow raised and her lips quivered with suppressed laughter. "A week's trial," she reminded him. "That's all I agreed to. By then I should know if I want to work for you."

Chapter Four

On Friday, Caleb left work a half hour early and started home. He'd finished the ornate Victorian oak bracket that he'd been fashioning all afternoon, and he didn't want to begin a new piece so late in the day. Three years ago, he'd switched from building custom kitchen cabinets to the handcrafted corbels, finials and other architectural items that he sold to a restoration supply company in Boise. Englishers who fixed up old houses all over the country spent an exorbitant amount of money to replicate original wooden details. Not that Caleb wasn't glad for the business, but he guessed his thrifty Swiss ancestors would be shocked at the expense of fancy things when plain would do.

He rarely left his workbench before five, but he was still uneasy leaving Amelia with the Yoder girl. Better to arrive early and check up on them. So far, Rebecca Yoder seemed capable, and he had to admit that his daughter liked her, but time would tell. Amelia sometimes went days without getting into real mischief. And then, it was Gertie, bar the door—meaning that his sweet little girl could stir up some real trouble.

The walk home from the shop took only a few minutes, but his new workshop was far enough from his house to be respectable. Otherwise, it wouldn't have been fitting for him to have an unmarried girl housekeeping and watching his daughter for him. He left in the morning when Rebecca arrived and she went home in the late afternoon when he returned from work. The schedule was working out nicely, and as much as he hated to admit it, it was nice to know that someone would be there in the house when he arrived home. A house could get lonely with just a man and his little girl.

When Caleb arrived home, Rebecca's pony was pastured beside his driving horse, and the two-wheeled, open buggy that she'd ridden in this morning was waiting by the shed. A basket of green cooking apples, three small pumpkins and a woman's sewing box filled the storage space at the rear of the buggy. As he crossed the yard toward the house, Caleb noticed that one of the kitchen windows stood open. Wonderful smells drifted out, becoming stronger as he let himself in through the back door into an enclosed porch that served as a laundry and utility room.

Fritzy greeted him, stump of a tail wagging, and Caleb paused to scratch the dog behind his ears. "I'm home," he called. And then, to Fritzy, he murmured in *Deitsch,* "Good boy, good old Fritzy."

Amelia's delighted squeal rang out, and Caleb grinned, pleased that she was so happy to see him. But when he stepped into the kitchen, he discovered that his daughter's attention was riveted on an aluminum colander hanging on the back of a chair.

"Again!" Amelia cried. "Let me try again!"

"Ne," Rebecca said. "My turn now. You have to wait until it's your turn."

"One!" Amelia yelled.

Caleb watched, bewildered, as an object flew through the air to land in the colander.

"Two!" Into the colander.

"Three!"

A third one bounced off the back of the chair and slid across the floor to rest at his feet.

"You missed!" Amelia crowed. "My turn!"

"Vas ist das?" Caleb demanded, picking up what appeared to be a patchwork orange beanbag. "What's going on?"

"Dat!" Amelia whirled around, flung herself across the room and leaped into his arms. "We're playing a throwing game," she exclaimed, somehow extracting the cloth beanbag from his hand and nearly whacking him in the eye with it as she climbed up to lock her arms around his neck. "At Fifer's Orchard they had games and a straw maid and—"

"A maze," Rebecca corrected. "A straw bale maze."

"And a train," Amelia shouted. "A little one. For *kinder* to ride on. And a pumpkin patch. You get on a wagon and a tractor pulls you—"

Caleb's brow creased in a frown. "A train? You let Amelia ride on a toy train like the Englisher children?" His gaze fell on a large orange lollipop propped on the table. The candy was shaped like a pumpkin on a stick, wrapped in clear paper and tied with a ribbon. "And you bought her English sweets?" Caleb extricated himself from Amelia's stranglehold, unwound her arms and lowered her gently to the floor. "Do you think that was wise?" he asked, picking up the lollipop and turning it over to frown at the jack-o'-lantern face painted on the back. "These things are not for Amish children."

"*Ya,* so I explained to her and I'd explain to you if you'd let me speak," Rebecca said, a saucy tone to her voice. "We weren't the only Amish there. And it was Bishop Atlee's wife who bought the lollipop for her. I could hardly take it back and offend the woman. I told Amelia that she couldn't have it unless you approved, and then only after her supper. I didn't allow her to go into the Fall Festival area with the straw maze, the rides and the face painting. I told her that those things were fancy, not plain."

"But…" he began.

Rebecca went on talking. "Amelia didn't fuss when I told her no, and she helped me pick a basket of apples." Rebecca flashed him a smile. "Three of those apples are baking with brown sugar in the oven. For after your evening meal or tomorrow's breakfast."

Caleb ran a finger under his collar. He could feel heat creeping up his throat and his cheeks were suddenly warm. Once again this red-haired Yoder girl was making him feel foolish in his own house. "So she didn't ride the toy train?"

"A wagon, Dat." Amelia tossed the orange beanbag into the air. "Rebecca said that we could…to pick pumpkins and apples."

"To find the best ones," Rebecca explained. "We had to go to the field, so we rode the tractor wagon. Otherwise we couldn't have carried it all back."

"Too heavy!" Amelia exclaimed, catching hold of his hand and tugging him toward the stove. "And we made a stew—in a pumpkin! For supper!" Amelia bounced and twirled, coming perilously near the stove. He caught her around the waist and scooped her up out of danger as she chattered on without a pause for breath. "I helped, Dat. Rebecca let me help."

Caleb exhaled, definitely feeling outnumbered and outmatched. The good smells, he realized, were coming from the oven. A cast-iron skillet of golden-brown biscuits rested on the stovetop beside a saucepan of what could only be fresh applesauce. "Maybe I was too hasty," he managed. "But the beanbags? The money I left in the sugar bowl was for groceries, not toys. The move from Idaho was expensive. I can't afford to buy—"

"I stitched up the beanbags at home last night."

Rebecca's expression was innocent, but she couldn't hide the light of amusement in her vivid blue eyes.

"From scraps," she continued. "And I stuffed them with horse corn. So they aren't really *bean*bags."

"Corn bags!" Amelia giggled. "You have to play, Dat. It's fun. You count, and you try to throw the bags into the coal-ander."

"Colander." Rebecca returned her attention to Caleb. "It's educational. To teach the little ones to count in English. Mam has the same game at the school. The children love it."

Caleb's mouth tightened, and he grunted a reluctant assent. "If the toy is made and not bought, I suppose—"

"You try, Dat," Amelia urged. "Rebecca can do it. It's really hard to get them in the coal…colander." She pushed an orange bag into his hand. "And you have to count," she added in *Deitsch*. "In English!"

"I don't have time to play with you now," Caleb hedged. "The rabbits need—"

"We fed the bunnies," Amelia said. "And gave them water."

"And fresh straw," Rebecca added. She moved to the stove and poured a mug of coffee. "But maybe you're tired after such a long day at the shop." She raised a russet eyebrow. "Sugar and cream?"

Caleb shook his head. "Black."

"My father always liked his coffee black, too," Rebecca murmured, "but I like mine with sugar and cream." She held out the coffee. "I just made it fresh."

"Please, Dat," Amelia begged, tugging on his arm. "Just one game."

His gaze met his daughter's, and his resolve to have none of this silliness melted. Such a little thing to bring a smile to her face, he rationalized…and he had been away from her all day. "Three throws," he agreed, "but then—"

"Yay!" Amelia cried. "Dat's going to try."

"You have to stand back by the window," Rebecca instructed. "Underhand works better."

With a sigh, Caleb took to the starting point and tossed all three beanbags into the colander on the first try, one after another.

"*Gut,* Dat!" Amelia hopped from one foot to the other, wriggling with joy. "But you forgot to count. Now my turn. You take turns." She gathered up the beanbags and moved back about three feet. "One… *zwei*…three!" She burst into giggles as she successfully got one of the three into the target.

"A tie," Rebecca proclaimed, and when he looked at her in surprise, she said, "Amelia gets a handicap." She shrugged and gave a wry smile. "Both on the English and on her aim." Rebecca stepped to a spot near the utility room door, a little farther from the colander than he stood, and lobbed all of the bags in. She didn't forget to count in English.

"Rebecca wins!" Amelia declared. "She beat you, Dat. You forgot to count."

Caleb grimaced. "I did, didn't I?"

Rebecca nodded. "You did."

"The lamb's tail," Amelia supplied and giggled again.

"Comes last," Rebecca finished for her.

He chuckled and took a sip of his coffee. It was good and strong, the way he liked it. But there was something extra. He sniffed the mug. Had Rebecca added something? "Vanilla?" he asked.

"Just a smidgen," Rebecca admitted. "My father liked his that way."

Caleb nodded and took another sip. "Not bad," he pronounced, and then said, "Since I'm new at this cornbag tossing, I think I deserve a rematch."

"The champion sits out," Rebecca explained merrily. "So you have to play Amelia."

Caleb groaned. "Why do I think that there's no way I can win this?"

"I go first," Amelia said, scooping up the bag. *"Eins."* She tossed the first.

"One," Caleb corrected. "You have to say it in English, remember?"

"Two! *Drei!*" she squealed, throwing the third.

"Three," he said. "One, two, three."

"I got them all in," Amelia said. "All *drei.*"

"She did," Rebecca said. "All *three* in. That will be hard to beat, Caleb."

He pretended to be worried, making a show of

staring at the colander and pacing off the distance backward. Amelia giggled. "Shh," he said. "I'm concentrating here." When he got back to his spot by the window, he spun around, turning his back to them and tossed the first beanbag over his shoulder. It fell short, and Amelia clapped her hands and laughed.

"You forgot to count again," she reminded him.

Caleb clapped one hand to his cheeks in mock dismay. "Can I try again?"

"Two more," Amelia agreed, "and then it's my turn again."

He spun back around and closed his eyes. "Two!" he declared and let it fly.

There was a *plop* and a shocked gasp. When Caleb opened his eyes, it was to see Martha Coblentz—the other preacher's wife—standing in the doorway that opened to the utility room, her hands full, her mouth opening and closing like a beached fish.

Well, it should be, Caleb thought as familiar heat washed over his neck and face. The beanbag had landed on Martha's head and appeared to be lodged in her prayer *kapp.* The shame he felt at being caught in the midst of such childish play was almost as great as his overwhelming urge to laugh. "I'm sorry," he exclaimed, covering his amusement with a choking cough. "It was a game. My daughter… We… I was teaching her English… counting…"

Martha drew herself to her full height and puffed up like a hen fluffing her feathers. The beanbag dislodged, bounced off her nose and landed on the floor. "Well, I never!" she said as her gaze raked the kitchen, taking in Rebecca, the colander, the biscuits on the stove and the pumpkin lollipop on the table. Martha sniffed and sent the beanbag scooting across the clean kitchen floor with the toe of one sensible, black-leather shoe. "Hardly what I expected to find here." Her lips pursed into a thin, lard-colored line. "Thought you'd want something hot…for your supper."

Caleb realized that Martha wasn't alone. A younger woman—Martha and Reuben's daughter, Doris, Dorothy, something like that—stood behind her, her arms full of covered dishes. She shifted from side to side, craning her thin neck to see past her mother.

"Come in," Caleb said. "Please. Have coffee."

"Aunt Martha. Dorcas." Rebecca, not seeming to be the least bit unsettled by their arrival, smiled warmly and motioned to them. "I know you have time for coffee."

"Your mother said you were only here while Preacher Caleb was at the shop," Martha said. "I didn't expect to find such goings-on."

"We came to bring you stuffed beef heart." Dorcas offered him a huge smile. One of her front teeth was missing, making the tall, thin girl even plainer. "And liver dumplings." The young woman had a slight lisp.

Caleb hated liver only a little less than beef heart. He swallowed the lump in his throat and silently chided himself for being so uncharitable to two of his flock, especially Dorcas, so obedient and modestly dressed. He had a long way to go to live up to his new position as preacher for this congregation.

"And molasses shoofly pie," Martha added proudly, holding it up for his approval. "Dorcas made it herself, just for you." She strode to the table, set down the dessert and picked up the questionable pumpkin lollipop by the end of the ribbon. Holding it out with as much disgust as she might have displayed for a dead mouse attached to a trap, Martha carried the candy to the trash can and dropped it in. "Surely, you weren't going to allow your child to eat such English junk," she said, fixing him with a reproving stare. "Our bishop would never approve of jack-o'-lantern candy, but of course, I'd never mention it to him."

"Pumpkin," Rebecca said, defending the lollipop. "We were going to wash off the face."

Martha sniffed again, clearly not mollified.

Amelia's lower lip quivered. She cast one hopeful glance in Caleb's direction, and when he gave her the father warning look, she turned and pounded out of the room and up the stairs. Fritzy—cowardly dog that he was—fled, hot on the child's heels.

Rebecca went to the stove and turned off the oven. "You're right, Aunt Martha," she said sweetly. "It *is* time I went home."

Martha scowled at her.

"Eight on Monday?" Rebecca asked Caleb.

"Eight-thirty," he answered.

Rebecca collected the colander and the beanbags, made her farewells to her aunt and cousin and vanished into the utility room. "See you Sunday for church."

Martha bustled to the stove, shoved Rebecca's pan of biscuits aside and reached for one of the containers Dorcas carried. "Put the dumplings there." She indicated the countertop. "They're still warm," Martha explained. "But they taste just as good cold."

Probably not, Caleb thought, trying not to cringe. He liked dumplings well enough, although the ones the women cooked here in Delaware—slippery dumplings—were different than the ones he'd been served in

Idaho. He certainly couldn't let good food go to waste, but he wasn't looking forward to getting Amelia to eat anything new. The beef heart would certainly be a challenge. His daughter could be fussy about her meals. Once she'd gone for two weeks on nothing but milk and bread and butter. That was her "white" phase, he supposed. And the butter only passed the test because it was winter and the butter was pale.

"We wondered how you were settling in," Martha said. "Such a pity, losing your wife the way you did. Preachers are generally married. I've never heard of one chosen who was a single man, but the Lord works in mysterious ways. He has His plan for us, and all we can do is follow it."

"Ya," Caleb agreed. The smell of the beef heart was strong, but fortunately not strong enough to cover the scent of Rebecca's stew baked in a pumpkin or the apples and cinnamon.

Martha eyed the biscuits. "I suppose you can eat those with your supper," she said. "Although my sister-by-marriage—Hannah Yoder, my dead brother's wife—has taught her girls to cook the Mennonite way. Hannah was born and raised Mennonite, not Amish," she said, wanting to make certain that he got her point. "Most prefer my recipe for baking powder biscuits. My Grossmama Yoder's way. She always used lard. Hannah uses butter." Martha curled her upper lip. "Too rich, by my way of thinking. Not plain."

"Ne," Dorcas agreed. "Mam's biscuits are better."

"But you'll love Dorcas's shoofly pie," Martha said, patting her daughter on the shoulder. "Extra molasses and a good crumb crust. That's the secret."

"Ya," Dorcas echoed. "That's the secret."

Caleb struggled to find something to say. Was he supposed to invite them to stay for supper? It was early yet, but he was hungry—hungrier than he could remember being in a long time. There was something about this mild Delaware autumn that put a spring into his step and made his appetite hearty. "I thank you for your kindness, Martha. And you, Dorcas. I'm not much of a cook myself."

"Just so," Martha agreed. "And why would you be? Cooking is a woman's gift. Men's work and women's are separate." Something that might have been a smile creased the lower half of her face. "We'll be by again on Sunday with something else. Can't let our new preacher starve, can we, Dorcas?"

"Ne." Dorcas blushed and averted her gaze. "Can't let him starve."

Martha started for the door and Dorcas followed. "We'll get the china on Sunday," the older woman said. She spared a glance at the trash can. "And, mind you, no more of those pagan sweets for Amelia. Our bishop is strict. I can't imagine what his wife would say if she knew that Rebecca Yoder gave such nonsense to your innocent daughter."

Chapter Five

Two weeks later, on the last Sunday in October, church was held at Samuel and Anna's home, and the community got to hear the new preacher's first sermon. Caleb had chosen to speak on Moses and how—with the Lord's help—he led the Israelites out of slavery in Egypt, through the wastelands in search of the Promised Land. Prayers and scripture readings by Rebecca's Uncle Reuben aided Caleb; the main sermon on faith and patience in the face of impossible odds was delivered by Bishop Atlee. Everyone had an opinion about Caleb's sermon, but most agreed that it was a good one for a beginner.

"Plainspoken is what I say," Lydia Beachy declared later as she collected dirty plates from the long table in the backyard and placed them in a tub of soapy water. The deep container fitted neatly in the back of a child's wagon pulled by Rebecca. Men, women and children had all finished eating, and the women and girls were busy cleaning up before a short prayer session that would end the day's worship. "The man is plainspoken."

"But that's a good thing in a preacher." Martha picked up a handful of dirty silverware, glanced across the yard toward the group of men lounging against the barn and lowered her voice. "My Reuben has a real gift for delivering a sermon, but he can let the time get away from him."

Rebecca averted her eyes and pressed her lips tightly together to keep from smiling. Uncle Reuben was known for his long sermons, preaching sessions that Bishop Atlee sometimes tactfully cut short by asking that the congregation rise for a hymn from the *Ausbund.* But Uncle Reuben had been chosen to minister to the flock, and such thoughts, she decided, were uncharitable—especially on a church Sunday.

Lydia nodded to give emphasis to her statements. She was tall and thin, and her head bobbing was so vigorous when she spoke that Rebecca always expected her *kapp* to fly off like a startled pigeon.

"No one could call Caleb long-winded," Lydia declared in her always-squeaky voice. "In my opinion, he might have been a bit nervous, but who wouldn't be his first time preaching?" She folded her arms and looked right into Aunt Martha's face. "Can you imagine standing up there and having to give a sermon?"

"Ne." Aunt Martha's mouth and eyes opened wide. "Wherever do you get those ideas, Lydia Beachy?" She scoffed. "A woman preaching a sermon? *Narrisch!"* *Crazy.*

And it was a strange idea, Rebecca had to agree. A baptized woman's vote was equal to a man's in the church, but women couldn't be preachers or bishops. And Rebecca wouldn't want to be. She'd been so nervous that when Caleb first stood up, his face pale, his hands clamped tight against his sides, she'd held her breath. But as he'd begun to talk, he'd looked out at his neighbors and began to speak naturally. He had a clear, strong voice, and a way of speaking that painted pictures of that long-ago time in her mind. If she closed her eyes, she could still see the Israelites, with all their children and their flocks, fleeing the Egyptian pharaoh's army. And she could almost hear the crash of waves as the sea closed around the soldiers and washed them away.

Aunt Martha said Caleb's sermon had lasted the better part of an hour, but for Rebecca the time had flown by. She felt that he deserved the praise that people were giving him.

"A blessing for us that the day remained so mild," her mother, Hannah, said as she whisked a food-stained tablecloth off the bare table, rolled it up and handed it to Rebecca's friend, Mary Byler. The table, really a series of folding tables, stretched more than thirty feet and required six tablecloths to cover it. Tomorrow, Anna would wash the linens and hang them out on the line to dry, but not today. No work, other than caring for livestock or what must be done for the family, was allowed on Sunday.

The day had been unseasonably warm, and much to everyone's delight, the church members had been able to share their communal meal outside in the yard— probably for the last Sunday of the autumn. Rebecca always loved eating outside at church. It made the afternoon almost a holiday.

Mam nudged Rebecca's elbow and motioned toward the back porch. Anna's daughter Mae, Amelia and two other little girls were gathered around Susanna, listening as she "read" a Bible story. Of course, Susanna couldn't really read all the words in the book, but she knew them by heart and could recite them well enough to satisfy the children. Vigorous play wasn't encouraged on the Sabbath, and it was sometimes difficult to keep active little ones suitably occupied.

"Amelia's been a good girl today." Hannah smiled. "You've done wonders with her."

Rebecca nodded. "I only had to take her out of service twice, once to use the bathroom and later when she was getting hungry. And so far, no temper tantrums."

"Just wait," Mary said. "That Amelia's a handful. Just when you think she's behaving and being nice… *Wham.* A dead mouse in your apron pocket." She rolled her eyes. "And the apple doesn't fall far from the tree. If you ask me, I'd say our new preacher has a sharp side, as well."

"I haven't seen it since I've been working there," Rebecca said. She felt that her friend had gone overboard in finding fault with the little girl and, for that matter, with her father. Other than a few setbacks, she'd made out fine at Caleb's house, and she had to admit, she looked forward to going every day. "Amelia's like any four-year-old," Rebecca defended. "She gets into mischief sometimes, but she's sweet natured."

"Sweet like honeycomb in the hive," Mary murmured, half under her breath. "Full of bee stings." Rebecca's mother handed Mary another soiled tablecloth, and Mary bundled an armload together. "I'll take these to the washroom and come back for the others."

"I'll get the rest," Lydia offered. "You can put the rest of those sandwiches in the refrigerator with the macaroni salad and wipe down the counters."

While work wasn't permitted on Sundays, necessary work like cleaning up dirty dishes and putting food away was.

"Services will be starting soon," Rebecca said.

"But you can't leave those hard-boiled eggs out." Aunt Martha pointed to a bowl. "It's too warm in the kitchen."

"We won't," Mary assured her as she started back toward the house with the armload of tablecloths.

Mam and Lydia exchanged looks. "I'm sorry that Mary had a difficult time with Caleb's daughter," Mam said, folding her arms. "But Rebecca hasn't come home with any complaints."

Lydia shrugged. "*Kinner* can be a handful. Especially at that age. I'll give credit where credit is due," she continued. "Rebecca, you've done well with that family." A smiled creased her thin face, making her look younger than her mid-forties. "From what Fannie told me..."

Roman's wife, round and rosy-cheeked Fannie, her hands full with a dishpan of coffee mugs, bustled toward them. "What did Fannie say?" she asked Lydia good-naturedly.

Mam and Lydia chuckled.

Rebecca liked both Fannie and Lydia. They were close friends of her mother's, and Rebecca had known them since she was a baby. They seemed more like relatives than neighbors. Although Fannie and Lydia loved gossip as well as most, there wasn't a mean bone in either one's body. And if someone needed help, Amish or English, Fannie and Lydia were likely to trample each other trying to get there to give assistance.

"Didn't I tell you Fannie had good hearing? You can't get anything past her," Hannah teased.

"I was only saying what you told me before services, Fannie," Lydia said. "That you were in Caleb Wittner's house on and off while Mary and then Lilly worked for him. You said that things were different since Hannah's Rebecca took over. You said that Rebecca had put that place in order. And the child is better behaved."

"*Ya,* I did say so, Hannah." Fannie nodded. "Not to be speaking ill of Caleb or of little Amelia. Wouldn't do that. Eli's cousin is a good man and a hard worker. It can't be easy for him to tend a house and care for a motherless girl. Poor man, he means well, but he just never seemed to have his household in order. Our Rebecca's made a world of difference."

"You shouldn't be saying such things. You'll puff her up with false pride," Aunt Martha warned.

Fannie shrugged. "Truth is truth, Martha. Mary and Lilly together couldn't do what Rebecca has done for Caleb's family."

Rebecca felt her cheeks grow warm. It was good to hear that Fannie approved of what she'd done with Amelia, but Mary and Lilly were her friends. It wasn't right to make light of their efforts. "*Ya,* Caleb's house did need readying up," she admitted. "But he'd just moved in when Mary and Lilly helped out. Just coming from Idaho to Delaware had to be upsetting to Amelia." Feeling uncomfortable, Rebecca glanced across to where the men stood and was surprised to find Caleb watching her.

"If Rebecca has such a touch with that girl, she'd better see to her," Martha retorted, pointing. "Looks to me as though the pot has just boiled over."

Rebecca turned in time to see Amelia, on the porch, give Mae a hard shove that sent her tumbling off the back step. Susanna protested and Amelia answered back. Then Mae began to wail and Amelia burst into tears.

Rebecca grimaced.

"Go on," Mam said. "Straighten it out."

By the time Rebecca reached the porch, Amelia had worked herself up into a full-blown fuss.

Susanna was attempting to quiet her, to no avail. "She hit Mae and pushed her off the step," Susanna said. "And…and Mae hurt her knee."

Mae's black cotton stocking was torn, and Rebecca saw a small scrape and a few drops of blood. Mae, naturally, was making the most of the incident, howling like a hound dog on the trail of a rabbit. "She hurt me," Mae blubbered.

"I hate her!" Amelia shouted between outbursts of angry tears.

Rebecca gathered her charge—kicking and screaming—and whisked her into the house. As she carried the child through the back doorway and into the kitchen crowded with women and babies, she ignored unrequested advice sent in her direction and hurried through the kitchen and the rows of benches set up in the living room for church services. She turned into a wide hallway and found the spacious downstairs bathroom. Rebecca closed and locked the door behind them, and deposited the still-hysterical Amelia on the floor.

The girl stomped her foot and swung a fist at her. "I hate you, too!"

"Shh, shh, sweetie, you don't hate anyone," Rebecca soothed. She knelt on the floor so that she was eye to eye with the frustrated child. "Now, tell me what's wrong."

Amelia's features crumpled and she began to cry in earnest. Rebecca held out her arms and the little girl first hesitated, then ran into them. "Mae said…said… I don't have a mother," she sobbed. "An…and I do so." Her thin shoulders trembled. "I do."

"Of course you do," Rebecca answered. "She's still your mother, even if she can't be here with you."

Amelia drew in a long, ragged sob. "Mae said…said she has a mother and I don't."

"Shh, shh," Rebecca soothed, cradling the child against her. "That wasn't very nice of Mae."

"She said…" Amelia pulled away and rubbed her eyes with her fists. "She said my Mam went to heaven because I was bad."

"Ne." Rebecca shook her head. "It was an accident. If you ask your *dat,* he'll explain it to you."

"Mae is mean. She wouldn't let me look at the book with the giraffe. She said she can read and I can't."

"I'll tell you a secret, Amelia. Mae was pretending. She can't read yet, either. But when you are a little older, you'll go to school and then you'll both learn."

"I hate her."

Rebecca sighed. "You don't hate her. Mae is your friend. She let you play with her Noah's ark, remember? Sometimes friends say unkind things to each other, but it doesn't mean that you stop liking each other."

Amelia sniffed. "I wasn't going to take her book home. I just wanted to look at the pictures."

"She should have shared with you." Rebecca gave Amelia another hug. "Let me wash your face."

"My tummy hurts."

"I know, but you'll feel better with a clean face." Rebecca stood up, ran cool water on a clean washcloth and wiped the tears and sweat from Amelia's face. "You know, Mae's first mother, the one whose tummy she grew in, died, too. She's in heaven with your *mam*. My sister Anna is Mae's new mother. So, for a long time, Mae was just like you."

Amelia's eyes widened. "She was? Did her *mam* die in a fire?"

Rebecca flinched. She hadn't known that Amelia was aware of the details of her mother's passing. Compassion made Rebecca's eyes blur with unshed tears. "*Ne,* sweet. Mae's *mam* was very sick and she couldn't get better."

"Will my *dat* get sick like that?"

Rebecca shook her head. "He is a big, strong man, Amelia. Nothing bad will happen to him." She wondered if it was wrong to say such a thing to an innocent child. Especially when her own father had been taken far too young. But she didn't have the heart to say otherwise. "You must trust in God, Amelia. Say your prayers and try to do what is right. And you mustn't hit or push or get angry with your friends."

"She was mean." Amelia pushed out her lower lip stubbornly. "She wouldn't let me share her book."

"That was wrong," Rebecca agreed, "but hitting and pushing were *two* wrongs. You'll have to think about that."

"And say I'm sorry?"

"Only if you really are," Rebecca pronounced. "Not if you don't want to."

Amelia chewed at the protruding lip. "Will I get a new mother, too?"

"Maybe," Rebecca said. "*Ya,* I think maybe you will."

"When?"

Rebecca shook her head. "Only God and your father know. And maybe your *dat* doesn't know, either. But someday, I'm sure you will."

"Will she be nice?"

"Absolutely. As nice as Anna is to Mae. And she will love you and take care of you."

"Like Mae?"

"*Ya,* just like Mae."

A sharp rapping on the bathroom door made the two of them jump.

"Amelia? Rebecca?" Caleb's voice.

"Yes?" Rebecca swallowed to dissolve the lump in her throat. Caleb sounded cross. Had he seen what happened with the children? "I was just—"

"Open the door."

Rebecca did as he asked. "Amelia's fine. She and Mae just had a little fuss and—"

"Amelia? Did Rebecca spank you?"

The little girl looked at her father and burst into tears.

Rebecca blanched. "Spank her? *Ne,* I just—"

"I thought you said she was fine," Caleb said. "Look at her." Amelia flung herself into her father's embrace and started sobbing again.

"She *was* fine until you…" Rebecca tried to maintain her composure. "It was just a children's spat."

"If there was a problem, you should have called me. I'm her father. It isn't your place to discipline my child."

Amelia's wails became a shriek.

"I didn't *discipline* her." Against her will, Rebecca's

eyes teared up. Caleb wasn't listening to her. He was judging her without hearing her side. "I was just trying to—"

"Your aunt told me what you were doing." He glared at her, his face contorted with anger.

"I don't care what anyone said. I would never—"

"When I need your help, I'll ask for it," Caleb said. Then he lifted Amelia into his arms and carried her out of the bathroom and down the hall.

Rebecca walked out of the bathroom, then turned, but not toward the parlor and living room where church members were already beginning to file in for the afternoon worship service. She went in the opposite direction.

She heard footsteps behind her and stopped, expecting to confront Caleb again. Instead she found that it was Mary.

"What happened?" Mary asked. "He yelled at you, didn't he? I heard him from the kitchen. What did he say?"

Rebecca shook her head. Mary was her friend, but she wasn't about to escalate the embarrassing situation. Bad enough that Caleb had been misinformed and believed it—believed that Rebecca would spank his child. She didn't want to distract the community from Sunday services and cause a bigger scene. "It doesn't matter what he said," Rebecca hedged. "Amelia was crying and Caleb thought I'd taken her into the bathroom to punish her."

"You wouldn't listen to me about him, would you?" Mary whispered with a satisfied expression. "But I told you so."

Chapter Six

The following morning, Rebecca arrived early at Caleb's house, not certain if she wanted to continue working for him—or if he wanted her. She'd gone over and over in her head what had happened the previous day, and she'd come to the conclusion that maybe she had overstepped her bounds in dealing with the incident between Mae and Amelia. As unusual as it was for a father to become involved in such a small matter in public, Caleb was Amelia's parent, her only parent. And if he believed that she'd overstepped her boundaries and interfered, he'd been right to be irritated with her.

Obviously, Aunt Martha had said something to Caleb that had agitated the situation. What she'd said Rebecca didn't know, but she could imagine. "Spare the rod and spoil the child." Aunt Martha loved to quote that, although Rebecca had never seen her aunt physically correct Dorcas or any other child. Rebecca had to believe that Aunt Martha hadn't meant to cause discord. Mam said Aunt Martha had a good heart under all her bluster; she just said whatever popped into her head without considering the harm it could do. Rebecca

liked to think that Mam was right, but sometimes...
sometimes it was difficult not to believe that her aunt
enjoyed making mischief—especially for her sister-in-
law Hannah and her daughters.

When Rebecca arrived at the farm, she found Caleb
in the kitchen attempting to pack his lunch. Amelia,
still in her nightgown and barefooted, was standing beside him, chattering away about Mae's giraffe book.
When Rebecca entered the room, the little girl gave
her a shy smile and ran to greet her.

"I'm hungry, Becca. Can I have pancakes for breakfast? I like pancakes. Blueberry. Can I?"

Rebecca removed her bonnet and hung it on a hook
near the door, then added her cloak. It was cool this
morning and the snap of autumn filled the air with the
scents of wood smoke, newly split kindling and falling crimson and gold leaves. "Good morning, Caleb,"
she said hesitantly.

Fritzy gave a happy yelp and wagged his tail before dropping into a sitting position and raising one
front paw.

"Good morning, Fritzy," Rebecca said. "Good boy."

Ignoring the dog, Caleb's eyes locked with Rebecca's, his steely gray gaze clouded with emotion. "I'm
glad you came this morning." He looked at the floor,
then back up at her. "I talked to Amelia. She told me
what happened with Mae and what you said to her in
the bathroom. I was wrong to jump to conclusions."
Tiny wrinkles creased his forehead. "I owe you an apology." He swallowed. "I let my temper get the best of me,
and I made a fool of myself. I hope you can forgive me."

"Ya," Rebecca murmured. "You did. Embarrass

me," she added quickly. "I didn't mean to imply you were a fool."

"Only right if you did," he answered. He spread his hands, palm up, and Rebecca noticed a smear of mustard on his fingers. "I'm a blunt man. It's a fault of mine, and I fear I'm too old to overcome it. But I wronged you, and I intend to say so—not just to you, but to the community. Someone said something that made me think—"

"Aunt Martha," she supplied, going to the sink and retrieving a clean washcloth.

He nodded.

"Your hand," she said, running water on the cloth. She held it out to him. "Mustard…from your sandwich."

Caleb took the offered washcloth and cleaned off the mustard. "I'm all thumbs in the kitchen. Always was." He indicated the lumpy sandwich with bits of cheese and roughly cut ham spilling from the sides of the bread slices. Neither of them mentioned the obvious. His scarred hand didn't work as smoothly as the other. Not that he was handicapped. He managed his woodworking business, but using the burned hand was more awkward. "I'm apparently not much better in the role of preacher," he added.

Rebecca smiled gently. "I thought your sermon yesterday was a good one." A basket of clean laundry stood on the counter and Rebecca rifled through pillowcases and towels in search of socks for Amelia.

"Your opinion or that of the other members?"

"I only know what some of the women say. Mam gave you a B plus." Rebecca had worn a lavender dress today with the usual white apron. The garment was new. She'd finished stitching it on Mam's treadle machine on Saturday. It was as plain as her other dresses, but the cotton was soft and it was just the right weight for a fall day.

Caleb chuckled. "Bishop Atlee said I was a little long on the flight from Pharaoh's army and a little short on scripture." Caleb grimaced. "Too short altogether. He said that it was a good thing that Preacher Reuben can always be counted on to bring an abundance of sermon."

Caleb wore navy trousers, a light blue short-sleeved shirt and navy suspenders over his high-top, leather work shoes. It was what he wore every day but Sundays. Rebecca noticed that, as usual, his shirt was wrinkled. This one was also marred at the shoulder by what looked like a burn mark in the shape of an iron. She washed and ironed Amelia's clothes, but not Caleb's. He'd said that it wasn't fitting, and he liked to do his own laundry. Rebecca thought that he needed, at the very least, either help or instruction in the art of ironing.

Looking at his shirt, she thought how strange it was that she noticed the burn on his shirt first, not the scars on his face. His scars had been a little frightening the first time she'd seen them, but now she accepted them as part of Caleb. She simply didn't notice them when she looked at him. One side of his face, one hand, were smooth, and it was easy to imagine the other half as a mirror image…the way he'd been before the tragic fire.

She met his gaze. "I liked the part where you spoke about Moses's doubts when the Israelites were crossing the Red Sea and the soldiers were right behind them. That was good."

"I think I can understand a little of how he felt. Moses. God had called him, but he didn't feel up to the task." He opened a plastic bag and began to gather up his sandwich to put it in. "It's all new to me, preaching. I can't help thinking there are other men in the church who would do a better job."

"I can help," Amelia said.

"Wait—" Rebecca put out her hand to take Amelia's, but it was too late. Amelia pulled her father's sandwich to the edge of the counter, knocking half onto the floor. Fritzy dove for the bread and meat and gobbled it up.

"Fritzy!" Caleb said. The dog trotted to the far side of the kitchen, lay down and licked the crumbs off his chin with a long, red tongue.

"Not much left of your ham sandwich, I'm afraid," Rebecca said. "Do you like tuna salad?"

Caleb's mouth twisted into a grimace. "Like it fine. Don't have a can of tuna in the house. It doesn't matter. I can do without—"

"You can't work without your midday meal. Take this." She went to where she'd hung her cape and removed a foil-wrapped package from the pocket. "Two tuna sandwiches on rye with lettuce and mayonnaise. Mam was pushing them this morning. We had a lot of tuna salad left over from yesterday."

Caleb's face reddened. "I can't take your lunch."

"Of course you can. I'll just make some macaroni and cheese at nooning. Amelia loves mac and cheese." She looked at the little girl. "Don't you, Amelia?"

"Ya," the child agreed.

Caleb hesitated. "If you're sure…"

"I'm sure. I like mac and cheese, too, and we had tuna sandwiches for supper last night."

"All right." Caleb reached for the foil-wrapped sandwiches. "Thank you."

"You're welcome." Rebecca lifted Amelia onto a chair and knelt to slip stockings on to her bare feet. "You need to find your shoes," she said. "The floor is cold." She glanced back at Caleb as Amelia jumped down off the chair. "What you said about you being a preacher. Grossmama says that God doesn't make mistakes. If He chose you for the job of preacher, it was the right decision."

"That's what I keep telling myself." He grabbed an apple off the counter and put it in a battered old black lunchbox, along with Rebecca's tuna sandwiches. "I may be a little late this afternoon. I have to finish cutting out some delicate pieces and pack them for a UPS pick up." In the doorway, he grabbed his straw hat and pulled it down over his forehead. He turned back to her. "I hope you'll accept my apology."

Rebecca looked at Caleb. "You've already apologized to me. There's no need to say anything more to me or to anyone else." *That would give people more to talk about,* she thought, but wisely didn't add.

"There's every need," he said gruffly as he reached for his denim jacket. "How can I point out the mistakes others make if I'm not willing to take responsibility for my own?"

"Is that how you think of it?" she asked. "A preacher's job is to point out mistakes?"

"Isn't it?"

She nibbled at her lower lip. "I think it's about being a shepherd, helping the flock to find water and a safe place to rest."

He shook his head. "People aren't sheep. I'm responsible for their souls."

She wasn't certain that she agreed his job was to point out the errors of people's ways, but it wasn't her place to argue. "I still don't think you need to say anything to anyone about what happened. It was such a small misunderstanding, Caleb. And I was partly in the wrong, too. I'm not Amelia's mother."

"*Ne.* You're not."

His face hardened and Rebecca wished she'd had the good sense to keep her mouth shut while she was ahead.

"Other than that, you're satisfied with my housekeeping and looking after Amelia?" she asked.

He shrugged. "Let's give each other a little more time." He patted Amelia on the head. "Be a good girl for Rebecca, pumpkin."

"Dat!" She giggled so hard that her nose wrinkled. "I'm not a pumpkin. I'm a girl."

"And a good thing, too, or Rebecca might be baking you into a pie." He tickled her belly.

And with that, Caleb was out of the house, leaving Rebecca confused and frustrated. What had just happened? He'd been so warm and friendly with her that she'd thought that everything was all right between them. And then he'd turned cold on her again.

She didn't know what to think, and she wished that she could talk the problem over with her mother or one of her sisters. One of the best things about having such a large family was that there was always someone to listen to you and share both good times and bad. But where Caleb was concerned, it didn't feel right. She was oddly reluctant to bring someone else, even someone she loved and trusted, into her confidence. Whether she kept the job or not, it was up to her to mend the breach with Caleb. The question was, how was she to do it?

"Rebecca. I'm hungry. I want pancakes."

"All right, pancakes it is," she agreed. "But we have no blueberries. I can make apple and cinnamon, if you like."

"*Ya!*" Amelia clapped her hands. "Apple."

Rebecca smiled to herself as she pulled out a mixing bowl, spoon, measuring cups and ingredients. Everyone in the community thought that Amelia was a problem child, but Rebecca felt that the problem lay with her father, the troublesome new preacher.

The week passed quietly for Caleb. When he'd met on Friday evening with Bishop Atlee, Deacon Samuel Mast and Reuben, he'd told them, "On Sunday, I raised my voice in anger to a young woman who'd done nothing wrong. I know that some of the congregation couldn't help but hear my foolish outburst. I think you should consider if my lapse in judgment is reason to dismiss me from my position as preacher."

For a moment, there'd been silence, and then Samuel laughed. "We're all as human as you," he had admitted. "And as likely to wade into muddy water when it comes to children's quarrels."

"Best to leave such matters to the women," Bishop Atlee had said.

"But as Amelia's father, isn't the responsibility mine?"

The bishop had stroked his gray beard thoughtfully. "And a heavy burden it must be for a man alone."

"Which is why you should find a wife," Reuben had advised.

"The sooner, the better." Samuel had leaned forward, elbows on the table. "I was widowed and left with young children, too, and the Lord led me to a good woman. The only regret that I have is that I didn't ask her to marry me sooner."

Samuel's words echoed in Caleb's head now, as he rode in his buggy to Hannah Yoder's farm. Rebecca had invited Amelia to have supper with her family and had taken her home with her in the afternoon. It worked out for the best because Caleb had been unsure how long it would take to go over the church business, and he didn't want Rebecca to be out late. It would be simpler to carry a sleeping child home in his buggy than to worry about getting Rebecca home safely.

She met him at the back door and urged him to come in. "We have fresh coffee and apple-cranberry pie," she said.

"I thought I'd just pick up Amelia and—"

"Don't tell me that you don't have time for a slice of pie." Rebecca rested one hand on her hip.

He was about to refuse when his stomach betrayed him by rumbling. Pie was his weakness, and he hadn't had time to make himself anything substantial for supper before the meeting.

Stepping into the kitchen, he glanced around for Amelia. He didn't see her, but his gaze fell on the pie. The crust was brown and flaky, and it was impossible to draw a breath without inhaling the wonderful scents of apple, nutmeg and cinnamon.

"Irwin churned ice cream tonight for the children. There's plenty left." Rebecca motioned toward the table, poured him a mug of coffee and began cutting the pie. "Ice cream on top?"

Caleb groaned an assent, and in what seemed like seconds, he'd shrugged out of his jacket and a large slice of pie covered in a mound of vanilla ice cream had appeared in front of him.

Rebecca picked up a ball of yarn and two knitting needles and settled into a rocking chair near the window. She didn't speak, and the only sounds in the kitchen were the warm crackle from the woodstove, the tick of a mantel clock and the click of her needles. She didn't launch into chatter as she usually did mornings and evenings at his house, but only rocked and concentrated on the scarf she was constructing.

The chair Caleb sat in at the head of the table was big and comfortable. The coffee was strong, and the pie the best he'd ever tasted. He hadn't sat down all day, and it felt good to relax in this warm, cozy kitchen, knowing that he'd put in a good day's work. If next week went as well, he was certain he could finish the contract on time.

Caleb pushed a forkful of pie into his mouth, thinking he shouldn't stay long. "Is Amelia ready?"

Rebecca looked up and smiled. "She's asleep. I tucked her in with Johanna's Katy, who is spending the night. The two girls had a great time putting together a puzzle and playing Go Fish. That was all right, wasn't it? To let her play the card game?" Old Amish didn't play adult card games that involved betting, but in most families, simple games were acceptable.

"Go Fish." He shrugged. "I don't see why not."

"I can go get Amelia if you'd like, but I was hoping you'd let her sleep over tonight. She wanted me to ask you. Johanna and Roland are picking Katy up in the morning after breakfast and they could drop Amelia off with you. Or I could take her with me to Ruth's. We're going to make applesauce. That way, if you want to go to the shop for a few hours…"

Caleb considered. He usually worked around the farm on Saturday, but an extra half day would certainly make his deadline more doable. "If you're sure that it's no trouble," he said. "I'll pay you extra."

"Ne." Rebecca shook her head and rose gracefully from the chair. "I invited her. Another slice of pie?"

He glanced down, surprised to see that only crumbs remained on the plate. He went to hand it to Rebecca just as she reached for it, and their fingers accidently brushed each other. A tremor of sensation ran up his forearm and he inhaled sharply. Instantly he felt his throat flush. "No need," he stammered.

But she was already across the room and cutting more pie. Had she even noticed his touch? Caleb picked up the mug and downed a swallow of coffee to cover his confusion. He couldn't decide if this was way too comfortable or too uncomfortable. Somehow, he felt an invisible line had been crossed.

"Amelia can spend the night—since she's already asleep." He rose, feeling awkward. "I'll be on my way."

"But your pie?" She indicated the slice she'd just cut.

"I've had plenty." He grabbed his jacket and started for the door. "It was good. The pie. Thanks."

"You're welcome." She followed him to the porch.

"Send Amelia home with Roland and Johanna. No need for you to care for her on your weekend."

"As you like," Rebecca answered from the back door. "But I wish you'd take part of this pie home for breakfast."

"I told you," he said from the porch. "I've had enough."

"Good night, Caleb."

He heard the door close behind him and went down the steps. In the middle of the dark farmyard, he stopped and took a deep breath. It had been nice sitting in the warm, cozy kitchen with Rebecca, having pie, listening to her knitting needles click.

Was Samuel right? Should he start thinking about finding a wife and a mother for Amelia?

As he unhitched his horse from the hitching post, he thought about the fact that his first instinct concerning Rebecca Yoder was that she wouldn't be an appropriate housekeeper and childcare provider. He should have listened to common sense.

Originally, he'd thought she was the wrong woman because of her age. He had assumed that she didn't have enough experience caring for children. At least not with a child like Amelia. He'd been right about her being the wrong one to have in his house, but maybe for the wrong reason.

Rebecca was the wrong woman to be his housekeeper because she was too…pretty. Too lively. She was…too…too much.

It had been a bad idea from the first day. What business did a respectable preacher have employing a single woman…one as pretty as Rebecca? If people weren't talking yet, they would be soon. Samuel was married to one of Rebecca's sisters. Had he been hinting that gossip was already circulating about Rebecca?

Did she have to go?

Of course, if he was going to go to the older women in the community and tell them he needed a different housekeeper, he'd need to give them a reason. Rebecca was an excellent housekeeper. He couldn't deny that any more than he could deny that Amelia liked her, and the child's behavior was improving under Rebecca's tutelage. What would he say to the women of the community?

That he was afraid that he could possibly be attracted to her? He couldn't do that. It would be completely inappropriate. He wasn't even sure it was true.

Caleb climbed up into the buggy. The one thing he did know to be true was that something had to be done about Rebecca Yoder.

Chapter Seven

"First breakfast, and then I'm sure Susanna will take you, Katy and Mae out to her library and let the three of you look at the children's books." Rebecca motioned for Amelia to take her place at the table between the other two girls.

She scrambled up into the chair, and after a burst of small female greetings and chatter, the little girls closed their eyes for a few seconds of silent grace. Once the blessing had been asked, Rebecca handed each an apple-walnut muffin, a cup of milk and sections of tangerines. "Now, who wants oatmeal?" Rebecca asked. "Mam made it this morning before she went to school."

Caleb had driven over in the buggy to drop his daughter off at the Yoder house this morning, a Wednesday, more than two weeks after the misunderstanding with Rebecca. Rebecca knew that pride was a fault, but she couldn't help being pleased with the little girl. Over the past weeks, she had come to adore Amelia. The child could be spirited, sometimes even naughty, but she had a loving heart, and she could be extremely helpful when she wanted to be. It was natural that a child raised without a mother could be difficult at times; all Amelia needed was a gentle but firm woman's guidance.

And…if Rebecca was absolutely honest with herself, she had to admit that she liked working for Caleb. Since he'd apologized for being cross with her the day Amelia pushed Mae off the step, he had been nothing but kind and pleasant. He had done as he'd said he would—he'd told other members of the community, including her mother, that he'd made a mistake in judgment and that he'd been hasty with Rebecca.

She'd been a little embarrassed that the whole incident hadn't been dropped. But at the same time, it pleased her that Caleb was true to his word, even if it meant taking public blame—something not all men were willing to do. Seeing what a good father he was and how seriously he took his church responsibilities made her admire Caleb's character even more.

Despite their awkward beginning—when he'd unnecessarily come to her rescue that evening in his barn loft—Rebecca was glad that she hadn't heeded her friends' warnings about how difficult Caleb and Amelia were. Mam was right. It was always better to form your own opinions and not listen to other people—especially when they had something unkind to say about strangers.

"Becca!" Susanna tugged at her arm. "You are not a good listener."

"*Ach,* I'm sorry. I was woolgathering." Rebecca glanced down at her sister. "What is it, honey?"

Something had clearly upset Susanna. Her nose and cheeks were red, and her forehead was creased in a frown. "Listen to me, Becca. I *said* I don't want to take the *kinner* out to my library."

Surprised at such an unusual declaration from Susanna, who was always so willing to help, Rebecca stared at her in confusion. "You don't?"

"Don't want to read books," Susanna said adamantly. "Don't want to watch Mae, Katy and Amelia."

"But you love taking care of the library." Anna poured milk on Amelia's oatmeal and sprinkled raisins and bits of chopped apple on top. "And it's your responsibility."

"The girls want to take home books," Rebecca reminded her. "Don't you want to show them—"

"Ne," Susanna cut her off. "I want to make applesauce with you."

At a loss for words, Rebecca glanced up. Ruth, Miriam, Anna and Johanna were all looking at Susanna, too. They'd joined her in Mam's kitchen this morning to make applesauce and can it for the five households. Usually, Mam was in the center of applesauce production, but this was a school day. The sisters had planned to take on the task as a surprise and finish before Mam arrived home. Naturally, Ruth, Johanna and Anna had brought their children—the babies and those too young for school—and everyone had expected Susanna to entertain the little girls, as she always did. Small babies were easy to feed and tuck into cradles, cribs and bassinets, but active four-and five-year-olds could pose problems during the canning process if they weren't kept safely occupied.

"We were counting on you." Ruth smiled at Susanna. "You know you love the girls."

"Ya." Susanna nodded her head firmly. "Love the

girls, but want to make applesauce. Today. For King David."

Susanna's speech was sometimes difficult for strangers to understand because she had Down syndrome. It was especially hard to follow her when she switched back and forth between *Deitsch* and English indiscriminately, but Rebecca had no trouble interpreting her little sister's meaning. Most of the time, Susanna was sweet-natured and biddable, but when she made up her mind to do something, she proved she was a Yoder. Susanna could be as stubborn and unmovable as Johanna.

Rebecca looked at Anna, who just shrugged.

"Susanna wants to make applesauce." Miriam chuckled. "So I guess we go to plan B and let her help."

"Me, too," Mae piped up from the table. "I want to make applesauce."

Katy chimed in. "And me! I can help!"

"I can, too." Oatmeal dribbled from Amelia's mouth.

Rebecca grabbed a napkin and wiped Amelia's chin. Amelia slid down from her chair, and Rebecca leaned over and gave her a hug. When Amelia's arms tightened around her neck, Rebecca felt a catch of emotion in her chest. She was making real progress with Amelia. She knew she was.

"I can help," Katy repeated.

"We're happy that you all want to be big helpers," Anna assured them with a motherly smile. "But you can help most now by finishing your breakfast so we can clear away the dishes." Seemingly mollified, at least for the moment, Amelia returned to her seat and the children went back to eating.

Ruth took Susanna's hand and turned it over to show a Band-Aid. "Remember what happened when you were peeling potatoes Saturday? You cut yourself. One time you cut your hand so badly that you had to go to the hospital for stitches. That's why Mam would rather you didn't use sharp paring knives."

"We love you," Johanna put in. "We don't want you to get hurt again."

"You can help us, if you want," Anna soothed. "You can wash the apples and jars and—"

"I want to peel apples," Susanna insisted. "Me. Make applesauce for King David. He likes applesauce. With *cimmanon.*"

Miriam rolled her eyes.

Rebecca sighed. The family had thought that Susanna's innocent infatuation with David King, a young man who also had Down syndrome, would pass. But to Mam's distress, and all of the sisters, it showed no signs of going away.

Amish girls grew to women and married and had families of their own. That was the way it had always been. But because sweet Susanna had been born with Down syndrome, in many ways, she would always remain a child. There would be no husband for Susanna. She would never have her own family. Her family would always be those who loved her most: her mother, her sisters and brothers-in-law, her aunts and grandmother and her nieces and nephews. Through the years, Mam had tried to explain this to Susanna, but she never understood.

The family had always cherished Susanna. Their father had called her their special blessing. If there were things Susanna couldn't do—like using sharp tools or driving a horse and buggy—God had given her special gifts. Susanna could see clearly into the hearts of others, and she possessed endless patience and compassion.

Susanna had a tender understanding of children and animals, and she seemed to possess her own store of sunshine that she carried with her. Just being near Susanna and seeing her joy in everyday things made other people happier. In Rebecca's mind, Dat had been right. Susanna was not only one of God's chosen; she was a blessing to the family because they all learned so much by knowing her.

For all those reasons and a hundred more, none of them wanted to deny her the pleasure of helping in the daily household tasks. She could help in making applesauce as she helped Mam in the garden and kitchen, as she helped at community gatherings. But there were things that weren't safe for Susanna to attempt, one of which had proved to be cutting or peeling. And, until recently, Susanna had seemed to accept those limitations.

But today, apparently, was going to be different. Susanna's lower lip stuck out. She folded her chubby arms and stamped her foot. "I want to peel apples," she said.

"Sorry," Johanna said firmly. "Mam says no."

"It's up to Mam," Anna agreed. "You'll have to ask her."

"Ya," Miriam said. "And she's at school."

Tears glistened in Susanna's eyes and one slid down her cheek. Angrily, she wiped it away. "No library books," she flung at them. "No washing apples." Turning abruptly, she trudged out of the kitchen and up the stairs, leaving her sisters astonished.

"I'm sorry she's upset," Ruth said, crossing the room to check on her sleeping twins. Mam and Irwin had

carried a cradle down from the attic, and when Ruth or
Anna visited, there was usually a baby tucked into it.
In Ruth's case, with her twin boys, there were two. "I
think someone is awake and hungry," Ruth murmured.
She picked up Adam and sat down in the rocker near
the window. Covering herself modestly with a shawl,
she began to nurse the baby.

"It's good to have so many little ones in the house,"
Anna said. Her own youngest, Rose, was asleep in
Hannah's bed. She wiped her hands on her apron and
walked over to smile down at Ruth's other sleeping boy.
"I know it makes Mam happy."

"Shouldn't one of us go up and talk to Susanna?" Johanna wiped off an already spotless counter and shifted
a large kettle from one burner on the stove to another.
"If she's really upset…"

"Maybe we should let her be," Ruth said. "Mam
would have our heads if she had another accident with
a paring knife, and once she's over her fuss, she'll be
fine."

"Can we go see the books?" Amelia ventured. "Is
there one about a giraffe?"

"I have a giraffe book," Mae said. "And a book about
chickens."

"I want a book about ponies." Katy tugged at her
mother's apron. "The brown pony with the black mane.
That book."

"Come on, *kinner*." Miriam indicated the door with
a nod of her head. "I'll take you out to pick books."

Giggling excitedly, the three girls followed Miriam
outside to the Amish community library, in what had
once been Dat's milk house.

"And that leaves us to start on the applesauce." Anna

placed her hands on her ample hips and glanced at the huge copper-bottomed pots that stood on both Mam's woodstove and the six-burner, propane gas range. "Do you two want to start carrying in the apples? We've got a lot of peeling and cutting to do before they're ready for the kettles."

"Sure," Rebecca agreed. Bushels of Black Twig, Granny Smith, Winesap and Jonathan apples waited on the porch. Making applesauce with her family was something that she looked forward to all year. She loved the heady smells of cooking apples and cinnamon, and she loved seeing the results—rows of quart jars of applesauce to line the pantry shelves. There was something so satisfying about knowing that a few days' work provided good food that would last them until next fall and the next crop of ripe fruit.

The baskets were heavy, but the Yoder sisters had done manual labor since they were young, and Rebecca didn't mind the lifting. Peeling was easy. Her fingers remembered what to do while she was free to sit and visit with her sister. They laughed and shared memories of their childhood as well as amusing or serious moments in their own homes.

This is a good day, a happy day. But how many days with my sisters do I have left?

Since Rebecca was fifteen, she'd been taking part in young people's singings and frolics. So far, while she watched her sisters, cousins and friends court and marry, she hadn't met a man with whom she wanted to spend the rest of her life.

An unmarried girl her age usually began to look farther afield; it wasn't uncommon to go to another community in another state to find a husband. It wasn't the thought of leaving her mother's house that bothered her as much as not having her sisters around her on a daily basis, as she did now. How could she marry and move away and not watch Anna's little Rose learn to talk, or see Ruth's twins start to crawl and then walk? What would she do without Miriam to tease and laugh with, or Johanna, who gave the best advice? How could she leave all those she loved to go away to be a wife and miss the remaining years of Grossmama's life?

If only there were someone here like...like Caleb.

Caleb was a fine man, of course. That went without saying. But she didn't want him for a husband. He was a preacher and too settled in his ways for her. Not old exactly, but thirty, at least.

A preacher's wife? she mused. *Impossible.* She couldn't imagine herself as a preacher's wife. The community expected a certain seriousness from the spouse of a religious leader. Dat had been Bishop and her mother had always been respected. Women came to Mam when they needed help or advice in their personal lives. Mam had always had a dignity, an instinctive manner that told even the English that she was an authority figure.

Rebecca sighed as she tossed another apple peel in the bucket. She was definitely too worldly and not humble enough to be a preacher's wife. Besides, Caleb didn't think of her as a candidate for courtship. Eventually, she knew that he would seek out a wife, but it would be some older woman, probably a widow with children. Someone Johanna's age. Johanna would have been a good match for Caleb if she and Roland hadn't fallen in love all over again and wed.

I could end up meeting some young man from Ohio

or Oregon or Virginia and going to make a new life among his family and friends, Rebecca thought.

"More apples," Susanna said as she dumped a dozen washed Jonathans into Rebecca's bowl.

As Ruth had said, Susanna had gotten over her huff and come downstairs as cheerful as always. She'd taken her turn at watching the children and rocking babies and changing diapers as the rest of them had. Susanna had said nothing more about peeling apples and no one had mentioned it to her. Rebecca hoped that she'd forgotten all about it.

"So how are you and Caleb getting on?" Miriam asked Rebecca.

"Fine. I like him," Rebecca answered.

Miriam glanced at Ruth. "What we were wondering is, how much does *he* like *you?*"

Rebecca glanced around to be certain Amelia, Mae and Katy hadn't crept into the room to listen to the adults as she and Leah used to do when they were that age. "It's not like that," she said quietly. Suddenly she felt anxious. "Caleb's my employer, not my beau."

"Still, he's a good-looking man," Anna pronounced, turning from the stove where she was stirring a pot of cooking apples. "And single."

"*Very* single," Johanna agreed. She placed Luke back in the cradle beside a sleeping Adam. "You have to be careful, Rebecca. Make certain that you never give people a chance to gossip about you."

"*Ya,*" Anna agreed. She took a long-handled wooden spoon and dipped out a spoonful of cooked apples to taste. "Samuel and I were always chaperoned when we were alone together."

"Caleb is my employer." Rebecca frowned. "He's

our preacher. He's the last person I'd be interested in. And he certainly hasn't shown any—"

"Ne?" Miriam raised her eyebrows. "I saw him watching you at service. He didn't look all that uninterested to me."

Flustered, Rebecca stood up, dropping apples onto the floor. "That's silly." She stooped to pick up the fallen fruit. "Caleb's too old for me." One apple rolled under the table and she had to get down on her hands and knees to retrieve it.

"Now who's talking foolishness?" Anna said. "You're twenty-one, and Caleb can't be much past thirty-one or thirty-two. There's a bigger age difference between me and Samuel." She chuckled. "And look how that turned out."

"No one would blame you if you set your *kapp* for him," Miriam chimed in. "Caleb Wittner is a good catch."

"Is that what people are saying?" Rebecca rose to her feet. She tried but couldn't keep the indignation out of her voice. "That I've set my *kapp* for him? Because that isn't true. He's the last man I'd want to marry."

Ruth and Johanna exchanged meaningful looks. "That's what I said about Roland Byler," her oldest sister remarked. "Sometimes a smart woman is the last to see what's plain as day to everyone around her."

Chapter Eight

That afternoon, Rebecca was attempting to open the outside cellar door of her mother's house while balancing a box of quart jars full of applesauce, when Caleb came around the corner of the back porch.

"You're here early." She hadn't expected him until four or so. What surprised her more was the warm pleasure she felt at seeing him unexpectedly.

"Let me take those for you," he offered. "They're heavy."

"Thanks."

It was kind of him to offer. Many men didn't do that sort of thing. They just expected their wives and daughters and sisters to manage the household tasks. Most Amish men considered the home a woman's domain, and they would be embarrassed to be caught carrying a dish or making a pot of coffee. Not that women were in any way inferior to men in their faith; men and women simply divided the daily work. Maybe their new preacher was more progressive than Rebecca had first thought.

Caleb took the case of jars, Rebecca unhooked the

latch on the door and they went down into the cellar. The dirt-floored cellar was a good place for storing potatoes, onions and rows and rows of home-canned fruit and vegetables because the temperature never dropped below freezing. Deep bins of straw held cabbage, winter squash, turnips and apples. Most English people got all of their groceries at the store, but among the Amish in their community, it was customary to buy only what couldn't be grown in a garden or purchased from neighbors.

Canning, drying and salting food was labor intensive, but Mam had taught her daughters well. Rebecca knew that when she had her own home, she would be as capable of preserving fruits, vegetables and meats as her older sisters and their mother.

"Watch your head," Rebecca warned Caleb. The old brick stairway was steep and the overhead beam low enough that he had to duck when he reached the bottom of the steps and entered the main room. Barred windows above the outside ground level let in light, but the cellar remained shadowy.

"Back here," she said, showing Caleb the way to a windowless chamber beyond the main room. She turned on a battery-powered lantern that stood on a shelf, illuminating the shelves built into the brick foundation. Quarts of applesauce already lined one shelf. On the other side of the passageway was an identical space with more shelving, and beyond that, there was another room where strings of sausage and preserved hams hung above kegs of curing sauerkraut.

"You girls have been busy," Caleb said. "Did you make all this applesauce today?"

"Ne." Rebecca began to take the jars one by one and

stand them carefully on the shelf, turning each one so that the cheerful labels faced outward. Each label bore the date and contents in her own handwriting. "This is our second batch."

"You wouldn't have any extra left over for a hungry man, would you?" he teased.

"A dozen quarts," she answered. "Waiting on the porch for you. Did you find Amelia? She was on the porch *reading* with Katy."

"I did." He smiled a slow smile that lit his eyes up. "She showed me a book about a burro. She said that she could take it home for two weeks. You don't mind?"

Rebecca shook her head and took two more jars from the box. "Oh, no. It's Susanna's library. She has books for the children...and adults. Some in the community wanted books for their little ones, but Bishop Atlee thought it best if they not borrow from the county library."

"Because not all of the Englishers' books are suitable for Amish children," he finished.

She returned his smile. "Exactly. Mam found a used bookstore, and they save books for us. We also buy books from the county library when they have their book sales. Susanna has collected more than two hundred. It makes her feel useful and it pleases the children and their families."

Caleb lowered the cardboard box as she took the last two jars from him and rested a hand against the wall. He seemed more relaxed than usual, and it made him look younger. The lines around his eyes had eased. In the shadowy light, it was easy to overlook the scars that marred his face. Rebecca wondered if they pained him, but she didn't want to ask. That seemed too forward.

"Amelia's mother hated canning," he said. "I used to help her with the tomatoes. We had a cellar in our Idaho house, the house... The one that caught fire. Our first place, though, was much smaller—only three rooms." He chuckled. "We were young and poor. That first winter, snow blew through the cracks around the kitchen window and covered our table."

"Brrr." Rebecca shivered. "That must have been tough."

"*Ya,* it was, but there were good times, too. My Dinah was an orphan, and that first house we rented, it was her first time having her own kitchen."

"Did she have other family?" Rebecca tried to imagine what Amelia's mother had been like. She must have been pretty, Rebecca thought, because Amelia was so pretty.

"A half sister and a brother in Missouri, but the sister was fifteen years older, and the brother was in a wheelchair. He had all he could do to provide for his own wife and children. Dinah was raised in an uncle's family. Six boys and no girls. Dinah had to work hard. Her aunt and uncle didn't want her to marry me because they counted on her help with the cooking and cleaning."

Rebecca didn't know what to say, so she remained silent. Caleb reached up and touched a label on one of the jars of applesauce. "Nice handwriting."

"Thank you." She averted her eyes, suddenly shy. Her fingertips tingled, and she felt a wash of warmth flow through her. She didn't want to be prideful, but she'd always taken pleasure in writing. "If you don't put what's in the jar on the label, you might get squash when you wanted beets," she said.

"Beets?" Caleb chuckled. "Beets are red. At least they were the last time I noticed."

"I guess you've never sent Irwin to the cellar for squash," she ventured.

"*Ach,* that one." Caleb's smile widened into a grin. "I saw him last church Sunday. Paying more attention to the King girl than to the sermon. He'll bear watching, that boy."

Rebecca smiled back, feeling more at ease talking about her foster brother than herself. "Mam says Irwin never seeks out mischief. It just sticks to him like flies to flypaper."

Caleb straightened one of the jars. "Samuel told me that you write more than just applesauce labels. He said that you are a regular correspondent for *The Budget*."

The Budget was an Amish newspaper published weekly in Ohio and circulated not only nationally, but internationally. It featured stories and classified ads pertinent to Amish life, but what everyone read it for was the newsy blurbs about what was happening socially in various Amish communities.

"Guilty," she admitted. Caleb was standing very close, so close that she was very aware of how tall he was and how broad his shoulders were. She liked his hands best of all: strong hands, even the one that the fire had scarred. And he smelled good. Of Ivory soap and freshly cut wood. "Just community news... The weather, who had visitors and the announcements of new babies."

"And frolics and deaths," Caleb said. "It's not everyone who has a way with words—to write accounts of neighborhood events and make it interesting. I read what you put in about my barn raising. It was good." He stepped back. "I've been reading the Delaware news in *The Budget* since Eli first suggested I come out here, but I never knew it was you writing it. I didn't know if it was written by a man or woman." He hesitated. "You don't sign your name."

"Most contributors do," she said, meeting his intense gaze. It was curious…but was it something else? Rebecca felt a little breathless as she explained, "I started submitting to *The Budget* when I was eleven, and Mam didn't think that I should take credit because I was so young. She was afraid it would make me proud. So I got in a habit of signing Delaware Neighbor or Kent County Friend, whatever seemed right that day." She hesitated. "Why would Samuel bring up my writing to you?"

"It was an accident, really," he said. "We were talking about a farm auction listed there. Abe Hostetler's in Lancaster? Abe's a second or third cousin of mine on my mother's side. I mentioned your article to Samuel, because it told about my barn raising. That's when he said you were the one who wrote it. I was just surprised. I wouldn't have guessed."

She wasn't sure whether that pleased her or not.

His eyes narrowed as he tucked the cardboard box under his arm. "I've always considered myself a good judge of character, but you…" He shook his head. "Maybe there's more to you, Rebecca Yoder, than I first thought."

Rebecca met his gaze.

"Has the cellar fallen in on you two?" Anna's cheerful voice came from atop the cellar entrance. "I've another case of applesauce here."

"Coming," Rebecca called, breaking eye contact with Caleb, feeling off balance and not sure why.

Caleb hurried ahead of her to the stairs. "I'll take those," he called up to Anna.

Rebecca waited until he came back down the steps with another box.

"Go on up. I know where they go," he said gruffly, avoiding looking at her.

Gone was the man who'd looked at her with such intensity…the man who seemed interested in her writing. Back was her…her employer, and the moment of closeness they'd shared receded into the shadows of the cellar.

"I guess I'll go back to the kitchen for more," Rebecca said.

Anna stood, hands on hips, one eyebrow arched in suspicious curiosity when Rebecca reached the top of the steps. "A long time it took the two of you to put twelve quarts of applesauce on a shelf." Her mouth pursed. "You should take care, Rebecca. It's just us here today, but you wouldn't want others to get the wrong idea."

"We weren't doing anything wrong," she protested. "And if you doubt me, don't forget, Caleb is a preacher. He wouldn't—"

"I trust you," Anna said quietly. She leaned close and kissed Rebecca's cheek. "I know you're a good girl." She motioned toward the cellar doorway. "And Caleb seems decent, but he's a man first, a preacher second."

"We were just talking." She pushed down a small tremor of guilt. She and Caleb *had* been just talking. It was unfair of Anna to assume that anything else had taken place between them. Back stiff with indignation, she walked quickly toward the back porch. "You're beginning to sound like Aunt Martha."

Anna caught up with her and took her arm. "I'm not accusing you of anything, Rebecca. I'm just warning you to be careful. Talk all you like where people can see you or when you have Amelia as chaperone. And if he wants to ask you to walk out with him—"

"He doesn't," Rebecca insisted, shaking off her sister's hand. "He wouldn't. It's not like that. Caleb asked me about the article I wrote for *The Budget,* the one about his barn raising. Innocent enough conversation."

Anna crossed her arms over her plump figure. "Just so you keep it that way."

The hasty reply on the end of Rebecca's tongue was cut off by a scream from the barnyard. She ran into the barnyard, vaguely aware of Anna and Caleb pounding after her. *Pray God none of the children are hurt!* she thought.

But the figure at the back gate was a white-faced and breathless Dorcas. "You have to come!" her cousin shrieked. "Dat... My *dat* is..." Her words were lost in a sobbing wail.

Rebecca reached Dorcas first and grabbed her by the upper arms. Her cousin was several years older than her, but the whole family knew that she was high-strung and useless in an emergency. "What's wrong?" Rebecca demanded. "I can't help if I don't know what's happened."

Dorcas fell forward and began to wail into Rebecca's ear. "The cow. She..." Another sob. "His leg... Kicked. He's hurt."

Caleb came to a halt beside them.

"Mam's not home. You have to come," Dorcas exclaimed.

Caleb's voice was calm and steady. "How serious is his injury? Dorcas, isn't it?"

Dorcas nodded. "I don't know, Preacher. He can't get up."

"Is he conscious?" Caleb asked. "Breathing all right? Awake and talking?"

"*Ya,* he told me to run here and get someone. I think he's hurt bad."

"Dorcas, you have to calm down," Anna told her, out of breath from running. "You'll be of no use to your father in this state."

Rebecca stepped back, passing Dorcas into her sister's embrace. "Maybe we should call an ambulance?" she told Caleb.

"Ne, ne." Dorcas's hands flew into the air, fluttering like a startled bird. "No ambulance. No doctor. Mam would never agree to such an expense."

"I'll go and see how bad the injury is," Caleb said. "If he needs medical help—"

"Ne!" Dorcas shook her head and began to cry again, this time on Anna's shoulder. *"Ne,"* she repeated. "Not without my mother's say-so. I couldn't."

Caleb looked at Rebecca. "You stay here with Dorcas. My buggy and horse are still hitched up. I'll drive over to see for myself."

"He's in the barn," Dorcas managed, still in Anna's arms. "The Holstein heifer… She kicked him."

"I'm coming with you," Rebecca told Caleb. "Do you want to come, Dorcas?"

Her cousin shook her head, working her hands together. "I couldn't. It's too awful. I'll wait here."

Rebecca laid a hand on Caleb's arm. "I can show you a shortcut through the orchard. It's faster than going by the road." She glanced back at the house. "Anna and my sisters will look after Amelia. She'll be fine with them." She caught Dorcas's hand and gave it a squeeze before hurrying after Caleb.

Rebecca scrambled up into Caleb's buggy at the hitching post. He unsnapped the rope, gathered his reins and got in. In less than five minutes, Rebecca was guiding him along the back lane to the woods road that led to her uncle's farm.

Caleb drove the horse at a sharp trot. Leaves crackled under the buggy wheels and the horse's hooves thudded softly on the packed dirt. Rebecca clung to the edges of the seat, and her heart raced. *Please God, let Uncle Reuben be all right,* she prayed silently. She hoped that Dorcas was just being Dorcas, overreacting to a minor incident, but there was no way to tell.

"Money is tight for everyone, but more so for Aunt Martha and Uncle Reuben," Rebecca explained. "That's why Dorcas didn't want us to call an ambulance. But knowing her, it wouldn't be reasonable to call without seeing for ourselves first." She glanced into Caleb's face. "Sometimes Dorcas exaggerates."

"Not about something as serious as this, I would hope." His hands were firm on the reins, his back straight.

It was clear to Rebecca that he wasn't a man who jumped to conclusions or made hasty decisions. She was glad that Caleb had been at the Yoder farm when Dorcas had come. It made her feel that whatever they found at her uncle's, they would be able to deal with the situation together.

"There's a gate around the bend, just ahead," she told Caleb. "This is where Uncle Reuben's property line starts. I'll get down and open it." He nodded and she went on. "The pasture is low-lying, but if you stay on the trail you won't get stuck."

Once they were through the gate and Rebecca had closed it to keep the cows in, it was only a short distance to her aunt and uncle's barnyard, where the buildings were in various states of disrepair.

Though he had never said so, Rebecca knew her father had always thought that his sister's husband had inherited a good farm but hadn't put in the work that was needed to maintain it. Both of Martha and Reuben's sons had married young and moved to Kentucky, leaving their parents with only a daughter to help out. Uncle Reuben had always held out hope that Dorcas would find a hardworking husband to take the place in hand, but so far, that hadn't happened.

Rebecca felt a twinge of guilt that she would have such uncharitable thoughts about her uncle at such a time, but at least she hadn't expressed them to Caleb. Truthfully, she was embarrassed by the peeling paint, loose shingles and sagging doors that caused her aunt and cousin so much unhappiness. Had Uncle Reuben been ill or handicapped, his church members would have gladly come to his aid, but her uncle was as healthy as a horse. And no farmer who rose at nine and left the fields at three could expect the results of others who were more industrious.

As one of two preachers in the congregation, Uncle Reuben commanded the respect of his flock because of his position. But Rebecca had often felt that Aunt Martha's criticism of her Yoder sister-in-law, Hannah, and nieces was as much envy as an honest wish to see them live a proper Amish life. If Uncle Reuben was a better provider, maybe her aunt would be a happier person and Dorcas might have found a husband, instead of remaining single.

When they reached the main barn, Rebecca and Caleb climbed out of the buggy and she led the way inside. They had to thread through an assortment of broken tools, a buggy chassis with a rotting cover and missing wheels, bales of old, mouse-infested hay and a rusty, horse-drawn cultivator that hadn't seen a field since Rebecca was a toddler. Pigeons flew from the overhead beams and chickens scattered. A one-eared tomcat hissed at them and Rebecca cautioned Caleb not to trip over a bucket of sour milk.

"Uncle Reuben?" she called. The shed where he kept the heifers leaned at the back of the barn, but reaching it by way of the paddock would have meant walking through a morass of cow manure. This path was strewn with obstacles, but high and dry.

"Reuben!" Caleb added his strong voice to her plea. "Are you there, Reuben?"

"Here!" came a pain-filled plea. "I'm here."

Rebecca ducked beneath a leaning beam and through a low doorway cut in the barn's back wall. Her uncle lay sprawled on the dirt floor in a pile of odorous straw. The culprit, a black-and-white heifer with small, mean eyes, stood in the far corner of the shed, chewing her cud.

"Uncle Reuben!" Rebecca cried, running to kneel by his side. One leg lay at an unnatural angle. A tear in the fabric of his trousers revealed an ominous glimpse of white that Rebecca feared was a broken bone protruding through the flesh. "Oh, Uncle Reuben." She glanced back at Caleb.

He stared down at her uncle's leg. "You need to get to the hospital, Reuben." He crouched down and took the injured man's wrist. After a moment, he asked, "Anything else hurt but the leg?"

"That's enough, wouldn't you say?" Uncle Reuben snapped.

Caleb released his wrist, glanced at Rebecca, and nodding reassuringly. "Good, strong, steady pulse. Any bleeding?"

"Some. Nothing a vet can't deal with," Uncle Reuben said. "You'd be doing me a favor to call one of the Hartmans. Set this and slap some plaster on it, it'll heal well enough." His talk was bold, but Rebecca could see the pasty hue of his face and the fear in his eyes.

"You don't need a veterinarian, Reuben. You need a doctor," Caleb pronounced. "And a hospital. Likely, you'll need surgery on that leg. I'm going to go down to the chair shop and call for an ambulance."

"You'll do no such thing," her uncle said. "I've no money for—"

"No need for you to worry yourself about money right now," Caleb assured him, getting to his feet. "And no need to take chances with your leg or your life."

"I told you, I'm not paying for any English ambulance or any of their fancy doctors," Uncle Reuben insisted.

"We'll worry about the doctor bills when they come in," Caleb said. "Your neighbors will help, as I'm sure you've helped others in your community. As for the ambulance, I think you need one and I intend to see it comes for you."

"You'll ruin me! Do you know what they charge to carry you ten miles?"

"Ease your heart, Reuben." He rested his hands on his hips. "I'm making the decision, and I'll bear the cost of the transportation myself."

Chapter Nine

By nine o'clock Saturday morning, Caleb, Samuel, Eli, Charley, Roland and a half dozen other men and teenage boys were hard at work in Reuben's cornfield. A field that should have been cut a month ago. Teams were cutting the drying stalks with corn knives, a sharp-bladed tool much like a machete, and stacking them in teepee-shaped structures. The English used massive machines to harvest their fields, but in Seven Poplars, the Amish still practiced the old ways whenever possible. If the crop was to be saved, it would be due to the work of Reuben's friends and neighbors, because it would be a long time before he would be physically fit enough to do manual labor again.

As Caleb had suspected, Reuben's leg had been badly broken. Once Rebecca's uncle had reached the hospital by ambulance, he'd been examined and rushed up to surgery. Reuben was still hospitalized, but was hoping to be discharged later that day. Calling the ambulance had been the right decision. According to the EMTs who responded, any attempt to transport Reuben by buggy could have resulted in the loss of his leg or worse.

When one of the congregation became ill or injured, it was the custom of neighbors and relatives to come to his or her aid. It wasn't considered charity; it was what was expected. To do otherwise would be unthinkable in the plain community. For the next weeks, perhaps months, volunteers would tend to Reuben's livestock daily, milk the cows twice a day, finish bringing in his harvest, cut firewood and ready the farm for winter.

Caleb had spent most of Wednesday night at the hospital with Reuben and had taken off work Thursday and Friday to look after the details of seeing that his family and farm were taken care of. Somehow, because Caleb had been the first of the elders in the church to respond, it fell to him to organize assistance for Reuben's family. He'd made a schedule of regular volunteers, plus arranged for backup when the regulars couldn't be there.

Paying for the ambulance as he'd promised would cut deeply into Caleb's savings, but he had given his word. It was the right thing to do for Reuben and his family, who were—from all appearances—in reduced financial circumstances. Fortunately, Caleb had some money left over after the purchase of his farm and the expense of moving, money that had come from an unexpected inheritance. A childless uncle had died in Wisconsin, leaving his entire estate to him, making the move to Delaware possible. Helping Reuben's family seemed little enough to ask, considering the gift he had received.

Caleb fell into a steady rhythm—swing and chop, step, swing and chop, step, moving down the row. Behind him, another man gathered armfuls of corn stalks and tied them together for stacking. Cutting corn was strenuous, but Caleb didn't mind. Since he was a boy, he'd worked long, hard hours in the fields. The repetitive motion taxed the muscles, but left a man's thoughts free to roam where they would. Today, however, that might not have been a good thing.

Somehow, Caleb couldn't keep his gaze from lingering on Rebecca Yoder as she strode gracefully from one laborer to another, carrying a ladle and a bucket of cool water flavored with slices of lemon. How fine she looked this morning in her robin's-egg-blue dress, dark sweater and crisp white apron and *kapp*. Modest black stockings flashed below the hem of her full skirt as she stepped lightly over the raised rows of cut stalks, and her laughter rang merrily in the brisk fall air.

Rebecca said something to her foster brother Irwin, and Caleb heard him chuckle. As she walked away, Irwin tossed a ball of fodder at her back, and Rebecca whirled around and threw a nubbin of corncob at him. The missile struck the brim of Irwin's felt hat and knocked it off. He yelped and made an exaggerated show of retrieving it.

"Watch yourself, Irwin," Eli teased good-naturedly. "Next, you'll be getting a dipper of ice water down the back of your shirt."

"Ya," Charley agreed. His wife, Miriam, approached and he quit cutting corn to lean close and speak to her. Whatever he said must have been funny because Miriam chuckled and pushed him playfully away. Then Charley began cutting again and Miriam tied the stalks into sheaves behind him.

I miss that, Caleb thought wistfully—having a wife to share private moments and jests. Charley and Miriam were obviously a good match, despite Miriam's unusual practice of working alongside the men. The couple were strong supporters of the Gleaners, the young people's group, and they often chaperoned or hosted youth singings. They also had strong family values. The two were about to embark on a journey to Brazil to spend time with Miriam's sister, Leah. Leah's husband was a Mennonite, currently serving as a missionary for his church.

It wasn't envy Caleb felt toward Charley, more a yearning for the family happiness he had. *Maybe it was time I started to look for another wife.* He would always hold a special place in his heart for Dinah, but a man wasn't meant to live without a partner. Once a suitable period of mourning had passed, Amish communities expected a man of his age to remarry or he was considered as going against the Ordnung.

"Thirsty?" Rebecca held up her ladle and favored him with a big smile. A drop of water clung to the rim of the utensil, sparkling in the sunshine. "Would you like a drink of water?"

Startled, Caleb missed the cornstalk he'd been about to slice off and dug into the dirt with the tip of his blade. "*Ne...* I mean, *ya,* I would." He'd been watching Charley and Miriam and hadn't noticed Rebecca coming up behind him.

Amusement lit her vivid blue eyes. "It's a simple question, Caleb. Are you thirsty or not?"

"I was thinking of something else," he said. The words came out more harshly than intended, and he reached for the ladle. She handed it to him, but when he brought it to his lips, he found it empty except for a slice of lemon.

Smothering a giggle, she pursed her lips and offered the bucket. He frowned and then scooped up some water and drank. Without saying anything more, he helped himself to a second dipperful. His face felt hot, but the water was marvelously cool in his throat, and by the time he'd swallowed the last drop, he'd regained his composure. "What did you say to Irwin to set him off?" he ventured, trying to think of something, anything, other than how her rosy lips curved into such a sweet smile.

"I asked him if he knew how to catch a blue hen."

Caleb waited, the back of his neck feeling overly warm, obviously the result of the bright sunshine. There were at least a dozen workers in the field, but it seemed as if he and Rebecca were all alone. He was acutely aware of just how vibrant and attractive a young woman Rebecca was.

She chuckled. "How else? A blue chicken net."

"A joke." Not smiling, he handed back the ladle.

She chuckled and shrugged. "Guilty."

He'd noticed that she sometimes told funny stories to the children and women at church Sunday meals. And more than once, he'd caught sight of Rebecca using her handkerchief to make a hand puppet to amuse Amelia during service. Come to think of it, Amelia had been regaling him with rhymes, word teasers and silly jokes in the evenings. He didn't have to look far to see where they'd come from. "You like to make people laugh?"

She rested the dipper in the bucket and used her free hand to tuck a stray lock of bright auburn hair behind her ear. Golden freckles sprinkled her nose and cheeks, freckles that made her look younger than her actual years. "Chores go easier with a light heart," she replied.

A light heart... Caleb suddenly felt as if it was hard to breathe. He cleared his throat and stepped away from her, rubbing his free hand against his pant leg.

It was a mistake to be drawn in by Rebecca's winsome ways and easy laughter. She wasn't the woman for him. She was too young...too pretty...too sprightly. A woman like Rebecca would never want a man like him. Certainly not with his scars...or his past. He'd not been able to save Dinah. Surely that made him unworthy of a woman like Rebecca.

What he needed was a more sensible wife, one more suited to a staid and practical preacher. "*Danke* for the water," he managed. "I can't stand here lazing when there's half a field to do."

A pink flush colored her fair complexion. "I'll leave you to your work then, Preacher Caleb." Back straight, *kapp* strings trailing down her neck, she moved away, leaving him oddly disconcerted.

Caleb began to swing the corn knife again, slashing with hard, quick blows that left a sharp line of stalk stubble behind him. *Ya,* he decided, he had put this off far too long. It was time a new wife came to fill his loneliness and tend his motherless daughter. Too long he'd clung to his grief for Dinah. She was safe in God's hands, free from all earthly pain and care, and it was his duty to pick up the reins of his life and carry on.

"What was that... You and Caleb?" Miriam whispered.

Rebecca and Miriam had returned to Aunt Martha's kitchen to help the other women set out the midday meal. Rebecca was slicing meatloaf, and Miriam had stepped close to her, a platter of warm *kartoffel kloesse,* potato croquettes, in her hand.

Rebecca's eyes widened. "What do you mean, me and Caleb?"

Miriam elbowed her playfully in the side. "Come on, it's me. I know you too well. Don't try to pretend you don't know what I'm talking about. I saw the two of you together in the field. You like him, don't you?"

Rebecca put down the knife, glanced around to be sure no one was watching them and pulled her sister into the pantry. "Do you want everyone to hear you? I took him water like I did every other man."

Miriam shook her head and chuckled as she set the platter on the counter in the pantry. "*Ne,* little sister. Not like every other man. If my Charley looked at you like Caleb did… Well, let's say he'd better not if he knows what's good for him."

The pantry was shadowy, the only light coming from a narrow window. High shelves filled with jars of canned fruit and vegetables lined the walls, and a wooden bin held cabbages, potatoes, onions and carrots. Aunt Martha was not known for her housekeeping skills, but this one room was always clean…if you didn't notice the cobwebs overhead or the fingerprints on the windowpanes.

"There's nothing between us."

"So why does he look like a lovesick calf and why are your cheeks as red as pickled beets every time his name is mentioned?" Miriam asked. She hesitated. "You know, he's perfectly acceptable, if you do like him. I could have Charley talk to him. He could—"

"What would make you say such a thing?" Rebecca grabbed her sister's hand. "Caleb hasn't said anything that would make me believe… At least, I don't think…" She let go of Miriam's hand and let her words trail off as she remembered the strange sensations she'd felt when she and Caleb had exchanged words in the cornfield.

Excitement made her giddy. Maybe it hadn't been her imagination. If Miriam had noticed the way Caleb looked at her…then maybe it wasn't just her own foolish fancy. Maybe he did like her.

Miriam planted a hand on her hip. "Do you like him or not?"

"I don't know," she blurted, looking up at her. "I think… Maybe I do…but…"

"He wouldn't be my choice for you," Miriam remarked. "He's too serious, too stuffy."

"Caleb isn't stuffy. He is serious at times, but he has a lighthearted side, too. You should see how he plays and laughs with Amelia. And he's had so many sorrows in his life. Can you blame him if he's sad sometimes?"

"The scars on his face? His hand? They don't bother you?"

Rebecca shook her head, thinking. "It's odd to hear myself even say it, but the truth is… I don't notice them. He has such nice eyes, and—"

"You don't *notice* them," Miriam groaned. "One half of his face and you don't see it." Then she smiled. "You've got it bad. I can have Charley talk to him and see what's what."

A little thrill passed through Rebecca. "Charley would do that for me?"

"Of course he would."

"Even if you don't think he would be a good choice for me?"

Miriam smiled kindly. "Love is love, little sister. There were some who would have chosen John over Charley for me…."

"But Charley was the right husband for you," Rebecca finished.

"He was. So say the word and I'll have Charley speak with Caleb. Of course, if he's interested in getting to know you to see if you might be a suitable match, different arrangements will have to be made with your job. It wouldn't be seemly for you to be working at the preacher's house and courting him at the same time."

Courting Caleb? Just the sound of the words made Rebecca nervous…and a little giddy. Was that what she wanted? Was that the direction God was leading her? She looked at her sister. "Let me pray about it for a day or two. It's too soon—"

"You know Mam would like it if you married close to home, and we all love little Amelia." Miriam chuckled softly. "Of all my sisters, you're the last one I'd expect to be a preacher's wife."

"I said I'd pray on it," Rebecca answered. "I'm not going to rush into anything. And don't you dare tell Anna or Johanna or—"

"I know, I know." Miriam grinned. "I'll keep your secret, but don't wait too long. A lot of mothers would consider Caleb Wittner a good catch for their daughters. You wait too long to make up your mind and someone could snatch him right out from under you."

When the dinner bell rang, Caleb walked back to the Coblentz house with the other men. As he approached, he couldn't help noticing that one of the back porch posts was leaning and the rails, on their last legs, were sagging. He climbed the rickety steps, thinking that while Reuben was laid up with his injury, it wouldn't hurt to have some of the neighbors do some work on his house. It pained him to think that a family in his church was living like this when others were clearly doing so much better financially.

Someone had set up a tub of water, a bar of soap and towels on the porch. Charley and Eli were there cleaning up. Charley was laughing at some nonsense and shaking his wet hands, splattering a protesting Eli with soapy drops of water. As they stepped aside, still teasing each other, Caleb pushed up his sleeves and washed his hands thoroughly. When he reached for a towel, Martha's daughter, Dorcas, handed him a clean one.

"It's good of you to come and help us. Get in our corn," Dorcas said. She was a tall, spare woman, plain in features, but with good skin. Unmarried, he remembered, and probably nearing thirty. He'd not exchanged more than a few words with her since her father's accident, and not many since he'd come to Delaware.

"I'm glad to help," he answered.

She covered her mouth with her hand and offered what he thought might be a smile. Had he ever seen her smile? No matter, she was obviously a devout and modest young woman, and it would do no harm to consider her in his search for a prospective bride.

Dorcas's mother, Martha, appeared at his side and tugged at his sleeve. He turned toward her. *"Ya?"*

"A word, if you would, Preacher Caleb." She smiled, showing sparkling white, obviously artificial uppers.

Caleb glanced into the kitchen where the other men

were taking seats at the long table. "Maybe after the meal? I think Samuel is about to—"

"Of course," Martha agreed. "After you've eaten. Actually, Grace Hartman, my niece… She's Mennonite. My brother's daughter. Not raised among us. Offered a ride to the hospital. If you'd like to join Dorcas and me to visit Reuben. He's not to come home until tomorrow now. Nothing to worry about. Just a slight fever. Such a terrible accident, a man of his years. So glad you were there to come to his aid in his time of—"

"The grace," Caleb reminded her. "The others are waiting."

"After the meal," Martha repeated, patting his arm. "You are more than welcome to—"

"It's kind of you to ask," Caleb replied, glancing toward the kitchen door. "But we need to finish that field today. The weather forecast calls for rain tomorrow night, and—"

"Tomorrow being the Sabbath, there will be no work," Martha finished for him. "*Ya,* you are right to remind me. My Reuben is such a devout member of the church, and we've tried to raise our Dorcas to be equally obedient to the rules of our community." Creases crinkled in the corners of her eyes as she beamed at him. "She's quite accomplished, our Dorcas. You've noticed her, I'm sure. As you would, a single man, a widower with a young daughter in need of a mother."

Caleb nodded. He could feel the impatient gazes of hungry men on him.

"No need to hold you back from your meal," Martha said. "You've worked so long and hard in the field today. You've earned your rest and a full stomach. But

I wondered, if we can't talk today, perhaps tomorrow evening. Supper. Bring your daughter, naturally. Reuben will be home. We would be honored to have you. Six o'clock?"

"Ya," Caleb agreed. "Six." He saw his opportunity and nearly bolted for the door. "Tomorrow." Three long strides and he was in the kitchen.

"About time," Charley grumbled. "We're starving."

Caleb slid into the only empty chair and closed his eyes.

"Let us give thanks," Samuel intoned.

When their silent prayers ended and they opened their eyes, the serious eating began. Biscuits, potato dishes and creamed celery were passed around. Women slid more bowls of vegetables and meats onto the patched white tablecloth.

Dorcas placed a bowl of gravy down with a thump directly in front of Caleb's plate. "For the meatloaf," she said. "My mother made it." Again, she smiled behind her hand.

He nodded, wondering exactly what he'd committed to by agreeing to come to supper. He had been able to tell by the look in Martha's eyes that she had more on her mind than a simple thank-you supper. But maybe this was God's plan for him. Maybe finding a new wife wouldn't be that difficult. He didn't know anything about Dorcas, but that was what courtship was all about.

"Lord, help me," he murmured silently. But as he glanced up, he saw Rebecca leaning over the table and pouring water into Eli's glass tumbler. And just for a second, he absently stroked the scar on his cheek and wished...

* * *

"Don't go far," Rebecca called to Amelia. "I just need to get an armload of kindling for the wood box."

The little girl and Fritzy were racing back and forth between the woodshed and the house. Amelia was throwing a leather ball Charley had sewn for her out of old scraps into the air. The dog would jump up and catch it in his mouth, and then the child would chase him. The big poodle ran in circles around her as she shrieked with laughter and tried to catch him to get the ball back. Only when Amelia stopped, breathless, would Fritzy drop the toy at her feet. Then the game would begin all over again.

With a final glance over her shoulder to see that dog and girl were where they were supposed to be, Rebecca entered the shed and began gathering small pieces of wood for the stove. She had almost all she could carry, then stooped to pick up one last piece. As she reached for it, she heard the door hinges squeak behind her.

She looked back and saw the tall silhouette of a man in the doorway. Startled by Caleb's sudden appearance, she stepped sideways onto a log and lost her balance. She quickly righted herself, but in the process lost control of the kindling, spilling half of it back onto the floor.

"I didn't mean to frighten you." Caleb stepped forward to steady her. "I'm sorry."

"*Ne,* it's nothing." She could feel the blood rising in her face. "I just…" Clumsily, she began to gather up the wood. "You just surprised me."

"Let me," he insisted, taking the wood from her arms. "The fault is mine. I thought I left the wood box full."

"I didn't realize it was so late." Rebecca kept her face turned away as she picked up some bigger pieces of wood. Caleb must think she was flighty, to be so startled by his arrival in his own woodshed. "Supper is on the back of the stove," she said.

Caleb carried his armload outside and she followed, carrying the additional logs she'd picked up. "I may be a little early," he said. "I finished the trim work for that fireplace surround I was telling you about, the fancy one with the columns. They want me to come to Lewes and mount it on-site. They're even going to pay for my driver."

"That's good," Rebecca said. The town in Sussex County had an area where old houses were being moved in and restored. A contractor had contacted Caleb about doing specialty pieces for some of his projects. It was different than the way he usually worked, but Caleb seemed pleased. He said the pay was twice what he normally made. Rebecca was happy that the English people realized what a craftsman Caleb was. Secretly, she was sure that, preacher or not, he took pride in his woodwork.

"I wanted to tell you that I'll be going out for supper on Wednesday. You won't have to make anything for us that night," Caleb said.

"Oh?"

"*Ya,* to Reuben and Martha's."

Again? Rebecca tried not to let the surprise she felt show. "Oh." Once was natural, after all that Caleb had done for her aunt and uncle, but he'd already had dinner with them on Sunday. Twice in one week? An uneasy thought rose in Rebecca's mind. "You and Aunt Martha and Uncle Reuben and…and Dorcas." She heard Fritzy barking and Amelia's squeal of laughter. The game was still going on. But the two seemed a long way off. Supper twice in one week usually meant...

"Caleb, are you courting my cousin?" she blurted out, louder than she intended.

He stopped short, turned and fixed her with that intense, dark stare. He suddenly looked as uncomfortable as she felt. "We're not courting, Dorcas and I. At least, not yet."

Rebecca was stunned. She gripped the wood, her fingers numb. "Not yet?" she repeated.

Only Saturday she had had the conversation with Miriam about the possibility of having Charley speak to Caleb about her. When Rebecca had said she wanted to pray about it first, Miriam had warned her not to wait too long, or someone else might snatch him up. But Dorcas?

Rebecca realized how uncharitable such a thought was. Why not Dorcas? She was the single daughter of a preacher. It was perfectly logical that she and Caleb would have much in common, wasn't it?

"We're trying to see if we're compatible," Caleb explained. "To find out if we want to walk out with each other." His eyes narrowed. "Why? Is there something wrong with Dorcas?"

"Ne, ne," she said quickly. She looked down at the frozen ground, feeling a sense of loss and not entirely sure why. She had prayed about Caleb, but she'd gotten no answer. Had Charley been standing here at this moment, ready to speak with Caleb about her, she wasn't sure she would have agreed to it. "She's a good girl, Dorcas. Very..."

Caleb cocked his head slightly. "Very what?"

Frantically, Rebecca searched her mind for something positive and truthful to say in her cousin's defense. "She's devout. And she's a dutiful daughter. Thoughtful and obedient to her parents."

"Admirable in anyone."

"Ya," Rebecca continued in a rush. "A hard worker, not lazy. And she makes good chowchow. The best. Everyone says so. She sells a lot of it to the Englishers at their stand at Spence's."

He chuckled. "A handy skill to have, I suppose. A good thing I have always been fond of chowchow."

Rebecca quickened her step, hurrying past him to the back porch and into the house. She dumped her load into the wood box beside the stove. Caleb came into the kitchen with Amelia and Fritzy on his heels. "Do you want me to stay and keep Amelia on Wednesday?" she asked him. "Or take her to Mam's?"

"I considered taking her. It's important to me that Amelia be comfortable with any young woman I care to…to consider as a wife."

"Naturally." Rebecca dusted her hands off on her skirts. She was trying not to be upset. What right did she have to be? If she'd been interested in Caleb, she should have spoken up sooner.

"But maybe I should wait. Courting is a big step." He dumped his own load into the box. "It isn't one I would take lightly. But I think it is time. Amelia should have a mother." He paused, and then his gaze met hers again. "And maybe it's time I stopped mourning Dinah and took a new wife."

Rebecca forced herself to smile and nod. "It is only right," she agreed. "A preacher should…" She took a breath. "Amelia does need a mother. Every child does." Her voice softened and she looked away. "You'll do what is right for her, Caleb. You always do."

Chapter Ten

The following Saturday, Rebecca, Ruth and Miriam went to Fifer's Orchard in the nearby town of Wyoming to get apples. They were picking from the seconds bins by the side of the building and chatted while they worked. It was the last chance they'd have to spend with Miriam for a while as she and Charley were headed to Brazil to spend time with Leah and Daniel that week, and would be gone almost a month.

Mam's orchard hadn't produced many sound apples this year, and despite the quarts and quarts of applesauce they'd put up, Mam wanted more fruit for apple pies and cakes and apple butter. They would purchase baskets of the best apples to store in the cellar for winter, but the slightly bruised or odd-shaped seconds would be fine for cooking.

"So I heard Caleb's courting Dorcas." Miriam propped her hands on her hips. "*Our cousin,* Dorcas? How did that happen?"

Rebecca glanced at Ruth and Miriam. She didn't want to talk about this with her sisters, and she certainly didn't want to talk about it in public. It had not been a good week. When Caleb had told her he was having supper with Uncle Reuben's family with the intention of trying to find out if he and Dorcas might be a suitable match, she'd been taken by surprise. Then, as the week had passed, she'd found herself growing more and more upset by the idea. And more certain she *did* have feelings for Caleb. Miriam had warned her she had to act fast, but it had never occurred to her that she'd have to act *that* fast. Even before she'd had the opportunity to consider what she felt, everything changed.

Ruth placed two apples into her brown paper bag. "I heard he went to supper at Aunt Martha's Sunday evening and again on Wednesday. Wearing his good coat. Sounds like courting to me."

"If Dorcas can land the new preacher, it will be a triumph for Aunt Martha," Miriam said. "She told Mam that she was afraid she'd have Dorcas on her hands forever."

"Mmm." Ruth picked up an apple, examined it and then rejected the apple. "Maybe it's the new tooth."

"Getting that broken tooth repaired certainly didn't hurt Dorcas's appearance," Miriam agreed. "You know I hate it when a woman's looks are more important than how beautiful she is inside, but Dorcas can use all the help she can get."

"That's not very charitable," Ruth admonished.

"I didn't mean it unkindly." Miriam looked up at her. "But the truth is, Dorcas is plain, and the way Aunt Martha insists she dress doesn't help. Amish men aren't all that different from any other. Most of the time, they'll pick the pretty girls first."

Ruth frowned. "It didn't stop our Anna from making a good match with Samuel. Her size didn't mean a thing to him."

"*Ya,* but who wouldn't want Anna? She has the biggest heart of any of us. She's a wonderful mother to Samuel's children—and she makes him happy. Not to mention that she's a better cook than even Mam."

"I think Dorcas could have married long ago if she took a page from Anna's book. It's no secret that Dorcas isn't always pleasant to be around. She can be…" Ruth nibbled at her lower lip "…critical, and…"

"Aunt Martha-ish?" Miriam suggested. "Maybe that's what Caleb is looking for. No one can fault Dorcas's devotion to the church. It could be that she's exactly the kind of wife Caleb is looking for."

Rebecca continued to sort apples and tried not to listen to her sisters. Then she tried to pretend that she didn't care whom Caleb was walking out with. If he chose her cousin, though… She swallowed, trying to dissolve the knot in her throat. Over the years, she and Dorcas hadn't always been the best of friends, but Dorcas was family and she was a member of their church. If Caleb asked Dorcas to marry him, Rebecca would have to find a way to be happy for them.

Ruth lowered her voice and moved closer to Rebecca. "You see Caleb every day. Did he say something to you about being interested in Dorcas?"

Rebecca didn't look up at her. "He said that he was visiting to see if he and Dorcas suit each other."

"Catch." Miriam tossed Rebecca an oversize green apple. "There's still time, little sister. I think you should let Charley speak to Caleb for you."

Rebecca felt tears sting the backs of her eyelids.

Ruth squeezed Rebecca's arm and looked at her. "You do care for him, don't you?"

Rebecca opened her mouth to answer, but before she could say anything, Susanna trotted down the wooden ramp toward them, waving a vegetable peeler.

"Look what I bought!" Susanna exclaimed. "With my own money. A peel-er. Now I can help peel apples. I won't cut myself." She thrust the green-handled utensil in Ruth's face. "Isn't it pretty?"

"It is." Ruth smiled back at her. "Where did you find such a good one?"

"By the reg-i-ter. King David's Mam. I saw her. In-side." Susanna was so excited that she was practically bouncing from one black athletic shoe to the other. "She helped me count my money."

"Great," Rebecca agreed, glad for a reason to change the subject. "Mam will be proud of you."

"Good job," Miriam said, admiring Susanna's purchase. "You didn't forget about wanting to peel apples, did you?"

"*Ne.* I didn't forget. I want to help," Susanna said. "Not just play with *kinner.* Help like you."

"We can always use another pair of hands," Ruth said.

Susanna nodded vigorously. "And…and when King David and me get married—" she took a deep breath "—I can make applesauce for him!"

Rebecca met Miriam's gaze, and suddenly their little sister's happy moment became a sad one for the older sisters. No matter how many peelers she bought, they all knew Susanna would never be able to marry and leave home. She would always live with Mam or one of them, and in some ways, she would always re-main a child.

I should be ashamed of myself, Rebecca thought. In-stead of being upset by Caleb's attention to her cousin, she should be thanking God that she wasn't born with Susanna's burden. Her sister was a precious and inno-cent soul, but she could never be a wife or a mother. *Someone, somewhere will surely ask me to be his wife.*

"Hi!" Grace joined them at the apple bins. "I didn't know you were coming here today. I could have picked you up in my car. I'm so glad I got to see you again be-fore you and Charley set off on your adventure." She kissed Miriam on the cheek and continued greeting each of her sisters affectionately. Because Grace was Mennonite, she didn't wear Amish clothing, but she was dressed in a long denim skirt, a modest blouse and a lace prayer cap.

"How's school?" Rebecca asked. Grace was attend-ing a college program for veterinary technicians and would soon be working beside her husband, John, at his animal hospital.

"Tough, but I love it." Grace flashed her a grin. "This one teacher I have is a real bear, but I can always count on John to help me study for her tests. I don't know what I'd do without him."

"You couldn't have found a better partner," Mir-iam said.

Miriam and John had been good friends for years, and she'd come close to marrying him. But he wasn't Amish, and in the end, Miriam had chosen Charley and remained true to her faith. *It was funny how things turned out,* Rebecca mused. Who would have believed that John was destined to be her brother-in-law, not by wedding Miriam as everyone expected, but by becoming the husband of a beloved half sister who'd recently come into their family? Proof that God truly had a plan for each of them.

She wondered what His plan was for her.

I thought it might have been Caleb, she thought with a pang of sadness. She'd been so certain that there was no hurry, no reason to rush the awakening feelings that stirred in her heart. Now, selfishly, she didn't want Caleb to become her cousin by marriage. She wanted more....

"So what's new at home?" Grace asked. "I kept thinking about all of you on Thanksgiving. Uncle Albert ordered a whole turkey dinner from a restaurant, and we all sat around and stuffed ourselves. Grandpa Hartman ate most of a sweet-potato pie all by himself."

"We missed you, too," Ruth said. "It was a quiet day of prayer and fasting for us."

"But we'll expect you all for Christmas dinner." Rebecca added one last apple to the bag. "Uncle Albert and his father, too."

"We wouldn't miss it. You know how 'Kota loves to play with his cousins." Grace picked up a bag of apples. "Let me help you load these in the buggy."

Ruth and Susanna went inside to pay while Rebecca, Miriam and Grace walked across the parking lot to the hitching rail.

"What's this I hear about Caleb Wittner and Dorcas?" Grace asked as they approached the buggy. "Is he really courting her? I thought that you..." Grace gave Rebecca a meaningful look. "You know. So I was surprised when John said that Noodle Troyer said—"

"Caleb isn't walking out with Dorcas." Rebecca shoved her bag of apples into the back of the buggy so hard that the brown paper split and apples spilled out and rolled across the floorboards.

Miriam chuckled. "Bad subject, Grace. I was just telling Rebecca last weekend that if she thought she might be interested in Preacher Caleb, I should have Charley speak to him before someone else beat her to him."

Rebecca whirled around. "If Caleb and Dorcas are suited to each other, I'd be the last person to—" She bit down on her lower lip.

Grace's eyes clouded with compassion. "I'm sorry. I didn't mean to…" She sighed. "It's just that…" She shrugged. "I don't understand. I'm a Yoder, and I should have learned all this stuff by now, but how the Amish choose a husband is just…just…"

"It must sound strange to you, being raised among the English," Miriam offered, "but it isn't odd to us. It's just the way things have always been done. What is it that you aren't clear about?"

"When John and I started to be interested in each other, we…we dated, sort of. He asked me out." She looked from Miriam to Rebecca. "John said that Amish boys don't ask girls to go out with them—they have someone else ask."

Rebecca nodded. "There's often a go-between. Amish boys are shy."

"Usually more so than the girls," Miriam put in. "And since our church is one of the more conservative, we like to see couples who are walking out be with other people, not alone."

"Chaperoned?" Grace said. "Even at Dorcas's age? Really?"

Miriam slid her bag in and began to gather the apples that had spilled out of Rebecca's bag before raising her gaze to meet Rebecca's. "I wanted to have Charley talk to Caleb to see how he felt about Rebecca. When there's a friend or relative asking, it's less embarrassing if the other person isn't interested."

"So Caleb had a go-between to ask Dorcas—" Grace began.

Rebecca shook her head. "*Ne.* Not exactly. Aunt Martha invited him to supper. What they are doing is visiting to see how they get along, if they want to court."

"And if they do like each other in that way, will they start going to singings and work frolics together?" Grace asked.

Miriam shrugged. "I doubt it. Both of them are older, and Caleb's been married before. I suppose the first thing people will notice is him driving her home from church services. And Caleb will keep visiting her at home."

"When Samuel was courting Anna," Rebecca said, "they went to a taffy pulling she wanted to go to, so he took her. What a disaster. Of course, the age difference isn't so great between Caleb and Dorcas. But neither of them seem the kind to want to go to young people's frolics."

Grace wrinkled her nose. "It doesn't seem very romantic."

"It's complicated." Miriam knotted the loosening ties of her blue wool scarf under her chin. "Respect, devotion to the faith and an ability to help the partner. That's what's important." She smiled. "As Grossmama always says, 'Kissing don't last. Cooking do.'"

"Maybe it's best I didn't become Amish," Grace said thoughtfully. "I married John because I loved him—because I couldn't live without him. Respect and friendship alone wouldn't be enough for me."

And maybe not for me, either, Rebecca thought. *I think I'd rather stay an old maid than settle for a man I couldn't love with my whole heart.*

"Are you almost done?" Amelia pleaded from the bale of hay where Caleb had placed her a half hour ago.

Caleb shook his head. "Just a little while yet. Stay where you are and play with your baby."

They'd been on the way to Dover to the hardware store, but he'd stopped at Reuben's farm long enough to see if the volunteers had come by for morning milking and chores. They had, but Martha had seen him and asked if he'd clean out the horse stall. By the time he finished, he'd be in no shape to be seen in public. He couldn't help wondering when Reuben had last cleaned it.

Caleb looked down at his shoes. They'd need a good polish before tomorrow's worship. Had he known he'd be pressed into service, he'd have brought along his muck boots.

"Dat, I'm hungry."

"You're not hungry. You had soup and a chicken sandwich before we left home." Rebecca never left on Friday afternoon without leaving food for the weekend. He didn't know how he and Amelia had managed without her. She didn't just cook and clean and look after Amelia, she was tackling bigger projects, too. She was working her way through the moving boxes that had been scattered throughout the house, unpacking his life and putting it in order.

"Dat, I want to go. I'm tired of sitting here. And I need you to tie Baby's bonnet strings."

Caleb emptied another hayfork full of dirty straw and manure into the wheelbarrow. "Not now, Amelia. I'm working." The soft rag doll that Dinah had made for her was his daughter's greatest treasure. She spent hours taking the doll's clothes off, putting them on and trying to tie the tiny bonnet strings. Usually, he ended up tying them for Amelia, but in minutes, she'd have them untied and the bonnet off again.

"I can tie them for her," came a thin voice from the shadows.

Startled, Caleb almost dropped his pitchfork. *Dorcas.* He hadn't known that anyone else was in the barn. She was standing only a few feet away. How long had she been watching him and how had she gotten behind him without him seeing her?

"Ne," Amelia whined. "I want Dat to do it." His daughter clutched the doll and bonnet against her chest. "I want Dat!"

"Amelia," he chastised. She was never on her best behavior around Dorcas or her family. And to Dorcas's credit, she'd shown more patience than was warranted. "Let Dorcas fix it for you."

"Ne. Don't want her to play with my doll. It's mine."

Caleb thrust his pitchfork into the muck. "Behave yourself, child. That's no way to talk to Dorcas."

"Mam says she's spoiled." Dorcas leaned on the upright post at the corner of the stall. "She says it's to be expected. Her having no mother to teach her right."

"Do so have a mother!" Amelia flung back. "Rebecca says so. My Mam is in heaven!"

Caleb frowned at her, and Amelia's face crumpled.

"My mother says…" Dorcas began.

Her shrill monotone grated on his ears and her next words were lost to him as he stuck the pitchfork into another clump of rotting straw.

I should be ashamed of myself, he thought. Dorcas isn't responsible for the nature of her voice anymore than the color of her eyes. She had nice eyes. They were her best feature. There was nothing flashy about her face or hair, but that wasn't what a man should be looking for in a wife.

Dorcas came from a respectable family, and she was modest and hardworking, according to Martha.

If Dorcas lacked somewhat in her cooking skills, that would come in time. Amelia's mother hadn't been the world's best cook when he'd first married her, but in time she'd improved. It was unfair to compare Dorcas's chicken stew to the one that Rebecca had put on his table this week. Rebecca had tucked it neatly into a golden brown piecrust, and it had been so good that he'd finished the last slice of it for breakfast this morning. Maybe, if he suggested it, Dorcas could ask Rebecca for her recipe.

Dorcas was kind to Amelia, and if Amelia was slow to respond, it was her nature. She spent every weekday with Rebecca; it was only natural that she had become so attached to her. Amelia was constantly telling him of new games Rebecca had taught her, and silly songs they'd sung.

Caleb almost groaned out loud. What was wrong with him? Why was he thinking of Rebecca Yoder when he should be paying attention to the very suitable young woman standing behind him? Rebecca would never be interested in him. It was Dorcas's good points he should be concentrating on. On the whole, she was a fine prospect for marriage. She was clean, reasonably intelligent and she seemed interested in him. And if she had a few minor traits that rubbed him the wrong way, doubtless she could find plenty of fault with him, as well.

"Caleb."

"*Ya,* Dorcas?" He had only a small corner of the stall to go. If he finished up quickly, he might have time to go home, change and still get to the hardware store before the afternoon got too late.

"My mother is out of sugar and cinnamon. She asked if you could take me to Byler's to get some. With Dat being so poorly, we can't get to the store."

"You don't drive the horse and buggy?" He shouldn't have said that, but the words just came out before he thought.

"*Ne.* Not me. I'm afraid of horses. Dat always drives. Mam does, sometimes, when we go someplace without him, but she has a sore throat. She doesn't want to go out of the house. And she needs cheese for casserole. For the midday meal. At meeting tomorrow. Mam says…"

"*Ya,* I can take you." She kept talking while he concentrated on the last of the stall. He would spread fresh straw when he was finished. The hardware store errand could wait. He probably had enough nails to finish the pigpen anyway. If Dorcas could take Amelia into Byler's with her, the child would be satisfied that she didn't get to go to Dover today.

"…eat supper with us tonight," Dorcas was saying. "I made snapper soup. We had a big old turtle that Dat caught in the pond. He put it in a barrel and we fed it table scraps and corn and…"

Caleb stiffened. Snapper soup? Snapping turtle? His stomach turned over. "Thank your mother," he said. "But I've stuffed peppers waiting at home. Another time, Dorcas."

He couldn't abide snapper soup. The bishop's wife had served it at the first meal he'd shared with them, and he'd forced it down and been nauseous all that night. It was a little embarrassing, being a man who didn't like the strong tastes of some traditional Amish foods.

Caleb shook off a shudder. He'd told Rebecca about his ordeal at Bishop Atlee's table one morning when they'd seen a snapping turtle crossing the road. Rebecca had laughed at the tale, but despite her teasing, he was certain that she would never invite him to share a pot of snapper soup.

"It's all right, Caleb," Dorcas went on, apparently picking up on his distaste. "We've got pigs' knuckles with sauerkraut and dumplings left over from Wednesday night's supper. You can eat that. It's still *gut*."

Wonderful, Caleb thought with dark humor. Pigs' knuckles were his second-most-hated food and he'd already lived through that experience once this week. *What will she and Martha serve me next? Blood sausage?*

Chapter Eleven

Tuesday evening, snowfall dusted the ground with a fine layer of white. The air was cold on Caleb's cheeks as he swung his legs over the rail fence that bordered his property. He was late coming home tonight, but he was so close to finishing a console bracket that he'd lost track of the time. It was the first time he'd attempted such an intricate design and he was greatly pleased with the results.

He knew a man of faith shouldn't be guilty of *hochmut*, but when a seasoned block of oak, cherry or walnut took shape under his hands and became an object of beauty, it was hard not to feel pride in his craft. And foolishly, he wanted to show it to Rebecca. In a way, she was partly responsible for the success of the piece, because if he didn't feel confident that Amelia was safe and well cared for, he couldn't have concentrated on his work.

Snow crunched under Caleb's feet and he began to sing an old hymn of praise. His voice was nothing beyond adequate, but with only the wind and the trees to hear him, he could open his heart and sing praise. As he walked and sang, it came to him that today he was truly happy for the first time in years. Coming East had been the right thing to do for him and his daughter. It had given them the new start that they'd needed to pick up their lives and move forward. This community was quickly becoming his own, and the conservative views and practices seemed right for him.

Thank You, God, he thought. *Thank You for guiding me to a safe place when my eyes were blinded by tears.*

He slipped a hand inside his leather bag and ran his fingers over the perfect curves of the pendant at the bottom of the bracket he had made. It was shaped like a child's top and sanded as smooth as glass. Later, someone would attach the bracket to a house and probably paint it in the garish colors that the Englishers favored, but for now, it was a deep red oak with lighter streaks of shading. It was strange how his craftsmanship had improved in the months and years since the fire. It was almost as if the flames had burned away his flesh, exposing ugliness but leaving him with a greater ability to create beauty in wood.

Caleb pushed back the wave of sadness that threatened to suppress his good mood. Those times were past, and the uncle and aunt who'd cared for him had been fair. From them he'd learned to be strong, to depend on himself and to be content with few material goods—all qualities that prepared him to be a good father.

And husband?

He grimaced. Tomorrow evening would be another strained visit at the Coblentz home. He wished that he could spend some time alone with Dorcas, to really get to know her, but Martha had made it clear that she wouldn't allow it.

"You're older. You've had a wife," she'd said ominously. "Dorcas is an innocent young woman. Best you remain under the watchful eye of her parents and not risk falling to temptations of the flesh."

He found several flaws in Martha's line of thinking. First, Dorcas wasn't that young. No one had mentioned her exact age, and he wasn't about to ask, but he guessed that she was probably close to thirty. And the fact that he had reached an age of maturity meant that he was far *less* likely to behave inappropriately with a young woman than he had been in his youth. Furthermore, he and Dorcas weren't yet courting, and if he didn't get to know her, how could either of them know if they wanted to take the arrangement further?

Caleb kicked at the snow. He wanted to take this whole thing with Dorcas slowly, especially since it had started so suddenly. He hadn't intended to commit himself to visiting every Sunday and Wednesday, but with Reuben laid up with his broken leg, it naturally fell to him to be at the Coblentz farm more frequently. Then Martha had brought up Dorcas's availability and it had snowballed from there. Now everyone seemed to assume that he and Dorcas were courting. Roman had even remarked on their impending marriage during the lunch break today, and Caleb had to make his position clear.

"There's nothing definite yet between us," he'd explained to Roman and Eli. "We're just *considering* walking out together."

Roman had shook his head and Eli had laughed. "Not what Martha's telling the womenfolk," Roman said between bites of his liverwurst sandwich. "My

Fannie talks about you two marrying like it's a done deal."

Eli had poured himself another cup of coffee from his Thermos. "Nothing wrong with Dorcas."

"I wouldn't be talking with her if there was," he'd defended. "Dorcas is a suitable prospect. Her being a member of our church makes it easier. If I picked a wife from another state, she'd be homesick for her family."

"Ya," Roman had agreed with a chuckle. "That's a fine reason for picking a bride. You don't have to go far to find her."

"Romantic," Eli added with a straight face.

"Marriage is a partnership," Caleb had defended. "For the family and—"

"Ya, ya." Roman snapped his fingers. "But a little spark between you never hurts."

Was there a spark between them? Caleb wondered as he reached the farmyard. Not so far. But maybe when she was a little more comfortable with him, Dorcas would have more to say. Not that she didn't talk; it was just that most of her sentences were prefaced by "Mam says." The thing was, he didn't want to hear what Martha thought. It was Dorcas he was considering as a wife and companion, not her mother.

Maybe he could invite her to his shop. Rebecca had been there several times, and she'd always been interested in what he was working on and his plans for increasing the business. Doubtless, Dorcas would be curious about his ability to support her and want to know exactly what he did. He didn't know how good her math skills were. If Dorcas was proficient in numbers and could learn to do his bookwork as Fannie did for Roman, it would free him to spend more time in the shop.

Caleb glanced ahead. In the darkness, golden lamp-light glowed from the kitchen windows of his house. Rebecca would have the woodstove burning, the table set and supper waiting. He'd hitch up the horse and drive her home before eating. It was too cold for her to walk home, and he worried about her on the road at dusk—too many cars and trucks passing by.

As he approached the farmhouse, Fritzy barked and Rebecca threw open the back door. "Come in out of the cold. You're late," she said. Red-gold curls escaped her scarf to curl around her rosy face. A smudge of flour streaked her chin, and she looked as sweet as a frosted ginger cookie.

Don't go there, Caleb thought. Rebecca Yoder was all wrong for him, and it did no good to allow himself foolish yearnings. If he was a younger man... If fire hadn't marred his features... If he hadn't been called as a preacher, or she was a more serious girl, then maybe. He caught himself up sharply. "Maybe or might fill no corncribs," his uncle used to say. He was the man he was, and Rebecca was the way God made her. A smart man didn't plague his mind with something that could never be.

"Dat!" As Caleb entered the house, Amelia ran and threw herself into his arms. "Rebecca showed me how to make biscuit pigs!" she cried. "A mama pig and baby pigs with raisin eyes. And we baked them in the oven, and—and I'm going to eat them for supper. With but-ter on their snouts. You can have one."

Stepping into the kitchen, Caleb swung his daughter high until the top of her head nearly brushed the ceiling. She squealed with excitement. "I'll eat your baby pigs," he teased in a gruff voice. "I'll gobble them up, one by one."

"*Ne,* Dat." She giggled. "One baby pig. You get one. Rebecca gets one. And I eat the rest!"

"We'll eat when we get back. I'll take you home, Rebecca. It's too cold for you to walk. Roads may be slippery."

Rebecca pulled a cast-iron frying pan full of biscuits from the oven. "Grace is coming by to pick me up at six, if you don't mind me staying a little longer. Her boy's school was closed today, and he was with Johanna."

"It's no bother." He slipped off his wet shoes and hung his coat and hat on hooks in the utility room. Then he padded in his socks to the kitchen sink to wash his hands. Wonderful smells filled the kitchen and his stomach rumbled with anticipation. "You're welcome to share our supper," he said.

"*Ne.* Thank you just the same, but Johanna invited us to eat with her." Rebecca lifted the top of a Dutch oven, revealing a roasted chicken with stuffing. "I hope you like scalloped sweet potatoes and apples."

"And apple cobber," Amelia supplied. "I put in the cinn-a-min."

"Amelia did help make the cobbler." Rebecca dished out a plate for him and a smaller one for his daughter. "She's going to be a wonderful cook."

Caleb took his seat at the table. "Will you at least sit with us?" he asked.

Rebecca shook her head. "I'll just slip into the parlor and finish the letter I've been writing to *The Budget.*" Her blue eyes sparkled with mischief in the lamplight.

"Uncle Reuben would be disappointed if I didn't share the news about his accident. I'm mentioning the auction you've arranged to help with his medical expenses, too. Some may want to come from out of state to attend." She went back to the stove and returned with the biscuits. As Amelia had claimed, there were a number of small, misshapen objects that could have been pigs.

"Mine!" Amelia said, reaching for one. "My baby pigs."

"Careful," Rebecca warned. "The pan is still hot. Don't burn yourself."

Caleb glanced at Rebecca. "Whatever possessed you to teach her to make biscuits shaped like animals?" he asked. "Learning to bake is a useful skill for a girl, but pigs?"

Rebecca's mouth tightened. "She's a child, Caleb. Sometimes she simply has to have fun. Not everything is about work."

"She's growing fast. She can't get away with the nonsense she did as a baby." With a twinge, he realized he was echoing a remark he'd heard Martha make when Amelia had tipped over the sugar bowl trying to dip her finger in. "Her mother would expect her to be brought up proper," he said. "Especially since I'm a—"

"*Ya, ya.* A preacher. I know. You've made that clear to me." Rebecca set a pitcher of milk on the table beside Amelia's empty glass—set it down hard enough to make the silverware rattle together. Her blue eyes darkened. "And, just so you know, Caleb, my father was a bishop. And he's the one who taught me to make pig biscuits." With a sharp nod of her chin, she turned and bustled, stiff shouldered, out of the kitchen.

Caleb stared after her, confused. What had he said

to set her off? Was she annoyed with him because he'd questioned the wisdom of her odd-shaped biscuits? His gaze fell on the leather case containing the carved bracket with the exaggerated pendant and disappointment settled over him like a wet coat. *I suppose she won't want to look at the piece now,* he thought, as some of the warmth seeped out of the room.

"Dat?" Amelia stared at him in bewilderment. "Don't you like my biscuits?"

"*Ya,* they are good biscuits. Remember, grace first, before we eat." Caleb bowed his head for a few moments and then nodded to Amelia and picked up his own fork. The chicken and stuffing had smelled so good, but now each bite tasted like sawdust in his mouth.

Thankfully, he didn't have to talk. Amelia couldn't remain silent long and soon began to chatter on about her day. Apparently, they had scrubbed the floors upstairs and polished the furniture. "Rebecca hung our laundry in the attic," she explained. "I helped."

"*Gut,*" he said absently. There was a large open space on the third floor with finished walls, but no furniture. He'd thought, when he'd bought the house, he could easily put several more bedrooms up there, if he ever had the need. Chimneys ran up on each end of the house, and when the stoves were in use, the attic was warm and dry. Why hadn't he thought of that instead of stringing clotheslines across his kitchen in bad weather?

"Rebecca says that—"

"Enough about Rebecca," he said. "Finish your supper."

"But—"

"Amelia."

Her face fell, and she sniffed.

Caleb stared at his plate. He hadn't meant to be harsh with her, but he'd heard quite enough about— A rap at the back door interrupted his thoughts. Thinking that must be Rebecca's sister come to pick her up, he rose from his chair to let her in.

He hadn't even heard Grace's car. He walked back through the utility room to let her in but to his surprise, he found not a Mennonite woman but three Amish men standing on his little back porch. Behind them, he saw a horse and buggy in the snowy yard.

"We've come to talk with you about an important matter, Preacher." The man extended his hand. "Ray Stutzman. Next district over."

"Ray." Caleb shook his hand and waved the visitors in. He recognized Thomas Troyer, a stout elder with a long white beard. "Thomas."

The three stomped the snow off their feet and removed their outer jackets and hats. "Samson Hershberger," Thomas said, indicating a big man of about forty, with dark hair and a full beard.

"Samson." Caleb exchanged handshakes with Thomas and Samson before showing them into the kitchen. Amelia slipped out of her chair and dashed out of the room. "Sit down," Caleb said, picking up the dinner plates to set them in the sink. "Coffee?"

"If it's no trouble." Thomas took a seat. "Sorry to bother you at suppertime, but the weather might get worse. We wanted to speak to you—"

"Tonight," Ray finished. "Samson and I are neighbors over on Rose Valley Road."

Rebecca appeared in the doorway, saw the visitors and immediately went to the cupboard for cups. "Thomas." She nodded a greeting to the other two before asking, "How is your wife, Samson? Doing well, I hope? And the new baby?"

"Both well," he said with a smile. "Heard you were cleaning for Preacher Caleb."

She poured coffee and served the men, quickly clearing away the last of the dinner and bringing sugar and milk and a tray of cookies. "I'll leave you to your business," she said and went back into the other room.

"Usually she doesn't stay this late," Caleb explained. "Her ride will be here any minute."

"She's half sister to John Hartman's wife, isn't she?"

Caleb nodded. He didn't want to be rude, but he was curious as to what urgent business he might have with these men from another church district so important as to bring them out on a snowy night. But these Amish were no different from those men he'd known in Idaho. No business could be contracted until small talk was out of the way. First, the weather, the price of hay and the scarcity of reasonable farm land had to be discussed, chewed over and commented on at length.

Finally, just when Caleb had nearly lost patience and was ready to come right out and ask why they were there, Thomas got to the point. "What do you know about the Reapers?" he asked.

"Reapers?" Caleb had no idea what he was talking about.

"You know about the Gleaners," Samson said. "The young people's church group?"

"Of course." One of his jobs was to meet with them twice a month and approve projects, frolics and community outreach. "Charley Byler and his wife are the sponsors. Surely, the Gleaners haven't done anything—"

"Ne," Thomas replied. "The Gleaners have always been a responsible group. We find no fault with them. It's this new group, the Reapers."

"Teenagers from three of our local districts gathering. Yours included. I've had a report from the Delaware State Police of underage drinking of alcohol," Samson said. "Boys are sneaking out at night and attending parties with Englishers. The policemen told me that they broke up a bonfire in a field near Black Bottom. They caught some of the English kids, but the Amish boys ran into the woods."

"There's no *Rumspringa* in Kent County," Ray said. "We don't allow it. Too dangerous. We need your support to settle this behavior before someone is hurt."

"I agree, but why come to me?" Caleb asked. "I have only the one child, and you saw her. She's not even old enough for school."

"We would have asked Reuben for help." Samson leaned forward on his elbows on the table. He wore long johns under his shirt, and the wrists were worn thin from wear. "He's been successful with wayward teenagers before, but Reuben's laid up with that broken leg. You're the other preacher for Seven Poplars. We were hoping you'd step in."

Caleb rose to pour another cup of coffee. His was still half full, but he needed the excuse to gather his thoughts. Bad enough that he'd been thrust into the position of preacher to his own district, a job he doubted he was up to. But this? If he failed to influence the boys and change their dangerous behavior, he'd disappoint his congregation and maybe shame their district in front of the others. "I'm not sure I'm the right man for this," he said hesitantly.

"I'd do it myself, but I'm too old," Thomas said. "The teens feel no connection to most of our elders. And Samson, here, he—"

"My boy Joe is one of the ringleaders of this bunch," Samson admitted. "I've tried talking to him, tried punishment, but Joe is eighteen and feeling his oats. It would break his mother's heart if he was arrested or got hurt in this nonsense."

Caleb looked at Ray. "You, Ray?"

Ray shook his head. "I was pretty wild when I was their age, and they all know it. My Paul said as much to me. He said they weren't doing anything wrong, but they are. The world is a temptation our kids aren't equipped to face. First it will be drugs, then who knows what? You've heard what goes on in Kansas with some of the young people? Drinking alcohol and worse."

Caleb nodded. "I have, and it troubles me. To think that children raised in the faith could stray so far."

"Amen to that," Ray agreed. "It's why we've come, why we ask you to meet with these kids, try to convince them that they are on the path to real trouble."

"You say some of our teenagers are involved?" Caleb asked. "Do you have names to give me?"

"Only three I know for sure," Thomas answered. "Vernon and Elmer Beachy and their cousin, Irwin Beachy. He lives with the schoolteacher, Hannah Yoder."

Chapter Twelve

"Irwin?" Rebecca said to Caleb. "I've heard rumors about these Reapers, but I had no idea that Irwin was involved. Mam will have him cleaning the stables until he's twenty-one!" It was all Rebecca had been able to do to remain out of sight in the parlor until the visitors were gone. But she'd heard every word the men exchanged.

"It's a bad business." Caleb glanced in the direction of the parlor.

"It's all right," Rebecca assured him, knowing he was concerned Amelia might overhear them. "She's playing with her doll on the rug near the fireplace where it's warm." The parlor and that section of the house were heated with a new pellet stove that stood on a tile platform in a fireplace. There was a child-protection screen to keep Amelia from falling against it and getting burned.

Caleb glanced up at the clock and then out the window. "Grace is late."

"I know." Snow was still falling, but there was no wind, and it didn't appear to Rebecca that a storm was brewing. "She's usually on time. Something must have delayed her." She began to take the dirty coffee mugs to the sink.

"Leave them," Caleb said, taking a seat at the kitchen table. "I can do that later."

She slipped into the chair across from him. "So, what are you going to do about the boys? It *is* just boys, isn't it? They didn't say any of our girls were involved, did they?"

Caleb's brow furrowed and he rubbed his fingertips along his scarred cheek. "*Ne,* no Amish girls, but some English. Maybe Charley would have some ideas of what to say to our kids."

She thought for a moment before she spoke. "You know I love Charley. He's been like a brother to me since he and Miriam married, but I'd trust your judgment before I would his—on something like this. Charley is…" She sought the right word. "Innocent. He's really like a big kid himself. I think you're a better choice in this situation. You'll find a way to guide these boys back to the right path."

Caleb folded his arms and looked at her. "You think I'm up to it?"

"I know you are," she answered.

He nodded. For once, the rigid mask slipped, and Rebecca could see the man behind it: the Caleb who wasn't bearing the weight of the world on his shoulders. "It's good you think so," he said. "I have doubts about myself, doubts about being chosen as a preacher for our church. I failed my family once, when it mattered, and I guess I'm always afraid that…"

"You didn't fail." She extended her hand across the table, and Caleb's lean, scarred fingers closed around hers. What was strange was that she barely felt the scars. Instead, she felt the strength. "What happened with your wife. You tried to save her, but bad things happen sometimes." She pressed her lips together. "I think trying to do the right thing now is what God wants of us."

He squeezed her hand and then released it, leaving her with a sense of loss. She could still feel the power and the warmth of his grip, and she wanted it again. "Caleb…"

Once, when she was small, when the family was just getting ready for dinner, Mam had asked her to keep an eye on Susanna. But she and her sisters were playing tag, and she forgot. When she remembered to look for Susanna, she found that she'd chased a duck out onto the frozen pond. Only, it was March, and the ice wasn't solid.

Ruth had run for Dat, but Rebecca had been afraid that the ice would crack and Susanna would fall in and drown. Instead of getting a clothes pole like Ruth had told her, she'd crept out on the pond. By the time she got to Susanna, ice had splintered under her weight in long thin cracks like spiderwebs.

Rebecca had been terrified, trying not to cry, and all the while, Susanna was laughing and pointing at the pretty patterns in the ice. Rebecca had gotten hold of her sister's hand and together they had crawled, inch by inch, back toward the bank.

"Stay where you are!" Leah had screamed. "Wait for Dat! Stay there!"

But, some inner voice had warned her that she had to keep moving. If they stopped, they'd sink into that deep, cold water. They'd reached solid land safely, but she had never forgotten the terrifying sensation of ice bending beneath her feet. She felt like that now, with Caleb, afraid to remain where she was and terrified to move forward.

"I *know* you can do this," she told him firmly.

He stood and began to pace the linoleum floor. "It seems you have more faith in me than I do." He paused near the doorway and glanced back at her. "How does a young woman gain so much confidence about a man she hardly knows?"

She leaned forward. "You weren't the only one surprised when you were chosen as our new preacher. Everyone was. You were new to Seven Poplars. No one really knew what you were like. And you were a widower who hadn't remarried. I've never heard of a preacher who didn't have a wife when he was called."

"And?"

"I'm just a woman, but I try to follow the teachings of the church. I read my Bible and I pray every day, but I'm not wise. All I know is that God chose you. And if He believes in you, Caleb, why shouldn't I?"

A smiled softened the curves of his lips. "It sounds so simple when you say it, Rebecca. Sensible." He chuckled. "I hope you're right—"

The sound of a car horn outside brought Rebecca to her feet. "That must be Grace." She reached for her cloak and the heavy mittens Mam had insisted she wear when she walked over this morning. "It will be all right," she told him.

He held her gaze for a long moment, then turned away. "Amelia! Rebecca's leaving. Come say good night."

"I'll see you tomorrow." Rebecca's feet felt heavy.

She didn't want to leave, but she knew she had to. Her hand still tingled where Caleb had touched her and her chest felt tight. Was this what it felt like to love a man? *Love?* She shivered, but it was a shiver of excitement, not fear. She knew that it was too late to go back. Coming here, being part of Caleb and Amelia's household had become more than a job.

Amelia came running for a hug and Rebecca bent to embrace her.

"Thank you," Caleb said.

"I didn't do anything," she answered breathlessly as they walked to the back door and she opened it.

"You did," he insisted, swinging Amelia up into his arms. He opened the back door for Rebecca. "More than you'll ever know. I just want you to know I appreciate it."

The driver's door opened and Grace stepped out of the SUV. "Sorry," she called. "I was held up on Route 1. A chicken truck jackknifed and both lanes were closed. There were chickens everywhere."

"How terrible." Rebecca hurried out of the house, closing the door behind her, putting distance between her and Caleb. "Was anyone injured?"

Grace shook her head. "I don't think so. It was just the truck, no other vehicles. It must have been the slippery road."

Big snowflakes coated the SUV, the ground, the house and buildings and Grace's mane of curly red hair, covered only by a tiny lace prayer cap. Rebecca hugged her.

Grace was dressed in a jean skirt, a sweater topped by a leather coat and boots to her knees. "Johanna will have our heads for delaying her supper," she said. "I hope she hasn't worried."

Rebecca went around to the passenger's door and got in. The heater was running, and the automobile was toasty warm. "Wait until you hear what I just found out about Irwin," she said. "He is in so much in trouble."

"He's not the only one." Grace pointed. "At the crossroads, I had to slam on my brakes and swerve to keep from hitting that old buggy that Elmer Beachy's been driving—the one decked out in red-and-green Christmas lights."

"What?" Rebecca stared at her. "Are you sure it was Elmer?"

"Certain. He had a bunch of other boys in there with him. Some of them were hanging out the back door, yelling and waving, acting stupid. I wondered what Lydia was thinking, letting them take a horse and buggy out on a night like this."

"What direction were they going?"

"They turned on to Thompson's dirt lane, the one that runs along the edge of his property line. I don't know where they were going. It's not likely the kids would be having a bonfire tonight, in this weather, is it?"

"Did you see Irwin with them?"

Grace shook her head as she turned the key in the ignition. "No, but I wouldn't have recognized Elmer if it wasn't for the Christmas lights and his horse. It was a paint. Almost every Amish man in this county drives a bay. Elmer's horse is brown and white. Plus he was wearing that beat-up cowboy hat of his." She put the SUV in Reverse. "I talked to John. He swung by and picked up 'Kota after work, so if Johanna's invitation is still open—"

"Stop!" Rebecca exclaimed. "Stop the car."

Grace applied the brakes. "What's wrong?" She squinted. "Chickens in the driveway?"

"*Ne,* worse. A lot worse." Rebecca unfastened her seat belt. "There's something Caleb and I have to do right away. Can you take Amelia to Johanna's?"

"Sure, but why?"

"I'll explain later," she said getting out of the car. "But if those Beachy boys are up to no good and Irwin is with them, I've got to try to stop it."

"How much trouble could they cause on a private dirt road?"

"You'd be surprised."

"I can't believe I let you talk me into this," Caleb said. "How are we ever going to find that buggy? It's been a good twenty minutes since Grace saw the boys at the crossroads." He slapped the reins over his horse's back and guided the animal down the blacktop.

There were few cars and trucks on the road. It was still snowing, and Rebecca hadn't seen a single Amish person since they'd left Caleb's house. She sat up straight on the cushioned buggy seat, very conscious of Caleb only inches away. Being unchaperoned with him on a woods road at night was definitely stretching the rules, but the members of the Seven Poplars church district were sensible. If she and Caleb could show they'd been on an errand of supervision—keeping Amish kids out of trouble—the breach would be forgiven.

"We might be able to catch up with them if they took the Thompson lane," she explained. The Thompsons were Englishers. "They may not know that there's a new gate on the far side of the woods. The owners just put it up this week. Mam heard at Spence's that Thompson's nephew had reported someone breaking into his uncle's abandoned farmhouse. The police advised him to put up a locked gate to keep people from driving back to the farm. They rent out the land to a farmer, but no one has lived in the house for twenty years. It doesn't even have electricity anymore."

"What makes you think Elmer Beachy and our boys would break into that house?" The lazy, fat snowflakes had given way to smaller flakes that were now coming down as if they had no intention of stopping until the snow lay six inches deep. The temperature had dropped in the past hour, and Rebecca was glad of the thick wool blanket that Caleb had brought from the house and insisted that she tuck around her lap and legs.

"You're new to Kent County, so there's no way you'd know. About five years ago, some English teenagers were using the farmhouse as a place to hold parties. They got pretty wild and even started a fire in the fireplace. Some parents caught on and called the authorities before someone was hurt or the house burned down. So it wouldn't surprise me if the same kids who were now having bonfire parties decided to use the old Thompson place. There are no neighbors, and the house is in the deep woods and has a really long lane. No one would hear them back there."

"You better be right, Rebecca. If you're wrong, I've sent my daughter to your sister's house to spend the night and compromised both our reputations to take a long, cold buggy ride in the snow."

"I'm afraid I am right. Think about it. Isn't it suspicious that the Beachy brothers are out on such a bad night? There isn't a singing, and neither of them are old enough to be walking out with girls." She paused long enough to draw in a quick breath and went on. "Besides, Grace said there was a buggy full of boys. Mam was just saying that Irwin was going to bed awfully early lately, but he still looks red eyed and tired in the morning. She was going to buy him some vitamins."

"So he could be sneaking out with his cousins?"

"Turn here." Rebecca pointed to an opening in a grove of cedar trees. "It's an old logging road and it can get muddy in wet weather, but the ground will be frozen solid tonight."

Caleb guided the horse off the paved road. "I don't see any tracks, Amish or English."

Rebecca shook her head. "Trust me, Caleb. I grew up here. There's a tangle of lanes and dirt roads that run for miles through woodland and back pastures. My sisters and I used to ride ponies back here when we were young, and before that, we went cutting wood and looking for wild bees with my *dat*. Most of the trails are grown over, but we can still squeeze through." She spoke with more confidence than she felt. "If they're headed for the Thompson house, we can still get there ahead of them."

The lane had deep ruts, and they couldn't see more than a few yards ahead of the horse, but once they were sheltered by the old growth forest, it was easier driving. Ten minutes stretched like thirty, and Rebecca was beginning to fear that she'd made a terrible mistake when the horse snorted and perked up its ears.

"Listen," Rebecca said. "Do you hear that?"

Caleb reined in the horse. Without the soft thud of

the animal's hooves and the creak of the buggy, Rebecca could clearly hear music up ahead. Loud, thumping music!

"Not hymns, for certain," Caleb remarked.

"Hurry," she urged. "This lane meets up with another one just beyond the trees. The house will be on the left in a clearing, and our kids should be driving from the right."

Caleb slapped the reins over the horse's rump, and the buggy lurched ahead. Rebecca's stomach rose in her throat, and she clutched the dashboard of the carriage.

The level of noise rose, and when they broke out of the woods, Rebecca wasn't surprised to hear the blare of a car horn and shrieks of laughter. Pickup trucks, SUVs and automobiles crowded the open space around the house and lined the dirt road on either side. Lights bobbed behind shuttered windows, and someone had built a huge fire of fence posts and logs near the front door—much too near the house for safety. English boys and girls ran across the clearing, whooping and shouting. Most seemed to be drinking out of cans, but Rebecca couldn't tell if they had soft drinks or something more inappropriate. As she stared, she heard the crack of glass and wood and saw something pitch through an upstairs window, followed by peals of shrill laughter.

"This is bad," Caleb said. "Do you see any buggies?"

"*Ne,* but it's so dark…." She scanned the area around the fire. From their clothes, most of the kids seemed to be Englishers, but she couldn't be sure. Amish kids were known to leave their house in their own homemade clothing and change into Englisher clothes on the way to this sort of thing. "What do we do?" she asked Caleb. "If our kids are here, we can't leave them."

"*We* will do nothing. You'll stay here and I'll go and see for myself," he answered. "Don't get out of the buggy. I'll turn the horse around first, so if…if anything frightens you, just drive back the way we came."

"I couldn't leave you," she insisted.

"*Ne,* Rebecca." His voice was firm. "I'm capable of looking after myself. If I'm not back in five minutes, you—"

"Look!" She caught his arm. "Coming up the lane. See!"

In the distance, she could see telltale blinking red-and-green Christmas lights. "Elmer's buggy. We got here ahead of them."

"*Ya,*" Caleb agreed. "Looks as though you were right. But what about that gate you mentioned? The one that was supposed to be locked?"

"With all these cars and trucks here, the English kids must have broken through. We can go out that way." She pointed left. "It's a good mile shorter to the main road."

"A mile? How's that possible?"

"The Thompson farm isn't on the hardtop. There's a right-of-way drive through Joe King's farm." She shivered as a clump of snow from an overhanging branch fell onto the dashboard and splattered over her.

"Walk on," Caleb said to the horse. "We've come this far. Best finish this mess as quick as we can." He glanced at her. She couldn't see the expression in his eyes, but she was certain that there was a hint of amusement in his voice.

She smiled in surprise. "You're enjoying this, aren't you?"

"Am not," he said brusquely.

Rebecca stifled a chuckle. Who would have thought that Caleb had a sense of adventure? "Now all you have to do is convince the Beachy boys and whoever else is with them to go home."

"Oh, they'll go home, all right," he assured her. "One way or another, they're going home." Caleb urged his horse faster, cutting off the approaching buggy a good fifty yards from the house and bonfire. "Stay where you are," he said as pulled up and jumped down from the seat.

A moment later, Rebecca heard Caleb's voice and the subdued ones of the boys, but try as she could, she was unable to hear exactly what was being said. She was tempted to get out and walk over, despite Caleb's warning her not to. But before she could get up the nerve, he came striding back, climbed up and turned his horse.

"Are they coming with us?" she ventured.

"What do you think?"

"Was Irwin with them?"

"Irwin, the two Beachy boys and two others. I don't know their names, but they're Amish."

"They haven't been drinking, have they?"

"*Ne.* Although I think those Englishers are. The boys have no alcohol or tobacco in the buggy."

"Good." A sense of relief swept over her. "What will you do? Will you go to their parents?"

"I will. I'd not try to keep this night's mischief to myself. But I told the boys I'd be meeting with them to discuss the matter further and that there would be consequences from the church."

"What will you say to them?"

Caleb sighed. "I'll pray on it, Rebecca. God sent you to show me the way tonight. I have no doubt that He won't abandon me when I talk with the boys later." He laid his hand over hers and she shivered again. This time, it wasn't from the cold. "I hope you don't mind. I'm going to take these boys home in the Beachy buggy. I'll follow you to your mother's, then be on my way. I told Irwin to come up and ride home with you. I'll come back for my buggy at your mother's place in the morning. The Beachy boys can come for their buggy when their parents see fit."

"Whatever you say, Caleb." She felt a twinge of disappointment that she wouldn't be riding home with him. She heard the shuffle of feet and saw a crestfallen Irwin appear at the side of the buggy. "Will you drive, or shall I?" she asked him.

"You best drive, Rebecca. Irwin hasn't shown the best of judgment tonight. I'm not sure I want to trust him with your safety."

Gathering the reins in her hands, she clicked to the horse. There wasn't a sound from Irwin as she headed for home. Soon, the house and the noisy party were behind them and only the snowy lane lay ahead.

"I'm sorry," Irwin began. "I didn't…"

"Save it for Mam," she said. "I'm too disappointed with you to talk about this tonight."

They were almost to the main road when Rebecca heard sirens and saw the flash of lights. Her heart raced and then sunk as a Delaware State police car turned off the blacktop and came directly toward her. Shaking, she reined the horse off the center of the lane to allow them to pass.

They didn't. The lead vehicle came to a stop beside her, and two state troopers got out. One shone a light into her face and looked at her for a moment. "Sorry to bother you, ma'am," he said. "We're investigating a report of trespassing and underage drinking. Where are you headed?"

"Home, with my brother."

"You be careful, then," the trooper instructed.

She nodded. "Have a good evening." Then she lifted the reins and urged the horse forward.

When she looked back, however, she saw that Caleb, driving the Beachy buggy with the garish red-and-green flashing Christmas lights, hadn't been so fortunate. The police had stopped him as well, but had not waved them on. Caleb and his passengers were climbing down onto the snowy lane, their pale faces illuminated by a glaring spotlight.

Chapter Thirteen

The following morning was cold and still, and a crust of snow crunched under the buggy wheels as Caleb drove the Beachy buggy up into the Yoder barnyard. He'd disconnected the battery so that the ridiculous red-and-green lights no longer blinked, something he wished he'd taken the time to do when he'd climbed up onto the bench seat the night before.

He'd taken down the big foam dice and removed the speakers for the boom box, but there was nothing he could do to hide the florescent orange triangles painted on each side of the carriage. Every Amish vehicle that was driven on the road had to have a large orange reflector on the back to satisfy Delaware traffic laws, but in Caleb's opinion the Beachy boys had gone overboard with their nonsense. He felt more conspicuous driving this hot-rod buggy in the daytime than he did at night.

A single set of fresh footprints crossed the yard from the back door of the house to the barn. The tracks were small and neat, definitely not left by Irwin's size-eleven muck boots. Anticipation made Caleb sit up a little straighter on the bench seat. He hoped the early riser might be Rebecca and not Hannah or Susanna. As part of the evening's escapade, Rebecca would be the last person to poke fun at him for being seen in the outrageous buggy.

He reined in the horse and swung down out of the seat. He'd turn the animal in to a box stall in the stable. Elmer could come for his horse later today. Caleb had dropped off the two brothers last night before taking the other two boys home, but he wasn't doing them any more favors by returning the horse and buggy. They could walk over to retrieve it, providing their father ever let them leave the house again. As it was, they'd gotten off easy. They hadn't been arrested and hadn't caused the community public shame—perhaps even unwanted pictures in the Dover newspaper. That would have been hard to live down.

Caleb unharnessed the horse and walked it to the barn, still deep in thought.

Immediate disaster had been avoided by getting the boys away from the party before the police arrived, but preventing future indiscretions would be more difficult. Caleb knew that teenage boys had short memories. The talking-to he'd given the miscreants the previous night was only the first step in changing their behavior. He had spent an hour on his knees this morning praying that God would give him the wisdom to live up to the task.

As Caleb entered the Yoder barn, he looked up to see Rebecca coming down the ladder from the hayloft. For a few seconds, he didn't call out to her. She was such a pretty sight, all pink cheeked from the cold, red curls tumbling around her face and small graceful hands—

hands that could bake bread, soothe a crying child and manage a spirited driving horse without hesitation.

"Caleb!" A smile lit her eyes and spread over her face. "I didn't expect you so early."

"Ya." Why did he always sound as though he was about to deliver a sermon when he spoke to her? Most times, he felt at ease around people he knew, but Rebecca often made him trip over his own tongue. "You, too," he added. "Up early."

She nodded. "I like mornings, when it's quiet. And when there's snow or rain, it seems even quieter. A barn can be almost like a church. Don't you think so? The contented sounds of the animals, the rustle of hay when you throw it down from the loft." She laughed softly. "I must sound foolish."

"Ne. I feel the same way. Not so much like when the bishop gives a sermon, but as if…as if God is listening."

"Exactly." She came down the last few rungs to the floor, folded her arms and stood there, smiling at him, almost as if she was waiting for something.

He cleared his throat. "Your mother? Did she ask what happened? Was she angry that you got home so late?"

"Not angry." The corners of Rebecca's eyes crinkled as her mood became more serious. "Concerned. But when I explained what we did, why we had to go and fetch Irwin and the others home, she understood." Rebecca arched an eyebrow. "She was very unhappy with Irwin, and she let him know it."

Caleb led the horse into a stall, backed out and closed the gate. "Will she punish him?"

Rebecca brushed hay off her skirt. "Mam has always been good at finding the right punishment for each of her children, and her pupils. I think she'll find extra work for him to do. He won't have so much free time to think up mischief." She went to a feed bin, lifted the wooden lid and scooped out a measure of grain.

"That's what I was thinking." Caleb walked over to stand nearer, and he caught a whiff of green apples. The scent was one he'd come to associate with Rebecca, and he supposed it must be her shampoo. Hannah was sometimes lenient with her daughters, but wouldn't allow Rebecca to wear perfume. Green apple was a plain smell, clean and honest. He liked it, maybe more than he wanted to admit. "What I thought would be best," he said.

She looked at him expectantly.

"I know the parents will want to reprimand their sons as they see fit, but I think that there should be something more." He swallowed, suddenly nervous that Rebecca wouldn't agree his plan was the wisest—that she might think he was too lenient. "That's to say, if the elders and the parents think that it's a good idea, I want to meet with the boys every Saturday. Not for punishment, but for counseling."

Rebecca's blue eyes sparked with interest, and he went on with more confidence. When she looked at him, he got the feeling she saw beyond the scars on his face and hand. It was almost as if she didn't see them at all. "I want each boy to take responsibility for another person or couple—elderly, or those with health problems. And not from the church district they belong to. That would be too easy. They should already be caring for their own grandparents, their own neighbors. I want them to help someone in another district. And not just for a few weeks. I want them to paint, repair, fetch and carry, do whatever's needed for a full year." He waited, unconsciously holding his breath for her reaction.

"Caleb, that's a wonderful idea," she pronounced. Understanding flooded her animated features, and her gaze grew warm. "A year of helping someone who needs it. That could make a difference, not just for the teens but for those receiving the help. You could change lives in a year."

"I hope so." He felt the tenseness drain from his shoulders. "These are good boys, just…"

"Just kids," she said. "It's not easy to grow up. But…" She fiddled with one of the ties that hung from her *kapp*.

"But what?"

"I wonder…"

"*Ya?* A suggestion?"

She nodded. "I think they need fun, too, a little excitement. Nothing the elders wouldn't approve of, but perhaps…" Now she looked at him hesitantly. "Maybe you could take them places like to a baseball game or a camping trip to a national park? Interesting places that they've never seen."

"Show them some of the English world?"

"*Ya,* Caleb. Let them see that ours is a good place, but that it isn't wrong to want to see elephants and eat cotton candy and watch trains."

"Trains?" He nodded, trying to hide a surge of excitement. As a boy, he'd been fascinated by trains, but he'd never gotten to ride on one. "They would like that, to ride on one, you think?"

"I'm sure they would. I know I would. You could take them on Amtrak to a work frolic in an Amish community in another state. It could be a reward for completing their year of service."

He grinned at her. "A reward for doing right. I like that idea, Rebecca. I like it a lot, and if we were going for a reason—say to help raise a barn or dig a well in another Amish community, I think the elders would approve." He chuckled. "And I would like the train ride, too."

"Caleb." He turned to see Rebecca's mother standing in the doorway. "I saw the horse and buggy." Hannah smiled at him, but Caleb sensed that she wasn't entirely comfortable to find him alone in the barn with her Rebecca.

"I was just about to ask Rebecca if she thought it was too early for me to pick up Amelia at Johanna's," he said.

"I can do that for you," Rebecca offered. She hurried to the nearest box stall and dumped a scoop of grain into the feed box. Blackie pushed his nose into the fragrant horse chow. "There's no sense in you being late for work. We can drive back to the chair shop and then I can go and get Amelia. I'd like to go to Byler's this morning, anyway. You need groceries."

"That will work out fine," he agreed. "It was kind of your sister to keep Amelia overnight. We don't want to wear out her welcome."

"Not to worry about that," Hannah assured him. "Katy loves Amelia, and her having someone to play with makes Johanna's life easier. Katy can be as full of mischief as her brother if she isn't kept busy." Hannah tilted her head. "There's just one thing I want to know."

"Ya?"

"When the policemen stopped you last night? What did you say to them?"

He glanced at Rebecca.

"I told Mam how scared I was when they made you get out of the buggy," she explained.

"I was pretty scared myself," Caleb admitted. "I just told the police that I was following you home, to see that you got home safe on such a snowy night."

Hannah chuckled. "That was the truth, I suppose. You *were* following Rebecca." She looked back at him. "And they didn't ask why you had so many boys with you?"

Caleb shook his head. "They looked them over to see if they'd been drinking and waved us back into the buggy. I couldn't lie, but the police didn't ask where the boys had been headed, and I didn't offer."

Hannah crossed her arms over her chest and studied Caleb for a moment. "I like you, Caleb. You're a man who knows when to speak and when not to." She gave him a smile and walked away.

Rebecca looked at Caleb. He looked at her, and they both laughed; for just a moment, Rebecca found herself lost in his merry brown eyes.

Sunday was a visiting day, and Mam had invited Grossmama, Aunt Martha, Uncle Reuben, Dorcas, Bishop Atlee, Aunt Jezzy and her husband, Nip, and Caleb and Amelia to dinner. Even though Ruth had come over the previous day to help with the salads, pies and ham, there were still a few things to do. The bishop's wife had gone to stay with a daughter who was expecting a baby, so the church members were taking turns having the bishop over for meals.

The truth was, Rebecca hadn't really wanted any company today. Although she usually loved visiting Sundays, today she was restless. It seemed as if she hadn't had a moment to herself all week, and since the night she and Caleb had gone to round up the boys, she needed time to think.

She liked Caleb—more than liked him—and she was beginning to realize that her interest went beyond respect and friendship. The previous weekend, she'd seen another side of him, and they'd shared a real adventure. Caleb had shown that he was willing to risk his reputation and bend the rules for a greater good. And then, the following morning, when he'd shared his plans and seemed genuinely interested in her opinion, she'd suspected that the weak feeling in her knees and the quickening heartbeat and giddiness she'd felt went beyond a parishioner's approval of her preacher. She realized she was falling in love with him.

No, she corrected herself sternly, not falling—had fallen in love with him. It had already happened, sometime in the days and weeks since she'd begun caring for Amelia and his house. Every instinct told her that Caleb felt the same about her. Of course, he hadn't said so in words. And certainly not his actions. Worse, everyone said he was courting Dorcas.

Rebecca felt so confused. Maybe he hadn't been completely honest with her; maybe Caleb really was walking out with her cousin. Grossmama believed it. Aunt Jezzy and all the neighbors already saw Caleb and Dorcas as a couple. And over the past few weeks, Aunt Martha had certainly told everyone who would listen what a fine match the new preacher would be for her daughter. Only Caleb continued to insist that he and Dorcas were spending time with each other to see if they wanted to court.

So Rebecca was in a quandary. What did she do

about these feelings for Caleb? It wasn't her place to initiate a conversation with him concerning their possible mutual feelings. Amish men were the ones responsible for starting such talk. Rebecca knew she could be bold at times, but she didn't think this was a time when she could step beyond the customs of her community. What if she was wrong, and Caleb really did care for Dorcas and not her? She'd embarrass herself and Caleb.

"Becca." Susanna tugged on her apron. "Becca. You're not listening." She was persistent and now was tugging at her sleeve. "Becca, Mam is mean," she said.

"What?" Rebecca sank down on the top step of the staircase. She'd been on her way upstairs to get a clean apron from her bedroom when she'd gotten sidetracked by her introspection. The sight of Susanna's tearstained face made her instantly ashamed. "What's wrong, Susanna banana?"

"I want King David to eat, too. Mam said, 'Not today.' But I *want* him to come. Not fair."

"David was here for breakfast just yesterday," Rebecca reminded her. She dug in her apron pocket for a tissue and handed it to her sister. "Blow."

Susanna did as she was told, blowing so hard that her eyes watered. "I want King David," she repeated. "Mam is mean if he can't…can't come." She thrust out her lower lip in a pout. "She wants to keep me and him…" Susanna's forehead creased with concentration as she searched for the right word. "Not together!" She sniffed and wiped at the end of her nose. "Mam hates him."

"Ne." Rebecca slipped an arm around Susanna's trembling shoulders. "Mam doesn't hate anyone, and she certainly doesn't hate David. She likes him."

Susanna looked up hopefully. "She does? He can come eat ham?"

Rebecca shook her head. "Not today. Another day. You can't see each other every day. It isn't proper. You aren't children. If you spend too much time together, people will talk."

"But…but King David and me…we're walking out. I'm going to marry him."

"Susanna. Hush, don't say such things. You aren't going to marry David. You can't."

Susanna's round blue eyes narrowed. "You're mean, too. You don't believe me. I love him."

Rebecca caught Susanna's chin in her hand and tenderly tilted it up. She wondered if this was a problem Mam ever thought she'd have to address with Susanna. Like Rebecca and all of her sisters, had she assumed Susanna would never have the inclination to marry? "It's complicated, sister. It's like we all have our jobs to do. You can't get married. You have to stay home and take care of Mam."

"Ne." Susanna shook her head so hard that her cap slipped sideways. "You think I'm stupid. I'm not stupid. I can peel apples and marry King David if I want." Rising to her feet, she pulled away and ran down the stairs, nearly colliding with their mother at the foot of the steps before veering off toward the kitchen.

"What's wrong with Susanna?" Mam said, coming up.

Susanna was already out of sight.

"She's upset that David can't come to dinner today," Rebecca explained. "I tried to—"

"I know," her mother answered. "Come with me. I was looking for you, and I wanted to talk to you about something." She pulled an envelope out of her pocket. "I got this from Leah yesterday."

"Is something wrong?"

"*Ne.* Nothing like that." Mam shook her head. "We should talk in your room."

Rebecca followed her into her bedroom and watched, puzzled, as her mother closed the door. Having her sister far away at a jungle mission in Brazil was worrisome. Leah was the sister she'd been closest to in age. They had gone together to care for Grossmama in Ohio before moving her to Delaware. Rebecca and Leah had never been apart until Leah's marriage.

"Your sister says that Daniel's aunt Joyce and her husband have been called to spend three months at a Mennonite orphanage a few hundred miles from the mission where she and Daniel live. They've booked passage on a container ship and they'll be going right after Christmas. They'll be taking a few truckloads of blankets, clothes, shoes and medical supplies to the orphanage, but they have room for two more passengers. Leah wants you and Susanna to come stay with her for the three months. She's says she's been lonesome for the sight of family, that she wants you to come, and I think you should."

"But Miriam and Charley—"

"Are already there. Yes, I know. But they can't stay long. Charley needs to get back to work. If you girls went, you'd go with Daniel's family and then return with them three months later."

"Susanna and I?" Rebecca caught hold of the end of the iron bed. "Go to Brazil?"

"You could be with your sister. Leah will be thrilled to have you and…" Mam's voice trailed off.

"And?" Rebecca looked at her suspiciously.

Mam nodded. "And I think it would be a good thing to get Susanna away from David King for a time. I know what she's been upset about for the past few months. She has this notion in her head that they're going to be married and I've tried to make her understand that's not going to happen."

"I tried to tell her, too." Rebecca met her mother's gaze and held it. "But is it Susanna you want to send away, or is it me?"

Chapter Fourteen

Her mother reached for her hand, and instantly Rebecca felt a twinge of remorse for the sharpness of her retort. "I'm sorry," Rebecca murmured. "I didn't mean to be rude. It's just that Ruth keeps bringing up Caleb, and even Anna and Miriam think—"

"That you had set your *kapp* for him?" Hannah's fingers closed around Rebecca's. "That you would like to have Caleb for yourself, even though he's courting your cousin?"

"He *isn't* courting her," Rebecca protested, pulling her hand free. She sat on the bed, slipped out of her shoes and tucked her feet up under her skirt. "Caleb says that they're getting to know each other, to see *if*—"

"I don't know how they do things in Idaho, but Dorcas thinks they're walking out." Mam frowned. "She told Charley's sister Mary that her mother wanted them to announce the banns soon so that they could marry in the spring." She hesitated. "Is there something going on I should know about?"

"*Ne.* Of course not." A heaviness settled on Rebecca.

"But I won't lie to you. I… I could have feelings for him."

Her mother sat beside her on the bed. "Has he told you that his affection for you goes further than friendship? That he looks on you as more than someone to clean his house and care for his child?"

Rebecca looked away. "Not in so many words." The heaviness had become a lump in the pit of her stomach. Maybe it was just her imagination that Caleb liked her. She looked back at her mother hesitantly. "You think I should go to Leah in Brazil?"

"I think it would be wise. Without you here in Seven Poplars," Hannah continued, "Caleb will make his intentions clear to Dorcas. If the two of them part ways after you leave, no one can say you ruined your cousin's chance at a good marriage." Mam's mouth tightened. "This may be Dorcas's only opportunity. She's my niece and I love her, but she's often at a loss as to how to show her good heart."

"Which is a nice way of saying Dorcas can be prickly."

Hannah smiled. "Some people find it more difficult to understand others. And Martha hasn't always been the best example. I don't mean to be critical, but if Dorcas would think before she speaks, I believe she would have more friends."

Rebecca gripped her mother's hand, feeling lost and confused. "You know I wouldn't want to hurt Dorcas." Thoughts of never seeing Caleb come home, of not sharing jokes and the day's events with him made her sad. "But if I leave, what will happen to Amelia?"

"I've already thought of that. Johanna will watch her during the day. We already discussed it." Mam sighed.

"And by the time you come home, you might feel differently about Caleb."

"And if I don't?"

"Then he will either be your cousin by marriage or the two of you will have a chance to start fresh—to court openly." Mam was quiet for a minute. "Whether you go or not, I think it may be time to make other arrangements for Amelia's care. I don't think it's wise for you to work for him anymore. You're thrown together too often. If he wasn't our preacher, it never would have been permitted. But even the faithful can be tempted into dangerous behavior."

"You really want Susanna and me to go?"

Her mother's expression softened. "I want to keep you close, of course. Every mother does. But my heart goes out to Leah, alone there in a strange land with only Daniel. Charley and Miriam's visit will do her heart good, but I know she would like to see you and Susanna. If his aunt and uncle weren't going down, I could never afford to send you. It may be Providence, a solution to more than one problem."

"God's plan for us?"

"I don't know. Perhaps. You don't have to decide today, but I'd like to write Leah as soon as possible. She'll be waiting for an answer."

"When will Daniel's aunt and uncle be leaving?"

"Right after Christmas. Just as Charley and Miriam will be returning."

"I'll pray on it," Rebecca agreed. "But I still think that Dorcas—"

"What about me?" came a familiar voice from the hallway.

Surprised, Rebecca looked up to see her cousin

standing at the open bedroom door, arms folded over her apron. "Dorcas. You're early."

"I know." Dorcas came into the room. She was wearing a rose-colored dress that had once belonged to Aunt Martha and black stockings with a hole at the ankle. Dorcas's black leather shoes were old and scuffed and badly needed polish. "My mother said I could walk over and see if you needed help with the meal. She and Dat took the buggy to fetch Grossmama from Anna's."

"We're about ready." Hannah rose from the bed, smiling at her. "I'll go on down and take the ham out of the oven. I was just warming it. You girls can sit here for a few minutes and catch up on your week."

Rebecca groaned inwardly. She didn't want to be left alone with Dorcas. She would rather shut herself in the attic where she could have a minute's peace to think this through. And if she did want company, Dorcas would be the last person she wanted to visit with today.

"*Ya,* Aunt Hannah. I'd like that," her cousin said in her shrill voice, a voice that sometimes had the same effect on Rebecca as fingernails on a blackboard.

But, no matter how she felt, Rebecca couldn't be unkind to anyone. She forced a smile. "It's nice having your family share our Sunday meal."

Dorcas twisted her chapped hands. Her bony hands and feet were large in proportion to her thin body, and as long as Rebecca could remember, Dorcas had chewed at her knuckles when she was anxious. She was obviously uneasy today, because the skin was red and sore on the middle of her right index finger.

"And Caleb," Rebecca added, when the silence stretched between them.

"*Ya,* Caleb is coming." Dorcas flopped on the bed beside her.

"Amelia, too," Rebecca added. "I hope your *dat* is feeling better."

Dorcas sighed. "I think he likes it, having the broken leg and everyone taking care of him. Caleb comes every day to help around the farm."

"He's a thoughtful person," Rebecca agreed. *Did they* have *to talk about Caleb?*

Dorcas nibbled at her raw knuckle. "I suppose."

Rebecca glanced at her cousin sitting beside her, surprised by her tone. "You don't sound very enthusiastic about him. Don't you like Caleb?" She couldn't help herself. She had to find out if they were really serious about each other. "Please don't do that." She caught hold of Dorcas's hand. "Look at your poor finger. It makes me hurt just looking at it."

Dorcas pulled her hand back and tucked it under her. "Mam says the same thing. She tells me it will turn black and fall off, but it never does. Most of the time, I don't even know I'm doing it."

Rebecca couldn't help but feel sorry for Dorcas. She looked so unhappy. "What's wrong?" she asked.

Dorcas raised her hand to her mouth, then tucked it under her again. "I know you will think I'm silly. Mam says I shouldn't be so choosy. She says that Caleb is a good catch." She sighed again. Dorcas's eyes were large and caramel brown and framed with long, light brown lashes. They were her most attractive feature, but they weren't lovely today. Dorcas looked as though maybe she'd been crying.

"I'm listening," Rebecca said, really meaning it.

"Caleb's the only boy—*man,*" she corrected herself. "The only man who's ever come to dinner, who's ever treated me like…" Her face flushed. "Well, you know. I'm not pretty like you and your sisters. Boys have never asked me to ride home from singings with them, and they've never tried to outbid each other to buy my pie at school auctions."

"Don't say such things," Rebecca protested, pulling Dorcas into her arms and hugging her. "There's nothing wrong with the way you look." The truth was, Dorcas finally having her front tooth fixed made a big difference in her appearance, but Rebecca didn't want to say that. "A person's looks shouldn't matter. It's what they are inside that counts."

"Shouldn't, but they do, and you know it." Dorcas pulled away. "I'll be thirty next November, and if I don't find a beau before that, people will call me an old maid."

"But you…" Rebecca's pulse quickened. "You don't like Caleb?"

"He's all right, I suppose." Dorcas frowned. "*Ya,* I do like him. I'm getting used to his face. You know, the scars. It used to frighten me looking at it, but not so much now. What really bothers me is he's…well…dull."

"Dull? Caleb?" The man who would walk a roof beam in the dark to rescue a woman? A father who threw himself wholeheartedly into sock fights with his daughter? Could they be talking about the same person?

Dorcas sighed dramatically. "He's *so* serious. I know he's not much older than me, but he *seems* old. Last time he came to supper, he wanted to tell me about something he was making at the shop. Some wood thing. He went on and on about it, and I had to sit there and pretend to be interested, even though I was bored to tears."

"Oh," Rebecca replied softly. "I didn't know you felt that way about him." She glanced at her cousin hopefully. "So the two of you aren't courting?"

"Not yet, but we'd be bundling if Mam had her way. She's really trying to push me into marrying him. As soon as possible."

"She said that?"

Dorcas shrugged. "It isn't what she says, it's the way she smiles at him, and how she wants everyone to know that the new preacher is calling on me." Dorcas rubbed at her irritated knuckle. "What do you think, Rebecca? Should we court? Should I look toward marrying him?"

Rebecca felt sick. The lump in her stomach had become a dull ache. She knew what her answer would be if Caleb asked *her* to be his wife. Feeling the way she did, could she be honest with Dorcas? "Have you prayed about it? What does your heart tell you?"

"I don't know if it's my heart or my head," her cousin answered. "I'm scared. I'm afraid that if I say no, I'll end up living the rest of my life with my mother, with people feeling sorry for me. I'll be another Aunt Jezzy."

"But Aunt Jezzy found someone who treasures her," Rebecca reminded. "She's happy."

"But it didn't happen until she was old. I don't want to spend my life fetching and carrying for my mother. I love my parents, but I want my own home, and babies, lots of babies. Caleb could give me all that. I'd have to be stupid to refuse him."

"Is that a reason to marry a man?" Rebecca managed.

"Maybe," Dorcas said. "*Ya,* I think it is. I can respect Caleb and be thankful for what he can give me. If I keep his house and raise his daughter, friendship will grow between us." A smile spread across her face and she looked at Rebecca. "Thank you, Rebecca." She let out her breath. "I feel so relieved. I knew you'd give me good advice."

"But I haven't," Rebecca protested.

"In time, love will come." Dorcas got up off the bed. "That's what my mother says. Marriage first, work as a team and everything else will fall into place."

But not for me, Rebecca thought. *Not for me.*

Dinner with Caleb, Amelia, Dorcas and her family was as miserable for Rebecca as she feared it would be. Dorcas and Caleb were seated across from one another, and each seemed to take great pains to avoid looking at the other. Amelia whined and fussed her way through the meal, breaking into tears when she spilled her milk and when she put her sleeve in the mashed potatoes while reaching for a biscuit. Grossmama commented loudly on poorly behaved children and questioned Caleb at length on the size of his property and the extent of his mortgage.

"Would you be able to support my granddaughter?" she asked before he could answer. "She has no dowry, you know. But she's a fine seamstress, none better, certainly not her mother. Martha was never handy with a needle."

"Lovina," Mam soothed. "Let the man eat. You can question Caleb to your heart's content after he's finished his dessert."

Grossmama frowned, popped another forkful of ham into her mouth and chewed noisily. An awkward silence settled over the table, a lapse that Caleb attempted to fill by describing his unease when the police had stopped him and the boys in the Beachy buggy.

Irwin clapped a hand over his mouth and stifled a chuckle.

Dorcas didn't seem to hear. Doggedly, she kept eating her macaroni salad and pickled beets. And when Rebecca managed to catch her gaze, Dorcas pursed her lips and shrugged, as if to say, "Didn't I tell you he was boring?"

After everyone was done eating, Mam and Rebecca got up to clear away the dirty dishes so the pies and cakes could be served. The bishop and Uncle Reuben stepped out on the back porch to get some air and talk.

"I want cookies," Amelia demanded, although she'd barely touched anything on her plate.

"No dessert until you eat all of your dinner," Dorcas admonished.

Amelia screwed up her face and began to wail.

"It's not a problem," Rebecca said, reaching for Amelia's plate.

"You're spoiling her," Aunt Martha told Caleb. "What she needs is—"

Amelia twisted on the bench, caught her plate with her sleeve and knocked it onto the floor. The dish broke and mashed potatoes, ham and applesauce went flying. Amelia threw herself into the mess and began to sob.

Caleb reached for his daughter, amid angry whispers from Aunt Martha. Dorcas got to her first and scooped her up. "Hush, now, Amelia," she said. "No need to fuss so about a broken plate."

Amelia kicked and screamed. "Don't want you! Want Becca!"

Caleb's face flamed as he took her from Dorcas. "Quiet down," he said. But Amelia's tantrum continued. "I'm sorry," he said to Dorcas. "I'll take her home."

Susanna stared wide-eyed.

"Better take her out behind the barn and warm her bottom," Aunt Martha advised.

"Ne, ne," Hannah soothed. "She's tired and feeling out of sorts."

"Becca!" Amelia howled, struggling against her father's embrace. "I want…want…my Maaam."

"Shh, shh," Rebecca said, putting out her arms. "Give her to me, Caleb."

With a look of helplessness, he passed the crying child to her, and Amelia clung to Rebecca with all her strength.

"What's wrong?" Rebecca asked. "Are you tired?"

Amelia buried her head in Rebecca's neck and sobbed great wrenching sobs of anguish that lapsed into hiccups. Her little face felt hot and sweaty against Rebecca's skin.

"Shh, shh," Rebecca continued to murmur as she patted the child's back. "No wonder she's acting out," she said, meeting Caleb's worried gaze. "She's burning up. I think she's running a fever."

Chapter Fifteen

Hannah's forehead creased in a concerned expression as she placed a hand on Amelia's forehead. "She does feel as though she has a fever. 102, maybe 103. Poor baby," she crooned, kissing her forehead. "No wonder you're cross."

"Are you sure? Do you have a thermometer?" Caleb's irritation with his daughter's awful behavior vanished, instantly replaced with dread. "Should we take her to the emergency room?"

Hannah shook her head. "I don't think that will be necessary. Children get fevers. I don't believe her fever is high enough that you can't wait to decide tomorrow if you should call her doctor."

"She doesn't have one," Caleb said. "I've been meaning to find one for her, but I've been so busy since we got to Delaware and I kept putting it off."

Rebecca hugged Amelia to her. "We do have a thermometer."

Caleb glanced in her direction, remembering that she'd urged him more than once to choose a pediatrician for Amelia. To her credit, she didn't mention that now.

"Susanna," Rebecca called. "Can you get the thermometer from the downstairs bathroom cabinet?" She gave him a reassuring nod. "You can trust Mam. She's tended enough sick children to know."

Caleb shook his head. "I wouldn't have brought her here if I'd known she was ill. I can't remember the last time she ran a fever." Illness was one of the things that made him feel helpless with Amelia. "Give her to me," he said.

This time, Amelia went willingly and put her arms around his neck. "I want to go home," she whimpered. "I want my baby doll."

Susanna returned with the thermometer and a bottle of rubbing alcohol. Rebecca took both to the sink, poured a little alcohol over the thermometer to clean it before rinsing it with cool water. "Here, sweetie," she said to Amelia. "Put this under your tongue."

Caleb rocked his child against his chest. He loved this child with every fiber of his being. Just the thought that she might have something seriously wrong with her terrified him. "Just for a moment," he soothed. "Be a good girl and let Rebecca take your temperature."

Rebecca removed the thermometer and held it up to the light. "102 degrees," she pronounced. "Not good, but not dangerous, either. She could be coming down with an ear infection or a cold."

"Or the flu," Martha said helpfully.

"Lots of flu going around," Rebecca's *grossmama* agreed. "My Jonas had it bad in the fall."

Caleb didn't respond. Rebecca had explained that her grandmother Lovina's memory was spotty at best, and that she often believed that her son, Jonas, Hannah's late husband, was still alive. Furthermore, Rebecca explained, no one corrected the elderly woman because when Lovina did remember, she mourned Jonas's death as deeply as if he'd just passed on, rather than dying years ago.

"I don't believe Amelia has the flu," Hannah said. "She's not throwing up, and she's not complaining of aching joints. Rebecca could be right. It could be no more than a cold."

Caleb let out the breath he'd been unconsciously holding. A cold or an ear infection, he could deal with. "I'd best get her home," he said. "Into her bed." He looked back at Hannah. "Thank you for dinner."

"No such thing," Lovina stated firmly. "It's cold outside. Take that baby outside and she could die of an ague. Why take the chance when Jonas and Hannah have all these empty bedrooms? You can just tuck her into bed here."

"She's right, Caleb," Hannah agreed. "We can put Amelia into one of the spare rooms and we can help you care for her."

Caleb felt uncertain. He didn't want to be a bother, but neither did he want to risk taking his daughter out of a warm house into the frigid air. What if Lovina was right and exposure made her worse? "If you're sure I won't be putting you out."

"If she's got a fever in the afternoon, you can be certain it will go higher tonight." Martha bustled around the table and gave Dorcas a small shove in his direction. "You and Amelia should stay here, Caleb. That way, Dorcas can assist you. It wouldn't be proper, her going to your house. My Reuben's always been careful of Dorcas's reputation, especially now that you've done her the honor of paying court to her."

Caleb didn't know what to say. "I'm not— We're not—" he began, but Dorcas cut him off.

"Ya," she agreed, giving him the most genuine smile he'd ever seen on her face. "It's *gut,* you and me talking like we are. It makes me pleased. But it wouldn't be right, me taking care of your Amelia." Her eyes glistened with hope. "Since we aren't strictly a couple yet."

Caleb didn't know what to say to clear things up without embarrassing her further, but he didn't want to give anyone the wrong impression, either. So he just repeated what Dorcas had said. "You're right, we aren't a couple yet." And then he added, "Nothing decided between us."

Dorcas lowered her head and blushed. "That's what I've been trying to get Mam to understand. We haven't come to an understanding yet. We're not really courting, just considering the possibility."

"Nonsense," Lovina insisted. "Of course you're courting. Dorcas is perfect for you. She's a preacher's daughter, isn't she? And she's been brought up properly." She glanced pointedly at Rebecca. "Not like Hannah's girls. A preacher has to remember his position. Dorcas is for you, Caleb Wittner, and the sooner you two quit stalling and cry the banns, the better."

Caleb didn't know what to say. No one seemed to notice.

"You don't think Amelia will be sick to her stomach, do you?" Dorcas's eyes widened as she backed away from him and Amelia. "I'm not much for tending sick people. If she throws up…" She shuddered. "I'd probably throw up, too." She covered her face with her hands. "I'm sorry, I just can't."

"No matter," Hannah said. "We'll manage just fine." She motioned to Caleb. "Bring the child into the bedroom and we'll get her tucked in."

"I have Fritzy at home, and my livestock." He looked down at Amelia. How small she seemed. Wisps of damp hair clung to her bright red cheeks. "I'm not sure what to do. I can't just leave."

"Irwin can go and get Fritzy, and Amelia's baby doll," Rebecca suggested. "I know right where it is. And he can do your evening chores, can't you, Irwin?"

"Ya." Irwin, still at the table, looked up from forking another piece of sweet-potato pie into his mouth.

"It's the least he can do." Hannah led the way past the parlor to one of her downstairs bedrooms. "If it wasn't for you, Caleb, Irwin would be in a lot more trouble than he is now."

Caleb followed Hannah's directions and tucked Amelia into a bed in a spacious room across from the downstairs bath. He'd never seen the private areas of Hannah's home before, but he was comforted by the homey feel of the chamber. The walls here were a pale blue, the furniture old and lovingly polished until the worn grain shone softly in the lamplight. A yellow-and-blue braid rug and several hand-worked quilts added color.

"Used to be my room," Lovina informed him as she walked into the bedroom behind them, her cane tapping. She settled herself into a high-backed rocking chair. "Before I went to live with Anna."

Hannah looked questioningly at her mother-in-law.

"You just have that Irwin boy go by Anna's and tell her I'm staying here with this sick child. Can't have the new preacher here alone with you and my granddaughters."

"Lovina—" Hannah began.

Rebecca's *grossmama* cut her off with a wave of her cane. "Oh, I know you think my mind wanders. Sometimes it does, but I'm staying as long as Caleb does, and that's that." She turned her cane around and used the hand grip to drag a footstool closer. "I'll prop my feet up and be as comfy as a hen in a nest."

Hannah stood in the doorway and sighed. "Of course, you're welcome to stay if you wish, Mam."

The older woman scowled. "Lovina. I'm not your mother."

Hannah averted her eyes. "*Ya,* Lovina." Going to a blanket chest, she removed a blanket and spread it over Lovina. "If there's anything you want—"

"If there's anything I need, he can fetch it for me. He'll have little enough to do, sitting here and watching the child sleep."

Hannah backed out of the room as Caleb drew an oak desk chair up beside the bed. Amelia's face looked pale against the pillow, but she was already getting sleepy. "Are you warm enough?" he asked.

"Don't leave me, Dat."

He pulled a soft blue coverlet up to her chin. "I won't, pumpkin." Caleb continued to stroke Amelia's hair. There was no sound but the child's breathing and the patter of sleet against the window.

"It's a fine thing you're doing, courting our Dorcas," Lovina said in her thin, raspy voice. "She never was as pretty as Hannah's girls, but pretty don't last. Dorcas will make you a *gut* wife."

Caleb didn't answer.

"We'd given her up for an old maid," Lovina continued. "Many a time she'd come crying to me, saying no decent man would ever have her. But I told her that God would see to her. I told her to pray for a husband, and here you come, a man with a solid house, two good hands and a voice for praising the Lord. He sent you to Dorcas, and don't you forget it."

"I haven't made up my mind yet," he said cautiously. "Dorcas is a fine young woman, but I'm not certain."

"None of that talk," Lovina warned, shaking an arthritic finger at him. "You drop her like a hot potato and it will break her heart. No decent man comes to her mother's table three weeks in a row and doesn't pop the question."

The creak of door hinges caught Caleb's attention and he glanced toward the hallway. Rebecca stood there, a basin of water in her hands. "I thought that a cool washcloth on her forehead might help."

"Go on with you, Rebecca," Lovina chastised. "The preacher and I are having a private talk about his marriage to Dorcas. You go find Jonas and help him with the milking. You're not needed here."

Rebecca set the basin and a clean washcloth and towel on the nightstand beside the bed.

Caleb looked up at her. "Stay," he said.

"No place for you." Lovina puckered up her mouth. "Dorcas should be here, being Caleb's intended," she muttered, seemingly speaking more to herself than to him or Rebecca now. "My Martha's right. Her *kapp*'s set for Preacher Wittner."

Before Caleb could think of how to stop her, Rebecca quietly slipped from the room, leaving him alone with Amelia and Lovina. The elderly woman soon dozed off. And then he had nothing to do but sit, worry about his sick child and try to think about how to untie the tangled reins of his life.

Blinking back tears, Rebecca returned to the kitchen. No one was there but Dorcas, who was putting on her cloak by the back door. "Are you leaving?" she asked.

"Oh, Rebecca!"

To her surprise, Dorcas threw herself into her arms. *"Danke. Danke,"* Dorcas said, hugging her fiercely. "I know it should be me with his girl, but I just can't!"

"It's nothing," Rebecca answered, hugging her back. "You know sick children don't bother me. And I adore Amelia."

Dorcas didn't let go. "Not just for this, for Caleb. For helping me see what's best, for helping me accept God's plan for me," she whispered.

Rebecca pried her cousin's hands loose and stepped back. She forced a weak smile.

"I'd have to be stupid to refuse him, wouldn't I? This is my chance. I have to take it, or I'll spend the rest of my life regretting it." Dorcas tugged her faded cloak into place and began to tie the string at the throat. "I'll get used to his face. I know I will. And he's a kind man, a man of substance that I can respect. It will be a good marriage."

Rebecca's heart sank. *Ne. Not you,* she wanted to say. *I want him for my husband!* But she couldn't. She couldn't bear to see the happiness on Dorcas's face turn to anguish. "If Caleb asks you," she reminded softly. "Nothing is decided yet. Not really."

"Not yet," Dorcas said. "But soon. Mam will insist on it. The season for weddings is past, but Caleb is a widower. We can marry whenever we please, the sooner the better, really. What do I need with a big wedding?"

"Dorcas!" Hannah called from the porch. "Your parents are waiting in the buggy."

"I have to go," Dorcas said. "I'll come again tomorrow to see how Amelia is. I'm sure it's nothing, just a cold. But I'll pray for her."

Rebecca nodded. "*Ya.* Prayer helps."

Her mother came into the kitchen and wiped her shoes on the mat. "Still nasty out there," Hannah told Dorcas as she went out the door. "Tell your father to be careful on the road. Blacktop may be slippery." She closed the door behind Dorcas and turned. "I definitely think you should go to Leah," she said firmly. "Give Caleb time to make his choice."

"I think you're right," Rebecca said. She looked down at the floor, then back up at her mother. "I'll go, but please, don't tell anyone. Let me decide when."

Hannah's shoulders slumped. "Daughter, daughter. How does that make it any easier on either of you?"

"Not yet, Mam, please. Amelia is what's important now. I promise I won't do anything rash. Just let me have a little more time to make certain that Amelia's Christmas isn't ruined. I won't be alone with Caleb, and I won't give anyone reason to think ill of either of us." She went to the cupboard and took down a white pottery pitcher. "Caleb will need cool water, in case Amelia is thirsty."

Hannah nodded. "All right. Just as long as you remember that happiness can't ever be found in the ashes of someone else's unhappiness."

A single tear welled up and splashed down Rebecca's cheek, but she turned away so that her mother wouldn't see it. "I keep telling myself that," she murmured. "Over and over."

Sometime after 2:00 a.m., Amelia's fever did rise higher, and together, while Grossmama slept on in her chair, Rebecca and Caleb cared for the sick child. They took turns holding her and wiping her forehead and body with cool washcloths, fed her sips of willow bark tea and baby aspirin.

"This is all my fault," Caleb confided when Amelia fell asleep in his arms. "I should never have brought her to dinner. I should have noticed that she wasn't feeling well when she didn't eat her breakfast."

Rebecca sat on the edge of the bed. The weather outside had changed from sleet to rain, and now a downpour rattled against the windows as the wind whipped around the house. She was tired and concerned for Amelia, but she cherished this time together, just the two of them. Not that they were alone. Her grandmother was here, preserving moral decency, and Hannah came in from time to time to check on the patient.

Rebecca kept her promise to her mother foremost in her mind. She and Caleb talked only about Amelia or everyday things that any neighbor might share. Twice, Caleb had read passages from the Bible, and they had prayed together for Amelia's safe recovery. They had been careful that they didn't sit too close or touch each other, yet she had never been more conscious of him as a man.

She rejoiced in the tenderness that Caleb showed toward Amelia. The only light in the room came from two propane lanterns, and the radiance of the love shining in Caleb's eyes as he looked down at his daughter. If Dorcas could see him now, Rebecca thought, she wouldn't see the scars that twisted the surface of his face, she would only see the goodness of this man and the depth of his character.

Selfishly, Rebecca was glad that Dorcas wasn't here. This was her time, and no matter what happened in the future, whether they could ever be together or not, no one could take this memory from her.

By 3:00 a.m., the fever had broken and the crisis had passed. An hour later, when Rebecca fetched warm water to bathe the sweat from Amelia's throat and chest, a small sprinkling of a rash was evident on the child's skin. "Look at that," Rebecca said.

"What is it?" Caleb asked.

"I'm not sure. It doesn't look like chicken pox or measles. We can take her to a doctor in the morning, but maybe it doesn't matter exactly what it is. Children get all kinds of things. What does matter is that her fever is gone and her color is better."

"You're sure?" Caleb demanded. "You're sure she's—"

"Dat." Amelia's eyelashes fluttered, and then opened wide. A smile spread across her face. "Dat, I'm hungry."

"You're hungry?" he asked in disbelief. "What do you want to eat?"

"Hush up," Grossmama wheezed. "I'm trying to sleep. She told you the fever had passed, didn't she? Men." She groaned, drifted off and began to snore again.

Rebecca met Caleb's gaze and stifled a giggle. "You heard her, didn't you?" she whispered. She smiled down at Amelia. "How about if I make you some toast with strawberry jam?"

"Ya," Amelia said. "And hot chocolate."

Rebecca shook her head. "No chocolate yet. Maybe some tea with honey."

"Okay."

Caleb reached over and clasped her hand. "Thank you," he said. "Without you…" His voice choked with emotion. "Rebecca." He swallowed visibly. "Rebecca, what are we going to do?"

She lifted her lashes to look at him in the dim light. Grossmama and Amelia were both present, but it suddenly seemed as if it was only she and Caleb. *"Do?* About what?"

He looked down at Amelia. "Rebecca and I will get your toast and jam. We'll be right back, sweetie." He rose from his chair, took Rebecca's hand and led her out of the room. He closed the door before he spoke again, keeping his voice low. No one else seemed to be awake in the house, but it was obvious he wanted their conversation to remain private.

"About us," he said. "What are we going to do about us?"

"Us?" she repeated. Her voice sounded breathy. Did he mean what she thought he meant?

He groaned aloud. "Must I say it?" he whispered. "What are we to do about these feelings between us? I've tried to deny them and I think you have, as well, but after tonight, I feel…"

Rebecca looked away from him. Part of her heart was singing; she had not been mistaken. Caleb *did* care for her. But part of her heart was breaking. What did he mean what were they going to *do?* They were going to do nothing. He was going to do the right thing. How could Caleb *not* propose to Dorcas? He had let the matter go on too long. Rebecca felt as if *she* had let it go too far. She could never hurt Dorcas or shame her family by stealing Caleb out from under her cousin.

Rebecca returned her gaze to Caleb's face. "What will we do?" she asked, slowly taking her hand from his. "What we have been doing. What is right. Trying to live as the faith teaches us."

This time, Caleb was the one who looked away. "Are you telling me you don't feel the same—"

She reached out and squeezed his big, warm shoulder, silencing him. Then she released him. She was afraid that if she didn't let go of him now, she would never be able to let go of him. "Dorcas expects you to ask to marry her. Her mother and father, Grossmama… Everyone, Caleb, expects you to ask Dorcas to marry you." She pressed her lips together, afraid she might cry, willing herself not to. "I can't hurt my cousin. And neither can you."

He hung his head. "You're right," he whispered. "I'm sorry."

"There's nothing to be sorry for. We've done nothing wrong, Caleb. Nothing to be ashamed of." Her voice quavered. "But this has to stop. Now." She took a deep breath. "You need to find someone else to look after your house." Her voice cracked. "And Amelia."

"But Amelia loves you."

"It's not fair to her. She should begin getting to know Dorcas. You'll have to find someone else to work for you until you can be wed." She almost blurted out that she was going to Brazil but she couldn't bring herself to do it. Instead, Rebecca made herself walk down the hall, away from Caleb. "I'll stay until Christmas, then I'm done."

Chapter Sixteen

It was just after lunch on December 24, the day before Christmas, and Rebecca was scrubbing the kitchen countertops in Caleb's house. She and Amelia had made trays of Moravian sand tarts, cinnamon crisps and black walnut cookies. Together, they'd packed assortments into brown paper bags, tied them with green yarn bows and were preparing to deliver them as gifts to her mother, sisters and their families.

Naturally, there would be holiday excitement and visiting at each home, so the process might take all afternoon. Rebecca was determined to leave the house and kitchen spotless, especially because she knew this would be her last day here. Wiping her hands on her apron, she paused to look around. Everything was in its place: dishes dried and put away, a chicken potpie staying warm on the back of the stove and the floor shiny clean.

She glanced at the large, colorful wall calendar with its cheerful painting of an old-fashioned, horse-drawn sled crossing a snowy farm field and felt a twinge of guilt. Where had the month of December gone? Every morning when she came to Caleb's, she'd meant to tell him that she would be leaving for Brazil a few days after Christmas. But somehow, it had never seemed the right moment. Rebecca's promise to her mother weighed heavily on her conscience, but still she'd held her secret, wanting just a few more days. The fault was hers and she took full responsibility, but Caleb hadn't made her unpleasant task any easier.

Amelia's illness that had worried them so had passed as quickly as most children's ailments. Her pediatrician diagnosed the rash as roseola. Children her age were generally too old to contract it, but the doctor had told Caleb there was nothing to worry about. Within a week the rash was gone and Amelia had been as bubbly as ever.

Caleb was a different story.

Since the night of Amelia's illness and the confession that Rebecca and Caleb had shared in the hallway, he had barely spoken to Rebecca. Before Amelia's fever, Caleb had often shown a lighthearted side. They'd laughed together over small things, and he'd brought home from the shop fine articles of woodwork to show her. He'd even told her about the doll cradle for Amelia's beloved doll and the small four-wheeled cart that Fritzy could pull that he was making for her for Christmas. Not only had Rebecca not seen Amelia's Christmas gifts, but when she'd hinted that she wanted to stop by to see the progress, Caleb had told her to stay away from the chair shop. He'd even started packing his lunch the night before and carrying it with him, putting an end to her and Amelia walking over at noon to bring him a hot meal. Now the only time he attempted a conversation with Rebecca was when he was forced to discuss a household matter, or one that related to Amelia.

"I'm ready! Can we go now? Can we?" Amelia dashed into the room with Fritzy right behind her.

"Ya," Rebecca answered. Her heart warmed at the sight of the child. It seemed as if she was growing every day, no longer a baby but a strong and healthy girl. How different Amelia seemed from what she'd been when Rebecca had first come to work for Caleb. The sulking and sullen face had been replaced by smiles and an eagerness to learn new skills and make new friends. Parting with Amelia would be so painful...as painful as parting with Caleb.

Rebecca knelt to retie Amelia's shoe and apron. How neat she looked in her new blue dress, white apron and black stockings. Mam had fashioned a white *kapp* just Amelia's size, and Susanna had carefully starched and ironed it. The hooded cloak was Rebecca's Christmas gift. It was calf-length, navy blue wool, lined against the cold and hand sewn with tiny, almost invisible stitches.

Amelia hugged her. "I love you, Becca," she cried.

Rebecca pulled the child into her arms and swallowed hard. "I love you, too, Amelia," she murmured. If only things were different, she thought, this would be her very own daughter.

Not that she'd completely given up hope. Because she truly believed God had a plan for her. But neither she nor Caleb had spoken of what had happened that night. Sometimes, she wondered if she'd imagined the whole thing. Caleb continued to accept Aunt Martha's invitation to Wednesday-night suppers. With every passing day, it had become clearer to Rebecca that Mam was right—she couldn't keep working for Caleb, feeling the way she did about him. She and Susanna would go to visit Leah, and when they came home, maybe…

The back door opened and the big poodle ran barking to welcome Caleb home. Rebecca looked up from where she was still kneeling on the floor. "Caleb? Is that you?"

"Who else would it be?" He removed his hat and hung it on a hook by the door. He looked at Amelia. "What are you doing down there?"

"Dat! Dat! We made cookies!" Amelia bounced from one foot to another. "We're taking them to Anna's and—"

"It's bitter cold. I'm not sure you should go out in this wind," Caleb said.

Hastily, Rebecca got to her feet. "We were going to deliver our Christmas cookies. I have our buggy, and I promise to keep her bundled up."

Caleb pushed a big cloth bag with something heavy in it into Rebecca's hands. "For you," he said brusquely.

"Thank you." She'd made him a fruitcake, but it was at home. Mam had invited Caleb and Amelia to come by tomorrow for dinner.

There was no Christmas Day church service. There would be family prayers and Bible readings in the morning, but the afternoon would be shared with friends and family. They would exchange gifts, sing songs together and enjoy each other's company. Most of the gifts were practical ones, but Mam always managed to provide something special for each of them. On Christmas, it was the men who washed dishes and made coffee, and the women sat around the stove and teased them.

"Are you going to look and see what it is?" Caleb stroked his close-cut beard.

Heart pounding, Rebecca reached into the bag and retrieved a cedar box inlaid with hearts and tulips in darker pieces of cherry, oak and walnut. The box was about twelve by fourteen inches and fastened with brass hinges and a brass latch. "Oh, Caleb, it's beautiful," she exclaimed. The box smelled of cedar, and she could see the hours of patient craftsmanship that had gone into making it. "It's wonderful."

"Nothing much," he said. "For your Bible." He absently rubbed the scarred side of his face as he scanned the stove. "There's no dinner?"

Rebecca clasped the box against her. "I... I didn't expect you. Didn't you take your lunch this morning?"

"I did, but I didn't have time for breakfast. I ate my sandwich." He scowled. "You and Amelia must have eaten something. Isn't there anything left?" His mouth formed a tight line.

Anger made her answer sharply. "Do you think I'm one of those snake-charming, crystal-ball-gazing gypsy women with rings in their ears? How was I supposed to know you'd come home and want lunch?"

He started to speak, but she didn't let him.

"Amelia and I had peanut-butter sandwiches and apple slices. You're welcome to that if you want to make your own. I promised her that we'd deliver our Christmas cookies, and that's what we're going to do."

He looked stricken. "*Ya*...but..."

"But nothing, Caleb. Thank you for the Bible box. It's the nicest thing anyone has ever given me." She glanced down at Amelia. "Honey, I think you need your gloves. Be a good girl and go upstairs and fetch them."

Once Amelia had scampered off, Rebecca took a breath and then blurted out what she'd been holding back for weeks. "I'm going to Brazil. To spend three months with my sister. I'm leaving the day after tomorrow."

"Brazil?" He couldn't have looked any more shocked if she'd told him that she was going to the moon. "You can't go to Brazil. I haven't found anyone to take care of Amelia yet."

"I told you weeks ago that I would only be working for you until Christmas. You've had plenty of time to find a replacement for me, Caleb." Her lower lip trembled, but her voice did not. "I have an opportunity to go to Brazil, and I'm going. And I think it's better this way—since you can't make up your mind whether you're courting my cousin or not."

"You're just leaving us? Abandoning Amelia when she's come to trust you? Abandoning *us?*" Caleb's voice choked with emotion and his eyes clouded with tears. Was he losing the woman he loved? Again? His first instinct was to forbid her to leave. "Rebecca. You can't go. I won't let you."

"Ne, Caleb," she answered. "It isn't up to you. I've made up my mind."

"This isn't fair."

"Ne, it isn't. Not to me. Not to Amelia, and certainly not to Dorcas. I'm going to my sister's, and while I'm gone, you can work out your own problems."

"But it's Christmas. I made the box for you. I thought…"

"I don't know what you thought." Rebecca folded her arms and glared at him. "How could I know *what* you think? You never say anything to me anymore."

"You must know…" Why were the words so hard for him? Why did it feel as though his world was crumbling? "…how much I care for you. I told you that night."

"And I told you that I care for you, but I can't hurt Dorcas and—"

Fritzy began to bark and scratch against the back door. Caleb heard the sound of a horse's hoofbeats and the creak of buggy wheels in the yard and went to the window in the utility room. "Someone's here," he said to Rebecca. "We'll talk about this later."

"*Ne,* we won't. I've said my piece," she replied. "If there's more you want to say, tell me when I get back from Brazil." She reached for her coat on the hook. "There's a chicken potpie for your supper. I'll bring Amelia home after we deliver the cookies."

He was still looking out the window. "It's Martha and Dorcas." *Not them,* he thought. He couldn't face them now—not when he was losing Rebecca. If only he'd told them weeks ago that Dorcas and he would never make a good match. He'd wanted to. He would have if it hadn't been for the happy expression on Dorcas's face that first Wednesday he'd come to supper. He'd seen something of himself there, had known what it felt like to be unwanted.

His childhood had been lonely, and he'd often wondered if he'd ever make a place for himself where he felt at home. When he looked at Dorcas, he saw the lanky, awkward boy he'd been, with big feet and bony shoulders, the man-child who'd been taken in out of duty rather than love.

Dorcas was a decent girl, getting no younger, ruled by an overbearing mother and shunned by eligible suitors in the community. Caleb had sensed that she had a loving heart, even if she sometimes spoke out thoughtlessly. She wasn't as pretty or as clever as Rebecca, but she was a devout daughter of the church. She had as much right as any other young woman to be a wife. And now, because he hadn't had the courage to reject her, things had escalated and people believed that his intentions were serious.

How could he have been such a fool? All the time he was searching for someone to fill the emptiness in his life, Rebecca had been right there in front of him. He'd misjudged her badly. He hadn't thought that she was the proper choice for a preacher, the one to heal his grief and fill his life with joy.

"Rebecca, wait," he said. "We can still fix this."

She stopped and met his gaze. "At what cost, Caleb? Do you think we could ever be happy if we break Dorcas's heart?" She glanced back toward the interior of the house. "Amelia! Let's go, sweetie!"

"Rebecca, please," Caleb said. He reached out to take her arm but she brushed past him, opened the back door and stepped from the utility room out onto the open back porch.

"Just the person I wanted to see," Martha said, trudging toward them. "*Ne,* not you, Caleb. My niece. We need to talk. Privately."

As she approached, Caleb saw that Martha's eyes were swollen and bloodshot. She looked as if she'd been crying. "What's wrong?" he asked. "Has something happened to Reuben?"

Martha's chin quivered and she brought a man's handkerchief to her nose and blew loudly. "I just need to…talk to Rebecca."

Bewildered, Caleb looked from her to a grim-faced Dorcas standing beside the buggy. "You're welcome to come into the house, too," he said to her.

"I want to talk to you," Dorcas called to him. "Alone."

"What is it? Is someone ill?" Wind cut through Caleb's shirt. He'd come out without his coat and the temperature was freezing. It was beginning to snow. Big flakes were falling on the ground, the horse and the buggy.

Dorcas shook her head. "The problem is you."

"Me?" He looked from Dorcas to Martha to Rebecca, then back at Dorcas. "Maybe we'd all better go inside," he suggested.

"Get in the buggy." Dorcas climbed back in.

"All right." He glanced toward the house, wondering if he should go back for his coat, but Martha was already pushing past him on the porch and through the doorway into the utility room. Deciding that freezing to death might be the lesser of evils, he hurried to the closed buggy and got up into the seat beside Dorcas. "What's wrong?" he asked her.

"Everything." She looked at him and scowled. "Where's your coat? Do you want to take pneumonia?"

He rubbed his hands together. "Say what you've come to say."

"Very well." She looked him in the eye. "I've come to break off our courtship."

Caleb blinked, certain he had misunderstood. "What?"

"You heard me." She held up her hand. "And you can't change my mind." Her cloth gloves were worn, one finger mended with an off-color thread. Her nose glowed scarlet in the cold.

"Dorcas."

"Now hear me out, Caleb. I don't mean to hurt you. You're a good, respectable man, even a passable preacher, although your sermons are still too short. But the truth is, I'm not romantically attracted to you, and I never will be."

He stared. Had she just said what he thought he'd heard? "I don't—"

Dorcas's right palm rose inches from his face, cutting him off in midsentence. "Give me the courtesy to allow me to finish. You won't change my mind." She pressed her chapped lips together. "I know that this will disappoint you. And I know that you may be my last chance to find a husband—not to mention how upset my parents are. But I refuse to settle."

"I—"

She eyed him sternly and then went on. "Think me foolish if you like, but I want a marriage like Ruth has, like Anna, Johanna and Miriam. I want what my Yoder cousins have. And if God doesn't send me a man that I can love with my whole heart, then it's clear He intends for me to remain single."

In the kitchen, Rebecca pulled out a chair and helped her weeping Aunt Martha into it. "What is it?" Rebecca asked. She'd never seen Aunt Martha cry. "Has something bad happened? Please tell me. You're scaring me."

Aunt Martha buried her face in her hands. She was still wearing her heavy wool cloak and bonnet. She'd refused to take them off.

Amelia and Fritzy wandered into the kitchen. Amelia was eating a cinnamon crisp. "Are we going now?" she asked.

"Not yet." Rebecca waved the child away. "I'm talking to Aunt Martha. Go up to your room and play. I'll call you when we're ready." She didn't let her argue. "Please do as I say, Amelia."

With a grimace, Amelia retraced her steps. Fritzy followed her, eyes watching the floor in case a crumb dropped.

"Now." Rebecca returned to stand beside her aunt and placed a hand on her shoulder. "Tell me what's wrong."

Aunt Martha groaned. "It's my Dorcas."

"She's not sick, is she?"

Aunt Martha shifted her black-rimmed glasses lower, turned her head and peered up over the top of them. "Dorcas is breaking off with Caleb."

"What?" Weak-kneed, Rebecca dropped into the chair nearest her aunt.

"I know it's hard to believe, but Dorcas refuses to court him. She's breaking the news to him now. Her father is furious."

"Uncle Reuben is furious?" Rebecca hadn't heard Uncle Reuben take a stand on anything as long as she could remember. She concentrated on what her aunt had just said, and hope made her heart race. "Dorcas doesn't want to marry Caleb?" she repeated woodenly.

"Are you deaf? It's what I said, isn't it?"

Rebecca nodded.

"I want her to be happy. My only daughter. Why wouldn't I?" Aunt Martha tugged on the strings of her black hat. "Foolish of me, I know." Her lower lip quivered. "What will we do if Caleb causes a scandal? He'll be disappointed, I know."

"Uncle Reuben?"

"Not your uncle," Aunt Martha replied sharply. "*Caleb.* Caleb will be disappointed. How will it look for his position? People will say she dumped him." She lowered her voice to a whisper. "That there's something wrong with him. More than the obvious," she added.

"Maybe not," Rebecca ventured.

"Oh, they will. I can hear it now. Everyone will be trying to guess what secret he's hiding." Martha rocked back and forth, a picture of misery. "A disaster. But I have to stand by my daughter. If she won't listen to reason, then we must make the best of her decision."

Rebecca reached for her aunt's hand. "You mean you and Uncle Reuben won't try to force her to reconsider Caleb?"

"What kind of mother do you think I am? I'm not like my *mam.*" Aunt Martha's eyes narrowed. "Dorcas thinks Caleb's dull. As boring as dried peas without pork fat, she said."

Rebecca started to defend Caleb and then thought better of it.

Her aunt glanced around and continued in a whisper. "You think I'm old and sour, but I had a young man once. Barnabas Troyer. We were young, and he was poor. Didn't even own a horse. Poorer even than we were, but we loved each other. Not a foolish fancy, but real love."

Compassion made her squeeze Aunt Martha's hand.

Martha sniffed and pried her hand loose. "Barnabas begged me to marry him, said we'd move to Missouri and start over, but I listened to my parents. I let him get away."

Rebecca exhaled softly. "I didn't know."

"Of course, you didn't. How would you know? How would anyone know? Eventually, I married Reuben. And you know how he is. A good enough man, a preacher, even, but never going to set the world on fire. Oh, we manage, all right. But, I'll say it once and never again. Your uncle was never one for hard work. It's his only weakness." She shook her head. "Mine was not taking real love when I found it."

Rebecca's heart was pounding so hard that she imagined Aunt Martha could hear it.

"I want more for Dorcas than making do. No matter what people say about her or our new preacher, I'm behind her one hundred percent. If she doesn't want to marry him, then she doesn't have to."

Rebecca's head was spinning. "But...why did you want to tell me?"

Aunt Martha lifted her head. "Because I know you can sway him. For whatever reason, he seems to listen to you. You need to make sure he doesn't make a fuss of this. Over my Dorcas rejecting him. Another woman will come along. He's a decent enough catch. Even with the—" she indicated the left side of her face "—you know."

"I—" Rebecca didn't know what to say. She could hardly believe what she was hearing.

"Maybe you should think about it. You're not getting any younger, you know." Aunt Martha rose. "Anyway, you'll have to forget all this nonsense about going to Brazil. You can't think of yourself, Rebecca. Your family needs you."

* * *

Five minutes later a stunned Rebecca and Caleb stood alone on the back porch as Aunt Martha's buggy rolled away through the falling snow. Speechless, Rebecca handed Caleb his coat that she'd snatched off the hook when she'd followed her aunt out of the house.

He slipped into it. "It's snowing," he said, turning back to her.

"Ya." She looked up into his eyes. "It is."

His cold hand closed around her waist and he pulled her into his arms. "I think I've been dumped," he murmured into her hair.

Trembling, she nodded. He smelled of cedar, wood chips, leather and molasses. She rested her head against his chest, not caring that allowing such liberties was reckless. She wanted to seize this moment and hold it forever. How right it felt, how safe and proper. How perfect.

"So I'm a free man," he continued.

"Ya, Caleb," she whispered. "I think you must be."

He tilted her chin up with cold fingers and pressed his warm lips against hers. The tender touch of his mouth and the nearness of him overwhelmed her and she felt giddy. "How will it look?" he asked.

"Look?" She blinked as clouds of snowflakes whirled around them.

A deep chuckle of laughter shook his chest. "Me, a preacher of the church, here alone with a beautiful woman on Christmas Eve? I suppose we'll have to remedy that and make it proper."

Hope made her daring, and she raised her head to meet his second kiss: tender, sweet and full of promise. "How could you make this proper?"

"Must I spell it out for you, girl?"

She smiled up at him through her tears of joy. "I think you must."

"Will you be my wife, Rebecca Yoder? Will you marry me and make me the happiest man in Kent County?"

"Just Kent County?"

A grin spread across his face. "I was going to say the happiest man in Delaware, but I thought that you'd accuse me of pride. And pride is not a good trait for a man of God."

"You mention marriage, but not love." She pressed her lips together. "Do you love me, Caleb?"

"I love you, and I want you to be my wife and Amelia's mother—as soon as the banns can be called."

"What?" she teased, already thinking the same thing. "No courting?"

"Rebecca, darling, don't you know? We've been courting since the evening when I saved you in my barn."

She laid her palm gently over the scarred side of his face and gazed up into his dark eyes. "Or, maybe," she ventured, "maybe I saved you."

The intensity of his embrace nearly took her breath away. "Say you'll be my wife, Rebecca, or we're both in a great deal of trouble."

"*Ya,* Caleb," she replied. "I'll marry you, but it will have to wait until I get back from Brazil. I promised my sister. Three months, and then we'll be together."

"All right," he agreed. "You drive a hard bargain, but I've waited a long time. A little longer won't matter."

"Dat!" Amelia called, coming out onto the porch.

"It's snowing! And we have to deliver our cookies for Christmas!"

"So we do," Caleb answered and then met Rebecca's gaze again. "Together, as a family."

And that's exactly what they did.

Epilogue

Christmas Eve, one year later

"Are you warm enough?" Caleb looked both ways before guiding the horse and buggy onto the blacktop. He, Rebecca and Amelia were on their way home after making several Christmas Eve visits to elderly members of their church community. He'd wanted to make certain that no one was alone or in need tonight. They'd brought pies, vegetable soup and apples to give as token gifts, and perhaps most important, they'd taken time to visit at each stop.

"*Ya,* Dat." Amelia's small voice came from the back of the buggy where she was snuggled down under a quilt with Fritzy and a new addition to the family, Joy.

The half poodle, half lab puppy, a stray that Rebecca's sister Grace had rescued and nursed back to health, had been an early Christmas gift for his daughter. When Grace and Rebecca had hatched the plan, he'd been a little skeptical, because he didn't know how Fritzy would take to a new dog. He should have known better. Most of Rebecca's ideas were good ones, and it was a toss-up as to whether Amelia or Fritzy was more taken with the pup.

"What about you?" Caleb asked, glancing over at his wife. "Warm enough?"

"*Ya,* Caleb," she answered. "Toasty warm. And why wouldn't I be in my new mittens and scarf?"

He'd found the scarf on a trip to the mall with some of the boys he'd taken under his wing after the incident the winter before. The scarf was long and blue, and as soft as duck down. The color was a little brighter than some might think suitable for a preacher's wife, but the price and practicality of the gift made it impossible to pass up. And fancy scarf or not, no one could find fault with Rebecca as a role model for other young women.

"I was wrong," he admitted. "When I thought you were too flighty."

Rebecca didn't answer. That was something else he valued about her. As quick as she was to stand up for herself or give an opinion, she knew when to listen and let a man say what was on his mind.

"When Clarence Troyer had to have his appendix out, you offered to keep their five children so that Margaret could stay at the hospital with him through it all," Caleb said. "And when Susan King wanted to die at home, it was you who organized the neighborhood women so that someone was always with her and Paul, day and night."

"It was little enough to do for them."

Caleb slipped his arm around her shoulders and pulled her closer to him on the seat. Their legs pressed against one another under the lap robe, and his heart swelled with happiness that he'd found this woman to be his partner and the mother of his child. "I misjudged you, Rebecca. I thought that a devout woman had to be a serious one, but I was wrong about that, too." He leaned nearer and kissed her forehead. "You've made my house a home," he whispered hoarsely, "and I love you for it."

"The two of us, working together as a team." Rebecca smiled. "That's what makes the difference. You and me and Amelia, a real family."

"Am I a good husband?" he asked. "Do I make you happy?"

"Every day I thank God for bringing you to me."

He chuckled and flicked the reins over the horse's back. "I've wondered, but I was afraid to ask if you were disappointed in me."

"Never. You're strong and smart and—"

"A little stuffy," he supplied.

She laughed. "Sometimes, but I know you'll always do what's right, like you did with Irwin and the others. Aren't you pleased with them? With how they are maturing? Yours was a good plan, Caleb. To have them fill their spare time with useful deeds instead of mischief."

"I credit you with any good I've done with those boys," he said to Rebecca. "It might have been my idea, but I doubt I'd have had the courage to follow through if you hadn't seen the value in it."

She snuggled closer to him. "Didn't I just say we made a good pair?" she teased. "You're too modest by half. And if I've made a passable preacher's wife, it's because you've been there every step of the way, holding me up." It wasn't like Caleb to open his heart to her, but she didn't need words to know that he loved her. Anyone who said that marriage was easy wasn't being honest, but she loved Caleb more tonight than she had on the day they'd pledged their vows to each other.

It was as cold as it had been on the previous Christmas Eve when he'd asked her to be his wife, but tonight there was no snow. The stars were bright against a velvet sky, and the horse's breaths made white puffs in the frosty air. She loved the familiar rhythm of the buggy wheels and the animal's hooves on the road. "I was hoping for a white Christmas."

"No snow in sight," Caleb answered. He'd turned into their lane. "There's something for you in the barn. Thought I'd give it to you tonight and leave Christmas morning for Amelia."

Rebecca sat up straight. "But you've already given me this beautiful scarf and new mittens."

"Snow boots for you under the bed. Fur lined, just for around the house. Wouldn't do for church. Not *plain* enough for—"

"For a preacher's wife?" she finished. They laughed together.

"Can't have you with wet feet, can I? Delaware doesn't get much snow, but we're good for rain and mud in winter."

"We are that," she agreed. "But you shouldn't have spent any more money on me. You've already hired Verna Beachy to come three days a week to help me with the housework."

"Made sense. You're doing more and more of my accounts for the wood-carving business. Not to mention the time you spend visiting those in need in the community. But I thought something else would come in handy." He drove to the barn and reined in the horse by the wide double doors. "Come see what I have in here,"

he said. He helped Rebecca down and then went around
to open the back doors. One small daughter, one small
dog and one bigger one spilled out. The dogs barked
and the girl giggled.

"I didn't tell, Dat," Amelia said. "I kept the secret."

"What secret?" Rebecca asked.

Caleb tied the horse to the hitching rail, took a battery lantern from the buggy and led the way into the
stable. Rebecca and Amelia followed him past the
empty stall, past where the cow was penned, to the
last stall in the row. A sorrel mare with a white nose
and a white blaze on her forehead hung her head over
the railing.

"You bought a new horse?" Rebecca cried, going
close enough to stroke the mare's head. "She's beautiful. What's her name?"

"Daisy. And she's not mine." He grinned at her.
"She's—"

"Yours!" Amelia squealed. "Dat bought her for you.
And she has a cart!"

"For me?" Rebecca cried. "Oh, Caleb, thank you."
She flung herself into his arms and hugged him. "I love
her, but why do I need a horse and cart?"

"So you can come and go as you see fit," he answered. "Bishop Atlee said you were busy enough to
need your own transportation, and I asked Charley to
keep his eyes open for a likely prospect." He stroked
the horse's nose. "She's six years old, traffic wise and
has no bad habits so far as I can see. Merry Christmas, Rebecca."

"Merry Christmas, Mam!" Amelia echoed.

Tears clouded Rebecca's eyes. This man… This
child… This farm and this wonderful present… How

could any woman ask for more? She caught Caleb's broad hand and squeezed it tightly. "I love you," she declared. "I love both of you!"

Amelia beamed and snatched up a handful of hay to feed Daisy. Daintily, the mare nibbled at the timothy.

"Come to think of it, I have a gift for you, too, Caleb." Rebecca raised a finger to her lips, and when he bent his head to hear, she whispered her secret into his ear.

A broad grin split his face, and the light from the lantern reflected in his eyes. "When?"

"Late July or early August," she murmured. "Merry Christmas, Caleb."

Laughing, Caleb swung Amelia up into his arms and enveloped both her and Rebecca in a big hug. And in that instant, there was no place else in the world that Rebecca would rather be.

* * * * *

A CHRISTMAS TO DIE FOR

Marta Perry

This story is dedicated to my supportive
and patient husband, Brian, with much love.

The salvation of the righteous comes from the Lord;
He is their stronghold in time of trouble. The Lord
helps them and delivers them; He delivers them
from the wicked and saves them, because
they take refuge in Him.
—*Psalms* 37:39–40

Chapter One

Rachel Hampton stood on the dark country road where, seven months ago, she'd nearly died. The dog pressed against her leg, shivering a little, either from the cold of the December evening or because he sensed her fear.

No, not fear. That would be ridiculous. It had been an accident, at least partially her fault for jogging along remote Crossings Road in the dark. She'd thought herself safe enough on the berm of the little-used gravel road, wearing a pale jacket with reflective stripes that should have been apparent to any driver.

Obviously it hadn't been. He'd come around the bend too fast, his lights blinding her when she'd glanced over her shoulder. But now she was over it, she—

Her heart pumped into overdrive. The roar of a motor, lights reflected from the trees. A car was coming. He wouldn't see her. She'd be hit again, thrown into the air, helpless—

She grabbed Barney's collar and stumbled back into the pines, pulse pounding, a sob catching in her throat as she fought to control the panic.

But the car was slowing, stopping. The driver's-side window slid smoothly down.

"Excuse me." A male voice, deep and assured. "Can you tell me how to get to Three Sisters Inn?"

How nice of him to ignore the fact that she'd leaped into the bushes when she heard him coming. She disentangled her hair from the long needles of a white pine and moved toward him.

"You've missed the driveway," she said. "This is a back road that just leads to a few isolated farms." She approached the car with Barney, Grams's sheltie, close by her side. "If you back up a bit, you can turn into a farm lane that will take you to the inn parking lot."

He switched on the dome light, probably to reassure her. Black hair and frowning brows over eyes that were a deep, deep blue, a pale-gray sweater over a dress shirt and dark tie, a glint of gold from the watch on his wrist, just visible where his hand rested on the steering wheel. He didn't look like a tourist, come to gawk at the Amish farmers or buy a handmade quilt. The briefcase and laptop that rested on the passenger seat indicated that.

"You're sure the proprietor won't mind my coming in that way?"

She smiled. "The proprietor would be me, and I don't mind at all. I'm Rachel Hampton. You must be Mr. Dunn." Since she and Grams expected only one visitor, that wasn't hard to figure out.

"Tyler Dunn. Do you want a lift?"

"Thanks, but it's not far. Besides, I have the dog." *And I don't get into a car with a stranger, even if he does have a reservation at the inn.*

Maybe it was her having come so close to death

that had blunted her carefree ways. Either that or the responsibility of starting the bed-and-breakfast on a shoestring had forced her to grow up. No more drifting from job to job, taking on a new restaurant each time she became bored. She was settled now, and it was up to her to make a success of this.

She stepped back, still holding Barney's collar despite his wiggling, and waited until the car pulled into the lane before following it to the shortcut. She'd walked down the main road, the way the car had come, but this was faster. She gestured Dunn to a parking space in the gravel pull-off near the side door to the inn.

He stepped out, shrugging into a leather jacket, and stood looking up at the inn. It was well worth looking at, even on a cold December night. Yellow light gleamed from the candles they'd placed in every one of the many nine-paned windows. Security lights posted on the outbuildings cast a pale-golden glow over the historic Federal-style sandstone mansion. It had been home to generations of the Unger family before necessity had turned it into the Three Sisters Inn.

Rachel glanced at the man, expecting him to say something. Guests usually sounded awed or at least admiring, at first sight. Dunn just turned to haul his briefcase and computer from the front seat.

Definitely not the typical tourist. What had brought him to the heart of Pennsylvania Dutch country at this time of year? Visiting businessmen, especially those who traveled alone, were more likely to seek out a hotel with wireless connection and fax machines rather than a bed-and-breakfast, no matter how charming.

"May I carry something for you?"

He handed her the computer case. "If you'll take this, I can manage the rest."

The case was heavier than she'd expected, and she straightened, determined not to give in to the limp that sometimes plagued her when she was tired—the only remaining souvenir of the accident.

Or at least she'd thought that was the only aftereffect, until she'd felt that surge of terror when she'd seen the car. She'd have to work on that.

"This way. We'll go in the side door instead of around to the front, if you don't mind."

"Fine."

A man of few words, apparently. Dog at her heels, she headed for the door, hearing his footsteps behind her. She glanced back. He was taller than she'd realized when he sat in the car—he probably had a good foot on her measly five two, and he moved with a long stride that had him practically on her heels.

She went into the hallway, welcoming the flow of warm air, and on into the library. She didn't usually bring guests in through the family quarters, but it seemed silly to walk around the building just to give him the effect of the imposing front entrance into the high-ceiled center hall. The usual visitor ohhed and ahhed over that. She had a feeling Tyler Dunn wouldn't.

"My grandmother has already gone up to bed." She led the way to the desk. "You'll meet her in the morning at breakfast. We serve from seven-thirty to nine-thirty, but you can make arrangements to have it earlier, if you wish."

He shook his head, glancing toward the glowing embers of the fire she'd started earlier. Grams's favorite chair was drawn up next to the fireplace, and her knitting lay on its arm.

"That's fine. If I can just get signed in now and see my room—"

"Of course." Smile, she reminded herself. The customer is always right. She handed him a registration card and a pen, stepping back so that he had room to fill it out.

He bent over, printing the information in quick, black strokes, frowning a little. He looked tired and drawn, she realized, her quick sympathy stirring.

"That's great, thanks." She imprinted the credit card and handed it back to him. "You indicated in your reservation that you weren't sure how long you'd want the room?"

She made it a question, hoping for something a little more definite. With all the work she'd been doing to lure guests for the holiday season, the inn still wasn't booked fully. January and February were bound to be quiet. In order to come out ahead financially, they needed a good holiday season. Her money worries seemed to pop up automatically several times a day.

"I don't know." He almost snapped the words. She must have shown a reaction, because almost immediately he gave her a slightly rueful smile. "Sorry. I hope that doesn't inconvenience you, but I have business in the area, and I don't know how long it will take."

"Not at all." The longer she could rent him the room, the better. "Perhaps while you're here, you'll have time to enjoy some of the Christmas festivities. The village is planning a number of events, and of course we're not far from Bethlehem—"

"I'm not here for sightseeing." His gaze was on the

dying fire, not her, but she seemed to sense him weighing a decision to say more. "That business I spoke of—there's no reason you'd recognize my name, but I own the property that adjoins yours on one side. The old Hostetler farm."

She blinked. "I didn't realize—" She stopped, not sure how to phrase the question. "I thought the property belonged to John Hostetler's daughter."

Who had annoyed the neighbors by refusing to sell the property and neglecting to take proper care of it. The farmhouse and barn had been invaded by vandals more than once, and the thrifty Amish farmers who owned the adjoining land been offended at the sight of a good farm going to ruin.

"My mother," he said shortly. His face drew a bit tighter. "She died recently."

That went a long way toward explaining the tension she felt from him. It didn't excuse his curtness, but made it more understandable. He was still grieving his mother's death and was now forced to deal with the unfinished business she'd left behind.

"I'm so sorry." She reached out impulsively to touch his arm. "You have my sympathy."

He jerked a nod. "I'm here to do something about my grandfather's property. My mother let that slide for too long."

It would be impolite to agree. "I'm sure the neighbors will be glad to help in any way they can. Are you planning to stay?"

"Live there, you mean?" His eyes narrowed. "Certainly not. I expect to sell as soon as possible."

Something new to worry about, as if she didn't have enough already. The best offer for the Hostetler farm might easily come from someone who wanted to put up some obnoxious faux Amish atrocity within sight of the inn.

"That's too bad. It would have been nice to hear that family would be living there again."

She'd made the comment almost at random, but Tyler Dunn's expression suggested that she'd lost her mind.

"I don't know why you'd think that." He bit off the words. "I'm hardly likely to want to live in the house where my grandfather was murdered."

Tyler closed his laptop and glanced at his watch. A little after eight—time for breakfast and another encounter with the Unger family.

He stood, pushing the ladder-back chair away from the small table, which was the only spot in the bedroom where one could possibly use a computer. He must be the first person who'd checked into the Three Sisters Inn for business purposes. Most of the guests would be here to enjoy staying in the elegant mansion, maybe pretending they were living a century ago.

The place looked as if it belonged in a magazine devoted to historic homes. The bedroom, with its canopy bed covered by what was probably an Amish quilt, its antique furniture and deep casement windows, would look right on the cover.

From the window in his room, he had a good view of Churchville's Main Street, which was actually a country route along which the village had been built. The inn anchored the eastern edge of the community, along with the stone church which stood enclosed in its walled churchyard across the street. Beyond, there was nothing but hedgerows and the patchwork pattern of plowed fields and pasture, with barns and silos in the distance.

Looking to the left, he could see the shops and restaurants along Main Street, more than he'd expect given the few blocks of residential properties, but probably the flood of tourism going through town accounted for that. The inn had a desirable position, almost in the country but within easy walking distance of Main Street attractions. It was surprising they weren't busier.

He opened the door. The upstairs landing was quiet, the doors to the other rooms standing open. Obviously, he was the only guest at the moment. Maybe that would make things easier.

Had it been a mistake to come out so bluntly with the fact of his grandfather's murder last night? He wasn't sure, and he didn't like not being sure. He was used to dealing with facts, figures, formulas—not something as amorphous as this.

At least he'd had an opportunity to see Rachel Hampton's reaction. He frowned. Her name might be Hampton, but she was one of the Unger family.

If his mother had been right—but he couldn't count on that. In any event, he'd understood what she'd wanted of him. The impossible.

He started down the staircase, running his hand along the delicately carved railing. The downstairs hall stretched from front to back of the house. To his right, the door into the library where he'd registered last night was now closed. On his left, a handsome front parlor opened into another parlor, slightly smaller, behind it, both decorated with period furniture.

He headed toward the rear of the building, where

Rachel had indicated he'd find the breakfast room. He'd cleared his calendar until the first of the year. If he couldn't accomplish what he planned by then, he'd put his grandfather's farm on the market, go back to his own life and try to forget.

The hallway opened out into a large, rectangular sunroom, obviously an addition to the original house. A wall of windows looked onto a patio and garden, bare of flowers now, but still worth looking at in the shapes of the trees and the bright berries of the shrubs. The long table was set for one.

Voices came from the doorway to the left, obviously the kitchen. He moved quietly toward them.

"...if I'd known, maybe I wouldn't have opened my mouth and put my foot in it." Rachel, obviously talking to someone about his arrival.

"There was no reason for you to know. You were just a child." An older voice, cultured, restrained. If this woman was hiding something, he couldn't tell.

A pan clattered. "You'd best see if he's coming down, before these sticky buns are cold."

That was his cue, obviously. He moved to the doorway before someone could come out and find him. "I'm here. I wouldn't want to cause a crisis in the kitchen."

"Good morning." The woman who rose from the kitchen table, extending her hand to him, must be Rachel's grandmother. Every bit the grande dame, she didn't look in the least bothered by what he might or might not have overheard. "Welcome to the inn, Mr. Dunn. I'm Katherine Unger."

"Thank you." He shook her hand gently, aware of bones as fine as delicate crystal. The high cheekbones, brilliant blue eyes, and assured carriage might have belonged to a duchess.

Rachel, holding a casserole dish between two oversize oven mitts, had more color in her cheeks than he'd seen the night before, but maybe that was from the heat of the stove.

The third person in the kitchen wore the full-skirted dark dress and apron and white cap of the Amish. She turned away, evading his gaze, perhaps shy of a stranger.

"It's a pleasure to meet you, Mrs. Unger. I suppose your granddaughter told you who I am."

"Yes. I was very sorry to hear of your mother's death. I knew her when she was a girl, although I don't suppose she remembered me. I don't remember seeing her again after she graduated from high school."

"Actually, she spoke of you when she talked about her childhood." Which hadn't been often, for the most part, until her final days. He'd always thought she'd been eager to forget.

"I'm sure you'd like to have your breakfast. Rachel has fixed her wild-mushroom and sausage quiche for you."

"You can have something else, if you prefer," Rachel said quickly. "I didn't have a chance to ask—"

"It sounds great," he said. "And I'm looking forward to the sticky buns, too." He smiled in the direction of the Amish woman, but she stared down at the stovetop as if it might speak to her.

Rachel, carrying the steaming casserole dish, led the way to the table in the breakfast room. He sat down, but before he had a chance to say anything, she'd whisked off to the kitchen, to reappear in a moment with a basket of rolls.

He helped himself to a fresh fruit cup and smiled at her as she poured coffee. "Any chance you'd pour a cup and join me? It's a little strange sitting here by myself."

This time there was no mistaking the flush that colored her cheeks. That fair skin must make it hard to camouflage her feelings. "I'm sorry there aren't any other guests at the moment, but—"

"Please. I need to apologize, and it would be easier over coffee."

She gave him a startled look, then turned without a word and took a mug from a mammoth china cupboard that bore faded stenciling—apples, tulips, stars. It stood against the stone wall that must once have been the exterior of the house.

Her mug filled, she sat down opposite him. "There's really no reason for you to apologize to me."

Green eyes serious in a heart-shaped face, brown hair curling to the shoulders of the white shirt she wore with jeans, her hands clasped around the mug—she looked about sixteen instead of the twenty-nine he knew her to be. He'd done his homework on the residents of Three Sisters Inn before he'd come.

"I think I do. You were being friendly, and I shouldn't have thrown the fact of my grandfather's death at you."

"I didn't know." Her eyes were troubled, he'd guess because she was someone who hated hurting another's feelings. "We left here when I was about eight, and I didn't come back until less than a year ago, so I'm not up on local history."

"I guess that's what it seems like." He tried to pull

up his own images of his grandfather, but it was too long ago. "Ancient history. I remember coming for the funeral and having the odd sense that conversations broke off when I came in the room. It must have been years before I knew my grandfather had been killed in the course of a robbery."

She leaned toward him, sympathy in every line of her body. "I'm sure it's hard to deal with things so soon after your mother's death. Is there any other family to help you?"

"I'm afraid not." He found himself responding to her warmth even while the analytical part of his mind registered that the way to gain her cooperation was to need her help. "I hate the thought of seeing the farm again after all this time. It's down that road I was on last night, isn't it?"

He paused, waiting for the offer he was sure she'd feel compelled to make.

Rachel's fingers clenched around the mug, and he could sense the reluctance in her. And see her overcome it.

"Would you like me to go over there with you?"

"You'd do that?"

She smiled, seeming to overcome whatever reservation she had. "Of course. We're neighbors, after all."

It took a second to adjust to the warmth of that smile. "Thanks. I'd appreciate it."

Careful. He took a mental step back. Rachel Hampton was a very attractive woman, but he couldn't afford to be distracted from the task that had brought him here. And if she knew, there might very well be no more offers of help.

* * *

The dog danced at Rachel's heels as she walked down Crossings Road beside Tyler that afternoon. At least Barney was excited about this outing. She was beginning to regret that impulsive offer to accompany Tyler. And as for him—well, he looked as if every step brought him closer to something he didn't want to face.

Fanciful, she scolded herself, shoving her hands into the pockets of her corduroy jacket. The sun was bright enough to make her wish she'd brought sunglasses, but the air was crisp and cold.

"There's the lane to the farmhouse." She pointed ahead to the wooden gate that sagged between two posts. If there'd ever been a fence along the neglected pasture, it was long gone. "Is it coming back to you at all?"

Tyler shook his head. "I only visited my grandfather once before the time I came for the funeral. Apparently, he and my mother didn't get along well."

From what Grams had told her this morning, John Hostetler hadn't been on friendly terms with anybody, but it would hardly be polite to tell Tyler that. "That's a shame. This was a great place to be a kid."

Her gesture took in the gently rolling farmland that stretched in every direction, marked into neat fields, some sere and brown after the harvest, others showing the green haze of winter wheat.

He followed her movement, narrowing his eyes against the sun. "Are those farms Amish?"

"All the ones you see from here are. The Zook farm is the closest—we share a boundary with them, and you must, as well." She pointed. "Over there are the Stolzfuses, then the Bredbenners, and that farthest one belongs to Jacob Stoker. Amish farms may be different in other places, but around here you'll usually see a white bank barn and two silos. You won't see electric lines."

He gave her an amused look. "You sound like the local tour guide."

"Sorry. I guess it comes with running a B&B."

He looked down the lane at the farmhouse, just coming into view. "There it is. I can't say it brings any nostalgic feeling. My grandfather didn't seem welcoming when we came here. If my mother ever wanted to change things with him—well, I guess she left it too late."

Was he thinking again about his grandfather's funeral? Or maybe regretting the relationship they'd never had? She knew a bit about that feeling. Her father had never spent enough time in her life to do anything but leave a hole.

"You said something this morning about conversations breaking off when you came in the room—people wanting to protect you, I suppose, from knowing how your grandfather died."

He nodded, a question in his eyes.

"I know how that feels. When my father walked out, no one would tell us anything." She shook her head, almost wishing she hadn't spoken. After all these years, she still didn't like thinking about it. But that was what made her understand how Tyler felt. "Maybe they figured because he'd never been around much anyway, we wouldn't realize that this time was for good, but the truth would have been better than what we imagined."

His deep-blue eyes were so intent on her face that it

was almost as if he touched her. "That must have been rough on you and your sisters."

She registered his words with a faint sense of unease. "I don't believe I mentioned my sisters to you."

"Didn't you?" He smiled, but there was something guarded in the look. "I suppose I was making an assumption, because of the inn's name."

That was logical, although it didn't entirely take away her startled sense that he knew more about them than she'd expect from a casual visitor.

"The name may be wishful thinking on my part, but yes, I have two sisters. Andrea is the oldest. She was married at Thanksgiving, and she and her husband are still on a honeymoon trip. And Caroline, the youngest, is an artist, living out in Santa Fe." She touched the turquoise and silver pin on her shirt collar. "She made this."

Tyler stopped, bending to look at the delicate hummingbird. He was so close his fingers almost touched her neck as he straightened the collar, and she was suddenly warm in spite of the chill breeze.

He drew back, and the momentary awareness was gone. "It's lovely. Your sister is talented."

"Yes." The worry over Caro that lurked at the back of her mind surfaced. Something had been wrong when Caro came home for the wedding, hidden behind her too-brittle laugh and almost frantic energy. But Caroline didn't seem to need her sisters any longer.

"The place looks even worse than I expected." Tyler's words brought her back to the present. The farmhouse, a simple frame building with a stone chimney at either end, seemed to sag as if tired of trying to stand upright. The porch that extended across the front sported broken railings and crumbling steps, and several windows had been boarded up.

"Grams told me the house had been broken into several times. Some of the neighbors came and boarded up the windows after the last incident. The barn looks in fairly good shape, though."

That was a small consolation to hold out to him if he really hadn't known that his mother let the place fall to bits. Still, a good solid Pennsylvania Dutch bank barn could withstand almost anything except fire.

"If those hex signs were meant to protect the place, they're not doing a very good job." He was looking up at the peak of the roof, where a round hex sign with the familiar star pattern hung.

"I don't think you'd find anyone to admit they believe that. Most people just say they're a tradition. There are as many theories as there are scholars who study them."

Tyler went cautiously up the porch steps and then turned toward her. "You'll have to climb over the broken tread."

She grasped the hand he held out, and he almost lifted her to the porch. She whistled to the dog, nosing around the base of the porch. "Come, Barney. The last thing we need is for you to unearth a hibernating skunk."

"That would be messy." Tyler turned a key in the lock, and the door creaked open. He hesitated for an instant and then stepped inside. She followed, switching on the flashlight that Grams had reminded her to bring.

"Dusty." A little light filtered through the boards on the windows, and the beam of her flashlight danced around the room, showing a few remaining pieces of furniture, a massive stone fireplace on the end wall, and a thick layer of dust on everything.

Tyler stood in the middle of the room, very still. His face seemed stiff, almost frozen.

"I'm sorry if it's a disappointment. It was a good, sturdy farmhouse once, and it could be again, with some money and effort."

"I doubt I'd find anyone interested in doing that." He walked through the dining room toward the kitchen, and she followed him, trying to think of something encouraging to say. This had to be a sad homecoming for him.

"There's an old stone sink. You don't often see those in their original state anymore."

He sent her the ghost of a smile. "You want to try out the pump?"

"No, thanks. That looks beyond repair. But I can imagine some antique dealer drooling over the stone sink. Those are quite popular now."

"I suppose I should get a dealer out to see if there's anything worth selling. I remember the house as being crowded with furniture, but there's not too much left now."

"My grandmother could steer you to some reputable dealers. Didn't your mother take anything back with her after your grandfather died?"

She couldn't help being curious. Anyone would be. Why had the woman let the place fall apart after her father died? Grief, maybe, but it still seemed odd. Surely she knew how valuable a good farm was in Lancaster County.

"Not that I remember." He turned from a contemplation of the cobwebby ice box to focus on her. "You spoke of break-ins. Was anything stolen?"

"I don't know. My grandmother might remember. Or Emma Zook, since they're such close neighbors. She's our housekeeper."

"The Amish woman who was in the kitchen this morning? According to the lawyer who handled my grandfather's will, the Zooks leased some of the farmland from his estate. I need to get that straightened out before I put the place on the market. I should talk to them. And to your grandmother."

Something about his intent look made her uneasy. "I doubt that she knows anything about their leases."

"According to my mother, Fredrick Unger offered to buy the property. That would make me think your family had an interest."

There was something—an edgy, almost antagonistic tone to his voice, that set her back up instantly. What was he driving at?

"I'm sure my grandfather's only interest would have been to keep a valuable farm from falling to pieces. Since he died nearly five years ago, I don't imagine you'll ever know."

"Your grandmother—"

"My grandmother was never involved in his business interests." And she wasn't going to allow him to badger her with questions. "I can't see that it matters, since your mother obviously didn't want to sell. Maybe what you need to do is talk to the attorney."

Her own tone was as sharp as his had been. She wasn't sure where the sudden tension had come from, but it was there between them. She could feel it, fierce and insistent.

Tyler's frown darkened, but before he could speak, there was a noisy creak from the living room.

"Hello? Anybody here?"

"Be right there," she called. She'd never been quite so pleased to hear Phillip Longstreet's voice. She didn't know where Tyler had been going with his questions and his attitude, and she didn't think she wanted to.

Chapter Two

Tyler didn't miss the relief on Rachel's face at the interruption. The speed with which she went into the living room was another giveaway. She might not know what drove him, but she'd picked up on something.

Or else he'd been careless, pushing too hard in his drive to get this situation resolved.

He followed her and found her greeting the newcomer with some surprise. "Phillip. What are you doing here?"

The man raised his eyebrows as she evaded his attempt to hug her. "Aren't you going to introduce me?" He held out his hand to Tyler. "Phillip Longstreet. You may have noticed Longstreet Antiques on Main Street in the village."

He was in his late forties or early fifties at a guess, but he wore his age well—fit-looking, with fair hair that showed signs of gray at the temples and shrewd hazel eyes behind the latest style in glasses.

"This is Tyler Dunn." She glanced at him, and he thought he read a warning in her eyes.

"Nice to meet you. Were you looking for Ms. Hampton?"

"It's always pleasant to see Rachel, but no, I wanted to meet the new owner." Longstreet shrugged, smiling. "I like to get in before the other dealers when I can."

"How did you know?" Rachel sounded exasperated. "If we had a party line, Phillip, I'd suspect you of eavesdropping."

"I have to be far more creative than that to stay ahead of the competition. If you want to keep secrets, don't come to a village. Emma's son, Levi, delivered the news along with my eggs this morning."

It was an insight into how this place worked. "Are you interested in the contents of the house, Mr. Longstreet?"

A local dealer might be the best choice before putting the house on the market, but Longstreet was obviously trolling for antiques, probably hoping to get an offer in on anything of value before his competition did. Or possibly before Tyler realized what he had.

"Phil, please. I'd like to look around." Longstreet's gaze was already scoping out the few pieces left in the living room. "Sometimes there are attractive pieces in these old farmhouses, although more often it's a waste of time."

"I'm afraid your time was definitely wasted this afternoon." He gestured toward the door. "I'm not ready to make a decision about selling anything yet."

"If I could just take a look around, I might be able to give you an idea of values." Longstreet craned his neck toward the dining room.

Tyler swung the door open and stepped out onto the porch, so that the man had no choice but to follow. "I'll be in touch when I'm ready to make a decision. Thank you for stopping by."

"Yes, well, thanks for your time." Longstreet stepped gingerly over the broken step. "Rachel, I'll see you at the meeting tonight."

Rachel, coming out behind him, bent to snap a leash onto the dog's collar. "Fine."

Tyler waited until Longstreet had backed out of the driveway to turn to her. "Is that one of the reputable dealers your grandmother might recommend?"

"Grams probably *would* suggest him. His uncle was an old crony of my grandfather."

"But...?"

Her nose crinkled. "Phil's nice enough, in his way. It's just that every time he comes to the inn, I get the feeling he's putting a price on the furniture."

"I'm not bad at showing people the door, if you'd like some help."

"I run an inn, remember?" She smiled, her earlier antagonism apparently gone. "The idea is to get people in, not send them away. Are you a bouncer in your real life?"

"Architect. Showing people the way out is just a sideline."

She looked interested. "Do you work on your own?"

He shook his head. "I'm with a partner in Baltimore, primarily designing churches and public buildings. Luckily I'm between projects right now, so I can take some time off to deal with this." Which brought him back to the problem at hand. "Well, if your grandmother recommends Longstreet, I'll still be sure to get offers from more than one dealer."

"That should keep him in line. He's probably easier

to cope with when he wants to buy something from you. I'm on the Christmas in Churchville committee with him, and he can be a real pain there."

He pulled the door shut and turned the key in the lock.

"Are you sure you're finished? You didn't look around upstairs."

"I've had enough for the moment." He tried to dismiss the negative feelings that had come with seeing the place again. This was a fool's errand. There was no truth left to find here—just a moldering ruin that had never, as far as he could tell, been a happy home.

The dog leaped down from the porch, nearly pulling Rachel off balance, and he caught her arm to steady her.

"Easy. Does he really need to be on the leash?"

"I wanted to discourage any more digging around the porch. I'm afraid you may have something holed up in there for the winter."

"Whatever it is, let it stay." He took the leash from her hand and helped her over the broken step to the ground. "I won't bother it."

She glanced at him as they walked away. "You must be saddened to see the place in such a state."

He shrugged. "I only saw it twice that I recall. It would have been worse for my mother than for me. She grew up here."

"Do you think—" She stopped, as if censoring what she'd been about to say.

"That's why she let it fall to pieces?" He finished the thought for her. "I have no idea. I'd have expected my dad to intercede, but—" he shrugged "—I didn't know she still owned the place until a few weeks ago, and by then she was in no shape to explain much. Maybe she just wanted to forget, after the way her father died."

Rachel scuffed through frost-tipped dead leaves that the wind had scattered over the road. "I don't think I've ever actually heard how it happened."

"From what my mother told me, he apparently confronted someone breaking into the house. There was a struggle, and he had a heart attack. He wasn't found until the next day."

She shivered, shoving her hands into her pockets. "It's hard to think about something like that happening here when I was a child. It always seemed such an idyllic place."

They walked for a few moments in silence, their footsteps muted on the macadam road. He glanced at her, confirming what he heard. "You're limping. Did you twist your ankle getting off that porch?"

"It wasn't that." She nodded toward the bend in the road ahead of them, the wind ruffling her hair across her face so that she pushed it back with an impatient movement. "I had an accident just up the road back in the spring."

He frowned down at her. "It must have been a bad one. Did you hit a tree?"

She shook her head. "I was jogging, too late in the evening, I guess. A car came around the bend—" She stopped, probably reliving it too acutely.

That explained why she'd stepped back into the trees when he'd come down the lane last night. "How badly were you hurt?"

"Two broken legs." She shrugged. "Could have been worse, I guess. It only bothers me when I'm on my feet too long."

"I hope the driver ended up in jail."

"Hit and run," she said briefly.

Obviously she didn't want to talk about it any further. He couldn't blame her. She didn't want to remember, any more than he wanted to think about the way his grandfather died, or the burden his mother had laid on him to find out why.

"I guess this place isn't so idyllic after all."

"Bad things happen anywhere, people being people."

"Yes, I guess they do." Of course she was right about that. It was only the beauty that surrounded them that made violence seem so out of place here.

Rachel was thankful when the business part of the "Christmas in Churchville" meeting was over. The strain of mediating all those clashing egos had begun to tell on her after the first hour.

Now the battling committee members wandered around the public rooms of the inn, helping themselves to punch and the variety of goodies placed on tables in both the back parlor and the breakfast room. She'd figured out a long time ago that if you wanted to keep people circulating, you should space out the food and drink.

She and Grams had put cranberry punch on the round table next to the fireplace in the back parlor, accompanied by an assortment of cheeses, grapes and crackers. The breakfast room had coffee, tea and hot chocolate on the sideboard, along with mini éclairs and pfeffernüsse, the tiny clove and cardamom delicacies that were her grandmother's special holiday recipe.

Would Tyler come down? Thinking of him alone in his room, she'd suggested he join them for refreshments. He'd know when the business meeting was over, she'd told him, when the shouting stopped.

Her committee members weren't quite that bad, but they did have strong opinions on what would draw the holiday tourists to spend their money in Churchville.

She checked on the service in the parlor and walked back toward the breakfast room. Tyler was in an odd position here—part of the community by heritage and yet a stranger. He probably wouldn't be around long enough to change that. He'd sell the property and go back to his life in Baltimore.

Hopefully he wouldn't leave problems behind in the form of whoever bought his grandfather's farm. The neighbors disliked seeing it derelict, but there were certainly things they'd hate even more.

"Rachel, there you are." Phillip intercepted her in the doorway, punch cup in hand. Fortunately the cup made it easier to escape the arm he tried to put around her. "I wanted to speak with you about the Hostetler place."

"So does everyone else, but I don't know anything. Tyler hasn't told me what his plans are for the property."

"You know I'm all about the furniture, my dear. I remember a dough box that my uncle tried to buy once from old Hostetler. If there's anything like that left—"

"You saw the living room. Most of the furniture is already gone."

"I didn't see the rest of the house." His voice turned wheedling. "Come on, Rachel, at least give me a hint what's there."

"Sorry, I didn't see anything else." She slipped past him. "Excuse me, but I have to refill the coffeepot."

Phillip was nothing if not persistent. That probably explained how he managed to make such a success of the shop. His uncle had been a sweet old man, but he'd never had much of a head for business, from what Grams said.

She snagged a mug of hot chocolate and a pfeffernüsse for herself, turning from the table to find Sandra Whitmoyer bearing down on her. As wife of Churchville's most dedicated, as well as only, physician, Sandra seemed to feel the chairmanship of the decorating subcommittee was hers by right. Luckily no one else had put up a fight for it.

"Rachel, we really must keep our eyes on the rest of the shop owners along Main Street. It would be fatal to allow anyone to put up a garish display."

"I'm sure you'll do a wonderful job of that, Sandra." She had no desire to turn herself into the decorating police. "I have my hands full already, preparing the inn and organizing the open house tour." Maybe a little flattery was in order. "You have such wonderful taste. I know everyone will be seeking your advice. And they've all agreed to go along with the committee's decisions."

"Well, I suppose." Sandra ran a manicured hand over sleek waves of blond hair. She was dressed to perfection tonight as always, this time in a pair of gray wool slacks that made her legs look a mile long, paired with a silk shirt that had probably cost the earth.

Glancing past Sandra, she spotted Tyler standing in the doorway. So he had come down. He looked perfectly composed in the crowd of strangers—self-possessed, as if he carried his confidence with him no matter where he was.

She'd seen him ruffled at moments that afternoon, though, and she'd guess he didn't often show that side to people. The derelict house had affected him more than she'd expected.

And there had been an undercurrent when he talked about his mother, something more than grief, she thought.

Sandra had moved to the window, peering out at the patio and garden. "I suppose you'll be decorating the garden for the open house."

"White lights on the trees, and possibly colored ones on the big spruce."

"It would be more effective without the security lights," Sandra said. "You could turn them off during the house tour hours. And maybe put a spotlight on the gazebo."

"I don't want to draw attention to the gazebo. I'd be happy to demolish it completely."

"You wouldn't have to do something that drastic."

She turned at the sound of Tyler's voice, smiling her welcome. "What would you suggest, other than a stick of dynamite? Sandra Whitmoyer, I'd like to introduce Tyler Dunn. He owns the Hostetler place, down the road from us."

Sandra extended her hand. "Welcome to Churchville. Everyone is curious about what you intend for the property. Well, not my husband, of course. As a busy physician, he doesn't have time for many outside interests."

Bradley Whitmoyer was as self-effacing a man as she'd ever met, but his wife had appointed herself his one-woman press agency.

Tyler responded, politely noncommittal, and turned back to Rachel. "I wouldn't recommend high explosives for the gazebo. You wouldn't like the results."

"I don't like it the way it is."

He smiled down at her. "That's because it's in the wrong place. If you moved it to the other side of the pond, it would be far enough away to create a view."

"Well, I still think you should decorate it for the house tour." Sandra put down her cup. "I have to go. There's Jeff looking for me. It was nice meeting you, Mr. Dunn." She nodded to Rachel and crossed the room toward the hallway.

"Is that her husband, the physician?" Tyler's tone was faintly mocking.

"No, his brother. Jeff Whitmoyer. He has a small construction company. It looks as if he didn't find it necessary to change before coming by for Sandra."

Jeff's blue jeans, flannel shirt and work boots were a sharp contrast to Sandra's elegance. There was a quick exchange between them before Sandra swept out the hallway.

Rachel dismissed them from her mind and turned back to Tyler. "About the gazebo—"

"Single-minded, aren't you?" His smile took any edge off the comment. "It might be possible to move it, rather than destroy it. If you like, I'll take a look while I'm here."

"I'd love to find a solution that makes everyone happy. Grams never liked the gazebo at all—she feels it doesn't go with the style of the house. But Andrea thinks it should stay because Grandfather had it put up as a surprise for Grams."

"And it's your job to keep everyone happy?" The corners of his mouth quirked.

"Not my job, exactly." Every family had a peace-maker, didn't they? She was the middle one, so it fell to her. "My sister says I let my nurturing instincts run amok, always trying to help people whether they want it or not."

"It's a nice quality." Those deep-blue eyes seemed to warm when they rested on her. "I wouldn't change if I were you."

"Thank you." Ridiculous, to be suddenly breathless because a man was looking at her with approval. "And thank you for the offer."

He shrugged. "It's nothing. We're neighbors, remember?"

It was what she'd said to him, but he seemed to invest the words with a warmth that startled her.

Careful, she warned herself. It wouldn't be a good idea to start getting too interested in a man who'd disappear as soon as his business here was wound up.

Rachel did not like climbing ladders. Any ladder, let alone this mammoth thing that allowed her to reach the top of the house. Unfortunately, there didn't seem to be another way of putting up the outside lights anytime soon.

Grams had suggested hiring someone to do the decorating, but Grams didn't have a grasp on how tight money was right now. Rachel could ask a neighbor for help, of course, but this was a business. It didn't seem right if she couldn't pay.

But she really didn't like being up on a ladder.

She leaned out, bracing herself with one hand on the shutter, and slipped the strand of lights over the final hook. Breathing a sigh of relief, she went down the ladder. In comparison to that, doing the windows should be a breeze.

Reaching the ground, she took a step back, reminding herself of just how many windows there were. Well, maybe not a breeze, but she could do it.

And what difference would it make, the voice of doubt asked. *You have one whole guest at the moment.*

Tyler had gone off to Lancaster this morning to see the attorney who'd handled his grandfather's estate. He'd seemed eager to resolve the situation with the farm. Well, why not? He probably had plans for Christmas in Baltimore.

Once he left, she'd have zero guests. There were a few people scheduled for the coming weekends, but not nearly enough. They'd hoped for a good holiday season to get them through the rest of the winter, but that wasn't happening.

If she could get some holiday publicity up on the inn's website, it might make all the difference. Andrea had intended to do that, but the rush to get ready for the wedding had swamped those plans. And she could hardly call her big sister on her honeymoon to ask for help. They had already invested all they could afford in print ads in the tourist guides, and the website was the only option left.

She fastened a spray of pine in place, taking satisfaction in the way the dark green contrasted with the pale stone walls. This she could do. Decorate, cook gourmet breakfasts, work twenty-four/seven when it was necessary—those were her gifts.

Her gaze rested absently on the church across the street, its stone walls as gold as the inn. Someone had put evergreen wreaths on the double doors, and the church glowed with welcome. That was what she'd sensed when she'd come back to Churchville. Welcome.

Home. Family. Community. She'd lost that when Daddy left and their mother had taken them away from here.

She paused with her hand on the burgundy ribbon she was tying. *Lord, this venture can't be wrong, can it? It seems right. Surely You wouldn't let me have a need so strong if it weren't meant to be satisfied.*

"Rachel, you look as if you've turned to stone up there. Are you all right?"

She glanced down from the window to see Bradley Whitmoyer standing on the walk, eyeing her quizzically. She scrambled down from the stepladder.

"I guess that's what they mean by being lost in thought, Dr. Whitmoyer. What can I do for you?"

She saw him occasionally, of course, when she took Grams for a check-up, at church, at a social event, but he'd never come to the inn.

"Bradley," he corrected. "I'm on an errand." He gave her his gentle smile, pulling an envelope from the pocket of his overcoat. "My wife asked me to drop this off on my way to the office. Something to do with this Christmas celebration you're working on, I think."

She took the envelope. "You shouldn't have gone out of your way. I could have picked it up." She knew how busy he was. Everyone in the township knew that.

"No problem." He drew his coat a little more tightly around him, as if feeling the cold. "I've been meaning to see how you're getting along. This is an ambitious project you and your grandmother have launched."

"Yes, it is." He didn't know how ambitious. "But Grams is enjoying it."

"That's good." His eyes seemed distracted behind the wire-rimmed glasses he wore, his face lined and tired.

He wore himself out for everyone else. People said he'd turned down prestigious offers to come back to Churchville and become a family doctor, because the village and the surrounding area needed him.

"I understand you have old Mr. Hostetler's grandson staying here." He rocked back and forth on his heels. "I suppose he's come to put the farm on the market."

"I don't know what his plans are. Probably he'll sell the land. The house is in such bad shape, I'm not sure anyone would want it."

"He should just tear it down. Every old house isn't worth saving, like this one. You're doing a fine job with it."

"Thank you." She resisted the urge to confide how uncertain she was about her course. She wasn't his patient, and her problems weren't medical. She waved the envelope—no doubt Sandra's notes on the town brochure. "Please tell your wife I'll get right on this."

"I'll do that." He turned, heading for his car quickly, as if eager to turn on the heater.

Even as he got into his sedan, she saw Tyler's car pulling into the driveway. If he'd arrived a few minutes earlier, she could have introduced them.

"Was that a new guest?" Tyler came toward her across the crisp grass.

"Unfortunately not. That was Dr. Whitmoyer. You met his wife last night."

"So that's the good doctor."

"He really is. Good, I mean. He's the only doctor in the village, and in addition to carrying a huge patient load, he's doing valuable research on genetic diseases among the Amish."

"I'll agree that he's a paragon if you'll come inside

for a few minutes." He was frowning. "I need to talk to you."

Now that she focused on him, she could sense his tension. Something was wrong.

She put down the ribbon she'd been holding. "Of course."

The warm air that greeted her when she walked inside made her fingers tingle. She led the way to the library, shrugging out of her jacket, and turned to face him. "What is it? Can I help you with something?"

He shoved his hands into his pockets, frowning, and ignored the invitation to sit. "I saw the attorney who's been handling things since my grandfather died. According to him, your grandfather tried to buy the farm at least six times since then."

She didn't understand the tone of accusation in his voice. "I suppose that's true. The neighbors weren't happy to see the place falling to pieces. It would be natural for my grandfather to make an offer for it."

"It sounds to me as if he was eager to snap up the property once my grandfather was out of the way. According to my mother, he and my grandfather had been feuding for years."

She planted her hands on her hips. There weren't many things that made her fighting mad, but innuendos about her family certainly did. "I'm not sure what you're driving at, Tyler. I don't know anything about any feud, but if it did exist, it's been over for twenty years or so. What does that matter now?"

His eyes seemed to darken. "It mattered to my mother. She talked to me about it before she died. She said her father told her someone was trying to cheat him out of what was his. That she didn't believe his death was as a result of a simple robbery. And that she believed the Unger family was involved."

Chapter Three

Rachel's reaction to his statement was obvious. Shock battled anger for control.

That was what he'd felt, too, since the attorney told him about old Mr. Unger's attempt to buy the place. He'd hoped the lawyer would say his mother had been imagining things. Instead, his words seemed to confirm her suspicions.

Rachel took a breath, obviously trying to control her anger. She held both hands out, palms pushing away, her expression that of one who tries to calm a maniac. "I think you should leave now."

"And give you time to come up with a reasonable explanation? I'd rather have the truth."

Her green eyes sparked fire. "I don't need to come up with anything. You're the one making ridiculous accusations."

"Is it ridiculous? My grandfather claimed someone was trying to cheat him. Your grandfather tried repeatedly to buy his property. How else do you add those things up?"

"Not the way you do, obviously. There's a difference

between buying and cheating someone. If your grand-father thought the offer low, he didn't have to sell." She flung out a hand toward the portrait that hung over the fireplace mantel. "Look at my grandfather. Does he look like someone who'd try to cheat a neighbor?"

"Appearances can be deceiving." Still, he had to admit that the face staring out from the frame had a quality of judicious fairness that made the idea seem remote.

She gave a quick shake of her head, as if giving up on him. "This is getting us nowhere. I'm sorry for your problems, but I can't help you. I'll be glad to refund your money if you want to check out." She stood very stiffly, her face pale and set.

He'd blown it. He'd acted on impulse, blurting out his suspicions, and now he wouldn't get a thing from her. Time to regroup.

"Look, I'm sorry for coming out with it that way. Can we sit down and talk this over rationally?"

Anger flashed in those green eyes. "Now you want to be rational? You're the one who started this with your ridiculous accusations."

He took a breath. He needed cooperation from Rachel if he were going to get anywhere. "Believe it or not, I felt as if I'd been hit by a two-by-four when I heard what Grassley, the attorney, had to say. Just hear me out. Then I'll leave if you want."

Rachel looked as if she were counting to ten. Finally she nodded. She waved him to the sofa and pulled the desk chair over for herself. She sat, planting her hands on its arms and looking ready to launch herself out of the chair at the slightest wrong word.

He sat on the edge of the sofa, trying to pull his

thoughts into some sort of order. He was a logical person, so why couldn't he approach this situation logically?

Maybe he knew the answer to that one. Grief and guilt could be a powerful combination. He'd never realized how strong until the past few weeks.

"You have to understand—I had no idea all this was festering in my mother's mind. She didn't talk about her childhood, and I barely knew her father. I'd been here once, before I came for my grandfather's funeral."

She nodded. "You told me that. I thought then that there must have been some breach between your mother and your grandfather."

So she'd seen immediately what he'd have recognized if he weren't so used to the situation. "I never knew anything about it. My father may have known, but he died when I was in high school."

"I'm sorry." Her eyes darkened with sympathy, in spite of the fact that she must still be angry with him.

"My mother had always been—" He struggled to find the right word. "Secretive, I guess you'd say. After my father died, she started turning to me more. Change the lightbulbs, have the car serviced, talk to the neighbors about their barking dog. But she never shared anything about her finances or business matters. I knew my father had left her well off, so I didn't pry. That's why I didn't have any idea she still owned the property here."

"I suppose she let the attorney take care of anything that had to be done. I'm surprised he didn't urge her to sell—to my grandfather or anyone else." Her voice was tart.

"He did, apparently, but he said she'd never even discuss it. She didn't with me until her illness." It had been hard to see her go downhill so quickly, hard to believe that none of the treatments were doing any good.

"What was it?"

"Cancer. When she realized she wasn't recovering, that's when she started to talk." He paused. "She'd left it late. She was on pain medication, not making much sense. But she said what I told you—that her father had insisted he was being cheated, that everyone was out to take advantage of him."

"That sounds as if he felt—well, that he thought he was being persecuted. How can you know that any of what he told her was true?"

"I can't. But she thought there were things about his death that had never been explained. She regretted that she'd never attempted to find out. She demanded my promise that I'd try to learn the truth."

His hands clenched. He'd told Rachel more than he'd intended. If she knew about what had happened then—but that was ridiculous. She'd been a child twenty-two years ago. At most, she'd oppose him now out of a need to protect her grandfather's reputation.

"I can understand why you feel you have to honor her wishes," she said, looking as if she chose her words carefully. "But after all this time, how can you possibly hope to learn anything?"

"I thought I might talk to your grandmother—"

"No!" She flared up instantly at that. "I won't have my grandmother upset by this."

A step sounded from the hallway, and they both turned. "That is not your decision to make, Rachel." Rachel's grandmother stood in the doorway, her bearing regal, her face set and stern.

* * *

Rachel's throat tightened. Grams, standing there, hearing the suspicions Tyler was voicing. She'd like to throw something at him for causing all this trouble, but that wouldn't help.

"Now, Grams…" She had to think of something that would repair this situation. Protecting Grams was her responsibility.

She stood and went to her, the desk chair rolling backward from the pressure of her hands. She put her arm around her grandmother's waist.

Grams didn't seem to need her support. She had pride and dignity to keep her upright.

"Don't 'now, Grams,' me, Rachel Elizabeth. I know what I heard, and I don't require any soothing platitudes."

Rachel shot a fulminating glance at Tyler. At least he had the grace to look unhappy at this turn of events. He'd look worse when she finished telling him what she thought.

"Grams, I'm sure you misunderstood." She tried for a light tone. "You always told us that eavesdroppers never hear anything good, remember?"

Grams ignored her, staring steadily at Tyler. "I must apologize. I'm not in the habit of listening in on other people's conversations, but you were both too busy arguing to realize I was there."

"I just want to protect you—" Rachel began.

Her grandmother cut her short with a look. "I don't require protection. I knew my husband well enough to be quite confident that he'd never have been involved in anything underhanded. I have nothing to fear from Mr. Dunn's inquiry."

"Of course not, but it's still upsetting. Please, Grams, let me handle this."

Her only response was to move to her armchair and be seated, folding her hands in her lap. "I'll answer any question you wish to ask." She glanced up at the portrait. "The truth can't harm my husband."

Grams might want to believe that, but Rachel wasn't so sure. Of course she knew Grandfather had been perfectly honest, but rumors, once started, could be difficult to stop.

She glanced at Tyler. He looked as if getting what he wanted had taken him by surprise.

"It's very good of you to agree to talk with me about this." He'd apparently decided on a formal approach. Good. If she caught the slightest whiff of disrespect, he'd be out of here before he knew what hit him.

Grams inclined her head graciously. "I don't know that I have much to offer. My husband only discussed business with me in very general terms."

Tyler's mouth tightened fractionally. "Start by telling me what you remember about John Hostetler. You must have known him, since you were such close neighbors."

"I knew him. Knew of him, certainly. He was a rather difficult person, from everything I recall. After his wife died, he became bitter, cutting himself off from the community."

"Do you know if your husband had any business dealings with him? Did he talk to you about wanting to buy the place?"

She frowned. "I don't remember, but if he did, it would be in his ledgers. Rachel will make them available to you."

She swallowed the protest that sprang to her lips.

Tyler could strain his eyes looking through decades of her grandfather's fine black script, and he wouldn't find anything wrong.

"That's kind of you." Tyler seemed taken aback by that kindness, but that was her grandmother. "Do you know of anyone he was on bad terms with?"

A faint smile rippled on Grams's expression. "It might be easier to ask with whom he didn't quarrel. I don't mean to speak ill of him, but it's fairly well known that he argued with just about everyone."

"I remember a visit we made when I was about six. Certainly he and my mother seemed to battle most of the time."

"I'm afraid that was his nature." Grams spread her hands. "I don't know what else I can say. After his death, the neighbors were concerned about the condition of the farm. Several of them came to Fredrick about it, I remember that." She glanced up at the portrait again. "If he did try to buy it, I'm sure that's why."

He nodded, not offering any comment. It was what Rachel had told him, too, but she didn't think he was convinced. He wouldn't understand her grandfather's almost-feudal-lord position in the community. Everyone, Amish and English alike, had come to him with their concerns.

"Do you remember anything about the robbery and his death?"

Grams moved slightly, and Rachel was instantly on the alert. This questioning bothered her grandmother more than she'd want to admit.

"I know we were shocked. Everyone was."

She put her arm around her grandmother. "Of course

they were." She darted him a look. "I think my grandmother has told you everything she can."

Grams gave Tyler a level look. "I have, but if there's anything else…"

"Not right now." Tyler seemed to know he'd pushed enough.

Grams rose. "We'll cooperate in any way we can. It's what my husband would wish." She turned toward the kitchen and walked away steadily.

Rachel hesitated. She wanted his promise that this wasn't going to be all over the township by sunset, but she didn't want to say that where Grams could hear. She'd better make sure Grams was safely in the kitchen with Emma.

"Would you mind sticking around for a minute or two while I speak to Emma? I could use some help moving that ladder."

He nodded, his expression telling her he understood what she wasn't saying. "I'll wait for you outside."

By the time she went out the front door a few minutes later, Rachel knew exactly how she should behave. She'd talk with Tyler very calmly, explaining the harm that could be done to her grandmother by careless talk. She'd make it clear that they'd already done everything he'd asked of them and that there really was nothing else they could contribute.

She would not express the anger she felt. She'd extended friendship to the man, and all the time he'd been using her to pry into her family.

He waited by the ladder she'd left propped against the house, his leather jacket hanging open in the warmth of the afternoon sunshine. He straightened when he saw her. "Is your grandmother all right?"

"She didn't like being cross-examined," she said sharply, and then snapped her mouth shut on the words. If she wanted discretion from Tyler, she'd better try a little tact of her own. "She was telling you the truth." Katherine Unger was not someone who'd lie to cover up her own or anyone else's misdeeds.

He gave her a slight smile. "I know. Do you think I don't recognize integrity when I see it?"

"I was afraid your judgment might be skewed by your need to find out about your grandfather."

"Look, I said I was sorry for jumping on you with it. I want to be fair about it."

Did he mean that? She hoped so. "There's one thing you said to me that you didn't mention to my grandmother."

He frowned. "What's that?"

He knew. He had to. "You said your mother didn't think her father's death had been adequately explained. You called it murder."

The word seemed to stand there between them, stark and ugly.

He was silent for a long moment, and then he shook his head. "I don't know, Rachel. That's the truth. I can tell you what my mother said. What she seemed to believe. As to whether it had any basis in fact—" he shrugged "—I guess that's what I have to find out."

"I hope—" She stopped. Would he think she was trying to control his actions? Well, in a way, she was.

"What do you hope?" He focused on her, eyes intent.

"I hope you'll be discreet with the questions you ask people around here, especially anything to do with my grandparents. It doesn't take much to set rumors flying in a small community like this."

"Your grandmother didn't seem to be worried about that."

No, she wouldn't worry about people talking when she felt she was doing what was right.

"Grams can be naive about some things. If the rumor mill starts churning, the situation will be difficult for her. So be tactful, will you please?"

"I'll try." He took a step back from the wooden stepladder as she approached it. "I'm not here to stir up trouble for innocent people."

"Sometimes innocent people get hurt by the backlash." She bent to plug the end of the string of lights into the outlet.

"I can't let that stop me from looking for the truth." His jaw set like a stone.

"And I won't let anything stop me from protecting my family," she said. "Just so we're clear."

"We're clear. Does that mean you want me to move out?"

It was tempting to say yes, but it was safer to have Tyler where she could keep track of him. "You're welcome to stay as long as you want." She started up the ladder, the loop of lights in her hand.

"Thank you. And since I'm staying, I'd be glad to climb up and do that for you. I wouldn't have to stretch as far."

"I can reach." If she stood on the top step on her tiptoes, she could.

She looped the string of lights over the small metal hook that was left in the window frame from year to year. Pulling the string taut, she grasped it and leaned toward the other side.

She stretched, aware of him watching her, and pushed the wire toward the hook—

"Wait!" Tyler barked.

The wire touched the hook—a sharp snap, a scent of burning, a jolt that knocked her backward off the ladder and sent her flying toward the ground, stunned.

Chapter Four

"I'm fine. Really." Rachel tried to muster a convincing tone, but if she looked half as shaken as she felt, it was hardly surprising that Tyler wanted to rush her to the hospital.

"You don't look fine." He had a firm hold on her arm, and he didn't seem inclined to let go any time soon. "My car's right there. If you won't go to the E.R., at least let that local doctor you were talking to have a look."

"I don't need Dr. Whitmoyer to look at me." She rubbed her hands together, trying to get rid of the tingling sensation. "It just knocked the wind out of me, that's all."

He still seemed doubtful, but finally he gave a reluctant nod. "I'll help you inside."

"No." She tried to pull her arm free, but he continued to propel her toward the door. "Look, I don't want my grandmother upset, okay? She's been worried enough about me since the accident, and the last thing she needs is any fresh reason to fear. Besides, she's already had her quota of crises today."

Tyler's face settled in a frown, but at least he stopped pulling her toward the door. "That's dirty pool, you know that?"

"I'll do whatever works where Grams is concerned. She may think she's still as tough as she always was, but that's not true."

After her accident and then Andrea's brush with death in the early summer, Grams had shown a fragility that had hit both of them hard. She was doing much better now—confident that the inn would succeed, happy about Andrea's wedding. Nothing must disrupt that.

Tyler urged her toward the step. "Sit down and get your breath back, at least. When I saw the power arc and you fly backward, I thought my heart would stop."

"Sorry about that." She managed a smile as she sank down on the low stone step. It was nice of him to be so concerned about her. "I felt a bit scared myself, not that I had time to think about it. Is it my imagination, or did you tell me to stop just before I touched the hook?"

He nodded, putting one foot on the step and leaning his elbow on his knee as he bent toward her. "A second too late. I caught a glimpse of bare wire where the sun glinted on it. Sorry I didn't see it sooner. And sorry you didn't think to check those lights before you plugged them in."

"I'll admit that wasn't the smartest thing I ever did, but I did look over them when I got the box out of the attic. At least—" She stopped, thinking about it.

"Well?"

She glared at him. "I think I checked them, but I was in a rush to get ready for last night's meeting." She'd shoved the box in the downstairs restroom when she'd realized how late it was. Maybe she had missed some of the strings.

Tyler, apparently feeling it wiser not to pursue the conversation, walked over to the stepladder and cautiously detached the string of lights. He frowned down at it for a moment before carrying it back to her.

"There's the culprit." He held the strand between his hands. Green plastic coating had melted away from a foot-long stretch of cord, and the wire between was blackened and mangled, shreds of metal twisting up like frizzled hair. The acrid smell of it turned her stomach.

"Guess I won't be using that string of lights anytime soon." It took an effort to speak lightly.

"Or ever." He was still frowning, the cord stretched taut between his hands. "That's a lot of bare wire."

She shrugged, trying to push away the creeping sensation on the back of her neck. "All's well that ends well. I'm relatively unscathed, and I'd better get back to work."

"Sit still." He softened the command with a half smile. "Sorry, but you look washed out."

"Gee, thanks."

Now he grinned, his face relaxing. "Just let me see if this blew a fuse before you do anything else."

She hadn't even thought of that, so she leaned back against the step, watching him test the heavy-duty extension cord on a fresh strip of lights.

"Looks okay. Actually that's surprising. Usually the wiring in these old places isn't in great shape."

"You should see the maze of wires in the cellar. It's an electrician's nightmare, but it all seems to work.

We did have to have the wiring checked out before we could open the inn, of course."

He gazed up at the house. "It's early eighteenth century, isn't it?"

"I guess an architect would know. The oldest part dates to 1725, according to the records."

"It's been in your family ever since?"

"Pretty much. My maternal grandfather's family, the Ungers, that is."

He was probably making conversation to distract her from the fact that he was going over each strand of lights in the box, checking all of them methodically with eyes and hands.

Well, she wouldn't object to that. She was happy enough just to sit here, feeling the sun's warmth chase the winter chill away.

"Satisfied?" she asked when he'd put gone through every one.

"They're in better shape than I expected." He frowned a little. "You'd think if one was that bad, some of the others would show similar signs."

"Maybe a squirrel tried to make a meal of it, didn't like the taste, and left the rest alone."

"Could be." He picked up a strand of lights and mounted the stepladder.

"What are you doing?" She stood, fighting a wave of dizziness at the sudden movement. "I'll take care of that."

"I've got it."

She'd keep arguing, but he really was getting the job accomplished more easily than she could, given his height. She watched, liking the neat efficiency of his movements, the capability of his strong hands. She was used to doing for herself, and in the months of running the inn she'd learned how to do all kinds of things she'd never dreamed of before, but it was nice to have some help.

She couldn't rely on him. Not Tyler, of all people, given what brought him here. That galvanized her, and she went quickly to the stepladder.

"I'm sure you have work of your own to do." Such as investigating his grandfather's death.

"This is the least I can do, since your grandmother offered your cooperation in dealing with my problem."

"That's not exactly what she said."

He smiled faintly but continued to thread the cord through the hooks.

And if she did help him, what then? She was as convinced as Grams that Grandfather hadn't done anything wrong.

She watched Tyler, frowning a little, trying to pinpoint the cause of her uneasiness. No matter how irrational it was, she couldn't help feeling that Tyler's determination to look into his grandfather's death was similar to poking a stick into a hornet's nest.

Rachel searched through the changes she was attempting to make to the inn's website. Did she have everything right? Andrea could probably have done this in half an hour, but she'd been working for what seemed like hours.

She glanced at the ornate German mantel clock that stood on one side of her grandfather's portrait above the fireplace. Nearly ten. It *had* been hours. Grams had gone up to bed some time ago, but Barney still dozed on the hearth rug, keeping her company.

She smiled at the sheltie, and he lifted his head and looked at her as if he'd sensed her movement. "Just a little longer, Barney. I'm almost finished."

He put his head back on his front paws, as if he'd understood every word.

Tyler had gone out earlier and hadn't come back yet. She certainly wouldn't wait up for him, although she'd had difficulty all summer going to bed when guests were still out. He had a key—he'd let himself in.

Thinking about that opened the door to thoughts of him, just when she'd succeeded in submerging her concerns about Tyler in her more prosaic worries.

If she could stay angry with him, dealing with the situation might be easier. Unfortunately, each time he had her thoroughly riled, he managed to show her some side of himself that roused her sympathy.

Tyler was determined to give this quest his best effort, and she'd guess he brought that same single-minded attention to every project he undertook. That would be an asset in his profession, but at the moment she wished he were more easily distracted.

He'd had a difficult relationship with his mother—that much was clear. She sympathized, given her own mother, who was as careless with people as she was with things. She'd always had the sense that her mother could have left her behind on one of their frequent moves and not even noticed she was gone. Not that Andrea would have let that happen.

She rubbed her temples, trying to ease away the tightness there.

I'm spinning in circles, Lord, and I don't know how to stop. Please help me see Tyler through Your eyes and understand how to deal with him in the way You want.

Even as she finished the prayer, she heard the sound of the door opening and closing, followed by Tyler's step in the hallway. She paused, fingers on the keyboard, listening for him to go up the stairs.

Instead he swung the library door a bit farther open and looked around it. "Still working? I didn't realize bed-and-breakfast proprietors kept such late hours."

"It's pretty much a twenty-four-hour-a-day job, but at the moment I'm just trying to finish up some changes to the webpage. Not my strong suit, I'm afraid."

"Mind if I have a look?" He hesitated, seeming to wait for an invitation.

"Please. I think I have it right, but I'm almost afraid to try and upload it."

He smiled, putting one hand on the back of her chair and leaning over to stare at the screen.

"Never let the computer know you're afraid of it. That's when it will do something totally unexpected."

"Just about anything to do with it is unexpected as far as I'm concerned. I'd still be keeping reservations in a handwritten log if Andrea hadn't intervened."

"Andrea. That's the older sister, right?" He reached around her to touch the keyboard, correcting a typo she hadn't noticed.

"Two years older." She tried not to think about how close he was. "She and her new husband are on their honeymoon. Somehow I don't think I can call and ask her computer questions at the moment."

"Probably wouldn't be diplomatic," he agreed. "As far as I can see, this looks ready. All you have to do is upload."

She hesitated, cursor poised. "That's it?"

"Just click." He smiled down at her, giving her a

slightly inverted view of his face, exposing a tiny scar on his square chin that she hadn't noticed before.

And shouldn't be noticing now. She was entirely too aware of him for her own peace of mind.

She forced her attention back to the computer and pressed the button, starting the upload. "I can see you're a fixer, just like my big sister. She's always willing to take over and do something for the inept."

As soon as the words were out of her mouth, she heard how they sounded and was embarrassed. She thought she'd gotten over the feeling that she would never measure up to Andrea. And if she hadn't, she certainly didn't want to sound insecure to Tyler.

"There's nothing wrong with admitting you don't know how to do something. I couldn't make a quiche if someone offered me a million bucks."

"It's nice of you to put it that way." She leaned back, looking with faint surprise at the updated website. "It actually worked."

"You sound impressed. The program you're using is pretty much 'what you see is what you get.'"

"I seem to remember Andrea saying that. She actually told me how to do it, but my brain doesn't retain things like that."

Tyler's smile flickered. "Maybe you should write it up as if it's a recipe."

"Just might work." She smiled up at him, relaxing now that the work was done. For a moment time seemed to halt. She was lost in the deep blue of his eyes, the room so quiet she could hear his breathing.

She drew in a strangled breath of her own and broke the eye contact, grateful he couldn't know how her pulse was pounding.

That was unexpected. Or was it? Hadn't the attraction been there, underlying the tension, each time they were together?

Tyler cleared his throat. "You know, you could hire someone to run the website for you." He seemed to be talking at random, as much at a loss as she was.

Oddly enough, that helped her regain her poise. "Can't afford it," she said bluntly. "We're operating on a shoestring as it is, and it's getting a bit frayed at the moment."

He blinked. "I didn't realize. I mean—" His gesture took in the room, but she understood that he meant the house and grounds, too. "People who live in places like this often don't have to count their pennies."

"That's why it's a bed-and-breakfast." She wasn't usually so forthcoming, but it wasn't anything that everyone in the township didn't already know. And probably would be happy to gossip about. "If Grams is going to keep the place, this seems her only option. Luckily, she's a born hostess, and she's enjoying it. Otherwise, she'd have to sell."

"She doesn't want to do that, so you feel you have to help her."

"Not exactly. I mean, I love it, too." Was it possible he'd understand her feelings? "But even if I didn't, Grams was always there for us when our parents weren't. I owe her."

"I take it your folks had a rocky marriage."

"You could say that. My father left more times than I can count, until finally he just didn't come back."

"That's when you lived with your grandparents?"

She nodded. "They were our rock. Now it's our turn.

I'll do whatever is necessary to make this work for Grams."

His face seemed to become guarded, although his voice, when he spoke, was light. "Even if it means learning how to do the website."

"Only until Andrea comes back." She frowned, thinking of yet another chore. "I guess I really should put some Christmas photos up, too. She and Cal won't be home in time to do that."

"If you get stuck, just give me a shout." He turned away, his expression still somehow distant.

Some barrier had gone up between them, and she wasn't sure why. Because of her determination to take care of her grandmother, and he equated that with interference in what he planned? If so, he was right.

He paused at the door, glancing back at her. "Good night, Rachel. Don't work too hard."

"Thanks again for the help."

He vanished behind the partially open door, and she heard his steady footsteps mounting the stairs.

If she let herself start thinking about Tyler's situation, she'd never sleep tonight. "Come on, Barney." She clicked her fingers at the dog. "Let's go to bed. We'll worry about it tomorrow."

It was unusual to be unable to concentrate on work. Tyler had always prided himself on his ability to shut out everything in order to focus on the job at hand, but not this time.

He closed the computer file and shut down his laptop. No, not this time. Before he came to Churchville, he'd thought the task he'd set himself, although probably impossible, was at least fairly straightforward.

Find out what he could about his grandfather's death, deal with the property, go back to his normal life with his conscience intact.

He hadn't counted on the human element. Everyone he'd met since he arrived seemed to have a stake in his actions—or at least an opinion as to his choices.

Restless, he moved to the window that overlooked the street, folding back the shutters, and leaned on the deep windowsill. The innkeeper, the antique dealer, the doctor's wife—it sounded like a ridiculous version of doctor, lawyer, Indian chief.

He glanced down the road in the direction of the antique shop, but there was nothing to be seen. Churchville slept. Not even a car went by to disturb the night. He'd heard of places so small they rolled up the sidewalks at night. Churchville was apparently one of them.

Presumably Rachel and her grandmother were asleep as well, off in the other wing of the building.

He couldn't help wondering how she'd adjusted from the pressure-cooker atmosphere of a trendy restaurant kitchen to the grueling work but slower pace of running a B&B in the Pennsylvania Dutch countryside. Still, she'd shown him how dedicated she was.

Dedicated to her family, most of all. And yet, from what she'd said, her relationship with her father had been as strained as his with his mother. Maybe that made her other relatives more precious to her.

At least he'd eventually grown up enough to pity his mother for resorting to emotional blackmail with the people she loved. He'd learned to look at her demands in a more objective way. But now he was back in the same trap, trying to fulfill her impossible dying request. No, not request. Demand.

Looked at rationally, the proposal was ridiculous. He'd known that from the start, even colored as the moment had been by shock and grief.

Still, he'd had to deal with the property, and he'd told himself he'd find out what he could about the circumstances of his grandfather's death and then close the book on the whole sad story.

Now that he was here, he realized how much more difficult the situation was than he'd dreamed. Rachel's grandmother's integrity was obvious, and he couldn't imagine her covering up a crime, any more than he could imagine the personality that dominated the portrait over the mantel committing one.

This was a wild-goose chase. A sad one, but nothing more. Moreover, it could hurt innocent people, if Rachel's opinion was true, and he saw no reason to doubt that.

He closed the shutters again, feeling as if he were closing his mind to the whole uncomfortable business. He'd make a few inquiries, maybe talk to the local police and check the newspaper files. And at the end of it he'd be no wiser than he was now.

The shutters still stood open on the window that looked out the side of the house, so he went to close them. And stopped, hand arrested on the louvered wood.

Where was that light coming from?

Below him was the gravel sweep of the drive, well-lit by the security lighting, his car a dark bulk. There was the garage, beyond it the lane that led onto Crossings Road.

The pale ribbon of road dipped down into the trees. From ground level, he wouldn't have seen any farther, but from this height the shallow bowl of the valley stretched out. As his eyes grew accustomed to the dimness, he could make out the paler patches of fields, darker shadows of woods. That had to be the farmhouse—there was nothing else down on that stretch of road.

A faint light flickered, was gone, reappeared again. Not at ground level. Someone was in the house, moving around the second floor with a flashlight.

He spun, grabbing his car keys, and rushed into the hall. He pounded down the stairs, relieved there were no other guests to be disturbed by him.

In the downstairs hall he paused briefly. He should call the police before heading out, should tell Rachel what was going on before she heard him and thought someone was breaking in.

He tried the library door, found it unlocked, and hurried through to the separate staircase that must lead to the family bedrooms. If she was still awake—

A light shone down from an upstairs hall.

"Rachel?"

Soft footsteps, and she appeared at the top of the stairs, clutching a cell phone in one hand. At least she was still dressed, so he hadn't gotten her out of bed.

"What's wrong?" Her eyes were wide with apprehension.

"Someone's in my grandfather's house. I could see the light from my window."

She didn't try to argue about it, but hurried down the steps, dialing the phone as she did. "I'll call the police."

"Good. I'm going down there."

She grabbed his arm. "Wait. You don't know what you might be rushing into."

"That's what I'm going to find out." He shook off her hand. "Just tell the cops I'm there, so they don't think I'm the burglar."

He strode toward the back door, hearing her speaking, presumably to the 911 operator, as he let the door close behind him.

He jogged toward the car, a chill wind speeding his steps. This could be nothing more than some teenage vandals.

And if it was someone else?

Well then, he'd know he'd been wrong. He'd know there was something to investigate after all.

He took off down the lane, gravel spurting under his tires. A clump of bushes came rushing at him as the lane turned, and he forced himself to ease off the gas. Wouldn't do any good for him to smash into a tree.

Rachel's accident slid into his mind, displacing his concentration on the prowler. An image of her, standing in the road, whirling, face white, to stare in horror at the oncoming car—

He shook his head, taking a firm control on both thoughts and reactions. Get to the farm in one piece. Find out what was happening. Hope the cops got there in time to back him up.

The car rounded the final bend, and the dilapidated gateposts came into view. He stepped on the brake, took the turn cautiously and then snapped off his headlights. He couldn't have done it earlier, not without smashing up, but he could probably get up the lane without lights. He didn't want to alert the prowlers to his presence too soon. They could hear the motor, of course, but they might attribute that to a car going past on the lane. Headlights glaring at them would be a dead giveaway.

If they were still there. He frowned, squinting in the dim light of a waning moon. He could make out the rectangular bulk of the house, gray in the faint light, and the darker bulk behind it that was the barn. No sign of a vehicle—no glimmer of metal to give it away. It looked as if he was too late.

He drew to a stop next to the porch, cut the motor, opened the door and listened. No sound broke the night silence, not even a bird. He got out, moving cautiously, alert for any sign of the intruder.

Still nothing. He walked toward the steps. Stupid, to have come without a decent torch. He had only the small penlight on his keychain to show him the broken stair. He stepped over it, mounting the porch, the wooden planks creaking beneath his feet.

He focused the thin stream of light on the door, senses alert. It seemed to be as securely closed as it had been on his first visit. A flick of the light showed him boards secure over the windows.

The urgency that had driven him this far ebbed, leaving him feeling cold and maybe a little foolish. Could the light he'd seen have been some sort of reflection? He wouldn't think so.

Well, assuming someone had been here, they were gone now. Maybe he could at least figure out how they'd gotten in.

He bent, aiming the feeble light at the lock. Had those scratches—

A board creaked behind him. Muscles tightening, he started to swing around. A shadowy glimpse of a dark figure, an upraised arm, and then something crashed into his head and the floor came up to meet him.

Chapter Five

Given the small size of the township police force, Rachel knew her call would go straight through to whoever was on duty. Thankfulness swept her at the sound of Chief Burkhalter's competent voice.

It took only seconds to explain, but even so she was aware of how quickly Tyler would reach the farm. And put himself in danger.

"My guest, Tyler Dunn, the one who saw the lights—"

"Owns the farm. Right, I know."

Of course he would. Zachary Burkhalter made it his business to know what went on in the township.

"He's gone down there. Don't—"

"I'm not going to shoot him, Ms. Hampton, but he's an idiot. I'll be there in a few minutes."

And she could hear the wail of the siren now, through the air as well as the telephone. She could also hear Grams coming out of her bedroom.

"I could go down—" Rachel began, with some incoherent thought of identifying Tyler to the chief.

"No." The snapped word left no doubt in her mind. "I'll call you back on this line when we've cleared the place. Then you can come pick up your straying guest, but not until then."

She had no choice but to disconnect. The change in tone of the siren's wail as it turned down Crossings Road was reassuring. They'd be there soon. Tyler would be all right.

Grams reached her. "What is it, Rachel? What's happening?"

Rachel put her arm around Grams, as much for her comfort as her grandmother's. "Tyler saw a light moving around in the farmhouse. He insisted on going down there by himself, but the police are on their way."

Grams shook her head. "Foolish, but I suppose he wouldn't be one to sit back when there's trouble."

No, he probably wouldn't. It didn't take a long acquaintance with Tyler to know that much about him.

"I still wish he hadn't. If he runs right into whoever's there—"

"I'm sure he'll be sensible about it." Grams's voice was matter-of-fact. "The police are probably there by now."

She'd thought she'd have to comfort her grandmother, but it seemed to be working the other way around. Grams patted her shoulder.

"I'll start some hot chocolate. He'll be chilled to the bone, I shouldn't wonder, running out on a cold night like this."

She followed Grams to the kitchen, phone still in her hand, watching as her grandmother paused for a moment, head bowed.

Dear Lord, I should be turning to You, too, instead of letting worry eat at me. Please, be with Tyler and protect him from harm.

Even as she finished the prayer, the telephone rang. Exchanging glances with Grams, she answered.

"You can come on down here now, if you want." The chief sounded exasperated, which probably meant they hadn't been in time to catch anyone. "Maybe help Mr. Dunn figure out what's missing."

Questions hovered on her tongue, but better to wait until she saw what was going on. "I'll be right there."

It took a moment to reassure Grams that she'd be perfectly safe, another to grab her jacket and shove Barney back from the door, and she ran out and slid into the car, shivering a little.

She shot out the drive and turned onto Crossings Road with only a slight qualm as she passed the place where she'd been hit.

Why? The question beat in her brain as she drove down the road as quickly as the rough surface would allow. If someone was in the house, why? More specifically, why now? It had stood empty all these years and been broken into more than once. Why would someone break in now, when surely most people knew that the new owner was here?

Lots of questions. No answers.

She turned into the rutted lane that led to the farmhouse, slowing of necessity. The police car, its roof light still rotating, sat next to Tyler's car. Its headlights showed her Chief Burkhalter's tall figure, standing next to the porch.

Tyler sat on the edge of the porch, head bent, one hand massaging the back of his neck.

She pulled to a stop and slid out, hurrying toward them. "Are you all right?"

"I'm fine." Tyler frowned at the chief. "There was no need for him to call you."

"There was every need." She hoped her tone was brisk enough to disguise the wobble in her tummy. "You're hurt. Let me see."

Ignoring his protests, she ran her hand through the thick hair, feeling the lump gingerly.

He winced. "Are you a nurse as well as a chef?"

"No, but I know enough to be sure you should have some ice on that."

"I offered to take him to the E.R. or call paramedics," the chief said. "He turned me down."

"I don't need a doctor. I've had harder knocks than that on the football field. And the ice can wait until we've finished here."

"Just go over it once more for me," Burkhalter said, apparently accepting him at his word. "You saw the lights from your window at the inn, you said."

Tyler started to nod, then seemed to think better of it. "The side window of my room looks out over Crossings Road. I can see the house—or at least, the upper floor of it. I spotted what looked like a flashlight moving around on the second floor."

"So you decided to investigate for yourself." Burkhalter sounded resigned, as if he'd taken Tyler's measure already.

"I figured I could get here faster than you could."

She wanted to tell Tyler how foolish that had been, but his aching head was probably doing that well enough. Besides, she had no standing—they were nothing more than acquaintances. The reminder gave her a sense of surprise. She'd begun to feel as if she'd known him for years.

"What did you see when you got here?"

"No vehicle, so I thought maybe they'd gone already. My mistake." Tyler grimaced. "I went to look at the front door, to see if it had been broken into, and while I was bending over, somebody hit me from behind."

"You didn't get a look, I suppose."

"Only at the floorboards." Tyler massaged the back of his neck again. "I heard the car come round the house then. They must have parked it in the back. The guy who slugged me jumped in, and off they went. I managed to turn my head at some point, but all I could see were red taillights disappearing down the lane."

"Vehicle was parked by the kitchen door." The patrolman who joined them gave Rachel a shy smile. "Looks like a big SUV, maybe, by the size of the tires. They broke in the back."

"I should have gone around the house first." Tyler sounded annoyed with himself. "I didn't think."

"Wait for us next time," the chief said. "Not that I expect there to be a next time. If these were the same thieves who have broken into other empty houses, they won't be careless enough to come back again, now that they know someone's watching."

"This has happened before?" Tyler's gaze sharpened. "What are they after?"

"Anything they find of value. Old-timers in country places often don't think much of banks, so sometimes it's been strong boxes broken open. Other times silver or antiques."

Burkhalter's lean face tightened. At a guess, he didn't like the fact that someone had been getting away with burglaries in his territory. Nobody blamed him, surely. The township was far-flung, the police force spread too thin.

"If there's nothing else Mr. Dunn can tell you, maybe he ought to get in out of the cold." She was shivering a little, whether from the cold or the tension, and Tyler had rushed out in just a shirt and sweater.

"If you wouldn't mind taking a look around inside first, I'd appreciate it. See if anything's missing."

Tyler stood, holding on to the porch post for a moment. "Ms. Hampton and I were here yesterday, but we didn't go upstairs. And Phillip Longstreet stopped while we were here, wanting to have a look around. I told him I'd let him know if I decided to sell anything."

Phillip wouldn't be delighted to have his name brought up in the middle of a police investigation. Still, there was no reason for Tyler to hold the information back.

The chief's expression didn't betray whether that interested him or not. He ushered them inside and swung his light around, letting them see the contents of the living room.

In the daylight the place had looked bad enough. In the cold and dark it was desolate, but as far as she could tell, nothing had been moved.

"I think this is pretty much the way it was. Tyler?"

He seemed tenser inside the house than he had sitting on the porch. He gave a short nod. "I don't think they were in this room."

They walked through the dining room, then into the kitchen. Everything seemed untouched, other than the fact that the kitchen door had been broken in.

The chief's strong flashlight beam touched the stairway that opened into the kitchen. "Let's have a look upstairs."

"I haven't been up there yet," Tyler warned. "I can't say I know everything that should be there."

"Anything you remember could help." The chief was polite but determined.

Tyler nodded and started up the stairs. She couldn't assist in the least, since she'd never been in that part of the house, but she didn't like the idea of staying downstairs alone. She followed them, watching her footing on the creaking stairs.

The flight of steps led into a small, square hallway with bedrooms leading off it. Tyler stopped, gripping the railing. "There used to be a slant-top desk there, I remember."

"Not recently." The chief swung his flashlight over the thick layer of dust that lay, undisturbed, where Tyler indicated.

They peered into one bedroom after another. There was more furniture up here, sturdy country pieces, most of it, some probably of interest to collectors. Tyler really should have it properly valued.

The thieves had evidently started in the master bedroom, where the dresser drawers gaped open and empty. A small marble-topped stand had been pulled away from the faded wallpaper, and a basin and ewer set lay smashed on the floor.

Rachel bent, touching a piece gingerly. "Too bad they broke this. There's been quite a demand recently for sets of this vintage."

"Maybe they weren't educated thieves," Tyler said.

"Or they just don't know about china."

Tyler stepped carefully over the pieces. "Seems like

a stupid place for them to hit. Obviously there's no money or small valuables left. My impression is that the rooms used to be fairly crowded with furniture, but that's hardly going to let you trace anything."

"I don't suppose there's such a thing as an inventory," the chief asked.

"My grandfather's attorney did give me a list, but I don't know how complete it is." Tyler's smile flickered. "And given how little I know about Pennsylvania Dutch furniture, I doubt I could even figure out what's being described on the list."

"I can probably help you with that. Furnishing the inn made me something of an instant expert on the subject." She was faintly surprised to hear the offer coming out of her mouth. Didn't she already have enough to keep her busy?

"Sounds like a good idea," Chief Burkhalter said. "Let me have a copy of the list, and mark anything you and Ms. Hampton think has gone missing. At least that gives us a start."

His light illumined Tyler's face briefly. Was Tyler really that pale and strained, or was it just the effect of the glaring white light?

"You folks might as well get home." Burkhalter swung his torch to show them the way out. "We'll be a bit longer. Ms. Hampton, if you wouldn't mind taking Mr. Dunn, I'll have my officer drop his car off later. I don't think he should be driving."

"That's fine," she said, grabbing Tyler's arm before he could protest. "Let's go."

He must have been feeling fairly rocky, since he let her tug him down the stairs. When they reached the front porch, she took a deep breath of cold air. Even its bite was preferable to the stale, musty scent of decay inside.

No wonder Tyler disliked the place. His grandfather had been an unhappy, miserable man, by all accounts, and that unhappiness seemed to permeate the very walls of the house.

They stepped off the porch, and Tyler shivered a little when the wind hit him. He shoved his hands into his pockets. "So that's it. Minor-league housebreakers." He sounded— She wasn't sure what. Dissatisfied, maybe?

"I suppose so." She led the way to the car.

Maybe Tyler was thinking the same thing she was. Thieves, yes. That seemed logical.

But why now? That was the thing that bothered her the most. Why now?

"Are you sure you want to do this?" Tyler glanced at Rachel as they walked down Churchville's Main Street the next morning, headed for the antique shop.

She looked up at him, eyebrows lifting. "Why not? It'll be much easier for you to understand the look and value of the furniture on that list if you actually see some examples of Pennsylvania Dutch furniture. And the inn's furnishings aren't really the plain country pieces your grandfather had, for the most part. I have to pick up the final draft of the house tour brochure from Phillip, anyway."

"You're forgetting that I gave Phil Longstreet's name to the police last night. If they've come to call, he may not appreciate the sight of me."

"I'm sure Phil realizes that after the break-in, you had to mention anyone who'd been there. You certainly didn't accuse him of anything."

But he thought he read a certain reservation in her green eyes. She needed the goodwill of her fellow business people in the village. He'd been so focused on getting what he wanted that he hadn't considered how her efforts to help him might rebound against her.

"I don't want you to get involved in my troubles if it's going to make things sticky for you with people like Longstreet. And I sure don't want you involved if it means putting you at any risk."

They were on the opposite side of the road from the inn, because Rachel had wanted to take a digital photo of the inn's exterior decorations. He paused, turning to face her and leaning against the low stone wall that surrounded the church and cemetery.

"Because of what happened last night?" A frown puckered her smooth forehead. "But that was just—" She paused, shook her head. "I was going to say an accident, but it certainly wasn't that. Still, anyone who goes charging into a deserted house at night to investigate a prowler—"

"Deserves a lump on the head?" He touched the tender spot and smiled wryly. "You may have a point there. I just can't help but wonder if last night's episode had anything to do with my reason for being here."

She leaned against the wall next to him, her green corduroy jacket bright against the cream stone. Two cars went by before she spoke.

"Why now, that's what you mean. After all this time of sitting empty, why would someone choose to burglarize the place just when you've returned? I've been wondering about that myself."

She had a sharp mind behind that sensitive, heart-shaped face.

"Right. Assuming it had something to do with my return, or my reason for being here—"

She shook her head decisively. "Not that, surely. No one knows except Grams and me, and I assure you, neither of us goes in for late-night prowling. Everyone else thinks you're here just to sell the property."

He found he wanted to speak the thought that had been hovering at the back of his mind. "If someone had guilty knowledge of my grandfather's death, my coming to dispose of the property might still be alarming." He planted his hands against the top of the wall. "If there's even a chance of that, I shouldn't involve you."

"First of all, I think the chance that last night's thieves were in any way related to your grandfather's death twenty-some years ago is infinitesimal. And second, I'm not offering to mount guard on the farm at midnight. Helping you identify the furniture hardly seems like a threatening activity, does it?"

"Not when you put it that way. You're determined to help, aren't you?"

She nodded, but her mouth seemed to tighten. "Andrea is the superstar. Caro is the dreamer. I'm the one who helps."

"I didn't mean that negatively," he said mildly. "It's a quality I admire."

Her face relaxed in a genuine smile. "Then you're an unusual man." She pushed herself away from the wall. "Come on, let's put my helpfulness to use and check out some Pennsylvania Dutch antiques."

"Rachel?"

She glanced back at the query in his tone.

"Thanks. For the help."

"Anytime."

She started briskly down the street. He caught up with her in a few strides, and they walked in a companionable silence for a few minutes. Rachel was obviously taking note of the decorations on the shops, and twice she stopped to take photos.

"They've done a good job of making the place look like an old-fashioned Christmas," he commented. "I like the streetlights."

Churchville's Main Street had gas streetlamps that reminded him of the illustration for a Dickens novel. Each one had been surrounded with a wreath of live greens and holly, tied with a burgundy ribbon.

"You're just lucky you weren't here for the arguments when we made that decision," she said. "I thought Sandra Whitmoyer and Phillip Longstreet would come to blows."

"I couldn't imagine people would get so excited about it."

She raised her eyebrows. "You mentioned that you sometimes design churches. Don't you get into some passionate debates on that subject?"

He thought of one committee that had nearly canceled the entire project because they couldn't agree on the shape of the education wing. "You have a point there. People do feel passionate about things that affect their church or their home. I suppose the same applies when you're talking about a village the size of Churchville. They all feel they have a stake in the outcome."

She nodded. "It surprised me a little, when I came back after spending a lot of time in an urban setting. At first it bothered me that everyone seemed to know everyone else's business, but then I realized it's not just about wanting to know. It's about caring."

He was unaccountably touched. "That's a nice tribute to your community."

"I like belonging."

The words were said quietly, but there was a depth of feeling behind them that startled him. He would like to pursue it, but they'd come to a stop in front of Longstreet's Antiques, and Rachel's focus had obviously shifted to the job at hand.

"Don't show too much interest in any one thing," she warned as he opened the door, setting a bell jingling. "Unless you want to walk out the door with it."

He nodded, amused that she thought the warning necessary, and followed her into the shop.

Chapter Six

Longstreet's Antiques always looked so crowded that Rachel thought Phil must use a shoehorn to fit everything in. When she'd said that to him, he'd laughed and told her that was one of the secrets of his business. When people saw the overwhelming display, they became convinced that they were going to find a hidden treasure and walk away with it for a pittance.

Even though she knew the motive behind it, the place exerted exactly that sort of appeal over her. She'd like to start burrowing through that box of odds and ends, just to see what was there. But she doubted that anyone ever got the better of Phil Longstreet on a deal. He was far too shrewd for that.

Thinking about bargains was certainly safer than letting her thoughts stray toward Tyler. She watched as he squatted beside a wooden box filled with old tools, face intent as he sifted through them. They'd gone so quickly to a level where she felt as if she'd known him for years instead of days.

But there was nothing normal about their friendship, if you could call it that. He'd come here for a purpose that involved her family, and she couldn't forget that. If anything he learned threatened her people—

He glanced up, catching her gaze, and smiled. A wave of warmth went through her. Maybe just for the moment she could shove other issues to the back of her mind and enjoy being with him.

"I'm ready for my lesson whenever you are, teacher." He stood, taking a step toward her.

Pennsylvania Dutch furniture, she reminded herself.

"Well, here's a good example of what's called a Dutch bench, which was on your list." She pointed to the black wooden bench with its decorative painting of hearts and tulips. "It's basically a love-seat-size bench with a back. It's a nice piece to use in a hallway."

He nodded, touching the smooth lacquer of the arm. "Now that I see it, I remember one like this. It was in the back hall. My grandfather used to sit there to pull his boots on before he went to the barn."

"It's not there now. I'd have noticed it when we were in the kitchen."

"No." He frowned. "Of course, it could have gone anytime in the past twenty years, and I wouldn't know the difference."

"A lot of small things might have disappeared without being noticed, even if the attorney visited the place occasionally. You should check on the dishes. According to the inventory, your grandfather had a set of spatterware."

His eyebrows lifted. "And I would recognize spatterware how?"

She glanced around, found a shelf filled with china, and lifted a plate down. "This is it. Fairly heavy, brightly painted tableware. Very typical of Pennsylvania Dutch ware."

Tyler bent over the plate, his hand brushing hers as he touched it. "So I'm looking for gaudy plates with chickens on them."

Laughter bubbled up. "I'll have you know that's not a chicken, it's a peafowl."

"I doubt any real bird would agree with that."

The amusement that filled his eyes sent another ripple of warmth through her. For a moment she didn't want to move. She just wanted to stand there with their hands touching and their gazes locked. His deep-blue eyes seemed to darken, and his fingers moved on hers.

She took a step back, her breathing uneven. It was some consolation that the breath he took was a bit ragged, as well.

"I... I should see where Phil has gotten to. Usually he comes right out when the bell rings." She walked quickly to the office door, gave a cursory knock and opened it. "Phil, are you in here?"

A quick glance told her he wasn't, but the door that led to the alley stood open, letting in a stream of cold air. She crossed to the door, hearing Tyler's footsteps behind her.

"Phil?"

A panel truck sat at the shop door, and two men were loading a piece of furniture, carefully padded with quilted covers. Phil stood by, apparently to be sure they did it right. He looked toward her at the sound of her voice.

"Rachel, hello. I didn't hear you. And Mr. Dunn."

"Tyler, please." He was so close behind her that

his breath stirred her hair when he spoke. And she shouldn't be so aware of that.

"I wanted to let you know we're here. I can see you're busy, so we'll look around." She glanced at the man lifting the furniture into the van, but his head was turned away as he concentrated on his work. Youngish, long hair—not anyone she recognized.

"Fine." Phil made shooing motions with his hands. "Go back in where it's warm. I'll be with you in a few minutes."

"Okay." Shivering a little, she hurried back to the showroom, relieved when Tyler closed the office door on the draft. "It's good that he's occupied. We can look at a few more things without listening to a sales pitch." She took the inventory from Tyler's hand. "Let's see what we can find."

By concentrating firmly on furniture, she filled the next few minutes with talk of dower chests, linen presses and pie cupboards, because if she didn't, she'd be too aware of the fact that Tyler stood next to her, looking at her as often as at the pieces of furniture she pointed out.

Finally the office door opened and Phil came in, rubbing his hands together briskly. "There, all finished at last. That lot is headed to a dealer in Pittsburgh."

"Do you have some new help?" she asked.

Phil shook his head. "Just a couple of guys I use sometimes for deliveries. Now, what can I show you today?"

"How about showing me the brochure for the Christmas House Tour?"

"Now, Rachel, didn't I tell you I'd bring it over?"

"You did. You also said I'd have it yesterday."

She was vaguely aware of Tyler taking the inventory from her and sliding it into his pocket. Well, fair enough. She could understand his not wanting to share that information with anyone.

Phil threw his hands up in an exaggerated gesture. "Mea culpa. You're right, you're right, it's not finished yet."

"Phil, that's not fair." She didn't mind letting the exasperation show in her voice. This house tour had turned into a much bigger headache than she'd imagined. "You know that has to go to the printer, and the tour is coming up fast."

He stepped closer, reaching out as if he'd put his hand on her shoulder and then seeming to think better of it. "Forgive me, please? I know I promised, but you wouldn't believe how busy the shop has been lately."

"I'm happy for you. But the house tour is designed to help everyone's business, remember?"

"I'll finish it tonight and bring it to the inn first thing tomorrow morning. I promise. Forgive me?" He made a crossing-his-heart gesture, giving her the winsome smile that had persuaded too many elderly ladies to pay more than they'd intended.

She was immune. "Only if you don't let me down. Tomorrow. By nine, so I can proof it and get it to the printer."

He sighed. "You're a hard woman. I'll do it, I promise. Now, did you come to buy or sell?" He looked expectantly at Tyler.

"Neither, I'm afraid. I just walked down with Rachel so I could have a look at your shop." Tyler smiled pleasantly. "Very impressive collection."

"Thank you, thank you. I'm always looking, you

know. Any chance I might see what you have at the farmhouse soon?"

The police must not have been around. Surely he'd mention the break-in if he knew about it. She was relieved. Knowing Phil, an encounter with the police would probably throw him off his game so much that he'd be another week getting around to the brochure.

"I'll let you know." Tyler took a step toward the door.

"I'd be happy to do a free appraisal. Anytime." Phil retreated toward the counter. "I'll get right on the brochure, Rachel. You're going to love it."

"I'm sure I will." Aside from his propensity to put things off, Phil had a genuine artistic gift. Once he actually produced the brochure, it would be worth the wait.

She pulled the door open and nearly walked into Jeff Whitmoyer. They each stepped back at the same time, surprising her into a smile. "Come in, please. We were just on our way out."

"Morning, Rachel." His gaze went past her. "You must be Tyler Dunn. I've been wanting to talk to you."

Apparently they weren't getting out so quickly, after all. "Tyler, I'd like to introduce Jeff Whitmoyer. Jeff, Tyler Dunn."

Reminded of his manners, Jeff stuck his hand out, and Tyler shook it.

It was hard to believe Jeff and Bradley Whitmoyer were brothers—she thought that each time she saw one of them. Bradley was a lean, finely drawn intellectual with a social conscience that kept him serving his patients in this small community in spite of other, some would say better, opportunities.

Jeff was big, buff, with a once-athletic frame now

bulging out of the flannel shirt and frayed denim jacket he wore—certainly not because he couldn't afford better. He might not be the brightest bulb in the pack, as she'd heard Phil comment, but he made a good living with his construction company and was probably a lot smarter than people gave him credit for.

"Well, shut the door if you're going to talk." Phil's tone was waspish. "I'm paying the heating bill, remember?"

Jeff slammed the door, making the bell jingle so hard it threatened to pop off its bracket. "Wouldn't want you to spend an extra buck." He focused on Tyler. "I'd like to talk to you about the property of yours. I hear you're going to sell."

Tyler seemed to withdraw slightly. "Where did you hear that?"

Jeff shrugged massive shoulders. "Around. Anyway, I've had my eye on that place. I have some plans to develop that land, so how about we sit down and talk?"

Tact certainly wasn't Jeff's strong suit, but she supposed he'd think it a waste of time where business was concerned.

"I haven't reached that point yet, but thanks for your interest." Tyler reached for the door.

"Don't wait too long. I'll find something else if your place isn't for sale."

"Will you?" Phil's voice was soft, but Rachel thought she detected a malicious gleam in his eyes. "Given the scarcity of prime building land, I wonder where."

"Call me anytime. I'm in the book. Whitmoyer Construction." Jeff shook off Phil's needling like a bull shaking off a fly. "Talk to you soon."

Rachel waited until the door had closed behind

them. Once they were well away from the shop, she spoke the thought in her mind. "You aren't seriously considering his offer, are you?"

"He didn't make an offer. But what's wrong with him? I thought those people were friends of yours."

"Nothing's wrong with him, except that I don't trust his taste. If he's talking about developing the land, he might have in mind a faux-Amish miniature golf course, for all I know."

His eyebrows lifted. "I should think a new attraction would draw more people. Isn't that what you want as a business owner?"

"Not something that turns the Amish into a freak show. Besides, our guests come to the inn for the peace and quiet of the countryside. How would you like your window to overlook a putting green or shooting range?"

"If and when I sell, I probably won't have much choice about what use the new owners make of the property. Any more than your neighbors could control your turning the mansion into a bed-and-breakfast."

He was being annoyingly rational, turning her argument against her in that way. She'd like to argue that at least her bed-and-breakfast, even if it benefited from its proximity to Amish farms, didn't make fun of them.

Maybe she shouldn't borrow trouble, but she couldn't help worrying how much Tyler's plans for the property were going to affect her future.

The strains of "Joy to the World" poured from the speakers of the CD player the next morning, filling the downstairs of the inn with anticipation. Rachel took a step back from the side table in the center hall to admire the arrangement of holly and evergreens she'd put in a pewter pitcher. The antique wooden horse toy next to it sported a red velvet bow around its neck.

"What do you think?" She turned to Grams and Emma, who were winding a string of greens on the newel post. "Should I add some bittersweet, too?"

"It looks perfect the way it is," Grams said. "I wouldn't change a thing."

Nodding, Rachel looked up at the molding along the ceiling, finding the eyehooks from which something could be hung. "Where's the Star of Bethlehem quilt? I'm ready to hang it now."

"The Star of Bethlehem quilt," Grams echoed. "I haven't seen it in ages."

Rachel blinked. "But we always hang it here. It's part of my earliest Christmas memories. We can't not have it." Absurd. She actually felt like bursting into tears.

Grams exchanged glances with Emma.

"I know chust where it is, *ja*," Emma said quickly. "I will get it."

How silly she was, to be that obsessed with recreating the Christmases of her childhood. "You don't have to. If you'd rather put something else here—"

"Of course not," Grams said quickly.

"Well, let *me* get it, at least."

But Emma was already halfway up the stairs, her sturdy, dark-clad figure moving steadily. "It makes no trouble." She disappeared around the bend in the stairs.

Grams smiled. "Don't worry about Emma. She enjoys the decorating as much as we do, even though it's not much of a tradition among the Amish."

"Not like you Moravians." Rachel smiled. "You're Christmas-decorating fanatics."

Grams's face went soft with reminiscence. "That's

what it is when you grow up in Bethlehem. Every aspect of Christmas has its own tradition."

Grams had brought those traditions with her when she married. The Moravian star, the peppernuts, the *putz,* an elaborate crèche beneath the Christmas tree—those were part of the lovely Christmas lore she'd passed on to her granddaughters.

All Rachel's memories of Christmas had to do with Grams and Grandfather, not her parents. Hardly surprising, she supposed. Her parents had been separated so much of the time, with her father always off pursuing some get-rich-quick scheme or another. And her mom—well, Lily Unger Hampton had used the holidays as an excuse for extended visits to friends in the city. It had been Grams and Grandfather who made up Christmas lists, baked cookies, filled stockings.

Then Daddy had left for good and Mom had fought with Grandfather and taken the girls away. And their childhood ended.

She smiled at her grandmother, heart full. "We should go over to Bethlehem some evening while the decorations are still up. You know you'd love it."

"If we have time," Grams said, avoiding an answer. "We still have a lot to do before Christmas. I hope this weekend's guests don't mind our decorating around them."

"I'm sure they'll want to pitch right in." She hoped. Two couples would be arriving tomorrow, and there was no possibility she'd have everything finished by then. So her idea was to turn necessity into opportunity and invite the guests to join in.

"I hope so. They might be more enthusiastic than Tyler is, anyway." Grams looked a little miffed. She had suggested that Tyler might want to help them today, but he'd left the house early.

"Tyler's not in Churchville to enjoy himself, is he?"

Grams must have read something in her tone, because she gave her an inquiring look. "You're worried about that young man. I've told you—there's nothing he can find about your grandfather that will hurt us."

"I'm not worried so much about that as about what he's going to do with the property. Jeff Whitmoyer approached him about buying it. Says he has plans to develop it."

"And you don't want that to happen?"

Rachel stared. "Grams, surely you don't want that either. He could put up something awful in full view of our upstairs windows. Fake Amish at its worst, if his other businesses are any indication."

"Oh, well, it won't bother us, and the Amish will ignore it as they do every other ridiculous thing that uses their name." Grams tweaked the ribbon on the newel post as Emma came down the stairs, the quilt folded over her arm.

Grams didn't seem too concerned, maybe because she didn't understand the possible effects. Their peaceful, pastoral setting was one of their biggest assets.

Emma unfurled the Star of Bethlehem quilt, and every other thought went right out of her mind. Here was the warmth of Christmas for her, stitched up in the handwork of some unknown ancestor.

Together she and Emma fastened the quilt to its dowel and climbed up to hang it in place. Once it was secure, she climbed back down and moved the step-stool away, then turned to look.

The star seemed to burst from the fabric, shouting

its message of good news. Warmth blossomed through her. It was just as she remembered. After all those years of trekking around the country with her mother, with Christmas forgotten more often than not, the years when she'd been on her own, working on the holiday out of necessity, she'd longed for Christmas here.

Now she finally had it, and she wouldn't let it slip away. She had come home for Christmas.

"Ah, that looks lovely. I don't know why we ever stopped putting it up." Grams smiled. "This will be a Christmas to remember. You here to stay, Cal and Andrea coming home soon—if we could get Caroline to come back, it would be perfect."

Rachel hugged her. "We'll make it perfect, even if Caro doesn't come."

Grams patted her shoulder. "It's just too bad Tyler doesn't have any sense of belonging here. I'm afraid his grandfather and mother took that away from him a long time ago."

As was so often the case when it came to people, Grams had it right. Thanks to a family quarrel, Tyler had been robbed of that. Small wonder he didn't care who bought the land.

"His grandfather was a bitter man." Emma entered the conversation, planting her hands on her hips. "Turned against God and his neighbors when his wife died, left the church as if we were all to blame."

Rachel blinked. We? "Are you saying John Hostetler, Tyler's grandfather, was Amish?"

"*Ja,* of course." Emma's eyes widened. "Until he came under the *meidung* for his actions. You mean you didn't know that?"

The *meidung*—the shunning. The ultimate act for

the Amish, to cut off the person completely unless and until the rebel repented. "How would I?" She turned to Grams. "You knew? But you didn't mention it to Tyler."

"Well, I just assumed he knew. Everyone in the area knew about it, of course. Do you mean he doesn't?"

She thought about their conversations and shook her head slowly. "I don't think so." Would it make a difference to him? To what he decided to do with the property?

She wasn't sure, but he should be told. And probably she was the one to tell him.

Chapter Seven

The office of the township police chief was tiny, with a detailed map of the township taking up most of one wall. Tyler sat in the sole visitor's chair, taking stock of his surroundings while he waited for Chief Burkhalter to return.

At a guess, the faded, framed photographs of past township events and the signed image of a former president were relics of the previous chief. He'd credit Zach Burkhalter with the up-to-date computer system and what seemed, looking at it upside down, to be a paperweight on the desk bearing the insignia of a military unit.

The door opened before he could follow the impulse to turn it around and take a closer look. Burkhalter came in, carrying a manila file folder and looking slightly apologetic.

"Sorry it took me so long to come up with this. My predecessor had his own method of filing that I still haven't quite figured out."

Tyler grasped the file, unable to suppress a sense of optimism. If there was anything to learn about his grandfather's death, surely it would be here, in the police report.

He opened it to a discouragingly small sheaf of papers. "It looks as if he also didn't care to keep very complete records."

Burkhalter sat down behind his desk. "Things were pretty quiet around here twenty years ago. I don't suppose he'd ever had occasion before to investigate a case of murder."

Tyler shot him a glance. Burkhalter's lean, weathered face didn't give anything away. He couldn't be much older than Tyler himself, but he had the look of a man who'd spent most of those years dealing with human frailty in all its forms.

"Murder? I was afraid you wouldn't see it that way, since the death certificate says it was a heart attack that actually killed him."

The chief's eyes narrowed. "Heart attack or not, he died in the course of a crime, so that makes it murder in the eyes of the law. Since no one was ever charged, we don't know what a jury would have thought."

"That bothers you?"

"I don't like the fact that it was never solved." He looked, in fact, as if the case would have been worked considerably more thoroughly had he been the man in charge then.

Tyler flipped through the papers, seeing little that he hadn't already known. Apparently the crime had been discovered the next morning when a neighboring farmer noticed that the cows weren't out in their usual field. His interest sharpened at the name of the farmer. Elias Zook. A relative of the current Zook family, probably. He'd have to ask Rachel.

"The state police were called in," Burkhalter said. "I'll get in touch, see if they've kept the files."

"I'd appreciate it." He frowned down at a handwritten sheet of notes. "Apparently there were indications that more than one person was involved."

The chief nodded. "Hardly surprising, if they intended to rob him. Since I talked with you, I've looked through the records for that year. There were a number of robberies reported, isolated farms, owners elderly folks who sometimes couldn't even be sure when things went missing. Sort of like what's been happening recently."

"There've been other incidents of break-ins, then?"

Burkhalter's gray eyes looked bleak. "Several. Always isolated farmhouses, usually when no one was home. They're slick enough not to overdo it—might be a couple in a month, and then nothing for several months." His hand, resting on the desktop, tightened into a fist. "I'd like to lay my hands on them. Surprising, in a way, that they'd strike your place after you'd come back."

"Yes." He frowned. "I can't help but wonder if it had anything to do with the earlier crime, although I guess that's not very likely."

"No." But he detected a spark of interest in the chief's eyes. "If they thought they'd left any hint to their identity, they've had twenty years to take care of it."

"You think it's a coincidence, then."

Burkhalter considered for a moment. "Let's say I think it's a coincidence. But that I don't like coincidences."

It would not be a good idea to get on this man's bad

side. Well, they both wanted the same thing, so that shouldn't be an issue.

He looked back down at the file. It contained a list of items that were presumed to have gone missing, the phrases so generic as to be useless. One side table. One rocking chair. He read a little farther. "There's mention here of a strong box that was found broken open and taken in for examination. No indication that it was ever returned to my mother. Any idea where that might be?"

Burkhalter held out his hand for the file, scanning it quickly. "If it didn't go back to the family, it's hard to tell. There are a few more files I can check. And the basement of this building is filled with all kinds of stuff that no one has ever properly documented. I'll have someone take a look around, but there's no guarantee we'll find it."

"I'd appreciate that." He rose. He'd been here long enough and found out very little. There wasn't much left to find after all this time. The sense of frustration was becoming familiar.

Burkhalter rose, too. "I'll let you know if we come up with anything. You're still at the inn?"

"Yes. I'm not leaving until I've disposed of the property. That's been left hanging for too long." Because his mother hadn't been able to forget how her father died, but she also hadn't known how to deal with it. Or hadn't wanted to.

"Folks will be glad to see that place taken care of." Burkhalter's eyes narrowed. "I just hope you're not planning to do any more police work on your own. If you know anything that might be helpful, even on a crime this old, you have a responsibility to divulge it."

Information? His mother's suspicions hardly fell

into that category, and revealing them could harm innocent people.

"There's nothing, I'm afraid."

He had a feeling that Chief Burkhalter didn't entirely buy that, but he seemed to accept it for the moment.

"You'll let me know if anything occurs to you." It was more of an order than a request. "I'll be in touch if I find any reference to that strong box."

Tyler shook hands, thanking him, but without any degree of confidence that the strong box, or anything else, would appear. Everywhere he turned, it seemed all he found was another dead end.

Rachel tugged at the blue spruce she was trying to maneuver through the front door. Even with gloves on, the sharp needles pricked her, and as wide as the doorway was, it didn't seem—

"Having a problem?"

She'd seen Tyler pull in and had hoped she'd have the tree inside before he felt he had to come to the rescue. With the knowledge of his grandfather's Amish roots fresh in her mind, she'd have liked a little more time to decide how to approach the subject.

She managed a smile. "Large doorway, larger tree. It didn't look this big in the field."

"They never do." He replied easily enough, but she had the sense that some concern lurked.

Where had he been? She'd love to ask, but that would be prying.

"I seem to be stuck for the moment." She eyed the tree, halfway through the door. "I'm afraid you'll have to go around to the side."

"We can do better than that." He brushed past her,

grasping the tree before she could caution him. "Ouch. You have one sharp Christmas tree."

She held up her hands, showing him the oversize gardening gloves she wore. "Blue spruce is my grandmother's favorite, and that's what I always remember being in the parlor when I was a child."

He paused in the act of pushing the tree through the door, turning to regard her gravely. "That's important to you, isn't it? Preserving the family traditions, that is."

Her throat tightened. If he knew a little more about her parents, he'd understand her longing to have the Christmas she remembered from her early childhood.

"I like family traditions." She could only hope she didn't sound defensive. "I just hope our guests will appreciate ours."

"It sounds as if you have plenty to choose from." With a final lift, he shoved the tree through into the entrance hall. Rachel followed quickly, closing the door against the chill air.

"True enough. Grams is of Moravian ancestry, and to them, celebrating Christmas properly is one of the most important parts of their heritage."

"What about the Amish?" He lifted the tree at the bottom, seeming to assume he'd help her put it up. "Don't they have a lot of Christmas customs?"

The casual way he asked the question affirmed her belief that he didn't know about his grandfather's background. The need to tell him warred with her natural caution. What if she told him, and that knowledge influenced his decisions about the property in a negative way?

She grasped the upper part of the trunk and nodded toward the parlor, where the tree stand was ready.

"The Amish, along with the other plain sects, don't do the type of decorating that the rest of the Pennsylvania Dutch do. Their celebration is focused on home and school. The children do a Christmas play that's a huge event for the Amish community."

He nodded, but again she had the sense that he was really thinking of something else.

"If I lift it into the stand, do you think you can steady it while I tighten the clamps?"

"You don't need to help, really." She shouldn't be relying on him, even for something as minor as this.

"I'm a better bet than enlisting your grandmother or the housekeeper." He hoisted the tree, lifting it into the stand.

"I'm sure you have other things to do." But she reached carefully through the branches to grasp the trunk where he indicated.

Tyler shed his jacket and got down on the floor, lying on his back to slide under the tree. The branches hid his face to some extent, and his voice sounded muffled.

"I've done all I can today, in any event. I had a talk with your police chief."

She wasn't sure how she felt about that, especially if he'd seen fit to tell Zach Burkhalter about his mother's suspicions.

"Was he helpful?" She hoped she sounded neutral.

She must not have succeeded, because Tyler slid out far enough to see her face.

"I didn't say anything about your family." He frowned. "He seems pretty shrewd. He probably knew I was holding something back."

"Yes, he is." Her thoughts flickered back to the problems they'd gone through in the spring. Burkhalter had suspected, correctly, that they'd been withholding information then. "Did he have anything you didn't already know?"

"He was open about sharing the files." Tyler's hands moved quickly, tightening the tree stand's clamps around the base of the spruce. It was a good thing. Her leg ached from the effort of holding the heavy tree upright.

"But…?"

"But apparently his predecessor wasn't very efficient. It looked to me as if he'd just gone through the motions of investigating."

"I'm sorry. I know how much that must frustrate you."

Tyler slid back out from under the tree, giving it a critical look. "Seems fairly straight to me. What do you think?"

She let go and stepped back. "Wonderful. Thank you so much." Her gaze met his. "Really, I'm sorry the chief wasn't able to help you."

He shrugged. "I didn't expect much, to be honest. If there'd been anything obvious, the case would have been resolved a long time ago."

"I suppose so." But she knew he wasn't as resigned as he'd like to appear. He struck her as a man who succeeded at things that were important to him, and fulfilling a promise to his dying mother must be one of those.

The fact that his grandfather had been Amish didn't seem to relate at all, but how could she judge what might be important to him? She had to tell him, and now was as good a time as any.

She took a breath, inhaling the fresh aroma of the tree that already seemed to fill every corner of the room. "There is something that Grams mentioned to me. Something I think you ought to know, if you don't already."

He shot her a steely look, and she shook her head in response.

"I don't think it can have anything to do with his death. But did you know that your grandfather had been Amish?"

His blank stare answered that. "Amish? No. Are you sure? I don't remember seeing any Amish people at the funeral, and I'd have noticed something like that at that age."

"He'd left the church by then." She suspected he wouldn't be content with that.

"Left the church? You mean they shunned him?" His voice showed distaste. "They wouldn't even come to his funeral?"

She was probably doing this all wrong. "From what Grams said, the choice was his, not theirs. Please don't think the Amish—"

"I don't think anything about them, one way or the other. Why should it matter to me? It's not as if my grandfather ever wanted a relationship with me. I'm doing this for my mother."

How much of his mother's personality had been determined by that bitter old man? Instinct told her Tyler needed to deal with those feelings, but she felt unable to reach him without crossing some barrier that would turn them into more than casual acquaintances.

"Families can be wonderful, but they can be hurtful, too." Like Daddy, leaving them without a goodbye. Or Mom, taking them away from the only security they'd ever known.

His hand came out and caught hers, holding it in a firm, warm grasp. "I guess you know something about it, don't you?"

"A bit. For me, my grandparents were the saving grace. I don't know who I'd be without them."

"My dad was the rock in our family. Anything I know about how to be a decent Christian man, I learned from him."

"You still miss him," she said softly, warmed by the grasp of his hand and the sense that he was willing to confide in her.

They had crossed that barrier, and it was a little scary on the other side.

He nodded. "He died when I was in my last year of high school, but I measure every decision against what I think he'd expect of me."

"If he knows, he must be glad that he had such an influence on your life."

"I hope he does." His voice had gone a little husky. He cleared his throat, probably embarrassed at showing so much emotion.

"You know," she said tentatively, "maybe knowing a little more about why your grandfather was the way he was would help you understand your mother, as well." She gave a rueful smile. "Believe me, if I could figure out what made my parents tick, I'd jump at the chance."

He seemed to become aware that he was still holding her hand, and he let go slowly. "I'll think about it. But there is something else you can do for me."

"Of course. What?"

"Your grandmother said you'd let me see your grandfather's ledgers. I'd appreciate that."

She felt as if someone had dropped an ice cube down her back. It took a moment to find her voice.

"Of course. I'll get them out for you." She turned away. She'd been wrong. They hadn't moved to a new relationship after all. Tyler still suspected her grandfather, and to him she was nothing but a source of information.

She had told Tyler she'd have the ledgers ready for him this evening, but that was beginning to look doubtful. Rachel looked up toward the ceiling of the church sanctuary, where a teenager perched at the top of a ladder, the end of a string of greenery in his hand. She was almost afraid to say something to him, for fear it would throw off his balance.

"That's fine, Jon. Just slip it over the hook and come back down."

He grinned, apparently perfectly at ease on his lofty perch. "Am I making you nervous, Ms. Rachel?"

"Definitely," she replied. "So get down here or I'll tell Pastor Greg on you."

Still grinning, he hooked the garland in place and started down, nimble as a monkey. She could breathe again.

She wasn't quite sure how she'd allowed herself to be talked into helping with the youth group's efforts to decorate the sanctuary for Advent. Supervising the teenagers' efforts might be harder than doing it herself, except that she'd never have gotten up on that ladder. The memory of flying off that stepladder when she'd put up the inn's Christmas lights was too fresh in her mind. She still didn't understand how that could have happened. How could she have missed something so obvious?

She moved back the center aisle, assessing their progress. In spite of a lot of horseplay and goofing off, the job was actually getting done. Swags of greenery cascaded down the cream-colored pillars that supported the roof, huge wreaths hung on either side of the chancel, and candleholders in each window had been trimmed with greenery. All that was left to do was to put new candles in all the holders.

She glanced at her watch. That was a good thing, since it was nearly nine, and she'd been told to send the kids off home promptly at nine.

"Okay, everyone, that's about it," she called above the clatter of voices. "You've done a fantastic job. Just put the ladders away, please, and you'd better cut along home."

Jon Everhart paused, holding one end of the ladder. "Do you want me to stay and turn off the lights for you?"

"Thanks anyway, Jon. I'll do it. After all, I just have to walk across the street to get home."

Of course the kids didn't leave that promptly, but by ten after nine the last of them had gone out the walk through the cemetery to the street.

She picked up the box of new candles and started along the side of the sanctuary, setting them carefully in the holders. Maybe it was best that she do them herself in any event. Not that the kids hadn't done their best, but she'd feel better if she made sure the tapers were secure in the holders. On Christmas Eve every candle would be aflame, filling the sanctuary with light and warmth.

The sanctuary was quiet—quieter than she'd ever experienced. She seemed to feel that stillness seeping into her, gentling the worry that ate at her over the problem presented by Tyler and her continuing anxiety about the financial state of the inn.

She looked at the window above her, showing Jesus talking with the woman at the well. His face, even represented in stained glass, showed so much love and acceptance. In spite of her tiredness, she felt that caring touch her, renewing her.

I've come so close to You since the accident. Maybe the person who hit me actually did me a favor. He couldn't have intended it, but the accident forced me to stop running away spiritually.

She knew why she'd done that, of course. She spent years unable to refer to God as Father, until she'd finally realized that it made her think of her own father, absent most of the time and fighting with Mom when he was around.

Tyler had his own issues with his parents, but at least he'd had a positive relationship with his father for most of his young life. Did he realize how fortunate he was in that? Or was he too wrapped up in his inability to satisfy his mother's demands?

She started down the opposite side of the sanctuary, securing candles in holders. She should finish this up and get back to the inn. It wasn't really all that late. She could still locate the pertinent ledgers and turn them over to Tyler. Let him strain his vision all he wanted, reading through her grandfather's meticulous notes. He wouldn't find anything to reflect badly on Grandfather, no matter how hard he looked.

She was putting the last candle in place when the

lights went out. A startled gasp escaped her. She froze, feeling as if she'd suddenly gone blind.

Slowly her vision adjusted. The faintest light filtered through the windows, probably from the streetlamp at the gate to the churchyard. Dark shadows fell across the sanctuary, though, and if she tried to cut across to where she knew the light switches were, she'd probably crash right into a pew.

Here she stood with a box full of candles and not a single match to light one. The sensible thing was to feel her way along the wall until she got to the front pew where she'd left her handbag. The small flashlight she kept in her bag would help her reach the light switches.

Running her left hand along the cool plaster, reaching out with her right hand to touch the pews, she worked her way toward the front of the sanctuary. Why would the lights go out, anyway? It wasn't as if they were in the midst of a lightning storm.

Still, Grams had often said that the church building, just about as old as the inn, had similar problems. Maybe the overloaded circuits had chosen this moment to break down.

Or the explanation might be simpler. Mose Stetler, the custodian, could have come in, thinking they'd all left, and switched the lights off.

She paused, one hand resting on the curved back of a pew, its worn wood satiny to the touch. "Mose? Is that you? I'm still in the sanctuary."

Really, he should have checked to see if anyone was here before going around switching off lights.

No one answered. If it was Mose, he apparently couldn't hear her.

She took another step and stopped, her heart lurching into overdrive. Someone was in the sanctuary with her.

Ridiculous. She was being foolish, imagining things because she was alone in the dark. She took another step. And heard it. A step that echoed her own and then stopped.

She should call out. It must be someone on a perfectly innocent errand—Mose, or even the pastor, come to see that the church had been properly locked up. She should call out, let them know she was there.

But some instinct held her throat in a vise. She couldn't—she really couldn't speak. Stupid as it seemed, she was unable to make a sound.

Or was it so stupid? She'd already called out, and no one had answered. Whoever was there, he or she seemed anxious not to be heard or identified.

She drew in a cautious breath, trying to keep it silent. Think. A chill of fear trickled down her spine. She'd become disoriented in the dark. How far was she from the double doors at the rear of the sanctuary? How far from the chancel door that led out past the organ to the vestry?

Her fingers tightened on the pew back, and she strained to see. Directly opposite her there was a faint gleam coming through the stained glass. Surely that was the image of Jesus with the woman at the well, wasn't it? She could just make out the shape of the figure.

All right. Be calm. If that window was opposite, then she was nearer to the chancel door, wasn't she?

She took a cautious step in that direction, then another, gaining a little confidence. She didn't know where the other person was in the dark, but if she could make it to the door and get through, she could close it. Lock it. She tried to form an image of the door. Lots of the sturdy old wooden doors in the church had dead bolts. Did that one?

She wasn't sure. But she'd still feel a lot better with a closed door between her and the unknown person. She could move quickly through the small vestry, and beyond it was the door that led out to the ramp. It had a clear glass window, so she'd be able to see to get out.

She took another step, groping for the next pew, and froze, her breath catching. A footstep, nearer to her than she'd thought. He was between her and the chancel door—a thicker blackness than the dark around him. Did he realize how close they were? Surely he couldn't see her any better than she could him. If he did, a few steps would close the gap between them.

Not daring to breathe, she inched her way backward, moving toward the outer wall this time. Follow the wall back to the rear of the sanctuary, work her way to the door.

Please, Lord, please. Maybe I'm being silly, but I don't think so. I think there's danger in this place. Help me.

A few silent steps, and her hand brushed the wall. Holding her breath, she moved along it. She'd be okay, she'd reach the back of the church—and then she realized that the footsteps were moving toward her, deliberately, no longer trying to hide.

How did he know—stupid, she was silhouetted against the faint light coming through the stained glass. Moving to the outer wall was the worst thing she could have done. Heedless of the noise, she dove into the sheltering blackness of the nearest pew, sensing the movement toward her of that other, hearing the indrawn breath of annoyance.

Her heart thudded so loudly she could hear it, and terror clutched her throat. She couldn't stay here, helpless in the dark, waiting for him to find her. Even as she formed the thought she heard him move, heard a hand brushing against the pew back, groping.

She scuttled toward the center aisle, praying he couldn't tell exactly which row she was in. If he came after her—yes, he was coming, she couldn't stop, she didn't dare hesitate—

She bolted along the row, giving up any idea of silence. Her knee banged painfully against the pew and then she was out, into the aisle, sensing the clear space around her.

No time to feel her way. She ran toward the back, a breathless prayer crying from her very soul. *Help me, help me.*

Running full tilt, she hit the door at the rear of the sanctuary. It exploded open, and she bolted out into the cold night, less black than the sanctuary had been. She flew down the few stairs and ran into a solid shape, heard a gasp and felt hard hands grab her painfully tight.

Chapter Eight

Tyler wrapped his arms around Rachel, feeling her slender body shake against him. The grip of her hands was frantic, her breath ragged.

"Rachel, what's wrong?" He drew her close, all the exasperation he'd been feeling gone in an instant. "Are you hurt?"

She shook her head, but her grip didn't loosen, and he found her tension driving his own.

"Come on, Rachel. You're scaring me. Tell me what's wrong." He tried to say it lightly, but the depth of concern he felt startled and dismayed him. When had he started caring so much about Rachel?

She took a deep breath, and he felt her drawing on some reserve of strength to compose herself. "Sorry. I'm sorry." She drew back a little. "I'm not hurt. Just scared."

"Why? What scared you?" Fear spiked, making his voice sharp.

She pushed soft brown curls away from her face with a hand that wasn't entirely steady.

"The lights went out. I was in the sanctuary, finishing up the decorating by myself, when the lights suddenly went out."

"There's more to it than that." He gripped her shoulders. "You wouldn't panic just because you were alone in the dark."

She shook her head. "That's just it. I wasn't alone." She drew in a ragged breath. "Someone was there. I know how stupid that sounds, but someone was in there with me."

The fear in her voice made him take it seriously. "Did someone touch you—say something to you?" His mind jumped to the dark figure who'd struck him down at the old farmhouse. But the two things couldn't be related, could they?

She seemed to be steadying herself, as if talking about it was relieving her fear. "I heard him. Or her. I couldn't be sure. And I saw—well, just a shadow."

He studied her face, frowning a little. He didn't doubt what she was saying, but it was hard to imagine a threat against her in the church.

"You don't believe me." Her chin came up.

"I believe you." He ran his hands down her arms. "I'll go in and have a look around." He hefted the torch Rachel's grandmother had given him when he'd said he'd come over to the church and walk her back.

"Not without me." Her fingers closed around his wrist. "Come around to the side. We can go through the education wing door and get to the light switches from there."

If someone was hiding in the sanctuary, that would give the person a chance to escape while they were going around the building. "Maybe we should call the police."

She hesitated, and he could almost see her weighing the possibilities. Finally she shook her head. "I guess it's not a crime to turn off the lights, is it? Let's see what we can find."

He nodded and let her lead him along the walk. Once they'd rounded the corner, they could see the lamp above the side door shining. "Looks like the power's still on in this wing. Could be only one circuit was shut off."

Rachel marched to the door and turned the knob. It wasn't locked. "This is the way we came in. I was supposed to lock it with the key when I left. The sanctuary doors are locked, but they open from the inside."

A good thing, given the way she'd erupted through them. He followed her inside. She reached out, flipping a switch, and lights came on down a hallway with what were probably classrooms on either side.

"Everything seems okay here."

She nodded. "The door to the vestry is around the corner at the end of the hall."

He started down the hallway, not attempting to be quiet. His footsteps would echo on the tile floor, in any event.

Rachel walked in step with him, her face intent but pale, her hands clenched. Obviously she was convinced that something malicious had been intended in the incident. He still wasn't so sure, but—

Footsteps. Someone was coming toward them, around the corner. He heard the quick intake of Rachel's breath. His hand tightened on the flashlight. He grasped Rachel's arm, pushing her behind him.

A figure came around the corner, and all of his tension fell flat. The man had to be eighty at least, and he peered at them through the thick lenses of his glasses.

"Rachel?" His voice quavered. "That you?"

"Mose." Relief flooded Rachel's voice. "I'm glad to see you."

He grunted. "Pastor told me you'd be hanging the greens in the sanctuary tonight. You all finished?"

"Yes, we're done. Why didn't you answer me when I called to you in the sanctuary?"

The old man blinked several times before replying. "In the sanctuary? Haven't been in the sanctuary yet. Just came in the side door and was on my way here when I heard you folks come in." He glanced at Tyler suspiciously.

The color she'd regained melted from Rachel's face. "You weren't? But someone was. The lights went off."

"Lights off?" He sniffed. "We'll just see about that." He turned and shuffled off the way he'd come.

They followed him, and Tyler realized that at some point he'd grasped Rachel's hand. Well, she was scared. Giving her a little support was the least he could do.

Around the corner, through a set of double fire doors, and they were abruptly in the old part of the building again. In the dark. He switched on his flashlight, and the old man's face looked white and startled in its glare.

"Must be a circuit. Just shine your light over to the right, so's I can see what's what."

Tyler did as he was told and the flashlight's beam picked out the gray metal circuit box, looking incongruous against a carved oak cabinet that must be at least a hundred years old.

The custodian flipped it open. "There's the problem,

all right. Breaker's thrown." He clicked it, and lights came on immediately, gleaming through an open door that led into the sanctuary.

"Let's have a look inside." Tyler moved to the door. "Rachel heard someone in there."

The elderly man followed them into the sanctuary. The lights showed evergreen branches looping around the columns and flowing around the windows. Everything looked perfectly normal.

Rachel stood close to him. "I'd like to walk back through, just to be sure."

He nodded, sensing that she didn't want to say anything else within earshot of the custodian.

Halfway back along the outside wall, she stopped. "This is where I was," she murmured. "When I realized he was coming toward me. I ducked into that pew, ran along it and out the center aisle to the doors."

"He didn't follow you then?"

"I'm not sure. I was pretty panicked by then. All I wanted was to get out."

Hearing a faint tremor in her voice, he found her hand and squeezed it. "You're okay now."

She nodded, sending him a cautioning look as the custodian came toward them.

"Well, if someone was here, they're gone now." He patted Rachel's arm. "Don't like to say it, but most likely it was one of them kids. Their idea of a joke."

"I guess it could have been." Rachel sounded unconvinced. "Thanks, Mose. Do you want me to go back through and turn off the lights?"

"No, no, you folks go on. I'm going that way anyhow."

Touching Rachel's arm, Tyler guided her toward the

door, still not sure what he thought of all this. That Rachel had been frightened by someone, he had no doubt. But was it anything more than that?

They walked side by side out into the chilly night and along the walk. He waited for Rachel to speak first. Their relationship was fragile at best, and he wasn't sure what he could say to make this better.

They reached the street before she spoke. She glanced at him, her face pale in the gleam of the streetlamp. "I suppose Mose could be right about the kids. Though I hate to think they'd be so mean."

He took her hand as they crossed the street toward the inn. "Kids don't always think through the results of their actions. I can remember a couple of really stupid things I did at that age."

She smiled faintly. "I suppose I can, too. Well, thank you for coming to the rescue. I hope I didn't look like too much of an idiot."

"You didn't look like an idiot at all." His fingers tightened on hers. "It was a scary experience, even if Mose is right and it was just intended as a joke. I'm just not sure—" He hesitated. Maybe he shouldn't voice the thought in his mind.

"What?" They neared the side door, and she stopped just short of the circle of illumination from the overhead light.

"I've only known you…what? A week? In that time you've been nearly electrocuted by Christmas lights and—well, call it harassed in the church."

Her face was a pale oval in the dim light. "And you've been hit on the head."

"Seems like we're both having a run of bad luck." He waited for her response.

She frowned, looking troubled. "It does seem odd. But the Christmas lights—surely no one could have done that deliberately."

"Not if they didn't have access to them. If they were safely up in your attic until the moment you brought them down to hang—"

"They weren't," she said shortly. "I brought them down the day before. I was checking on them when I realized it was time for the committee meeting."

He didn't think he liked that. "Where were they during the meeting?"

"In the downstairs rest room."

"Where someone could tamper with them," he said.

"Why would anyone do that? They're all my friends. Anyway, how could they have known I'd be the one to put them up?"

"Anyone who's been around the inn would know that."

She took a quick step away from him, into the pool of light. "I can't believe that someone I know would try to hurt me." But her voice seemed to wobble on the words.

"I'm not trying to upset you." An unexpected, and unwelcome, flood of protectiveness swept through him. "I'm just concerned."

"Thank you. But please, I don't want Grams to know anything happened. She worries about me."

"She loves you," he said quietly, prompted by some instinct he wasn't sure he understood. "That's a good thing."

She tilted her face back, a smile lifting the corners of her lips. "Most of the time," she agreed.

"All of the time." Without thinking it through, he

brushed a strand of hair back from her face. It flowed through his fingers like silk.

Her eyes widened. Darkened. He heard the faint catch of her breath. Knew that his own breathing was suddenly ragged.

He took her shoulders, drawing her toward him. She came willingly, lifting her face. The faintest shadow of caution touched his mind, and he censored it. His lips found hers.

Astonishing, the flood of warmth and tenderness that went through him. The kiss was gentle, tentative, as if Rachel were asking silently, Is this right? Do we want to do this? Who are you, deep inside where it's important?

She drew back a little at last, a smile lingering on her lips. "Maybe we'd better go in."

He dropped a light kiss on her nose. "Maybe we'd better. Your grandmother will be worrying."

But he didn't want to. He wanted to stay out here in the moonlight with her as long as he could. And he didn't care to explore what that meant about the state of his feelings.

Barney trotted along Crossings Road next to Rachel, darting away from her from time to time to investigate an interesting clump of dried weeds or the trunk of a hemlock. She smiled at his enthusiasm, aware that they were coming closer to the farm with every step.

And that Tyler was there. She'd really had no intention of coming back here or seeing Tyler this afternoon. But Grams had said Rachel was driving them crazy tinkering with the Christmas decorations, and that everything was as ready as it could be for the guests who'd be arriving late this afternoon. Why didn't she take Barney for a walk and get rid of her fidgets?

The dog, apparently remembering their last excursion, had promptly led her down Crossings Road to the Hostetler farm. They reached the lane, and Barney darted ahead of her. She could see Tyler's car, pulled up next to the porch. He'd told Grams he was trying to identify the rest of the furniture today.

To say that she had mixed feelings about seeing Tyler was putting it mildly. She'd appreciated his help the previous night. He'd managed to submerge whatever doubts he had about her story and given her the help she needed.

As for what had happened—she stared absently at the clumps of dried Queen Anne's lace in what had once been a pasture.

Surely she could think about it rationally now. Little though she wanted to believe it, Mose's suggestion was the only sensible one. One or more of the teenagers, motivated by who knew what, could easily have flipped the switch to turn the lights off. Maybe they'd thought it would be funny to give her a scare in the dark.

Well, if so, she'd certainly gratified them by bolting out the way she had. She should have turned the tables on them and grabbed that person in the sanctuary.

She couldn't have. Cold seemed to settle into her. Even now, in the clear light of day with the thin winter sun on her face, she couldn't imagine reaching out toward that faceless figure.

Her steps slowed, and Barney scampered over to nose at her hand. She patted him absently.

Maybe it had been her imagination. She sincerely hoped it had been. But that sense of enmity she'd felt, there in the dark in what should have been the safest of places, had simply overpowered her. She'd reacted like any hunted animal. Run. Hide.

She forced her feet to move again. Just thinking about it was making her feel the fear again, and she wouldn't let fear control her.

Remembering what had happened afterward was disturbing in a different way. She couldn't stop the smile that curved her lips when she remembered that kiss. It had held a potential that warmed her and startled her. It certainly hadn't clarified things between them—if anything, she felt more confused.

And then what he'd suggested about the Christmas lights—well, it couldn't be, that was all. Except that his words had roused that niggling little doubt she'd felt every time she looked at the lights.

And he was right. Anyone who was there that night could have guessed she'd put them up. It would have been the work of a minute to strip the wires.

Not a surefire way of hurting her, but a quick and easy impulse.

Tyler had left someone out, though. Himself.

He'd had access to the lights, too. And he'd come here convinced that her family was guilty of something in relation to his grandfather's death.

Was he really just after the truth? Or did revenge figure in somewhere?

Ridiculous, she told herself firmly. He wasn't that sort of devious person.

But still—maybe that was all the more reason not to see Tyler alone today. She'd reached the house, but he wasn't inside. Instead she spotted him where the ground sloped up behind the barn.

For a moment she didn't know what he was doing, but then she realized. That tangle of brush and rusted fence was a small cemetery, of course. There were plenty of them, scattered throughout the township, most of them remnants of the earliest days of settlement. Some were well kept, others abandoned. This one fell into the abandoned category.

Tyler seemed totally absorbed. He hadn't noticed her. Good. She'd turn around and go back to the inn—

But before she could move, Barney spotted Tyler and plunged toward him, tail waving, letting out a series of welcoming barks. Tyler looked up and waved. Nothing for it now but to go forward.

Tyler climbed over the remnants of the low wrought-iron fence and stood, waiting for her. Barney reached him first, and Tyler welcomed him, running his hand along the dog's back and sending Barney into excited whines.

"Hi." He surveyed her, as if measuring the amount of strain on her face. "How are you doing? I wondered when I didn't see you at breakfast."

"I'm fine," she said quickly. "Just fine. Grams thought I could use a sleep-in day before the weekend guests get here, that's all."

He nodded, as if accepting that implication that she didn't want to discuss the previous night.

"How did you make out with the furniture?" she asked quickly. "Grams said you were trying to get through the list today."

"I managed to do that, but I'm not sure how far ahead it gets me. There are certainly plenty of things missing, and I can make up a list to give the chief. But there's no way of knowing when anything disappeared.

My grandfather could have sold some of it himself, for all I know."

She could understand his frustration. He was finding dead ends everywhere he turned.

"So you're investigating the family cemetery, instead."

"Not so much family, as far as I can tell. Most of the people buried here seem to be Chadwicks, dating back to the 1700s."

"The land probably originally belonged to a family called Chadwick. Once it came into Amish hands, they'd have been buried in the Amish cemetery over toward Burkville."

He knelt, straightening a small stone that had been tipped over. "Miranda Chadwick. Looks as if she was only three when she died."

She squatted next to him, heart clenching, and shoved a clump of soil against the marker to hold it upright. "So many children didn't survive the first few years then. It's hardly surprising that people had big families." She touched the rough-cut cross on the marker, unaccountably hurt by the centuries-old loss. "They grieved for her."

He nodded, his face solemn, and then rose, holding out his hand to help her to her feet.

She stood, disentangling her hand quickly, afraid of what she might give away if she held on to him any longer.

He cleared his throat. "So you said the Amish are buried elsewhere?"

"The Amish have a church-district cemetery—at least, that's how it's done here. Just simple stones, most of them alike, I guess showing that even in death, everyone is equal."

"But my grandfather had left the church by the time he died." Something sharp and alert focused Tyler's gray eyes. "So where would he be buried?"

"I don't know. Maybe my grandmother—"

But Tyler was already moving purposely through the small graveyard, bending to pull the weeds away from each stone. Feeling helpless, she followed him.

Chadwicks and more Chadwicks. Surely he wasn't—

But Tyler had stopped before one stone, carefully clearing the debris from it, and she realized the marker looked newer than the others.

Why this sudden feeling of dismay? She struggled with her own emotions. It didn't really make a difference, did it, where Tyler's grandfather was buried?

She came to a stop next to him, looking at Tyler rather than the stone. His face had tightened, becoming all sharp planes and angles.

"Here it is. John Hostetler. Just his name and the dates. I guess my mother held to Amish tradition in that, at least."

She couldn't tell what he was feeling. She rested her hand lightly on his shoulder. Tension, that was all she could be sure of. She focused on the marker.

John Hostetler. As Tyler said, just date of birth. Date of death.

Date of death. For an instant her vision seemed to blur. She shook her head, forcing her gaze to the carved date. It was like being struck in the stomach. She actually stumbled back a step, gasping.

Tyler was on it in an instant, of course. He shot to his feet, grasping her hands in both of his. "What is it?"

She shook her head, trying to come up with something, anything other than the truth.

Tyler's grip tightened painfully. He couldn't have known how hard he was holding her. "What, Rachel? What do you see when you look at the tombstone?"

She couldn't lie. Couldn't evade. Couldn't even understand it herself.

"The date. The date your grandfather died." She stopped, feeling as if the words choked her. "My father deserted us at just about the same time."

Chapter Nine

Tyler could only stare at Rachel for a moment, questions battering at his mind. He reached out, wanting to hold her so that she couldn't escape until he had all the answers. How could she land a blow like that and then stand looking at him as if it didn't matter?

Then he realized that it wasn't lack of caring that froze her face and darkened her eyes. Shock. Rachel was shocked by this, just as he was.

A cold breeze hit them, rustling the bare branches of the oak tree that sheltered the few tilted gravestones. Rachel shivered, her whole body seeming to tremble for a moment.

He grasped her arm. "Come on. Let's get back to the car and warm up."

She walked with him down the hill, stumbling a little once or twice as if not watching where she was going. Barney, darting around them in circles in the frostbitten field, seemed to sense that something was wrong. He rushed up to Rachel with small, reassuring yips.

They reached the car. He tucked her into the pas-

senger seat and started the ignition, turning the heater
on. Barney whined until he opened the back door so
the dog could jump in.

Tyler slid into the driver's seat, holding out his hand
to the vent, grateful for the power of the car's heater.
Already warmth was coming out, and he turned the
blower to full blast. He couldn't possibly get any answers until Rachel lost that frozen look.

For several minutes she didn't move. He should take
her back to the inn, but he'd never have a better time
than this to find answers.

She stretched her hands out toward the heater vent,
rubbing them together, and the movement encouraged
him. She seemed to have lost a little of that frozen look.

"Feeling better now?" He kept his voice low.

She nodded, darting a cautious, sideways glance at
him. To his relief the color had returned to her cheeks.

"I'm sorry. I don't know what got into me."

"Shock," he suggested.

"I don't—" She stopped, shook her head, made an
effort to start again. "I'm being stupid, letting the coincidence upset me so much."

He discovered his hand was gripping the steering
wheel so hard the knuckles were white, and he forced
his fingers to loosen.

"Do you really think it's a coincidence that your father deserted you about the time of my grandfather's
death?"

"What else could it be?" Defiance colored the words.

Plenty of things, most notably a guilty conscience.
But he suspected she would come to that conclusion
on her own if he didn't push too hard.

She moved, as if the silence disturbed her. "I was

only eight. I might be remembering incorrectly." Her voice was so defensive that he knew there was more to it than that.

"You must know around when it was. Didn't you tell me that your mother took you and your sisters away shortly after that?"

Her mouth was set, but she gave a short nod.

"Kids usually have their own ways of remembering when things happened. Connecting the experiences to being off school or holidays or—"

He stopped, because a tremor had shot through her, so fierce he could feel it. He reached out, capturing her cold hand in his. "What is it, Rachel? You may as well tell me, because you know I'm not going to give up."

She stared through the windshield at the bleak landscape. Barney whined from the backseat, seeming to sense her distress.

"My birthday would have been a week after your grandfather's death." The words came out slow. Reluctant. "I was excited because Daddy had promised to stay for my birthday and give me a gold cross necklace, like the one Andrea had." She seemed to be looking back over a dark, painful chasm. "But he was gone before then."

"Promised to stay? You mean he wasn't usually there?"

"Our parents were separated so much it's hard to keep track. Daddy would be gone for months at a time, and then show up. He and Mom might get along for a few weeks, then something would blow up between them and he'd leave." She threaded her fingers through her hair. "Not the most stable of parents. I sometimes wonder why they had us."

He willed himself to go slow, to think this through. Hampton had deserted his family at about the time of his grandfather's death; that was clear. But connecting the two incidents with any sureness was iffy, given what Rachel said about her father's absences.

"Had your dad been around much that summer?"

She frowned, shaking her head. "I'm not sure. It seems to me that he had, but—" She shrugged. "He could be so charming, although I don't think my grandparents saw it. Life seemed exciting when he was here."

She'd wanted to be loved, of course. Any child knows instinctively that a parent's love is crucial.

"Do you remember anything about when your dad left?" He tried to keep his voice gentle.

She stared down at her hands. He sensed that she was pulling her defenses up, figuring out how to cope with this situation.

"I don't know much." Her voice was calmer now, as if she were able to detach her grown-up self from the little girl who'd been looking forward to her birthday. "I'm sure the adults were all trying to protect us, but of course Andrea and I speculated. We crept out on the stairs at night. I remember sitting there, holding her hand, listening to my mother shouting at my grandparents, as if it was their fault he'd gone."

Her fingers twisted a little in remembered pain, and he smoothed them gently, hurting for her.

"Your mother must have explained things to you in some way."

A wry smile tugged at her lips. "You didn't know our mother if you think that. She just announced that Daddy was gone and that we were going away, too. She hauled us out of the house with half our belongings. For a while Drea and I thought we were going to join our father, but that didn't happen. Every time we asked, she'd tell us to be quiet." She shrugged. "So finally we stopped asking."

He struggled to piece it together. It sounded as if her family had been far more messed up than his. "So your parents never got back together?"

She shook her head. "Being taken away from our grandparents hurt the worst. Daddy had been in and out of our lives so much, always trying some great new job that was going to make all the difference. It never did."

"So your grandparents were the stable influence." And probably only her grandmother, or possibly Emma, could tell him the story from an adult perspective.

"They were. If Mom had let us see them more often—but she nursed her own grudge against them. It really wasn't until we were in college that we had much contact with them. Still, we always knew they were there." She brushed back a strand of silky hair, managing to give him something approaching a normal smile. "When I came back a year ago, just for a visit, I realized this place was what I'd been longing for all along. It's home, even though I left it when I was eight."

He nodded, understanding. Wanting to make it better for her, even at the same time that he knew he'd have to find out more about her father.

He touched the strand of hair she fiddled with, tucking it behind her ear. His fingers brushed her cheek, setting up a wave of longing that he had to fight.

"I'd have to say you turned out pretty well, in spite of your parents. What happened to them? Are you still in contact?"

She shook her head. "Mom died in a car accident three years ago in Nevada."

"I'm sorry." Although it didn't sound as if she'd been much of a loss as a mother. "What about your dad?" Casual. Keep it casual.

She blinked. "I thought you realized. We haven't heard a word from him from that day to this."

Maybe the worst thing about running an inn was the fact that no matter what was going on in her personal life, Rachel had to be smiling and welcoming for the guests. She could only be thankful that at the moment, Grams had their weekend guests corralled in the front parlor, serving them eggnog and cookies and regaling them with Pennsylvania Dutch Christmas legends, while Rachel had the back parlor to herself, getting the nativity scene ready to go beneath the Christmas tree.

If only she'd had a little more self-control, Tyler would never have known about the coincidence in dates between her father's leaving and his grandfather's death. That was all it had been. A coincidence. She'd never believe that her feckless, generous father could have been involved in that. Never.

She frowned at the low wooden platform that was meant to hold the *putz*. That end didn't seem to be sitting properly.

Keeping her hands busy unfortunately allowed her mind to wander too much.

I guess I couldn't have kept it from Tyler, could I? She had a wistful longing that God would come down on her side in this, but in her heart she knew it wouldn't happen. "Be ye wise as serpents and innocent as doves." Hiding the truth from Tyler was hardly an act of innocence.

Still, the fear existed. What would he do with the information he now had? She already knew part of that answer, didn't she? He'd want to talk to Grams. She hadn't remembered much about that time, but Grams would.

All her protective family instincts went into high gear at the thought, but there was nothing she could do. Tyler wouldn't be deflected, and Grams would do what was right.

Having arranged the molds to hold the hills and valleys on the wooden platform, she spread out the length of green cloth that was meant to cover them. The fabric fell in graceful folds, looking for all the world like real hills and valleys.

And then the end of the platform collapsed, sending her neat little world atilt. For a moment she felt like bursting into tears. Her world really was falling around her, and there seemed to be nothing she could do to stop it.

"Looks as if you need a carpenter."

Her heart jolted at the sound of Tyler's voice. She didn't look up. "My brother-in-law is a carpenter, but he moved his shop to the property he and Andrea bought in New Holland. And he's off on his honeymoon, anyway."

Tyler knelt beside her, his arm brushing hers as he righted the platform. She caught the tang of his aftershave and resisted the instinct to lean a little closer to him.

"I think I can manage to fix this. Will you hand me that hammer?"

She passed it over to him. With a few quick blows he firmed up the nails that had begun to work themselves loose.

She caught his sideways, questioning glance, as if he wanted to ask how she was but was afraid to start something.

"This is the foundation for the nativity scene, I take it."

"We call it the *putz*." She spread the cloth out again, aware of his hands helping her. "If you want to hear about it, you should go to the front parlor. Grams is giving the details to the other guests."

Was that ungracious? Grams would certainly think so.

"I'd rather hear it from you." Tyler's voice was low, pitched under the chatter from the other room.

"That's not what you want, and you know it." She couldn't seem to help the tartness in her tone.

Tyler nodded, blue eyes serious as he studied her face. "All right. That's true. You realize I have to talk to your grandmother, don't you?"

She paused in the act of removing one of the clay nativity figures from its nest of tissue paper. Even without seeing it, she could identify the shape of a camel through the paper.

She'd been anticipating this moment—getting out the familiar old figures, setting up the scene until it was just perfect. Irrational or not, she couldn't help but resent the fact that Tyler was spoiling it for her.

"I know you need to hear the story from Grams." Her words felt as fragile as the crystal ornaments on the tree. "I'd appreciate it if you'd wait until we've gotten through this evening."

"I'll wait, but later we have to talk." The implacability in his tone chilled her. He wouldn't be turned back, no matter what.

Even if what he was trying to do implicated her father.

"And now we're ready to set up the *putz,* or nativity scene." Grams came through the archway, shepherding the four new couples firmly. "We hope you'll enjoy doing this traditional Pennsylvania German tradition with us."

Both mother-daughter pairs looked enthusiastic. The other two couples were from Connecticut. The women seemed pleased, the men bored. How long before they made some excuse to get out of this? They looked slightly heartened at the sight of Tyler—another male to support them, she supposed.

But Tyler would want to get this over as quickly as possible, so he would corner Grams.

"You've already met my granddaughter Rachel when you checked in." Grams performed introductions. "And this is our friend, Tyler Dunn."

How did Tyler feel about being promoted from guest to friend? It wouldn't stop him from finding out all he could about her father.

While Grams explained the tradition of the *putz,* the elaborate Nativity scene that went under the tree, Rachel unwrapped the six-inch clay figures, setting them out on the folding table she'd brought in for the purpose.

"…not just a manger scene," Grams explained. "We start at the left and create little vignettes of the events leading up to the birth of Jesus—Joseph in his carpentry shop, Mary with the angel, the trip to Bethlehem. The stable scene goes front and center, of course, and then the shepherds with their flocks, the wise men following the star, even the flight to Egypt."

"These are beautiful figures." One of the women grabbed an angel, holding it up in one hand.

Rachel had to force herself not to take it back. That was the angel with the broken wing tip. She'd knocked it over the year she was six and been inconsolable until Daddy, there for once, had touched it up with gilt paint, assuring her that no one would ever notice.

"Antique," Tyler said smoothly, "and very fragile. Difficult to replace."

The woman seemed to take the hint, holding the angel carefully in both hands. "We actually get to help set this up? Well, if that isn't the sweetest thing."

She knelt by the platform. The others, seeming infected by her enthusiasm, gathered around to take the delicate figures or the stones and moss Rachel had brought in to add realism to the scene. In a few moments everyone was happily involved. Tyler even enlisted the two men to create a miniature mountain, and she thought she caught a serious discussion about how one might add a running stream.

She stood back a little, watching the scene take shape, handing out a figure where needed. Funny, how sharp the memory had been when she'd seen the angel with the chipped wing. She hadn't thought of that in years.

Maybe it had been so strong because it involved her father. Funny. You'd have expected the oldest daughter to be Daddy's girl, but instead it had been her. The whole time they'd lived here, everyone had known that Andrea was Grandfather's little helper and she was Daddy's girl.

Was it because Andrea was less guided by sentiment? A little more clear-sighted about their parents? The thought made her uncomfortable, and she tried to push it away.

"Rachel?"

She blinked, realizing that one of the guests must have said her name several times. "Yes? Peggy," she added, pleased to have pulled the woman's name from her memory banks.

"Will you show me how to put these Roman soldiers together? It looks as if the shield should hook on, but I don't quite see…"

"Let me." Tyler took it from the woman. She looked up at him, obviously flattered at his attention. "I think we can figure this out together, can't we?"

The woman fluttered after him in an instant, kneeling at the base of the tree next to him.

Rachel pinned a smile to her face. She couldn't let her private worries distract her from her duty to her guests. But Tyler—

Tyler had been watchful. Sensitive. Seeming to know what she was feeling, quick and subtle about helping out.

Even as she thought that, she caught him taking a clay donkey from Grams and handing her a star to be nestled in the branches instead, so that she didn't attempt to get down on the floor.

The simple gesture gripped her heart. Without warning, the thought came. This was a man she could love.

No. She couldn't. Because whether he wanted to or not, Tyler threatened everything that was important to her.

* * *

Rachel clearly didn't intend to let him talk to her grandmother tonight. The other guests had lingered long after the Nativity scene was finished. As it happened, one of the women was an accomplished pianist, and she'd entertained them with Christmas music while a fire roared in the fireplace and tree lights shone softly on the *putz*.

It was lovely. He'd had to admit that—admit, too, that he'd enjoyed watching the firelight play on Rachel's expressive face.

Too expressive. She probably didn't realize how clearly her protectiveness toward her grandmother came through. Once the last of the guests had wound down, she'd put her arm around the elderly woman's waist and urged her toward the stairs with a defiant look at him.

Well, much as he needed to talk to Katherine Unger, he had to agree with Rachel on this one. She had looked tired, and it was late. Tomorrow would have to do.

He put the book he'd been leafing through back on the shelf and headed for the stairs. As he did, the door into the private wing of the house opened. It wasn't Rachel who came through—it was her grandmother.

"Mrs. Unger." He stopped, foot on the bottom step. "I thought you'd already gone to bed."

"That's what my granddaughter thinks, too." She stepped into the hall, the dog padding softly behind her, and closed the door. "I think it's time we had a talk about whatever it is you and Rachel have been trying to keep from me all day."

"I'm not sure—"

She took his arm and steered him back down the

hall toward the kitchen. "My granddaughter is too protective. Now, don't you start, too. Whatever it is won't be improved by making me wait and wonder about it until morning."

A low light had been left on in the kitchen, shining down on the sturdy wooden table that had undoubtedly served generations of the family, and a Black Forest clock ticked steadily on the mantelpiece. Mrs. Unger sat at the table and gestured him to the chair next to her.

"Now. Tell me." She folded thin, aristocratic hands in a gesture that was probably her way of armoring herself against bad news. "You and Rachel learned something today that upset her. What was it?"

He hesitated. "I don't think Rachel is going to like my talking with you alone."

"I'll deal with Rachel." She waited.

"All right." Actually, this might bother her less than it did Rachel. "I was in the small cemetery at the farm today. The one where my grandfather is buried. Rachel saw the date he died. I think you know why that upset her."

Her face tightened slightly at the implied challenge, but she nodded. "It reminded Rachel of when her father left."

"That's what she said." He frowned, trying to find the right way to ask questions that were certainly prying into her family's affairs. "She didn't remember the sequence of events exactly. Maybe she didn't even know, at the time."

"But you knew I would." She said the words he'd omitted, shaking her head as if she didn't want to remember. "That was a difficult time. Rachel's father had been around for nearly a month—long for him.

The quarrels were starting up. We knew it was only a question of time until he left. The fact that it happened shortly after your grandfather's death doesn't mean they were related."

"Perhaps not. But you must know I won't be satisfied unless I get some answers."

She inclined her head, conceding the point. "You have that right, I suppose." A faint, wry smile flickered. "Oddly enough, I've waited for years for Rachel to ask the questions. Why did her father leave? Why did their mother take them away? She never has."

That was strange. He'd think the questions would burn in her. "I don't want to hurt her. Or you. But I need the truth."

"The truth always costs something. Probably pain." She held up her hand to stop his protest. "I'm not refusing to tell you. I'm just pointing out that you can't always protect people." She sighed, her fingers tightening against each other. "Maybe that was my mistake. Trying to protect everyone."

Yes, he could see that. She was someone who would always try to protect her family. Rachel was exactly the same. As much as it might annoy him at times, he had to admire it, too.

"We only had the one child, you know." Her voice was soft. "Perhaps things would have been different if we'd had more. As it was, Lily was the apple of her father's eye—spirited, willful and headstrong. My husband liked those qualities in her, until she met Donald Hampton."

"He didn't approve." He'd only had Rachel's child's-eye view of her father, but he hadn't been too impressed.

"No. Oh, Hampton was charming. Good-looking,

polite. It was easy to see why she fell in love with him. But Frederick didn't think there was much character behind the charm."

His mind flickered to his own father. Maybe not long on charm, but he'd been a sound man and a good father. Odd, to be sitting in this quiet room with this elderly woman, pulled willy-nilly into a bond with her.

She sighed, the sound a soft counterpoint to the ticking of the clock. "Frederick would have stopped the marriage if he could have, but she was determined. And afterward there were the babies—" Her face bloomed with love. "He adored those girls. Hampton was just as unreliable as my husband predicted, but Frederick managed to keep his opinions to himself, for the most part. And we were happy when they moved in here. Then it didn't matter when Hampton took off, supposedly in search of some wonderful deal. We could take care of the children."

It seemed to him that their mother should have done that, but apparently she hadn't, from what Rachel said, been especially gifted as a mother.

"They were living here when my grandfather was attacked." Maybe best to move things along.

"Yes. As I said, Hampton had been back for about a month, supposedly trying to find a decent job around here, although Frederick always said he would run at the sight of one. Still, he was here, and Rachel adored him."

He'd seen that, in her eyes, when she spoke of him. "Maybe that's why she's never asked. She wants to hold on to her image of him."

She nodded. "We thought he'd be here until Rachel's birthday, at least."

"How long after the attack on my grandfather did he leave?" That was the important point to him.

"Two days." Her face tightened until the skin seemed molded against the bone. "We woke up to find him gone. He left a note, telling Lily he'd heard of some wonderful job opportunity out west. He left, never even saying goodbye to the girls. I don't think they ever heard from him again."

The timing was certainly suspicious. "I understand your daughter left soon after that."

"There was a terrible quarrel between them—my daughter and my husband. Frederick was rash enough to say what he thought of her husband, never imagining she'd carry out her threat to leave." She shook her head, the grief she'd probably carried since that day seeming to weigh her down. "I tried to reason with them, but they were both too stubborn to listen. There was a time when I thought I'd never get my granddaughters back again."

"But you have," he said quickly. "They never stopped loving you." Love. Connections. They went together, didn't they? Binding people together for good or ill. Like it or not, his family and hers were bound, too.

"I do." She looked at him then, and he saw the pleading in her lined face. "I have Rachel, and through her Andrea came back, too. But Rachel is the vulnerable one. She always has been. Family is everything to her."

What could he say to that? She didn't seem to expect anything. She just leaned across the table, putting her hand over his.

"Please," she said. "Please don't do anything that will take family away from Rachel. Please."

Chapter Ten

Rachel charged up the stairs the next morning, fueled by a mix of rage and betrayal. Tyler had gone too far this time.

Imagine the nerve—he'd sat there at breakfast calmly eating her cream-cheese-filled French toast, listening to the other guests talk about their planned day in Bethlehem, and he hadn't shown her by word or look that he had talked to Grams last night.

Some latent, fair part of her mind suggested that he could hardly have brought up something so personal in the presence of strangers, but she slapped it down. She wasn't rational about this. She was furious.

She paused on the landing, catching her breath, calming her nerves. Her sensitivity where her father was concerned was probably getting in the way of her judgment, but she couldn't seem to help it.

If only Andrea were here. She knew her big sister well enough to know that if she called Andrea's cell phone and told her what was going on, she and Cal would be on their way home immediately. But that wasn't fair—not to Andrea, who deserved to have her honeymoon in peace, and not to herself. It was time she stopped depending on her big sister.

She went quickly up the rest of the flight, running her hand along the carved railing. The square, spacious upstairs hall looked odd with the bedroom doors closed. All of their guests had gone out for the day. Except Tyler.

She swung on her heel toward his door just as it opened.

"Rachel." His face changed at the sight of her.

Small wonder. She probably looked like an avenging fury. She certainly felt like one.

"We have to talk." She said the words with control, but her nails were biting into her palms.

He nodded, opening the door wide. "I know. Do you want to come in?"

Instinct told her not to have this conversation in the privacy of the bedroom. "Out here is fine. Everyone's left. We won't be overheard." No matter what she had to say to him.

"Right." He stepped out into the hallway, closing the door behind him, and just stood, waiting for her to say what she would.

All the insults she'd been practicing in her head seemed to fly away at the sight of his grave face. She could only find one thing to say.

"How could you? How could you talk to my grandmother without me?" Saying the words seemed to give her momentum. "You must have known how tired she was and how much that was bound to upset her. I can't believe you'd do that."

It was true, she realized. At some level, she couldn't

believe that the Tyler she'd grown to know and care for would go behind her back that way.

"If you've talked with your grandmother, you know I didn't go to her," he said calmly. "She came to me."

"Yes. I know. I also know that you could have made some excuse. You could have waited until today at least. Why was it so important that you had to talk about it last night? Grams—" To her horror, she felt tears welling in her eyes. She blinked them back.

But he saw. He took a step toward her, closing the gap between them, his face gentling.

"Don't, Rachel. Please. I don't want to hurt you. I didn't want to hurt her. But your grandmother is one smart lady. She knew we were hiding something from her, and she wasn't going to rest until she knew what it was."

She drew in a breath, trying to ease the tension in her throat. "She is smart. And stubborn."

His fingers closed over hers for a brief moment. "Like her granddaughter."

Another breath, another effort to gain control of the situation that seemed to be slipping rapidly away from her. Or maybe there had never been anything she could do about this, but it had taken her this long to realize it.

"Grams told me what she'd told you. About my father leaving, the fight between my grandfather and mother." She shook her head slightly, not liking the pictures that had taken up residence there. "She's convinced that his leaving didn't have anything to do with what happened to your grandfather." She forced herself to meet his eyes. "So am I. Maybe he was just as charming as I remember and just as weak as my grandparents thought, but he wasn't a man who'd turn to violence."

"I hope you're right, Rachel." His fingers brushed hers again in mute sympathy. "I hope you're right about him."

She nodded, throat clogging so that she had to clear it. Unshed tears would do that to a person. "Well. I guess I'm not angry enough to slug you after all."

His smile was tentative, as if he were afraid of setting her off again. "I'm sure there are things for which I deserve it, anyway, so feel free."

Her tension drained away at the offer. "Not today. Grams said I should thank you for bringing it out in the open—about my father leaving, I mean. I'm not quite ready to do that."

"Not necessary," he said quickly. "I know things I have no right to about your family. And you about mine. Neither of us can do anything about it."

He was right about that. She didn't have to like it, but she had to accept it. He probably felt the same way.

"I am grateful for your help last night with the guests." She managed a smile that was a bit more genuine. "You really picked up the slack for me."

He shrugged, seeming to relax, as well. "My pleasure. I have to hand it to you and your grandmother. You certainly have a hit on your hands with the Pennsylvania Dutch Christmas traditions. Those people will tell their friends, and before you know it, every room will be full for the holidays."

"I just hope everything will go more easily once we've had a little practice." Realizing how close they were standing, she took a step back, bumping into the slant-top desk that stood between the doors.

"Easy." He reached out to steady her and then seemed to change his mind about touching her again and put his hand on the satiny old wood instead. "Don't want to harm either you or this beautiful thing."

"I'm not sure which is more valuable." She straightened the small vase of bittersweet that stood on the narrow top.

"You are," he said, and then nodded toward the desk. "But that is a nice piece. I remember something like it in my grandfather's house." He frowned, and she thought memory flickered in those deep-blue eyes.

"What is it?"

He shook his head. "Funny. I guess being here has brought back more memories. It's as if a door popped open in my mind. I can actually picture that desk now. It used to stand in the upstairs hall." He shook his head. "I'm sure it wasn't a beautiful heirloom like this one, though."

The air had been sucked out of the hall, and she was choking. She couldn't say anything—she could only force a meaningless smile.

The slant-top desk wasn't the family heirloom he obviously supposed it to be. She'd found the piece stuffed away in one of the sheds and refinished it herself when she was getting the inn ready to open.

Coincidence, she insisted. It had to be. The desk was a common style, and surely plenty of homes in the area had one like it.

"Rachel?" Tyler stared at her, eyes questioning. "Is something wrong?"

"No, not at all." She had a feeling her attempt at a smile was ghastly. "Nothing—"

She broke off at the sound of footsteps coming up

the stairs. Sturdy footsteps that could only belong to Emma.

Emma rounded the turn at the landing, saw them, and came forward steadily. Rachel glanced at Tyler. He might not have noticed it, but Emma had been doing a good job of avoiding speaking with him. Now, it appeared, she was headed straight for him.

Emma came to a halt a few feet from them, her face square and determined, graying hair drawn back under her white kapp.

"I would like to speak with Tyler Dunn, *ja?*" She made it a question.

"Of course." Rachel took a step back. "Do you want to be private?"

"No, no, you stay, Rachel." She looked steadily at Tyler. "Mrs. Unger tells us that you are John Hostetler's grandson. That you might want to know about him. My Eli's mother, she minds him well. You come to supper Monday night, she will be there, tell you about him, *ja?*"

Tyler sent her a quick glance, as if asking for help. She tried not to respond. She'd already let herself get too involved in Tyler's search for answers, and look where it had gotten her. She'd been leading the trail right where she didn't want it—back to her own family.

"That's very kind of you, Mrs. Zook." Tyler had apparently decided she wasn't going to jump in. "I appreciate it."

Emma gave a short, characteristic nod. "Is *gut*. Rachel, you will come, too. That will make it more easy."

Not waiting for an answer, Emma turned and started back down the stairs, the long skirt of her dark-green dress swishing.

Rachel opened her mouth to protest and closed it again. Emma was bracketing her with Tyler, apparently assuming that she was helping him in his search. But Emma didn't know everything. Rachel carefully avoided glancing at the desk. She'd think that through later. In the meantime—

"Look, I'll understand if you don't want to go with me," Tyler began.

"No. That's fine. I'll be happy to go."

Well, maybe "happy" was a slight exaggeration. But like it or not, she seemed to be running out of choices. The circle was closing tighter and tighter around her family.

Staying close to Tyler was dangerous, but not knowing what he was doing, what he was finding out—that could be more dangerous still.

Rachel tried to focus on Pastor Greg's sermon, not on the fact that Tyler Dunn was sitting next to her in the small sanctuary. She'd resigned herself to the necessity of working with Tyler. She just hadn't expected that cooperation to extend to worshipping next to him.

Sunday morning with guests in the house was always a difficult time. She'd served breakfast, hoping she wasn't rushing anyone, and then scrambled into her clothes.

When she'd rushed out to meet Grams in the center hallway, Tyler had been there, wearing a gray suit tailored to perfection across his broad shoulders, obviously bound for church as well. They could hardly avoid inviting him to accompany them.

She took a deep breath, trying to focus her mind and heart. Unfortunately the heady scent of pine boughs sent her mind surging back to the night she'd faced fear in this place.

And Tyler had been there to help her. She stole a glance at him. His strong-boned face was grave and attentive. He didn't seem to be experiencing any of the distraction she felt.

Maybe he had better forces of concentration than she did. That was probably important to an architect. She wasn't doing as well. Because of the trouble he'd brought into their lives, still unresolved? Or whether because of the man himself?

She folded her hands, fingers squeezing tight, and emulated Grams, serenely focused on the pastor's sermon.

Grams would show that same attention and respect no matter who was in the pulpit. She hoped she would, as well, but Pastor Greg always gave her some sturdy spiritual food to chew on.

Today the topic was angels—not fluffy, sentimental Victorian Christmas card angels, but the angels of the Bible. Grave messengers from God, exultant rejoicers at Jesus's birth. Her wayward imagination caught, she listened intently, rose to sing the closing hymn and floated out of the sanctuary at last on a thunderous organ blast of "Angels We Have Heard on High."

The spiritual lift lasted until she reached the churchyard, where Sandra Whitmoyer grabbed her arm. "Rachel, I must speak with you about the open house tour."

Of course she had to. Rachel stepped out of the flow of exiting parishioners, buttoning her coat against the December chill.

"I thought we were all set. You received the brochures, didn't you?" Phillip had finally responded to her prodding and produced a beautiful brochure, which she'd dutifully delivered to the printer.

"Yes, yes, the brochures are fine." Sandra tucked a creamy fold of cashmere scarf inside the lapel of her leather coat. "But Margaret Allen wants to serve chocolates along with her other refreshments at The Willows. Now, you know we can't risk having people put sticky, chocolaty hands on antique furniture when they go on to the next house."

"It will be all adults on the tour," she pointed out. "I'm sure they'll be responsible about touching things."

Besides, she had no desire to take on the owner of a competing bed-and-breakfast. They'd had their run-ins with Margaret in the past, and she didn't want to reopen hostilities.

"You don't know that," Sandra said darkly. "Some people will do anything. I won't have people touching the Italian tapestry on my sitting room love seat with sticky fingers."

Sandra was caught between a rock and a hard place, Rachel realized. She'd been the first to offer her lovely old Victorian home for the tour, but she'd been worrying ever since that some harm would come to her delicate furnishings.

"If I might make a suggestion—" Tyler's voice was diffident. She might have forgotten that he was standing next to her, he'd been so quiet, but she hadn't.

Sandra gave him a swift smile instead of the argumentative frown she'd been bestowing on Rachel. "Of course. Any and all suggestions are welcome."

Especially when they came from an attractive male. Rachel chastised herself for her catty thoughts. And practically on the doorstep of the church, no less.

"You might have each stop on the tour offer a container of hand wipes at the entrance. It's only sensible during cold and flu season, in any event."

"Brilliant." Sandra's smile blazed. "I don't know why I didn't think of that myself. Or why my husband didn't suggest it—"

"Didn't suggest what?" Bradley Whitmoyer slipped his arm into the crook of his wife's arm.

While Sandra was explaining, Rachel took another quick glance at Tyler's face. Could he possibly be interested in all this? His gaze crossed hers, and her heart jolted.

He looked so serious. Worry gnawed at her. If he'd found out about the desk—

But that was ridiculous. How could he? He'd hardly go around asking Grams or Emma about the provenance of a piece of furniture.

She'd asked both of them herself, cautiously, if they knew where the piece had come from. Emma had shaken her head; Grams had said vaguely that perhaps Grandfather had bought it at an auction.

Impossible to tell. The outbuildings were stuffed with furniture. Andrea had been after her to have a proper inventory made, but who had time for that?

Maybe she should be up-front with Tyler about the desk. After all, even if it had come from his grandfather's farm, that meant nothing. He could have sold it—

She was rationalizing, and she knew it. She didn't want to tell him because it was one more thing to make him suspect her father. First her grandfather, now her father. Where was it going to end?

She forced her attention back to the conversation in time to find that Tyler's suggestion had been adopted and that Sandra, thank goodness, would take care of it herself.

"I think we've kept these people standing in the cold long enough." Bradley nudged his wife toward the churchyard gate.

He was the one who looked cold. Maybe it went along with being overworked, which he probably was now that flu season had started.

Rachel turned away, feeling Tyler move beside her. She probably should have suggested that he go on back to the inn—after all, none of this would matter to him. But before they'd gone more than a couple of yards, Jeff Whitmoyer stepped into their path, his face ruddy from the nip in the air.

"Hey, glad I ran into you, Dunn." He thrust his hand toward Tyler. "You have a chance to give any thought to my offer? I'd like to get my plans made, be able to break ground as soon as the ground thaws in the spring."

"I don't recall your saying what you planned for the property, if you should buy it." Tyler sounded polite but noncommittal.

Jeff glanced from one side to the other, as if checking for anyone listening in. "Let's say I have an idea for an Amish tourist attraction and leave it at that. When can we sit down and talk it over?"

"Not today," Tyler said. "I don't do business on Sunday."

Before Jeff could suggest another day, Rachel broke in. "Speaking of work to be done in the spring, Jeff, I'd like to get on your work schedule to get that gazebo in the garden moved."

"Moved?" Jeff looked startled. "Who told you that thing could be moved?"

"I did," Tyler said smoothly.

"Tyler is an architect," Rachel added. "He suggested moving the gazebo to the far side of the pond, and I'd like to do that. If you can handle it."

"Of course I can handle it," Jeff said, affronted. "I just don't see why you'd want to move it. I thought you told me last spring you wanted it torn down. Still, if that's what you and your grandmother want, I'll get it on my schedule. I'll stop by and take a look at it this week—maybe talk to you at the same time, Dunn."

Tyler gave a quick nod and took her arm. "We'd better get your grandmother back to the house." He steered her toward Grams, who broke off a conversation with one of the neighbors when she saw them.

Well, she'd gotten Tyler away from Jeff Whitmoyer for the moment, but she didn't know what good that had done. Sooner or later Tyler would settle for whatever truth he found about his grandfather. He'd sell the property and go back to his own life. He probably wouldn't care what use was made of the property after that.

They'd reached the curb when one more interruption intercepted them, in the shape of the police cruiser, pulling to the curb next to them. Chief Burkhalter lowered the window and leaned out.

"Some information for you, Dunn." He shook a keen, assessing glance toward her and Grams. "That lockbox we were talking about—it's turned up. You can stop by my office tomorrow, if you want, and pick it up."

"Thanks. I'll do that."

She caught the suppressed excitement in Tyler's voice, and tension tightened inside her. Box? What box? He hadn't mentioned this to her. She wasn't the only person keeping secrets, it seemed.

"I hope you don't mind driving over to the Zook farm." Rachel glanced at him as he held the door of his car for her, her soft brown curls tumbling from under the knitted cap she wore. "It's an easy walk from the path beyond the barn, but not in the dark. I'd hate to have you arrive with burrs on your pant legs."

"That wouldn't look too good, would it? Am I appropriately dressed?" He hadn't known what the Amish would consider decent attire for an outsider supper guest, so he'd settled on gray flannels and a sweater over a dress shirt.

"You're fine." She pulled her seat belt across. "One thing about the Amish—they don't judge outsiders by what they wear."

How did they judge, then? He closed Rachel's door, walked around the car and slid in. He wasn't nervous—the fact that his grandfather, even his mother, apparently, had been Amish was curious, that was all.

Rachel glanced at him as he started the car. "Relax. They'll be welcoming, I promise."

He turned out onto Main Street. "It's odd, that's all. If not for my grandfather's break with the church, my life might have turned out differently."

He stopped. Impossible to think of himself being Amish. Tonight's visit was going to be meaningless, but he'd hardly been able to refuse Emma's invitation.

Rachel seemed content with the silence between them as he drove past the decorated houses and shops. Or was *content* the right word? He'd sensed some reservation in her in the past day, and he wasn't sure what that meant.

"Looks as if your Christmas in Churchville committee is doing a good job. The only thing missing to turn the village into a Christmas card scene is a couple of inches of snow."

"It does look lovely, doesn't it?" The eagerness in her voice dissipated whatever reserve he'd been imagining. "This is exactly how I've pictured it. Like coming home for Christmas. Don't you think?"

It wasn't the home he'd known, but he understood. "That's it. You'll send visitors away feeling they have to come back every year for their Christmas to be complete."

He understood more than that. That her pleasure and satisfaction was more than just the sense of a job well done. It was personal, not professional. Rachel had found her place in the world when she'd come back here.

It wasn't his place, he reminded himself. His partner was already getting antsy, emailing him to ask how soon he'd be coming back.

He deserved the time off, he'd pointed out to Gil. And it certainly wasn't a question of Gil needing him in the office. They had a good partnership, with Gil Anders being the outgoing people-person while he preferred to work alone with his computer and his blueprints.

Baltimore is not that far away, a small voice pointed out in the back of his mind. It would be possible to come back. To see Rachel again.

Always assuming Rachel wanted to see him once this whole affair had ended.

Rachel leaned forward, pointing. "There's the lane to the Zook farm."

He turned. "The Christmas lights seem to stop here."

"No electricity." He sensed Rachel's smile, even in the dark. "The Amish don't go in for big displays, in any event. Christmas is a religious celebration. The day after, the twenty-sixth, they call 'second Christmas.' That's the day for visiting and celebrating."

He nodded, concentrating on the narrow farm lane in the headlight beams. "You certainly have a lot of different Christmas traditions going in this small area. I like your grandmother's Moravian customs."

"You'd see even more of that if you went to Lititz or Bethlehem. That reminds me, I want to run over to Bethlehem sometime this week to take more photos and pick up a stack of brochures before the next weekend guests come in."

The farmhouse appeared as they passed a windbreak of evergreens, lights glowing yellow from the windows.

"Just pull up by the porch," Rachel instructed. "The children are already peeking out the windows, watching for us."

While he parked and rounded the car to join Rachel, he went over in his mind what she'd told him about the family. Emma and Eli, her husband, now lived in a kind of grandparent cottage, attached to the main house, while their son Samuel and his wife, Nancy, ran the farm with their children. There was another son, Levi, who was mentally handicapped. Nobody seemed to be considered too young, too old or too disabled to contribute to the family, as far as he could tell from what Rachel had said.

The front door was thrown open as they mounted the

porch, and they were greeted by five children—blond stair steps with round blue eyes and huge smiles. The smallest one, a girl, flung herself at Rachel for a hug.

"You're here at last! We've been waiting and waiting. Maam says that you might hear me do my piece for the Christmas program. Will you, Rachel?"

Rachel tugged on a blond braid gently. "I would love to hear you, Elizabeth. Now just let us greet everyone."

The adults were already coming into the room. In rapid succession he was introduced to Eli, their son Samuel, and his wife, Nancy, a brisk, cheerful woman who seemed to run her household with firm command. If he'd imagined that Amish women were meek and subservient, she dispelled that idea.

"This is my mother, Liva Zook." Eli held the arm of an elderly woman, her hair glistening white, her eyes still intensely blue behind her wire-rimmed glasses. "She will be glad to talk with you about your grandfather."

He extended his hand and then hesitated, not sure if that was proper. But she shook hands, hers dry and firm in his.

"You sit here and talk." Nancy ushered him and Eli's mother to a pair of wooden rockers.

He nodded, waiting for the elderly woman to sit down first and then taking his place next to her. The room initially seemed bare to his eyes, but the chair was surprisingly comfortable, the back of it curved to fit his body and the arms worn smooth to the hand.

Eli pulled up a straight chair and sat down next to his mother. "Maam sometimes does not do well in English, so I'll help." He reached out to pat his mother's hand, and Tyler could see the bond between them. Eli's ruddy face above the white beard had the same bone structure, the same round blue eyes.

He'd begun to get used to the Amish custom of beards without mustaches, and the bare faces with the fringe of beard no longer looked odd to him.

"Thanks." Now that he had the opportunity, he wasn't sure how to begin. "If you could just tell me what you remember about my grandfather—"

For a moment he was afraid she didn't understand, but then she nodded. "I remember John. We were children together, *ja*." She nodded again in what seemed a characteristic gesture.

"What was he like?" Was he ever different from the angry, bitter man who had turned everyone away from him?

She studied his face. "Looked something like you, when he was young. Strong, like you. He knew his mind, did what he wanted."

He glanced from her to Eli. "The Amish church doesn't like that, does it?"

"He was young." Her lips creased in an indulgent smile. "The young, they have to see the other side of the fence sometimes."

"Rumspringa," Eli said. "Our youth have time to see the world before they decide to join the church. So they know what they are doing." His eyes twinkled. "Some have a wilder *rumspringa* than others."

Sensible, he thought. It surprised him, in a way, that the Amish would allow that. They must have a lot of confidence that their kids wouldn't be lured away by the world.

"Ja, that was John Hostetler. Always questioning. Always wanting to know things not taught in our

school. Folk worried about him." She frowned slightly, folding her hands together on the dark apron she wore. "But then he began courting Anna Schmidt. They had eyes for no one else, those two."

It was odd, he supposed, that he hadn't even thought about his grandmother. "I never knew her."

"She died when her daughter was only twelve." Her eyes clouded with sympathy. "Your maam, that was."

"What was she like? My grandmother?"

Pert and lively like young Elizabeth, who was bouncing up and down as she recited something for Rachel on the other side of the room? Nurturing, like Emma, or brisk and take-charge, like Nancy?

"Sweet-natured. Kind." The old woman smiled, reminiscing. "She was very loving, was Anna. Seemed as if that rubbed off on John when they married. But when she died—" She shook her head. "He turned against everyone. Even God."

Something in him rebelled at that. "Maybe if people had tried to help him, it would have been different."

"We tried." Tears filled her eyes. "For Anna, for himself, for the community. Nothing did any good. He would not listen. He turned against everything Anna was." She shook her head. "She would have been so sad. You understand. She was one who couldn't stop loving and caring."

He nodded, touched by the image of the grandmother who'd barely entered his mind before this. Someone sweet. Loving. Dedicated to family.

He glanced across the room at Rachel, her face lit with laughter as she hugged the little girl.

Like Rachel. Loving. Nurturing. Dedicated to family. Emotion flooded him. He had feelings for her. What was he going to do about that?

"It was in his blood," Liva Zook said suddenly. "Rebellion. He held on to that adornment out of pride, hiding it away and thinking no one knew about it. It took him on a dangerous path, like his grandfather before him."

He blinked. "I'm sorry?" He glanced at Eli. "I don't understand."

Eli bent toward his mother, saying something in a fast patter of the Low German the Amish used among themselves.

She shook her head, replying quickly, almost as if she argued with him. Then she stopped, closing her eyes.

It was unnerving. Had she gone to sleep in the middle of the conversation?

"What did she say?" Eli must know.

Eli shrugged, but his candid blue eyes no longer met Tyler's so forthrightly. "Old folks' gossip, *ja.* She has forgotten now. That's how it is sometimes."

There was more to it than that. His instincts told him. Eli knew perfectly well what his mother meant, but he didn't want to repeat it.

He could hardly cross-examine an elderly woman, but Eli was another story. "It was you who found him, wasn't it?"

Eli's face tightened. *"Ja,"* he said. "Heard the cows, I did, still in the barn and not milked. I looked inside, saw him."

Eli was the closest thing to an eyewitness he'd find, then. "Where was he?"

"Chust inside the door he was. I could see things was

messed up—a lamp broke, his strongbox lying there open. I went for help, but it was too late."

His mouth clamped shut with finality on the words, and for a moment he looked as grim as an Old Testament prophet. Tyler would get nothing else from him.

He thought again of what the elderly woman had said, frowning. He hadn't expected much from this visit. But what he'd heard had raised more questions than it answered.

Chapter Eleven

Rachel leaned against the car window to wave good-bye to Elizabeth, who stood on the porch, her cape wrapped around her, waving vigorously until the car rounded a bend and was lost to her sight.

"She's such a sweetheart." She glanced at Tyler, wondering if he'd say anything to her about what Eli's mother had told him.

The conversation had been general during supper. His manner had probably seemed perfectly natural to the others, but she knew him well enough to sense the preoccupation behind his pleasant manner.

"She certainly is. What was the piece she was talking about? Something she had to memorize?"

So apparently they were going to continue on a surface level. They turned onto the main road, and the Christmas lights seemed to blur for a moment before her eyes.

"The Christmas program in the Amish school is one of the most important events of the year for the children. The families, too. The kids practice their pieces for weeks, and the day of the program you'll see the buggies lined up for a mile."

"Do they ever invite non-Amish?"

She smiled. "As a matter of fact, we both have an invitation from Elizabeth to attend. It's the Friday before Christmas."

"If I'm still here—" He left that open-ended.

Well, of course. He probably had a wonderful celebration planned back in Baltimore. He wouldn't hang around here any longer than was necessary.

She cleared her throat. "I'm glad you had a chance to try traditional Amish food tonight. Nancy is a great cook."

"I thought if she urged me to eat one more thing, I'd burst. I hope I didn't offend her by turning down that last piece of shoofly pie."

"I expect she understood." She gestured with the plastic food container on her lap. "And she sent along a couple of pieces for a midnight snack."

"She obviously loves feeding people. She could go into business."

They were passing The Willows at the moment, and she noticed, as always, what her competition had going on. The Willows looked like a Dickens Christmas this year.

"I wonder—" The idea began to form in her mind, nebulous at first but firming up quickly.

Tyler glanced at her. "You wonder what?"

"What you said about Nancy's cooking made me think. If we could offer our guests the opportunity to have dinner in an Amish home, that might be really appealing."

"Sounds like a nice extra to pull people in. Why

don't you go for it, if Nancy and her family are willing?"

"It's a bit more complicated than that." The light was on in the back room of Phil Longstreet's shop. He must be working late.

"Why complicated? Just add it to the website, and you're in business."

"Not complicated at my end. At theirs. Even if Nancy and Samuel are interested, they'd have to get the approval of the bishop first."

He turned into the inn's driveway, darting her a frowning look as they passed under the streetlight. "Don't the Amish have the right to decide things for themselves? Seems pretty oppressive to me."

"They wouldn't see it that way." How to explain an entire lifestyle in a few words? "The Amish way is that of humility, of not being prideful or trying to be better than their neighbors. If something comes up that is not already part of the local Amish way, then the question would be taken to the bishop, and they'd abide by his decision."

"Still seems restrictive to me." He pulled into his usual parking space. "Maybe it would have to my grandfather, too."

"Do you think that's why he left the community?"

For a moment he didn't answer. Her hand was already on the door handle when he shook his head. "No, probably not. Will you stay awhile? I'd like to talk."

"Of course."

He stared through the windshield for a moment. Warmth flowed from the car heater, and the motor sound was a soft background. The windows misted, enclosing them in a private world of their own.

"Eli's mother told me a little about my grandfather. And my grandmother." His shoulders moved restlessly under his jacket. "Funny that I never really thought much about her. But if Mrs. Zook was right, she was really the key to understanding him."

"How do you mean?" She put the question softly, not wanting to disturb the connection between them.

"The way she described her—loving, warm, gentle. It sounds as if she melted his heart. When she died, he apparently turned against everyone."

"That's the last thing she would have wanted."

He shot her a glance. "That's what Mrs. Zook said, too. How did you know?"

"If she was the person you described, then his bitterness was a betrayal of everything she was." Her throat tightened. "So sad. So very sad."

"Yes." His voice sounded tight, as well. He turned toward her, very close in the confined space. "I'm not sure I like knowing this much about my family. They didn't do a good job of making each other happy, did they?"

"I'm sorry." She reached out impulsively to touch his hand, felt it turn and grasp hers warmly. "Sometimes people just make the wrong choices."

He nodded. "Speaking of choices—" He hesitated, and she sensed a moment of doubt. Then his hand gripped hers more firmly. "I didn't tell you about the strongbox that Chief Burkhalter found. Apparently, it's been shoved in a storeroom all these years."

"Did it—did it give you any ideas about what happened?" She held her breath, half afraid of the answer.

"It had apparently been broken into the night my grandfather died. The police chief at the time must have asked my mother what had been in it. I found a list inside. In her handwriting."

She smoothed her hand along his, offering wordless comfort. How hard that must have been for him, still struggling with his grief.

He cleared his throat. "Apparently he'd kept money in there, but there was no way of knowing how much. One thing she seemed sure was missing, though. It was a medal, a German military decoration. There was a pencil rubbing of it, still fairly legible after all this time. Apparently it was something of a family heirloom." He glanced at her. "Seems funny, doesn't it? I mean, the Amish are pacifists, aren't they?"

"Yes, but I suppose it could date from a time before the family became Amish. Or from a non-Amish relative. He might have kept it out of sentiment."

"Or pride. I get the feeling my grandfather really struggled with the whole humility aspect of his faith."

"That's tough for a lot of people, Amish or not."

His square jaw tightened. "There's something else. Something Eli's mother said, about him being rebellious. She said it was in his blood. Talked about him keeping some adornment, keeping it hidden."

"She may have meant the military medal, then." She wasn't sure why that seemed to bother him.

"Maybe." He tapped his hand on the steering wheel. "I could be imagining things, but I thought Eli didn't like her mentioning that. He denied knowing what she was talking about, but I wasn't convinced. He was the one who found my grandfather. Did you know that?"

"You can't imagine Eli had anything to do with your grandfather's death." Her voice sharpened in protest. "He's the most honest, peaceful person I know."

"There could be more involved than you know."

"I know that's ridiculous." Who would he suspect next?

"Maybe so." He didn't seem to react to the tartness in her tone. "In any event, the medal, whatever it means, gives me something that might be traceable. Another road to follow."

"Good. I hope you find something." She also hoped it was something that led away from her family.

"Sorry." He smiled, a little rueful. "I guess I sound obsessed. I can't help following this wherever it takes me. But I do hope——"

"I know." He was very close in the confines of the car, and she could sense the struggle in him. "I know you don't want to hurt me. I mean, us." She felt the warmth flood her cheeks. Thank goodness he wouldn't be able to see in the dim light.

"You." His hand drifted to her cheek, cradling it.

Her breath caught. She could not possibly speak. Maybe there wasn't anything to say. Because his lips lowered, met hers, and everything else slipped away in the moment.

He drew back finally. "I guess maybe we should go in. Before your grandmother wonders what we're doing out here."

It took a moment to catch her breath. To be sure her voice would come out naturally.

"I guess we should." She had to force herself to move, because if she stayed this close to him another moment, they'd just end up kissing again.

She slid out, waiting while he walked around the car to join her. The chill air sent a shiver through her, and she glanced around.

Imagination. It was imagination that put shadows within shadows, that made her feel as if inimical eyes watched from the dark.

Tyler put his arm across her shoulders. The spasm of fear vanished in the strength of his grip, and together they walked toward the house.

"It should be down just a couple of blocks on the right." Rachel leaned forward, watching as Tyler negotiated the narrow side street in Bethlehem late Wednesday afternoon. "I don't see any numbers, but I'll look for the sign."

"It's a good thing we came together. I didn't expect this much traffic. I'd never have found it alone." He touched the brake as a car jolted out into traffic from a parking space.

"Christmas in Bethlehem. It's a magnet for tourists, and the shoppers are out in full force this afternoon."

They were several blocks away from the attraction of the Moravian Museum and the Christkindlmarket, the Christmas craft mart for which Bethlehem was famous, but the small shops in this block had drawn their share of people.

"Are you sure this is the same medal?" She'd been surprised, to put it mildly, when Tyler told her that an internet search had already turned up the medal, or one like it, in a military memorabilia shop in Bethlehem. Since she'd planned to come anyway, it made sense that they do the trip together.

"No, I'm not sure. The dealer had a blurry photo on his website, tough to compare with a pencil rubbing." He frowned, glancing down at the printout that was tucked into the center console. "Still, it's worth checking out—same decoration, turning up in the same general area."

She nodded, not sure how she felt about this. "If it is the medal—well, I suppose if he valued it as much as you say, he probably wouldn't have sold it. But if the medal was stolen that night, where has it been all this time?"

"Might have been in the dealer's hands for years, and he just now got around to putting it up on a website."

He might be overly optimistic about that. The chances of finding the object so easily seemed doubtful to her. But if it was the right medal, and if the dealer remembered who'd sold it to him—

"There it is. In the next block." She couldn't help a thread of apprehension in her voice.

Tyler flipped on the turn signal and backed smoothly into a parking space that she wouldn't even have attempted. "Good. Let's see what we can find out."

A chilly wind cut into her as she stepped out of the car, and she wrapped her jacket tighter around her. Tyler tucked his hand warmly into the crook of her arm as they hurried down the sidewalk, passing antique shop and a craft store.

Military Memorabilia, the sign read. Joseph Whittaker, Owner. Dusty display windows revealed little of what lay inside.

"It'll probably be mostly Minnie balls and shell fragments," she warned. "There are plenty of places where a Civil War enthusiast with a metal detector can come up with those."

"Nothing ventured," Tyler murmured, and pushed open the door.

The shop was just as crowded and disorganized inside as it appeared from the street. Wooden shelves and bins held a miscellaneous accumulation of larger items, while a few glass cases contained what might have been military insignia and decoration. A Union Army uniform hung from a peg near the door, exuding an aroma of wool and mothballs.

An elderly man sat on a stool behind the counter. He unfolded himself slowly, straightening with a smile, and pulled a pair of wire-rimmed glasses from atop scanty white hair to settle them on a pointed nose.

"Welcome, welcome." He dusted off his hands as he came toward them. "What are you folks looking for today? Anything in the military line, I'm bound to have it. The best collection in the county, if I do say so myself."

"I'm looking for a military decoration you have listed on your website." Tyler obviously saw no reason to beat around the bush. He'd be as straightforward in this as in everything else.

"The website." For a moment the man looked confused. "Yes, well, my nephew did that for me. I'm afraid I'm not really up on such things. What was it you were looking for?"

She could sense Tyler's impatience as he pulled the printout from his pocket. "This medal."

The man squinted at the image for a long moment. "Ah, you collect Bavarian military memorabilia. Quite a specialty, that is. I have several pieces you might care to see."

"Just this piece." The impatience was getting a bit more pronounced. "Do you have it?"

He peered again at the sheet. "Well, yes, I'm sure I do. Let me just have a look around." He moved along behind the counter, peering down through the wavy glass and muttering to himself.

Rachel tried not to smile as he vanished around the corner of the shelves, still murmuring. "The White Rabbit," she whispered.

Tyler's frown dissolved in a surprised smile. "Exactly. I suspect he hasn't the faintest idea—"

"Ah, I know." The shopkeeper popped his head around the corner. "My nephew took some things in the back when he photographed them for the website. His new digital camera, you see. Just a moment while I check." He went through a door that was hidden by what seemed to be half of a medieval suit of armor.

"If he doesn't keep track of his stock any better than that…" she began.

"…he's unlikely to know where it came from. Well, all I can do is try." Tyler drummed his fingers impatiently on the countertop.

It couldn't be this easy. That was what she wanted to say, but it hardly seemed encouraging.

The shopkeeper hustled back in, something dangling from his hand.

"Here we go. I knew I had it somewhere."

Tyler leaned forward, his face tight with concentration. The man put the medal on the glass-top counter, where it landed with a tiny clink.

Dull silver in color, the shape of a Roman cross, with something that might have been a laurel wreath design around it and a profile in the center. Tyler turned it over, frowning at some faint scratches, and then flipped it back. "What can you tell me about it?"

"Fairly rare, I assure you. Early eighteenth-century

Bavarian. I'm not an expert on the period, I'm afraid. Civil War is more my area."

Minnie balls, she thought but didn't say.

"How did you come by this?" Tyler's voice sounded casual, but his fingers pressed taut against the glass.

She held her breath. Suppose he said— Well, that was impossible. Her father could not have been involved.

"Came from the collection of Stanley Albright, over at New Holland. Quite a collector, he was, but after he passed away, his widow decided to sell some things off."

"And do you know where he got it?" Tyler's gaze was intent.

The man shook his head. "I'm afraid not, but I assure you it's genuine. Albright knew his stuff, all right."

Since Mr. Albright was no longer around to be questioned, his expertise didn't help. She didn't know whether to be relieved or disappointed.

"Do you think his widow might have any records of his collection?"

"She might," he conceded. "I'm sure I have her number somewhere." He looked around, as if expecting the number to materialize in front of him. "Now about the medal—"

Rachel watched, a bit dissatisfied, as Tyler agreed to the first price that was named. He wasn't used to the routine haggling that the shopkeeper had probably looked forward to. She could have gotten it for at least fifteen percent less, but it wasn't her place to interfere.

She couldn't help commenting when they were back on the street with the medal and Mrs. Albright's phone number tucked into Tyler's pocket. "He didn't expect you to agree to the first amount he named, you know."

"Didn't he?" He looked startled for a moment, and

then smiled. "No, of course not. I was just so obsessed with getting it that I didn't think."

"You're convinced this medal is the right one, then." It all seemed too easy to her. Still, the dealer's account held together. Apparently the police hadn't even tried to trace the medal at the time.

He nodded, the smile vanishing. "It's identical to the rubbing, right down to the small chip on one of the points." He put his hand over the pocket containing the medal.

It meant something to him, that memento of the grandfather he'd barely known. Something other than a clue to the thief who'd stolen it.

She glanced at Tyler's face, his brow furrowed in concentration. Thinking about the next step, no doubt.

And where would that next step lead? If Mrs. Albright did indeed have a record of where her husband had gotten the medal, whose name would be it be?

Rachel came out of the second-floor office where she'd picked up the brochures she needed. After they'd been unable to find a parking place on Bethlehem's busy downtown streets, Tyler had dropped her off and gone in search of a lot.

At least this gave her a few moments to compose herself and think this situation through rationally. What did it say about her faith in her father, in her grandfather, that Tyler's discoveries disturbed her so much?

She was being ridiculous, letting his suspicions taint her own belief. Of course, her father, her grandfather, hadn't been involved with the theft of that medal, any more than Eli Zook had been. The very idea was preposterous.

Someone bumped into her, murmuring an apology, and she realized she was blocking traffic in the hallway. People had begun pouring from the display rooms toward the stairs. It must be a tour group, or there wouldn't be so many at once.

Clutching the awkward box firmly against her, she stepped back to let them pass, pressing against the nearest wall. She'd wait until they were gone, and then she'd go down.

She felt it then. The hair lifted on the back of her neck, as if a cold draft blew on her, but there was no draft. Someone was watching her.

She shrugged, trying to push off the feeling. She was in the middle of a crowd. Of course people looked at her as they went by, probably wondering why she was so inconsiderate as to stand there when they were trying to get down the stairs. She could hardly make an announcement, citing the awkward box she carried and the leg that was not always stable on stairs. She wouldn't if she could—she didn't care to let anyone know that.

But this wasn't just a sense of being frowned at by someone who wished she'd move. This was a return of the feeling she'd had that dark night in the sanctuary—the automatic response of the mouse that glimpses the hawk.

Turning a little, she scanned the crowd. Lots of gray heads—this was probably a seniors' tour group, come to enjoy a day of Bethlehem's Christmas celebration. A scattering of families, too—a father in a bright-red anorak carrying a toddler in a snowsuit on his shoulders, a pair of parents wrestling with a stroller and a balky preschool-age child. And a few students, laughing, jostling their neighbors even as they ignored them a bit too obviously. No one stared at her, and there wasn't a soul she knew.

But the feeling persisted, growing stronger by the moment. Then a fresh group swept around the corner, also headed for the stairs, clogging the corridor, and Rachel was carried along with it, helpless as a leaf in the current.

She struggled for a moment and then gave up and let herself be taken along. She had to meet Tyler downstairs in any event, and at least this would take her away from that feeling, whatever caused it.

Maneuvering through the crowd, trying to find something to hold on to, she reached the balcony railing just as she was pushed toward the top step. She grabbed the railing, clutching it with a sense of relief.

At least she had something to hold on to. She'd make it down the stairs all right. Goodness knew it would be impossible to fall—the packed bodies in their winter coats would certainly keep her upright no matter what she did.

An eddy in the crowd pressed her against the railing. It pushed uncomfortably into her side, sending the corner of the box poking into her ribs. She lifted the container, trying to get it out of the way, taking her hand from the railing for a moment.

The crowd lurched, for all the world like a train about to go off the track. Irrational fear pulsed through her. She hated this. She had to get out of it, get away from this feeling of helplessness.

Another, stronger push from behind her, this time doubling her over the waist-high railing. The box flew from her hands, flipping into the air and then going down, down, until it spattered on the tile floor below.

She tried to hold on to the railing, but it was round, smooth, shiny metal, sliding under her fingers. She didn't have breath to cry out. Someone shoved her again, harder, she was going to go over, she couldn't stop herself, she'd go plummeting down to that hard tile floor, she glimpsed Tyler's startled face in the crowd below, looking up at her—

And then a strong hand grasped her arm and pulled her back. "Easy, now. Are you okay? Get a little dizzy, did you?"

A bronzed face, looking as if its owner spent most of the year on a golf course. He gripped her firmly, smiling, but with apprehension lurking in his eyes.

"Of course she got dizzy." His wife, probably, a small round dumpling of a woman with masses of white hair under a turquoise knit cap. "No wonder, with this crowd. Just take it easy, my dear, and Harold will get you down safely."

Harold was as good as his wife's word, piloting her down the rest of the stairs with a strong hand on her arm. It was a good thing, because it seemed her balance had gone over the railing with the brochures.

And then they reached the bottom, and Tyler's arms closed around her. She lost the next few minutes, hearing a jumble of concern, recommendations that she go somewhere and have a nice cup of tea, Tyler's deep voice assuring her rescuers that he'd take good care of her.

Somehow, in spite of everything that stood between them, she didn't doubt it.

* * *

Tyler held Rachel firmly as the helpful couple left, pulling her close against his side. His breathing wasn't back to normal yet, and he was torn between the desire to kiss her and a strong urge to shake her for scaring him so badly.

"Are you okay? I thought for a minute you were going to take a header all the way to the floor." He tried for a light tone, hoping to disguise the panic he'd felt in that moment when he'd seen her falling and been unable to help her.

"So did I." Her voice trembled a little, and she shook her head impatiently. "Silly to be so scared, but it's such a helpless feeling when you're losing control."

His hand tightened on her arm. "Are you hurt?"

"No, not at all." Her smile wasn't quite genuine. "But my brochures—"

"They're over here." He led her into the shadow of the soaring staircase. "About where you'd have landed if someone hadn't grabbed you."

His uneasiness intensified. Either Rachel was accident-prone, or she'd been having a surprising run of misfortune lately.

He gathered up the brochures, stuffing them back into the box, his hands not quite steady. Coincidence, that bad things seemed to be happening to Rachel since his arrival? But not entirely—her accident had occurred before they met. That didn't reassure him.

He kept a firm grip on her as they exited the building. The streets were still crowded, and a band played Christmas carols on the corner. In the glow of the streetlamp and candles from the windows, her face was pale. He read the tension there, and something jolted inside him.

"What is it?" Anxiety sharpened his tone, and he drew her into the shelter of a shop doorway. "There's something more, isn't there?"

She pressed her lips together, staring absently down the crowded street. "It... I must have imagined it." She looked up at him, the color drained from her face. "I thought someone was watching me, upstairs. And when I nearly went over the railing, it felt as if someone pushed me." She shook her head. "I must have imagined it."

The shop door opened behind him, and they had to move to let a couple come out. The irresistible aroma of cinnamon and sugar wafted out with them. The place was a bakery, with several small round tables, empty now.

"Let's get inside and have some coffee. We need to talk about this."

His heart seemed to lurch at her answering smile. The smile trembled for an instant, and her eyes darkened as if she saw right into his heart.

He cleared his throat. He couldn't give in to the urge to kiss her here and now, could he? He held the door, touching her arm to steer her inside.

For an instant she stopped, half in and half out, her eyes focused on the street beyond the plate glass.

"What is it?" He glanced in that direction, seeing nothing but the flow of traffic and the jostling crowds.

"Nothing, I guess." She shook her head, moving past him into the shop. "I thought I saw someone staring at us. I told you my imagination worked overtime."

"Man or woman?"

"Man—youngish, wearing a dark jacket."

He paused, holding the door, scanning the street beyond. Someone had knocked him out trying to break into the farmhouse—someone had frightened Rachel with that stupid trick at the church. Maybe someone had even tampered with the Christmas lights.

Still, why would anyone care what they were doing in Bethlehem today?

He led Rachel to a table, placed the order, ending up getting hot chocolate and an assortment of cookies, and all the while his mind busied itself with the answer to that question.

Someone might well care what they were doing in Bethlehem, because they were following up on his grandfather's murder. And if someone had tried to push Rachel over that railing, it was his fault.

She wrapped her hands around the thick white mug, lifting it to sip gingerly and coming away with a feathering of cream on her lip. She looked at him, eyes wide and serious.

"I might feel better if you told me that was a ridiculous fear, and that no one could possibly have pushed me."

He captured one hand in his. "I might, but I don't like the way things are going. Someone might be worried about what we found out at the shop today. Might think we're getting too close."

She looked down at the frothy liquid. "In that case, you'd think it would be you they'd try to push down the stairs. You're the one who's determined to learn the truth."

"Yes." That bothered him, more than he wanted to admit. "The attack on me seems pretty explainable.

Thieves or vandals, hitting me so that they could get away. But you. Why would anyone want to frighten or hurt you?"

"I don't know. I'm not convinced that someone does, not really." Her brow furrowed. "Except— Well I still feel the Christmas lights could have been an accident. But someone was in the church that night." She shivered a little. "And I can't prove it, but someone did push me on the stairs."

"If so—" He felt in his pocket for the medal and pulled it out. "You'd think they'd have been better served by trying to pick my pocket if they're worried about this."

She nodded, watching as he unwrapped the medal. "Let me have a look at it."

He shoved it across the table to her, and she bent over it, studying the surface and then turning it over. Maybe the distraction was good for her. The color seemed to return to her cheeks.

She frowned, staring at the back of it. "Is this some sort of worn inscription, or is it just scratched?"

He held it up to the light, rubbing it with his finger. "I don't know. Maybe if I clean it, we'll be able to make it out." He fingered it a moment longer and then wrapped the tissue paper around it again. "If it could talk, it might give me the answers I need."

"Maybe it will anyway." She seemed to make an effort to meet his eyes. "I'll ask Grams the best way to approach Mrs. Albright. She knows everyone."

"It might be better if you and your grandmother didn't get involved in this. I don't want you put into any further danger."

"Assuming the danger is real, and not just a figment

of my imagination or a series of unfortunate accidents." She shook her head. "If I went to Zach Burkhalter—well, he might take it seriously, but what could he do?"

His fingers tightened on hers. "I should move out. Not see you again. Make sure that anyone who's interested knows you have no connection with me."

"And what good would that do?" Her voice was remarkably calm. "If this incident was real, not yet another accident, then it means that the target isn't you. It's me. And I don't know why."

Chapter Twelve

"Thank you, Mrs. Albright, but I really don't care for any more tea. Now if we could just—"

Rachel's frown didn't seem to be working, so she silenced Tyler with a light kick on the ankle. She smiled at the elderly woman across the piecrust tea table, holding out the delicate china cup.

"I'd love another cup. What a nice flavor. It's Earl Grey, I know, but it seems to have extra bergamot."

Mrs. Albright beamed as if Rachel were a favorite pupil. "That's exactly right. I get it from a little shop in Lancaster. If you think your dear grandmother would like it, I'll give you the address."

"That would be lovely." Rachel could feel Tyler seethe with impatience, and she gave him a bland smile. He didn't understand in the least how to deal with someone like Amanda Albright. He undoubtedly saw her as a contemporary of her grandmother, but she was at least ten or fifteen years older, and as delicate and fragile as a piece of the bone china on the tea table.

Elderly ladies in rural areas had their own rules of proper behavior. What Tyler didn't realize was that if he'd come alone, he'd never have gotten in the door, let alone be having tea in a parlor that was as perfect in its period detail as its mistress. Only her own vague memories of having been taken to tea with some of Grams's friends as a child had come to her rescue.

"You're running a bed-and-breakfast inn at the Unger house now, I understand. Just a nice, genteel occupation for a young girl, and I'm sure your grandmother is delighted to have you there."

Normally she'd have choked at the prospect of being called a young girl, but in this case it was best just to smile and nod. "I'm glad to be settled at home again."

Mrs. Albright nodded, eyes bright and curious as she looked from Rachel to Tyler. "And you, young man. What do you do?"

"I'm a partner in an architectural firm in Baltimore. Now about the collection—"

Rachel kicked him again. "Tyler has family ties here, though. His maternal grandparents were John and Anna Hostetler."

"Ah, of course." One could almost see the wheels turning as she ticked through the possibilities. "John had his faults, no one could deny that, but generally good, sturdy stock. Very appropriate."

Tyler had his mouth full of butter cookie at the time, and a few crumbs escaped when he sputtered in response.

Rachel set her cup down, hoping the tiny clatter masked his reaction and trying to stifle a smile of her own. She'd known what was going on from the moment they'd sat down on the petit-point chairs. Amanda Albright was sizing up Tyler's potential as a match for her dear friend Katherine's granddaughter.

Explaining that she and Tyler didn't have that kind of relationship would only confuse the issue, and Mrs. Albright probably wouldn't believe it, anyway. She had her own agenda, and nothing would deter her. It was different probably, in Tyler's brisk urban life, but in country places like this, the gossip around any young couple would include the suitability of the family lines for several generations back.

"Tyler is settling his grandfather's estate, and in the process he's located a piece that originally belonged to the family." Now that she had firmly linked their mission to the personal, it was time to broach the subject.

She nodded to Tyler. Finally recognizing his cue, he took a tissue-wrapped package from his pocket and opened it to divulge the medal.

"The dealer said that he'd purchased it from your husband's collection." He held it out for Mrs. Albright to see.

She raised the glasses that hung on a gold chain around her neck. "Yes, indeed, that was part of my Stanley's collection." She shook her head. "I didn't want to part with any of it, but my niece persuaded me to begin clearing a few of the things that don't have personal meaning to me."

"Did your husband happen to keep records of the origin of the items he acquired?" Tyler sounded as if he had faint hope of that.

"Certainly he did." She was obviously affronted that he would think otherwise.

"That was very wise of him," Rachel soothed. "So few people are as organized as he was. Do you think we might be able to find out when and from whom he purchased this medal? It was certainly help Tyler in—"

she could hardly say in investigating his grandfather's
death "—in understanding his family history."

"That's very proper. I wish more young people took
an interest, instead of leaving genealogical research to
their elders." She rose with a faint rustle of silk. "Just
come into my husband's library, and we'll have a look."

Tyler had sprung to his feet as soon as she moved,
and he stepped back to let her pass. Behind Mrs. Albright's back, he clasped Rachel's hand for a quick
squeeze.

She retrieved her hand and followed their hostess
into the next room, hoping she wasn't blushing. Well,
if she was, Mrs. Albright would just think—

She stopped, struggling with the idea. Mrs. Albright
would think there was something between them. She
already thought that. And there was certainly something, but the chances of it leading to a real relationship were slim, maybe nonexistent.

Mrs. Albright leaned over file cabinets against the
wall, peering at the labels. "Your eyes are better than
mine, young man. You check for it. He organized every
item in his collection and each antique in the house by
type, and kept a file with its provenance."

Tyler moved with alacrity, running his finger down
the file drawer labels and then pulling out one of the
drawers. He paused, glancing at Mrs. Albright. "Would
you like me to look through the files, or would you
prefer to do it?"

She shook her head, waving her hand slightly. "You
find it. I think I'll just sit down for a bit."

"Are you all right?" Rachel grasped her arm. "Would
you like me to get you something?"

"No, no, I'm fine." But she let Rachel help her to

the nearest chair. "This was Stanley's province, you know. I can't come in here without seeing him sitting in that chair, his nose buried in a book, his pipe on the table beside him."

Rachel patted her hand. "It must be so difficult."

"Sixty-one years, we had." She sighed. "I never thought I'd be the one to go on without him."

"I'm sorry if our coming has been difficult. Perhaps we could come another time to look for it—"

"That won't be necessary." Tyler's voice had an odd note. "I've found it." He carried a manila file folder to her.

She took it, almost afraid to look. *Please Lord. Not my father. He couldn't have, could he?*

She forced herself to scan the page. The medal was listed, with a minute description. The date Albright had purchased it. Her heart thudded. A year after John Hostetler died.

And the seller. Phillip Longstreet, of Longstreet's Antiques.

Tyler came down the stairs, suppressing the urge to take them a couple at a time. The Unger mansion, even in its incarnation as an inn, seemed to discourage that sort of thing. Nothing wrong with that, except that at the moment his muscles tensed with the need to do something—anything that would resolve this situation and lead him to the truth.

Rachel came out of the family side as he hit the hallway, almost as if she'd been listening for him. Her green eyes were anxious as they searched his face.

"Did you talk to Chief Burkhalter? What did he say?"

His jaw tightened. There was nothing, he supposed, that dictated that he had to tell Rachel. But she'd gone out of her way to help him, in spite of what must have seemed like very good reasons to tell him to get out.

Besides, he'd gotten to like the idea that he wasn't in this alone. "I talked to him." He grimaced. "He pointed out that there could be several perfectly innocent ways for Longstreet to come by that medal."

"And one guilty one." She shook her head. "I couldn't believe it when I saw his name. And I still can't, not really. He's been a fixture in the community his entire life. Surely, if there was anything to be known, someone would have talked about it by now."

"People can do a good job of keeping a secret when their lives depend on it."

She paled, as if she hadn't considered that outcome. "Your grandfather died from a heart attack, but if it was brought on by the robbery, it could be considered murder."

"Exactly." He shrugged. "I can't blame Chief Burkhalter for moving cautiously. Longstreet is well-known around here. But I've had the sense from you that he's not entirely respected."

"I certainly never meant he was dishonest. Just—maybe a bit too eager to make a good deal. If there had been rumors of anything else—well, I haven't heard them. But Zach Burkhalter would have. He knows what's going on. You can rely on him."

"He said he'd investigate."

"But you're not satisfied." She seemed to know him as well as he knew himself.

"No." His hands curled into fists. "I can't just wait

around, hoping he's asking the right questions. I have to do something."

Rachel put her hand on his arm, as if she'd deter him by force, if necessary. "What?"

"See Longstreet. Get some answers myself, before he has time to make up some elaborate cover story."

Her fingers tightened. "Tyler, you can't do that. The chief would have a fit. You'd be interfering in his investigation."

"That's probably true."

"But you're going anyway." She shook her head. "Then I'm going with you."

He frowned. "I don't want to be rude, but I didn't invite you."

"I'm not going to let you confront Phil Longstreet and get yourself in trouble." Her smile flickered. "It would reflect badly on the inn if you were arrested while staying here."

"Or on you? You've been seen in my company quite a bit."

Her eyes widened and then slid away from his. "All the more reason to keep you out of trouble." Her voice wasn't quite steady.

He resisted the impulse to touch her. What was wrong with him? He couldn't pursue a romantic relationship and confront a thief at the same time.

"I'm not going to be violent. Just talk to him."

"You should still have an independent witness," she said. "I'll get my jacket. Are you going to walk over?"

He nodded, waiting while she hurried off to get a jacket. He could leave without her, but she'd just follow him. And what she said made a certain amount of sense. If Longstreet let anything slip, it would be as well to have a third party hear it.

He heard her coming, saying something firm to the dog, who probably scented a walk in the offing.

"Later," she said, pushing an inquiring muzzle back and shutting the door. She turned to him. "I'm ready."

Outside, the air was crisp and cold. It was already dusk—they'd been longer getting back from their meeting with Mrs. Albright than he'd expected. Christmas traffic, Rachel had said.

"I hope Mrs. Albright wasn't tired too much by our visit." Rachel seemed to be reading his thoughts.

"She wouldn't have needed to turn it into a tea party." A few flakes of snow touched his face, and he tilted his head back to look up. "Snow. Are they predicting much?"

"A couple of inches by morning. Good thing we went over to New Holland today." She smiled. "As far as the tea party was concerned—you have to understand that's her way. She wouldn't have talked with you at all, probably, if Grams hadn't been the intermediary."

"Something else I owe to you and your grandmother. I appreciate it." Especially since none of them knew where this investigation would lead. Would it stop at Longstreet? Somehow he doubted it.

"About Mrs. Albright—" Rachel's mind was obviously still on their encounter with the elderly woman. The Christmas lights on the window of the florist shop they were passing showed him her face in images of green and red. "She jumped to some conclusions. About us, I mean. I hope that didn't embarrass you."

"No. But you look as if it did you." The rose in her cheeks wasn't entirely from the Christmas lights.

Her gaze evaded his. "Of course not. Setting young people up in pairs is a favorite local hobby of elderly women. I didn't want you to think—well, it's ridiculous, that's all."

Without a conscious decision, his hand closed over hers. "Is it so ridiculous, Rachel?"

She looked up, and a snowflake tangled in her hair. Another brushed her cheek. "We hardly know each other." She sounded breathless.

"Timewise. But we've come a long way in a short period of time." All the more reason to be cautious, the logical part of his mind insisted, but he didn't want to listen.

"Maybe too far." It came out in a whisper that seemed to linger on the chill air.

"I don't think so." He wanted to touch the snowflakes that clustered more thickly now on her hair. Wanted to warm her cold lips with his.

But they'd reached the corner. And across the street was the antique shop, its lights spilling out onto the sidewalk that was covering quickly with snow.

He'd come here for answers, he reminded himself. Not romance. And some of the answers had to be found inside that shop.

The bell over the door jingled, announcing their arrival. Rachel could only hope that Phil would attribute her red cheeks to the temperature outside, instead of seeing the hint of something more. He was usually far too observant about the state of other people's feelings—probably part of what made him a success as a dealer.

Still, in a few minutes he'd have far more to think

about than the state of her emotions. Apprehension tightened her stomach and dispelled the warmth that had flooded her at Tyler's words.

As for Tyler—a swift glance at his strong-boned face told her he'd dismissed it already. Well, that was only appropriate. They had far more serious things to deal with right now.

"Rachel. Tyler." Phil emerged from behind the counter, a smile wreathing his face. He came toward them, hands extended in welcome. "How nice this is. I was beginning to think I might as well close early. The threat of snow sends people scurrying to the grocery for bread and milk instead of to an antique shop."

"We walked over, so the snow wasn't an issue." She brushed a damp curl back from her cheek. Maybe she shouldn't have said anything, but she could hardly avoid greeting a man she'd known for years.

"Well, what can I do for you this evening?" He rubbed his hands together. "A little Christmas shopping for your grandmother? I have some nice porcelain figures that just came in."

She glanced at Tyler, willing him to take the lead. His face was taut, giving nothing away but a certain amount of tension.

"Actually there was something I wanted to talk with you about. A piece of military memorabilia that I ran across recently."

Phil shook his head, his smile still in place. "Afraid I can't help you there. China, silver, period furniture, that's my area. You'd have to see someone who specializes in military."

He was talking too much, being too helpful. The instinctive reaction was so strong she couldn't doubt it.

Phil's normal attitude with a customer who expressed interest in something he didn't have was to try to turn them to something he did.

Did Tyler realize that? Probably so.

"I already know about the object. A Bavarian military medal, early 1700s. Sound familiar?" His tone wasn't quite accusing.

Phil turned the question away with a smile. "Sorry. As I said, not my area."

It wasn't, Rachel realized. That made it all the more unusual that it had passed through his hands.

"It came from the collection of Stanley Albright, over in New Holland. You've dealt with him, I suppose?" Tyler would not be deflected or halted. He just kept driving toward his goal.

Phil's smile finally faded. "I knew Albright, certainly. Every dealer in the area knew him. Just like every dealer knows his widow is starting to sell off some of his things. I keep up with the news, but that's too rich for my blood, I'm afraid."

He tried a laugh, but it wasn't convincing. Rachel's heart chilled. Up until this moment she'd convinced herself that there was some mistake, that Phil would explain it all away.

He'd try, she knew that much. But she wouldn't believe him.

"You didn't sell him anything?" Tyler's tone was smooth, but she sensed the steel behind it.

"No, can't say I ever had the pleasure." Phil took a casual step back, groping behind him to put his hand on a glass display case filled with a collection of ivory pillboxes.

"Odd. Because Mrs. Albright says you sold him just such a medal about twenty-two years ago."

Phil was as pale as the ivory. "That's ridiculous. I tell you I never handled anything like that. Mrs. Albright must be—what, ninety or so? She's probably mixed up. She never knew anything about his collection, anyway."

He was talking too much, giving himself away with every defensive word. Tyler should have left this to Chief Burkhalter, or at least made sure Burkhalter was around to hear this. Zach Burkhalter would know Phil was lying, just as she did.

"That might be true." Tyler's voice was deceptively soft. "The thing is, I'm not taking her word for it. If you know anything about Albright's collection, you should know he kept meticulous records. It was there—his purchase from you, a description of the medal, even the date he bought it."

Phil turned away, aimlessly touching objects on the countertop, but she saw his face before he could hide his expression. He looked ghastly.

"I suppose you know what significance this is supposed to have, but I'm sure I don't. I suppose it's possible that the odd military piece might have passed through my hands at some point in my career. I really don't remember."

"Don't you?" Tyler took a step closer, his hands clenched so tightly that the knuckles were white. "Funny, I'd think you'd remember that. The medal belonged to my grandfather. It was stolen from his house the night he died."

He'd gone too far—she knew that instantly. He couldn't be positive the medal had gone missing that particular night, even if he were morally sure of it.

Phil straightened, grasping the significance as quickly as she did. He swung around to face Tyler, his face darkening.

"I've been accused of a lot of things, but this is a first. I doubt very much that you could convince anyone, including the police, that the medal was stolen, or that it disappeared the night he died. Your grandfather could have sold it himself."

"Are you saying you got it from him?"

"No, certainly not. But he could have sold it to someone else."

"He didn't. He wouldn't. It was important to him. He wouldn't have let it go."

Phil shrugged, seemingly on surer ground now. "We just have your opinion for that, don't we? The old man was on the outs with everyone, even his own family. Who knows what he might have done? All your detective work, running from Bethlehem to New Holland—"

Before she could guess his intent, Tyler's hand shot out, stopping short of grabbing the front of Phil's expensive cashmere sweater by an inch. Phil leaned back against the showcase, losing color again.

"I didn't mention Bethlehem. How did you know we went there?" He shot a glance at Rachel, but she wasn't sure he saw her. At least, not her as a person, just a source of information. "Could he be the man you saw watching us?"

Startled, she stared at Phil, certainty coalescing. "No. Not him. But I know who it was. I knew he looked familiar. It was one of those men who were loading the truck that first time we came. The men you said worked for you, Phil."

Now Tyler did grab the sweater. "Did you send

him to watch us? Did he try to push Rachel down the stairs?"

"No, no, I wouldn't. If he—if he was there, it didn't have anything to do with me."

"You were involved. You had the medal. You sold it, months after my grandfather died. I suppose you thought it would disappear into a private collection and never surface again. But it did. Now, where did you get it?"

"Tyler, don't." Her heart thudded, and she tugged at his arm. "Don't. You shouldn't—"

He wasn't listening. Neither of them were.

Phil shook his head from side to side. "I didn't. I didn't do anything. I bought it." He glanced at Rachel, a swift, sidelong gaze. "I bought it like I bought a lot of little trinkets around that time."

"Who?" She found her voice. "Who sold it to you?"

"I'm sorry, Rachel."

He actually did sound sorry. Sorry for her. Her heart clutched. She wanted to freeze the moment, to stop whatever he was going to say next. But she couldn't.

He cleared his throat, looking back at Tyler. "I bought the medal from Rachel's father."

Chapter Thirteen

If her head would just stop throbbing, maybe Rachel could make sense of what everyone was saying. Her mind had stopped functioning coherently at the instant Phil made that outrageous claim about her father. The next thing she knew, she was sitting in the library at the inn, Grams close beside her on the couch, clutching her hand.

Zachary Burkhalter sat across from them. The police chief should look uncomfortable with his long frame folded into that small lady's armchair, but at the moment he was too busy looking annoyed with Tyler.

Tyler. Her heart seemed to clench, and she had to force herself to look at him. He sat forward on the desk chair that had been her grandfather's, hands grasping its mahogany arms, waiting. If he was moved by the chief's comments, he wasn't showing it. He simply waited, face impassive, emotionless.

That was a separate little hurt among all the larger ones. Such a short time ago, he'd said—hinted, at least, that there was a future for them. Now, he thought her father was a murderer.

"I told you I'd investigate." Burkhalter's tone was icy. "If you'd been able to restrain yourself, we might have been able to gather some hard evidence. You can't just go around accusing respectable citizens of murder."

"*You* can't." Tyler didn't sound as if he regretted a single action. "I'm not the police. At least I got an admission from him. What hard evidence do you expect to unearth at this point?"

"Probably none, now that you've jumped in with both feet and tipped Longstreet off that he's under suspicion. If there is anything, he had a chance to get rid of it before I could get a search warrant."

"Is Phillip under arrest?" Grams's voice was a thin echo of her usual tone, and her hands, clasped in Rachel's, were icy.

Burkhalter's expression softened when he looked at her. "No. The district attorney isn't ready to charge him with anything at this point. We're looking for the man who works for him—the one you thought was following you in Bethlehem. He may shed some light. And it's possible we might trace some of the things that have been stolen recently to him."

Rachel cleared her throat, unable to remember when she'd last spoken. Shock, probably. Anger would be better than this icy numbness, and she could feel it beginning to build, deep within her.

"What does Longstreet say now?" Impossible to believe she was talking about someone she'd considered a friend, someone she'd worked with and argued with on a project that had been so important to both of them.

And all the time—all those meetings when he'd sat across from her, when they'd shared a smile at some ridiculous suggestion from Sandra, when they'd talked plans for Churchville's future—all that time he'd been hiding this.

"He sticks to his first statement. Says he bought the medal, and some other small collectible pieces, from your father shortly before he left town. Claims to have been guilty of nothing more than not inquiring too closely where the objects came from."

Tyler stirred. "He knew. He had to."

"He's confident we won't prove it at this late date." Burkhalter turned to Grams. "I don't want to distress you, Mrs. Unger, but I have to ask. Longstreet implied that some of the things he bought might have come from this house. Did you ever suspect your son-in-law of stealing from you?"

Grams's hands trembled, and Rachel's anger spurted to the surface. "Leave her alone. Can't you see how upset she is? You have no right—"

"No, Rachel." Her grandmother stiffened, back straight, head high, the way she always met a challenge. "Chief Burkhalter has his duty to do, as do I." The fine muscles around her lips tensed. "We had suspicions, that summer. Things disappeared, perhaps mislaid. A silver snuffbox, an ivory-inlaid hand mirror, a few pieces of Georgian silver. My husband thought that my daughter's husband was responsible."

"Did he accuse Hampton?" Tyler was as cold as if he spoke of strangers. Well, they were strangers to him. Just not to her. Her heart seemed to crack.

Grams shook her head slowly. "Not at first. He wanted to, but I was afraid."

"You're never afraid," Rachel said softly. She smoothed her fingers over her grandmother's hand, the bones fragile under soft skin.

"I was afraid of losing you and your sisters." Grams's eyes shone with tears. "I was a coward. I didn't want an open breach. But we lost you anyway."

"Not at first?" Burkhalter echoed. "Did there come a time when that happened?"

"Something vanished that my husband prized—a cameo that had been his grandmother's, supposedly a gift from a descendant of William Penn. He'd intended it for one of our granddaughters. That was the last straw, as far as he was concerned. But before he could do anything, Donald was gone. Maybe he guessed Frederick was about to confront him."

"Didn't people wonder about it?" Tyler asked. "Hampton disappearing so soon after my grandfather's death?"

Burkhalter shrugged. "I've done some inquiring. As far as I can tell, Hampton came and went so much that nobody questioned his leaving at that particular time. You don't automatically suspect someone of a crime for that."

"Of course not!" The words burst out of Rachel. She couldn't listen to this any longer. "This is my father you're talking about. My father. He wouldn't do anything like that."

Grams patted her hand. Tyler said her name, and she turned on him.

"This is your fault. You're trying to make yourself feel better by blaming all this on my father." She was standing, body rigid, hands clasped, feeling as if she'd go up in flames if anyone tried to touch her. "He didn't do it. He wouldn't do anything to hurt anyone. He was gentle, and charming, and he loved his children. He loved me." She was eight again, her heart breaking, her world ripping apart. "He loved me."

She spun and raced out of the room before the sobs that choked her had a chance to rip free and expose her grief and pain to everyone.

Rachel came down the stairs from her bedroom, glancing at her watch. Nearly seven and dark already, of course, although the lights on Main Street shone cheerfully and pedestrians were out and about, probably doing Christmas shopping. The house was quiet, the insistent voices that had pushed her to the breaking point silenced now.

She rounded the corner of the stairs into the kitchen. Grams sat at the table, a cup of tea steaming in front of her, Barney curled at her feet. He spotted her first, welcoming her with a gentle woof.

Grams looked up, her blue eyes filled with concern. "Rachel, you must be hungry. I'll get some soup—"

Rachel stopped her before she could get up, dropping a kiss on her cheek. "I'll get it. It smells as if Emma left some chicken pot pie on the stove."

"She sent Levi over with it. She knows it's your favorite."

Rachel poured a ladleful into an earthenware bowl, inhaling the rich aroma of chicken mingled with the square pillows of dough that were Emma's signature touch. "That was lovely of her. Please tell me the entire neighborhood hasn't found out about our troubles so soon."

"People talk. And I'm sure quite a few heard a garbled version of the police searching Longstreet's antiques and saw the police car parked in our driveway."

Grams sounded resigned to it. She'd spent her life in country places and knew how they functioned. "Did you sleep any, dear?"

Rachel sank into the chair opposite her, pushing her hair back with both hands. "A little." After she'd cried her heart out—for her father, for the trouble that would hurt everyone she loved, for what might have been with Tyler and was surely gone now. "I guess I made an exhibition of myself, didn't I?"

"Let's say it startled everyone," Grams said dryly. "Including you, I think."

She nodded and forced herself to put a spoonful into her mouth, to chew, to swallow. The warmth spread through her. Small wonder they called this comfort food.

"I thought I'd accepted it a long time ago. Maybe I never did." She met her grandmother's gaze across the table. "This business of Daddy taking things from the house—did Mother know?"

"She never admitted it if she did." She sighed, shaking her head. "That was what precipitated her taking you away. She was upset and angry over your father leaving, and Frederick—well, his patience ran out. He said, 'At least we no longer have a thief in the house.'"

She'd thought she was finished crying, but another tear slid down her cheek. "You tried to stop them from fighting. I remember that." They'd huddled at the top of the stairs, she and Andrea, listening to the battle raging below, understanding nothing except that their lives were changing forever.

"It was no good. They were both too stubborn, and things were said that neither of them would forget." She took a sip of the tea and then set the cup back in the saucer with a tiny *ching*. "I thought all that unhappiness was over and done with, and that with you and Andrea back, we could just be happy."

"I guess the past is always ready to jump out and bite you. If Tyler had never come—" That hurt too much to go on.

"Perhaps it was meant to be. I know we can't see our way clear at the moment, but God knows the way out."

The faintest smile touched her lips. "When I was little, you told me God was always there to take my hand when I was in trouble."

"He still is, Rachel. Just reach out and take it." Grams stood, carrying her cup to the sink. "I believe I'll read for a while, unless you'd like company."

Rachel shook her head. "After I finish this, I'll take Barney out for a little walk. The cold air will do us both good."

"Don't go on Crossings Road, dear. Not after dark."

"I won't." Grams couldn't help remembering her accident. "We'll take a walk down Main Street, where the shops are still open."

Grams came to pat her cheek and then headed for the steps. "Look in on me when you get back."

"I will. I love you, Grams."

"I love you, too, Rachel."

Barney trotted happily at her heels a few minutes later as she pulled jacket, hat and mittens from the closet. He knew the signs of an impending walk, even if no one said the word.

She stepped outside, the dog running immediately to investigate the snow, not content until he'd rolled over several times in it. Must be close to four inches, but it had stopped at some time since she'd come back from the antique shop. The sky above was clear now, and thick with stars.

She whistled to Barney and started down the street. Grams hadn't mentioned Tyler's whereabouts, but his car wasn't in its usual spot, so he was probably out to dinner. Or even moving out.

She tried to ignore the bruised feeling around her heart. Tyler believed her father guilty of killing his grandfather. They could never get past that in a million years, so it was better not to try.

She tilted her head back. The stars seemed incredibly close, as if she could reach out and pick a frosty handful.

Why did You bring him into my life, when it was bound to end so badly? I thought I was content with things the way they were, and now—

God is always there to take your hand. Grams's words echoed and comforted.

I don't see my way through this. Lord. I don't know how many more hard lessons there are to learn. Please, hold my hand.

Comforted. Yes, that was what she felt. She didn't see any farther, but she didn't feel alone.

Barney danced along the sidewalk, dodging shoppers—some locals that she knew, a few tourists. The Christmas lights shone cheerfully, and in every window she saw posters for the Holiday Open House Tour.

Funny. It had occupied an important place in her mind for weeks, as if its success marked her acceptance as part of this community. Now it was almost here, and she didn't feel her customary flicker of panic. There were too many more important things to worry about.

The tour would go on, no matter what happened in the private lives of its organizers.

She passed Sandra and Bradley Whitmoyer's spacious Victorian, ablaze with white lights and evergreens, a lighted tree filling the front window. Across the snowy street, Longstreet's Antiques seemed to be closed, the shop dark.

Would the police have searched thoroughly? She couldn't imagine Zach Burkhalter undertaking anything without doing it well, and he'd probably love to tie recent antique thefts to Phil. But he didn't think there was enough evidence to charge Phil with anything from the past. That had been clear from his manner.

It had also been clear that he pitied her. That he agreed with Tyler's assessment. That her father had been guilty of that terrible thing.

She stopped, staring at the shop. Barney pressed against her leg, whining a little.

Odd. The shop was dark, but she could glimpse a narrow wedge of light from the office. Phil must still be there.

If she talked to him again—just the two of them. Not Tyler. Not the police. Just two people who had been friends. Would he tell her about her father? Would he help her understand this?

She shouldn't. Chief Burkhalter had been angry enough with Tyler for his interference. He'd be furious with her if she did any such thing.

It was her father. She had a right to know. And the idea of being afraid to talk to Phil, of all people, was simply ridiculous. Snapping her fingers to Barney, she crossed the street, her boots crunching through the ruts left by passing cars.

She reached for the knob, expecting the door to be locked, but the knob turned under her hand. She'd have expected Phil to stay open tonight, like the other shops, but if he'd closed, why hadn't he locked up?

She stepped inside, reassured by the tinkle of the bell over the door and the feel of the dog, pressing close beside her.

"Phil? It's Rachel. Can I talk with you for a minute?"

No answer. The door to the office was ajar, a narrow band of light shining through it, reflecting from the glass cases.

"Phil?" she shivered in spite of the warmth of the shop, starting toward the light.

And froze at a rustle of movement somewhere in the crammed shop.

Her hand clenched Barney's collar. She felt the hair rise on the ruff of his neck, heard a low, rumbling growl start deep in his throat.

Danger, that's what he was saying. *Danger.*

She held her breath, though it was too late for that. If someone lurked in the shadows, she'd already announced herself, hadn't she?

She took a careful step toward the outside door, hand tight on Barney's collar, trying to control him. He strained against her, growling at something she couldn't see in the dark.

A step matched hers. Someone on the other side of an enormous Dutch cabinet moved when she did. Fear gripped her throat. Scream, and hope someone on the street heard before he reached her? Let Barney go?

She hesitated too long. Before she could move, a dark figure burst from behind the cabinet, arm upraised. She stumbled backward, losing her hold on the dog, she was falling, he'd be on her—

Barney lunged, snapping and snarling. Something crashed into a glass display case, shattering it, shards of glass flying. Dog and man grappled in the dark, and she fled toward the office, bolted inside, slammed and locked the door, breath coming in sobbing gasps.

Barney— But she couldn't help him. She had to call—

She turned, blinking in the light while she fumbled in her bag for her phone. And stopped.

Phil Longstreet lay on the floor between his elegant Sheraton desk and the door. His arms were outflung, hands open. Blood spread from his head, soaking into the intricate blue-and-wine design of the Oriental carpet.

Tyler wrenched the steering wheel and spun out of the snowy driveway at the inn, tension twisting his gut. He'd come back to the inn from supper to find Katherine in shock. Phil Longstreet was in the hospital, and Rachel was at the police station.

Incredible. Surely the police couldn't believe that Rachel—gentle, nurturing Rachel—could harm anyone. But he doubted that the police made their decisions based on someone's apparent character.

Think, don't just react, he admonished himself. Katherine Unger had rushed to him the instant he walked in the door. Her incoherent explanation of events had been interspersed with Emma's equally hard-to-understand pleas for her to be calm, to go and lie down, to stop exciting herself.

Finally he'd gotten both of them enough under control to get the bare facts they knew. Rachel had gone out with the dog for a short walk on Main Street. A half hour later, just when her grandmother was starting to worry, a policeman had appeared at the inn with the dog, saying that Phillip Longstreet had been injured and that Rachel was at the station, helping the police inquiry.

Emma had to restrain Katherine from rushing out into the snowy night without even a coat.

"Go after her, please, go after her." She'd grasped his arm, holding on to him as if he were a lifeline. "Someone has to be with her, to protect her. Please, Tyler. She needs you."

He clasped her hands between his. "I'll take care of her." He glanced at Emma. "And you'll take care of Mrs. Unger."

"*Ja,* I will." Emma put her own shawl around Katherine's shoulders and drew her toward the library. "Come. You come. Tyler will do it."

Now he was forced to slow down, watchful of the small group of pedestrians who hovered on the edge of the street, trying to see what was happening inside the antique shop. He passed a police car and then pulled to the curb in front of the police station, heedless of the No Parking sign.

He raced across the sidewalk, up the two steps and shoved the door open. A young patrolman looked up from the desk, telephone receiver pressed against his ear.

"Rachel Hampton. Where is she?"

"She's with the chief." He glanced toward the door to the inner office with what seemed a combination of fear and excitement. "They can't be disturbed."

"Is there an attorney with her? Because if not, I'm certainly going to disturb them."

"Now, sir—"

The door opened and Zach Burkhalter came out, closing it behind him, looking at Tyler with an annoyed glare.

"Mr. Dunn. Now, why am I not surprised that you've turned up here?"

"You're talking to Rachel Hampton. If she doesn't have an attorney with her—"

"Ms. Hampton isn't being charged with anything. And she said she doesn't want an attorney."

Tyler's eyes narrowed. "I'd like to hear that from her." Maybe it was better if he didn't look too closely at the emotions that drove him right now.

Burkhalter's annoyance seemed to fade into resignation. He opened the door. "Go ahead."

A few more steps took him into the room, and the sight of Rachel sent everything else out of his mind. She sat on a straight-backed chair in the small office, huddled into the jacket that was wrapped around her shoulders. It wasn't cold in the room, but she shivered as she looked up at him.

"Tyler." She blinked, as if she were close to tears. "Phillip…did you hear about him? About what happened?"

"Shh. It's all right." He knelt next to her chair, taking her icy hands in his and trying to warm them with his touch.

A sidelong glance told him that Burkhalter had left the door open, and there was no sound from the outer office. They'd hear anything that was said here.

"But Phillip—"

He put his hand gently across her lips. "Don't. Just tell me what the chief asked you."

The truth was that he liked Burkhalter—he judged him a good man and probably a good cop. But he *was* a cop, and that's how he thought.

"He wanted me to tell him exactly what happened." Her eyes were wide and dark with shock. "I told him. I was out for a walk with Barney, and I saw that the office light was on at the antique shop. I thought I should talk to Phil. Just as a friend, that's all, to try and understand."

"The shop was unlocked?" His mind worked feverishly. She'd already told this to the police, so it was as well that she told him, too. He had to understand what they were dealing with.

She nodded. "I went in, calling his name. He didn't answer. And then I realized someone else was there, in the shop."

Fear jagged through him. "Did he hurt you?"

"I'm all right." But she didn't sound all right. "Barney went after him. Gave me time to run into the office and lock the door."

"Did you see his face? Who was it?"

She shook her head. "I never got a look at him. And then I saw Phil lying on the floor. His head—" She stopped, biting her lip.

He smoothed his hands over hers. "What did you do next? Did you try to help him?"

"I was afraid of making things worse. I thought I shouldn't touch the things on his desk, so I used my cell phone to call the police."

If she hadn't touched anything else in the office, that

was good, but she'd undoubtedly been in there before, maybe touched things then.

Her fingers gripped his suddenly. "The paramedics wouldn't tell me anything, but it didn't look good. They took him to the hospital. Someone must know by now how he is."

Burkhalter came back into the office on her words, as if he'd been listening. For an instant he eyed Tyler, kneeling next to Rachel, as if he weighed their feelings for each other.

Well, good luck figuring that out. He didn't know, himself. He just knew that Rachel needed help and he was going to make sure she got it.

"What about it, Chief?" He rose, standing beside Rachel, his hands on her shoulders. "The hospital must have been in touch with you."

The chief's stoic expression didn't change for a moment. Then he shrugged. "Longstreet is in serious condition with a head injury."

"Is he conscious?"

"No." He bit off the word.

That meant that the police had no idea when or if Longstreet would be able to talk to them. He tightened his grip on Rachel's shoulders. "I'm sure Ms. Hampton has already helped you as much as she can. It's time she was getting home."

"If we went over her story again, we might—"

"She's told you everything. She's exhausted and upset, and she probably should be seen by a doctor. Is she being charged with anything?"

Rachel moved at that, as if it was the first time she'd realized that she might be under suspicion. His grip warned her to be still.

Burkhalter leaned against his desk, arms crossed, looking at them. "Charged? No. But from my point of view, she quarreled with Longstreet earlier in the day. She was upset about his accusations against her father. She went to the shop."

"But I didn't—"

His grip silenced her. "She's not saying another word without an attorney present." Somehow he didn't think Burkhalter wanted to press this, not now, at least.

Burkhalter eyed him. "Actually, you had a quarrel with Longstreet today, too. And a reason to have a grudge against him."

"And I was at the Brown Bread Café having dinner this evening, which you can easily check."

The chief looked at him for a long moment, then he nodded. "You can go now, both of you. We'll talk again. Please be available."

He took Rachel's arm as she rose, but she seemed steady enough now. She looked at Burkhalter with something of defiance in her eyes.

"I won't be going anywhere, Chief Burkhalter. I have a business to run." She turned and walked steadily out of the office.

Tyler followed her through the outer office, holding the door while she went out into the street. It was dark, cold and still. The crowd had dissipated, so Rachel wouldn't have to endure their curious gazes.

"My car is right here." He piloted her to the door. "Your grandmother—"

Her knees seemed to buckle, and he caught her, folding his arms around her and holding her close. "It's okay," he murmured. "It's okay."

She shook her head, her hair brushing against his face. "I don't know what to do. Why is this happening?"

He pressed his cheek against her hair. "It's going to be all right. Don't worry."

Fine words. The trouble was, he didn't have any idea how to make them come true.

Chapter Fourteen

It took a gigantic effort to keep smiling when she felt that everyone who came through the door for the open house was staring at her. Rachel handed out leaflets about the history of the Unger mansion to the latest group, hoping that their curiosity was about the house, not her.

"Please enjoy your visit. If you have any questions, be sure to ask one of the guides."

A couple of her volunteer guides had, oddly enough, become unavailable today, probably as a result of last night's events. But Emma and Grams had stepped into the breach. She'd worried about letting Grams exert herself, but she'd actually begun to regain some of her zest as she talked to people about the house she loved.

And then there was Tyler. She was aware of him moving quietly through the visitors, lending a hand here, there and everywhere. They'd managed a few minutes alone to talk earlier, trying to make sense of all this.

If Phil feared that Tyler's investigations might reveal he'd bought stolen property, he might have a reason to try to stop him. But why would he have anything against her?

Everything that happened to her could have been coincidence. Accident.

Except that someone who worked for Phil had been there, in Bethlehem. And someone had attacked Phil and her.

Her head ached with trying to make sense of it. Tyler had listened to her attempts at explanation, but he hadn't offered any of his own. Because he believed her father guilty of murder? Even so, last night he hadn't hesitated to leap to her defense.

She'd been emotionally and mentally shattered, finding Phil in that state after everything else that had happened. Tyler had had every excuse to cut her adrift, even to suspect her of the attack on Phil, but he hadn't. He'd rushed to the rescue. Without him, she might well have stumbled into saying something stupid that would make Chief Burkhalter even more suspicious.

She smoothed out a wrinkle in the Star of Bethlehem quilt, trying to make herself think of something—anything—else. Christmas was only a few days away. Andrea and Cal would be back soon. She should call Caroline and urge her again to come home for Christmas. And wrapping the gifts—

It was no use. She could think of other things on the surface, but the fear and misgivings still lurked beneath. She was caught in a web of suspicion and pain, and she didn't see any way out.

The sound of the front door opening yet again had her turning to it, forcing a smile even though her face felt as if it would crack. Her expression melted into something more genuine when she saw Bradley Whitmoyer, bundled up against the cold, pulling his gloves off as he closed the door behind him.

She went forward, hand extended. "Dr. Whitmoyer, it's a nice surprise you could make it. I thought you'd be completely tied up helping Sandra with the visitors at your house."

"Bradley, remember?" The doctor managed a smile, but she thought it was as much a struggle as her own.

"It's all right," she said impulsively. "Maybe we should both agree to stop smiling before our faces break."

"That is how it feels, isn't it?" He seemed to relax slightly. "I thought I'd go mad if I heard another person say what a lovely tree we have. The only way I could get out of the house was to agree that I'd see how you're doing and report back to Sandra."

She'd take Sandra's interest as a gesture of support. That was better than assuming there was anything negative about her interest.

"As you can see, we're busy, but I think it's starting to dwindle down now. We've had a steady stream of visitors all afternoon, up and down the stairs, determined to see everything."

The fine lines of his face tightened. "I drew the line at that. Guests to our house may see the downstairs, that's all. The upstairs is strictly off-limits."

"Well, yours is a private house. We have to keep business in mind, and some of our house-tour people may be potential guests."

She was faintly surprised that he was willing to stand here talking so long. The busy-doctor persona seemed to be in abeyance at the moment, but she suspected he'd been out early, checking on any patients in the hospital.

"Will you tell me something?" She asked the question before she could lose her nerve.

"If I can."

"Phillip Longstreet. Do you know how he's doing?"

His face seemed to close. He wouldn't answer. He'd plead professional ethics and say he couldn't. But then he shrugged.

"He's not my patient, so I don't know any details. But then, if he were, I couldn't tell you anything." His smile had a strained quality. "The police have a guard on his door, so I didn't see him, but I spoke with a resident who said he's stable. Not awake yet, but otherwise showing signs of improvement."

Something that had been tight inside her seemed to ease. *Thank You, Lord.* "I'm glad. Do you think, when he wakes up, he'll be able to identify his attacker?"

But there Bradley's cooperation halted. "I couldn't begin to guess. I understand the police think they can trace a few things stolen in the recent robberies to the shop, so it may have been some thief he was involved with." He took a step through the archway into the front parlor. "The *putz* looks very nice. Are you getting tired of explaining it to people?"

Obviously Bradley had been as indiscreet as he would let himself be. "It does get a little repetitive after a while, doesn't it?" she said. "Refreshments are set out in the breakfast room. I hope you'll go back and help yourself, although people do seem to come to a halt there."

He nodded and disappeared from view into the back parlor. She turned around, the smile still lingering on her face, and drew in a startled breath. Jeff Whitmoyer stood behind her.

He didn't seem to notice her reaction. "Sending my brother back to have something to eat? He won't. He avoids sweets, along with most everything else that makes life fun."

"I should probably follow his example. I've already been dipping into the snickerdoodles." Nerves, probably. She'd had an irresistible urge for sugar all day. "Have you taken the tour of the house yet?"

"I'll pass. No offense, but I'm not really into admiring the *decor*." He exaggerated the word. "It drives my sainted sister-in-law crazy when I refer to her eighteenth century étagère as 'that thing against the wall.'"

"I can see how it would." Both Whitmoyer brothers were unusually talkative tonight. Jeff usually only talked this long when it was a matter of a job to do.

"I heard you were the one who found Phil last night," he said abruptly.

Probably everyone who'd come through the door had heard that, but no one else had ventured to bring it up. A headache she hadn't noticed before began tightening its coils around her temples. Jeff stood there, waiting for an answer.

"That's right. I'm afraid I can't talk about it. Chief Burkhalter asked me not to say anything."

Before Jeff could pry any further, Emma bustled up to her.

"Rachel, you are needed in the kitchen, please. I will watch the door." She took the handful of brochures and gave Rachel a gentle shove.

"Thank you, Emma." She gave Jeff a vague smile and escaped with a sense of thankfulness.

Nancy Zook was in the kitchen, washing dishes, her oldest daughter standing next to her, drying.

"Nancy, you needn't do those by hand. We can use the dishwasher."

"It makes no matter. We can be quick this way." She passed a dripping plate to her daughter.

"Your mother said I was wanted?"

"Oh, *ja,* Tyler thought we should stop putting more food out."

"Tyler?"

"Here." He leaned in the doorway at the mention of his name. "According to my watch, the house tour hours are about over. But if Nancy keeps feeding those people, they're never going to leave." He nodded toward the chattering crowd clustered around the table at the far end of the breakfast room.

She glanced at Black Forest mantel clock. "It really is time." Her whole body seemed to sag in relief. "Nancy, I agree. No more food for them. Take the rest of it home for your family, all right?"

"That will be nice for our second-Christmas visitors, it will," Nancy said. "You don't worry about the kitchen. We will finish the cleanup in here."

"But—"

"Don't argue." Tyler's hand brushed hers in a gesture of support that seemed to reverberate through her entire body. "When you get a chance, I want to show you the medal." He lowered his voice, stepping back into the hallway and drawing her with him. "Those scratches on the back—there was something there. Faint, but it looks like someone scratched a triangle with something else inside it."

She tried to focus her tired brain on it. "Does that mean something?"

He shrugged. "I'm not sure. The triangle is a symbol of the Trinity, of course. Maybe my grandfather felt better about having a military decoration if he added a Christian symbol." He frowned. "It doesn't have anything to do with the robbery, but I can't help thinking about what Eli's mother said. Wondering what she really meant."

"Maybe I can talk to Emma after everything calms down." If it ever did. "She might have some insight."

"Good idea." He touched her shoulder, a featherlight brush of his fingers. "I'm going upstairs to get that last group moving. Just sit down and put your feet up for a moment."

She couldn't do that, but she appreciated the thought. "Thank you."

For a moment longer he stood motionless, his hand touching her, and then something guarded and aware came into his eyes. He turned and headed for the stairs.

Rachel swallowed hard, trying to get rid of the lump that had formed in her throat. To say nothing of the hot tears that prickled her eyes.

No matter how kind and helpful Tyler was, the events of the past still stood like a wall between them. And she was afraid they always would.

It had taken more than a few minutes, despite Tyler's best intentions, to clear the house of visitors, but finally the last of them were gone. Nancy and Emma had insisted on cleaning up the kitchen. Rachel had intended to leave some of the cleanup until tomorrow, but her helpers wouldn't hear of it.

And she had to admit they were right. Dirty dishes left in the sink, chairs pulled out of their proper places, a glass left on a tabletop—all offended her innkeeper's sense of what was right. Andrea might consider her the least-organized person in the world where record-keeping was concerned, but the house had to look right or she wouldn't sleep.

Once the Zook family had taken their leave, chattering as happily as if they'd been to a party instead of working hard for hours, she tucked Grams up in bed, Barney dozing on the rug next to her.

She went back downstairs, knowing she couldn't go to bed yet. Sleep wouldn't come, and she'd just lie in the dark and worry.

She walked into the library, where the last embers of the fire were dying in the fireplace. She sank down on the couch facing it, too tired to throw another log on. Silence set in, and with it came the fear that was becoming too familiar. And the questions.

I don't know what to think, Lord. How could the father I idolized have done these things?

One of the words she'd just used stopped her. *Idolized.* That was not a word to be used lightly, was it? Natural enough for a child to love her father, even if he hadn't been what the world would consider a good father.

But idolize? That smacked of something forbidden in her faith. Thoughts crept out of hiding, images from the past. How often had she let her feelings about her father's abandonment get between her and a relationship with someone else?

Is that really what I've been doing, Lord? I didn't mean to. I just never saw it.

Before she could pursue that uncomfortable line of thought, she heard a step. Tyler came in. One look at his face told her this endless day was not yet over. It was set in a mask, behind which she could sense something dark and implacable moving.

"We have to talk."

She steeled herself. What now? "If this is about the attack on Phillip—"

He dismissed her idea with a curt gesture of one hand. "No. Not Longstreet. You."

"Me?" Her voice came out in a squeak. "What about me?"

His jaw was hard as marble. "Showing people around the house was educational. Very. One woman in that last group especially admired the desk in the upstairs hall."

"It's a nice piece." She had to struggle to sound normal.

"Yes. And you let me believe it had been sitting in that spot for a couple of generations. But it hasn't, has it?"

"I didn't—" The attack, coming on ground she'd totally forgotten in the sweep of other events, took her off guard.

"I told you it reminded me of one that had been in my grandfather's house. When that woman was babbling on about the style and finish, I remembered it. I remembered hiding under that desk while my grandfather and mother shouted at each other. I had a brandnew penknife that my father had given me, and I used it to carve my initials on the underside, in the corner, where no one would see. T.D. Guess what, Rachel? They're still there."

She could face this attack better on her feet. She stood, facing him. She wouldn't be a coward about it.

"I didn't know. How could I know that the desk came from your grandfather's house?"

"You knew that it hadn't been standing in the upstairs hall for a hundred years. You could have told me that."

She could have. She hadn't.

"Tyler, try to understand. I didn't know, then, what you—"

What you would come to mean to me. No, she couldn't say that. Not now.

"I didn't know whether it meant anything that it was here. I found the desk in one of the outbuildings when I was decorating the inn. You've seen those buildings—they're crammed with cast-off furniture. It was just another piece."

He wasn't buying it. "After I mentioned the similarity to my grandfather's desk, you had to have known it might be significant. You should have told me."

"And could I have trusted you not to make too much of it?" Anger and tears were both perilously near the surface. "You've been so obsessed with finding out the truth, that you haven't cared who got hurt in the process. Our having the desk could be perfectly innocent. My grandfather might have picked it up at a sale anytime."

"Or not. It could be confirmation that someone from this house was involved in my grandfather's death." He was armored against her by his anger and determination. "You didn't tell me the truth, Rachel. All along, you've only been helping me as a way of protecting your own family. Isn't that right?"

Her head was throbbing with the effort to hold back tears. "You can't believe that."

"I can't believe anything else." The words had an echo of finality about them. He turned toward the hall. "In the morning I'll look for another place to stay until all of this is settled."

He walked out, and she heard his steps mounting the central staircase. She listened, frozen, until they faded away. Then she sank back onto the sofa and buried her face in her hands.

Forgive me, Father. Please forgive me. I know that Tyler never will. I'll try to accept that. I was wrong. But I have to protect my family, don't I?

Tears spilled through her hands, dropping to her lap. *Do you?* The question formed in her heart. *Can you protect your family by hiding the truth?*

I need this, Father. The cry came from her innermost heart. *I lost my family, and I need to bring it back together again. Isn't that the right thing to do?*

The answer was there. It had been all along, but she hadn't been willing to face it. She couldn't go back and recreate the family that she imagined they'd been once. That idealized image had probably never really existed.

And she couldn't build a future based on a lie. Her heart twisted, feeling as if it would break in two. She'd already lost Tyler, and whatever might have been between them. She couldn't go on trying to cover up, trying to pretend her way back to an imaginary family.

I've been wrong, Father. So wrong. Please, forgive me and show me what to do.

She already knew, didn't she? If her father was guilty, the truth would have to come out. And if evidence of that guilt lay anywhere in the house or grounds, she'd have to find it.

She leaned against the couch back, too tired to move. She couldn't start searching attics and cellars now. Even if she had the strength, she couldn't risk waking Grams.

In the morning. She pushed herself wearily to her feet. She'd start in the morning, assuming the police didn't decide to arrest her by then for the attack on Phil. She had the list of items that were missing from the farmhouse. If any of them were on Unger property, she'd find them, and let the truth emerge where it would.

And in the morning Tyler would leave. She rubbed her temples. Lying awake all night worrying about it wouldn't change anything. She'd take a couple of aspirins and have a cup of the cocoa Emma had left on the stove. Maybe, somehow, she'd be able to sleep.

Tyler had been staring at the ceiling for what seemed like hours. Probably had been. He turned his head to look at the bedside clock: 4:00 a.m.—the darkest watches of the night, with dawn far away and sleep not coming. It was the hour of soul searching.

He got up, moving quietly to the window that looked out on the lane and drawing back the curtain. It was snowing again, the thickly falling drifts muffling everything. The lights in front of the inn were misty haloes, and nothing moved on the street.

Was he being unjust to Rachel? He understood, only too well, her need to protect her family. She'd been eight when she'd lost all the stability in her life. Small wonder that she was trying desperately to protect what she had left of family.

But she'd lied to him. Not overtly, but it was a lie all the same. If she'd just told him, the day he'd talked about the desk—

What would he have done? He hadn't remembered, then, about the initials. He wouldn't have been able to identify it any sooner. But if she'd been honest, they could have searched for the truth together.

That was the worst thing about it. That he'd begun to trust her, care for her, maybe even love her, and she'd been keeping secrets from him.

He moved away from the window, letting the curtain fall. There was no point in going over it and over it. Facts were important to him, concrete facts, not emotions and wishful thinking.

The desk was certainly concrete enough. It had seemed huge to him when he was a child playing underneath it, imagining it alternately a fort and a castle. He'd needed a shelter during that visit, with his mother and grandfather constantly at each other's throats.

Giving in to the urge to look at it again, he opened his door and stepped out into the hall. No need to worry about anyone seeing him in his T-shirt and sweatpants—he was the only person in this part of the house tonight. When he moved out in the morning, it would be empty.

The thought didn't give him any satisfaction. He ran his hand along the smooth surface of the slanted desktop. Rachel had done a good job with it, as she had with everything she'd touched in preparing the inn. She'd taken infinite care. Did she even realize that she was trying to recreate the family and security she'd lost?

He stiffened, hand tightening on the edge of the

desk. That sounded like the dog, over in the other wing of the house. But Barney never barked at night.

A cold breath seemed to move along his skin. The barking was more insistent. Something was wrong. Someone—Rachel or her grandmother—would have silenced the dog by now. His heart chilled. If they could.

He was running, moving beyond rational thought, knowing he had to get to Rachel. Down the stairs two at a time, stumbling once as his bare feet hit the polished floor. The dim light that Rachel always left on in the downstairs hallway—it was off.

His fear ratcheted up a notch. He grabbed the door handle, already thinking ahead to how he'd get into the east wing if it were locked, but it opened easily under his hand.

Race through the library, pitch-black, stumbling into a chair, then a lamp table. Out into the small landing at the base of the stairs. Up the second set of steps, no breath left to call out, just get there. The dog's barking changed to a long, high-pitched howl, raking his nerves with fear.

Get to the upstairs hall, and now he knew his fears were justified. Barney clawed at Rachel's door, frantically trying to get in. From the crack under the door came a blast of cold air. One of the windows must be wide-open in the room. Or the door onto Rachel's tiny balcony.

Grab the knob. Locked. He'd known it would be. No time to analyze or plan. Draw back. Shove the hysterical dog out of the way. Fling himself at the door. Pain shooting through his shoulder. Throw himself at it again, wordless prayers exploding in his mind.

The lock snapped; the door gave. He stumbled into

the room. The balcony door stood open, Rachel's slender body draped over the railing, a dark figure over her, pushing—

He hurtled himself toward them, out into the night, snow in his face, grabbing for Rachel, pulling her back, fending off the blows the other man threw at him, the dog dancing around them, snarling, trying to get his teeth into the attacker. Rachel struggling feebly, trying to pull herself back. But the man was strong, Tyler's bare feet slid on the snowy balcony, he couldn't get a grip, they were going to go over—

The railing screamed, metal tearing loose, giving way. He fell to his knees, grabbing Rachel's arm, holding her even as her feet slid off the balcony. Holding her tight and safe as the other figure windmilled on the edge for an agonizing second and then went over, a long, thin scream cutting off abruptly when his body hit the patio.

He pulled Rachel against him, his arms wrapped around her. Safe. She was safe.

She pressed her face into his chest. "Who?" Her voice was fogged with whatever had been used to drug her. "Who was it?"

He leaned forward cautiously, peering down through the swirling flakes to the patio. The man lay perfectly still, sprawled on the stones, face up. The ski mask he'd worn must have ripped loose in the struggle. It was Jeff Whitmoyer.

Chapter Fifteen

Would this never end? Rachel sat at the kitchen table, still shivering from time to time, her hands wrapped around a hot mug of coffee. The coffee was slowly clearing her fogged mind, but it produced odd things from time to time.

"The cocoa," she said now.

Tyler seemed to know what she meant without explanation. "That's right. He drugged the cocoa Emma had left on the stove."

"Imagine the nerve of the man." Nancy topped off the mug Tyler held. She and Emma had just appeared, as they always seemed to at times of crisis, and Nancy had taken over the kitchen, apparently feeling that food was the answer to every issue. She slid a wedge of cinnamon coffeecake in front of Tyler. "Eat something. You need your strength."

Well, the police who swarmed around the place would probably eat it, if they didn't.

Emma was upstairs with Grams, refusing to leave her alone even though the paramedics had seen her and declared that she hadn't had enough of the drug to cause harm.

Tyler had dressed at some point in the nightmare hours before dawn. He wore jeans and a navy sweatshirt, his hair tousled. She'd put on her warmest sweater, but it didn't seem to be enough to banish the cold that had penetrated to her very bones when she'd been fighting for her life.

Not that she'd managed to fight very hard. "If it hadn't been for you—"

"If it hadn't been for Barney," he said quickly. "It was easy enough to drop something in the cocoa for you, but Barney had already been fed, so he had to take his chances that no one would hear the dog."

He didn't identify the person he spoke of. He didn't need to. They all knew.

The door opened, and Bradley Whitmoyer stepped inside. Usually he looked pale. Now he looked gray— as gray as a gravestone. He'd probably had to identify his brother's body.

She found her voice. "I'm so sorry."

Bradley shook his head. "I didn't come for that."

The words sounded rude, but she didn't think he'd meant them that way. He was just exhausted beyond reach of any of the conventions.

"You'd better sit down." Tyler didn't sound very happy at the prospect.

Bradley ignored the words. Maybe he didn't even hear them. "I have to tell you. I can't hold it back any longer. It will kill me if I don't speak."

She started to protest, but Tyler's hand closed over hers in warning.

"If this is something the police should hear, maybe you'd better wait until the chief comes in," he said.

"I'll tell them." He looked surprised at the comment. "But Rachel has the right to know first. And you. It was my fault, you see."

Tyler seemed to recognize the terrible strain Bradley was under. He looked at her, shaking his head slightly as if to say he didn't know what else they could do but let the man talk.

"I was home from college that summer." Bradley didn't need to say what summer. They knew. "I was desperate for money for my education, you see. I wouldn't have gotten involved with him, otherwise."

Her heart clutched. Was he going to name her father?

"Who?" Tyler's voice was tense.

"Phil Longstreet." He looked surprised that they had to ask. "He had this scheme—he would talk people, elderly farmers, mostly, into selling things, usually for a fraction of their value. While he was in the house, he would identify the really desirable items."

"And then you'd go back and steal them." Tyler finished it for him.

"We did." Bradley looked faintly surprised at the person he'd been. "I didn't… I didn't see any other way I could stay in school. I don't suppose Phil expected to get away with it for long. He was always talking about leaving here, he and Hampton both."

Her heart hurt. *Oh, Daddy. Why did you have to get involved in that?*

"They did all right, for a while. Then they tried it on John Hostetler." His gaze touched Tyler. "Your grandfather sold them some pieces of furniture. Then we went back when we thought the house was empty. He met us with a shotgun. He knew what we were doing. He was going to tell Phil's uncle, tell everyone—" His voice seemed to fade out for an instant. "There was a struggle. I don't know how it happened. I knocked him down. He lay there, clutching his chest. He was having a heart attack. I knew it, and I didn't help. I let him die."

His face twisted with anguish, and he seemed to struggle to control it, as though revealing his pain was asking for sympathy he didn't deserve.

"So you made it look like a robbery and you ran." Tyler didn't seem to have any sympathy to spare.

"The next day I was going to go to the police. I couldn't stand it. But I told Jeff, and he said he'd take care of everything. I couldn't ruin my future. So I kept quiet."

"My father?" She was amazed that her voice could sound so level.

"I heard he'd left town. The investigation died down. No one ever asked me anything. I went back to college, then medical school, and then I came back here to practice."

That was why, she realized. He'd come back as some sort of atonement for what he'd done, as if the lives he saved could make up for the one he'd taken.

Bradley's hands closed over the back of a chair. "I kept expecting to be exposed. Sometimes I thought it would be a relief. But years went by, and no one ever knew. And then you came back." He looked at her, eyes filled with pity. "And Jeff told me you had to be taken care of. And he told me why."

She shook her head. "I don't understand." But she knew something terrible was coming, and she couldn't get out of its way.

"It was because of what you wanted to do. You wanted to get rid of the gazebo. He couldn't let you, because if you did, they'd find your father's body, where Jeff buried it the night he killed him to keep him quiet."

It was Christmas Eve before Rachel thought she'd begun to understand everything. Andrea and Cal had rushed back from their honeymoon, and Andrea's calm good sense had helped her get through all of the things that had to be done. Even Caroline had come, all the way from New Mexico, making light of it but seeming to feel that all of the Hampton girls had to be together at a time like this.

The police had superintended the removal of the gazebo, and the family had had a quiet memorial service for their father at the church. She'd only broken down once—when the police gave her the tarnished remains of a child's gold cross on a chain that had been in her father's pocket.

The numbness that had gotten her through the past week had begun to thaw, and she wasn't quite sure what was going to take its place. She looked around the faces reflected in the lights of the Christmas tree. Grams, Andrea and Cal, Caroline.

And Tyler. With every reason for him to leave, Tyler had stayed.

"Now that Longstreet is awake and talking, it sounds as if he's blaming everyone but himself for what happened." Cal, Andrea's husband, leaned back in his chair, a cup of eggnog in one hand. "According to what I heard, he now says that your father decided to go to the police instead of leaving town, as they'd agreed. Jeff Whitmoyer had been working on the construction project, so he knew it was ready at hand. And he wasn't going to let anyone spoil the bright future he saw for his little brother."

"We don't need to talk about it now." Andrea, leaning close to her new husband, reproved him gently.

"It's all right." Rachel knew Andrea was trying to protect her, as she always did. "I'm over the worst of it." She couldn't suppress a shudder. "I guess I'm just lucky Jeff didn't do a better job of it back in the spring when he ran me down. I certainly never connected that to asking him for a quote on removing the gazebo."

Grams put a hand over hers, patting it gently. "How could you? I knew the man since he was a child, and I never suspected a thing."

"You seemed to give up your plans then, and I suppose they thought they were safe." Tyler rested one hand on the mantel, maybe too edgy to sit down. "Then I came and stirred them up again."

Caro brushed dark red curls back over her shoulder. Her bright, speculative gaze went from Rachel to Tyler. "Good thing you were here the other night."

"Good thing Barney was here," Tyler said dryly. The dog, hearing his name, looked up from his nap on the hearth rug and thumped his tail.

"Longstreet won't get off scot-free," Cal said. "The police know he's been behind the recent thefts of antiques. I suppose he thought it worked so well twenty years ago that he'd start it up again, with a couple of hired thugs. He apparently got nervous when you two started nosing around and tried to dissuade you. But his efforts backfired when Jeff decided he was a liability."

"He's lucky to be alive." She remembered that pool of blood around him on the office floor.

"He may not think so after the district attorney gets through with him," Tyler said. "But he'll fight it every step of the way, unlike Whitmoyer. I understand Sandra's trying to have her husband declared mentally unfit to defend himself."

She could actually feel sorry for Bradley, in a way. He'd been trapped by what happened twenty-two years ago, and all his good works hadn't been enough to make up for that.

"So the medal really didn't have anything to do with it, except that it left a trail to Phil." She'd probably be trying to figure out all the ramifications of what happened for months, but it was starting to come a little clearer.

"Funny thing about that." Tyler set his punch cup on the mantel and pulled something out of his pocket. He walked over to put it on the coffee table where they could see it. The medal. "I had it professionally cleaned. The jeweler brought up what was on the back, and did a little detective work on it."

He turned it over. Rachel leaned forward, staring at the symbol incised on the reverse. "It looks like a triangle with an eye inside it."

"Not a triangle. A pyramid. Turns out this was a symbol used by a number of odd little groups back in the late 1600s in Germany and Switzerland. Rosicrucians, Illuminati, the Order of the Rose—apparently my grandfather's ancestor was part of one. Small wonder the Amish didn't want to talk about it. They'd consider that heresy."

"But surely your grandfather didn't believe in that."

He shrugged. "I have no way of knowing. I wouldn't think so, but—" He picked the medal up again. "Somehow I don't think I want this as a memento after all. It can go back into somebody's collection. We exposed the truth about his death. That's enough for me."

There was finality in his words. Did everyone else hear it, or was she the only one? This was over. Now he would go back to his life.

"I think that cookie tray needs to be refilled." She got up quickly, before anyone else could volunteer to do it. She needed a moment to herself.

She went through to the kitchen, and when she heard a step behind her, she knew who it was.

"Are you okay?" Tyler was close, not touching.

"I guess." Talk about something, anything, other than the fact that he's leaving. "You know, if Bradley had gone to the police right away, my father wouldn't have died. But he would still have left us." She tilted her head back, looking at him. "I'm not going to lie to myself any longer about who and what he was."

"I'm sorry." His voice was soft and deep with emotion. "Sorry he's gone, and sorry he wasn't the man you wanted him to be."

"I'm all right about it. Really. It's better to have the truth out. I can't find my happiness in recreating a past that never existed. It's the love we have for each other as a family that's important, not the mistakes our parents made." She took a breath, wishing she knew what he was thinking. "At least you fulfilled your promise to your mother."

"I found out more than she intended. Knowing something about her childhood, I understand her better. Her mother died, and then her father shut her away from the only support system she had left."

"It's sad. If he hadn't taken her out of the church,

the Amish would have been family for her, no matter what he did." It was such a sad story, but at least now Tyler seemed content that he'd done what he could.

"Enough of that." His gaze seemed to warm the skin of her face. "I have a gift for you, and I'd like to give it to you without the rest of your family looking on, if that's okay."

She nodded, unable to speak. Her heart seemed to be beating faster than a hummingbird's.

Tyler took something from his pocket and dangled it in front of her. "I picked this up when I ran back to Baltimore yesterday. It belonged to my father's mother. I want you to have it. Not to replace the one your father would have given you, but because—well, just because it seemed the right gift."

She touched the delicate, old-fashioned gold cross, her heart almost too full for words. "It's beautiful. Thank you."

He fastened it around her neck, his fingers brushing her nape gently. "My grandmother was like you—loving, nurturing, filled with goodness. If my father knew, he'd be happy I found someone to give it to."

Her eyes misted as she traced the graceful design. "I don't know what to say."

"Then let me say it." He took both her hands in his, lifting them to his lips. "I know there are a lot of questions to be answered about the future, and I'm not sure how it will all work out. I'll move as slowly as you want, but I know right now that I want to share the rest of my life with you."

He was being careful, not pressuring her, but there was no need. She wasn't afraid anymore of what the future held. She reached up to pull his face toward hers, seeing the love blossom in his eyes.

She'd come back to this house to find something she'd lost years earlier. God had given her not only that but much more besides. She didn't have to look for home any longer. She'd found it.

* * * * *

WE HOPE YOU ENJOYED THESE **LOVE INSPIRED**® AND **LOVE INSPIRED**® **SUSPENSE** BOOKS.

Whether you prefer heartwarming contemporary romance or heart-pounding suspense, Love Inspired® books has it all!

Look for 6 new titles available every month from both Love Inspired® and Love Inspired® Suspense.

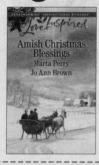

Love Inspired

Save $1.00

on the purchase of any
Love Inspired®,
Love Inspired® Suspense or
Love Inspired® Historical book.

Available wherever books are sold, including most bookstores, supermarkets, drugstores and discount stores.

- ✂

Save $1.00

on the purchase of any **Love Inspired®, Love Inspired® Suspense or Love Inspired® Historical book.**

Coupon valid until February 28, 2017. Redeemable at participating retail outlets in the U.S. and Canada only. Limit one coupon per customer.

52614460

Canadian Retailers: Harlequin Enterprises Limited will pay the face value of this coupon plus 10.25¢ if submitted by customer for this product only. Any other use constitutes fraud. Coupon is nonassignable. Void if taxed, prohibited or restricted by law. Consumer must pay any government taxes. Void if copied. Inmar Promotional Services ("IPS") customers submit coupons and proof of sales to Harlequin Enterprises Limited, P.O. Box 3000, Saint John, NB E2L 4L3, Canada. Non-IPS retailer—for reimbursement submit coupons and proof of sales directly to Harlequin Enterprises Limited, Retail Marketing Department, 225 Duncan Mill Rd., Don Mills, ON M3B 3K9, Canada.

U.S. Retailers: Harlequin Enterprises Limited will pay the face value of this coupon plus 8¢ if submitted by customer for this product only. Any other use constitutes fraud. Coupon is nonassignable. Void if taxed, prohibited or restricted by law. Consumer must pay any government taxes. Void if copied. For reimbursement submit coupons and proof of sales directly to Harlequin Enterprises, Ltd 482, NCH Marketing Services, P.O. Box 880001, El Paso, TX 88588-0001, U.S.A. Cash value 1/100 cents.

5 65373 00076 2   (8100)0 12237

® and ™ are trademarks owned and used by the trademark owner and/or its licensee.

© 2016 Harlequin Enterprises Limited

LIINCICOUPI116

SPECIAL EXCERPT FROM

Love Inspired

Could a Christmastime nanny position for the ranch foreman's son turn into a full-time new family for one Texas teacher?

Read on for a sneak preview of the third book in the
LONE STAR COWBOY LEAGUE: BOYS RANCH
miniseries, THE NANNY'S TEXAS CHRISTMAS
by *Lee Tobin McClain.*

"Am I in trouble?" Logan asked, sniffling.

How did you discipline a kid when his whole life had just flashed before your eyes? Flint schooled his features into firmness. "One thing's for sure, tractors are going to be off-limits for a long time."

Logan just buried his head in Flint's shoulder.

As they all started walking again, Flint felt that delicate hand on his arm once more.

"You doing okay?" Lana Alvarez asked.

He shook his head. "I just got a few more gray hairs. I should've been watching him better."

"Maybe so," Marnie said. "But you can't, not with all the work you have at the ranch. So I think we can all agree—you need a babysitter for Logan." She stepped in front of Lana and Flint, causing them both to stop. "And the right person to do it is here. Miss Lana Alvarez."

"Oh, Flint doesn't want—"

"You've got time after school. And a Christmas vacation coming up." Marnie crossed her arms, looking determined. "Logan already loves you. You could help to keep him safe and happy."

Flint's desire to keep Lana at a distance tried to raise its head, but his worry about his son, his gratitude about Logan's safety, and the sheer terror he'd just been through, put his own concerns into perspective.

Logan took priority. And if Lana would agree to be Logan's nanny on a temporary basis, that would be best for Logan.

And Flint would tolerate her nearness. Somehow.

"Can she, Daddy?" Logan asked, his face eager.

He turned to Lana, who looked like she was facing a firing squad. "Can you?" he asked her.

"Please, Miss Alvarez?" Logan chimed in.

Lana drew in a breath and studied them both, and Flint could almost see the wheels turning in her brain.

He could see mixed feelings on her face, too. Fondness for Logan. Mistrust of Flint himself.

Maybe a little bit of… What was that hint of pain that wrinkled her forehead and darkened her eyes?

Flint felt like he was holding his breath.

Finally, Lana gave a definitive nod. "All right," she said. "We can try it. But I'm going to have some very definite rules for you, young man." She looked at Logan with mock sternness.

As they started walking toward the house again, Lana gave Flint a cool stare that made him think she might have some definite rules for him, too.

Don't miss
THE NANNY'S TEXAS CHRISTMAS
by Lee Tobin McClain, available December 2016
wherever Love Inspired® books and ebooks are sold.

www.LoveInspired.com

REQUEST YOUR FREE BOOKS!

2 FREE INSPIRATIONAL NOVELS
PLUS 2
FREE
MYSTERY GIFTS

READERSERVICE.COM

Manage your account online!

- Review your order history
- Manage your payments
- Update your address

We've designed the Reader Service website just for you.

Enjoy all the features!

- Discover new series available to you, and read excerpts from any series.

- Respond to mailings and special monthly offers.

- Connect with favorite authors at the blog.

- Browse the Bonus Bucks catalog and online-only exculsives.

- Share your feedback.

Visit us at:

ReaderService.com